Titles include:

Palgrave Studies in the Enlightenment, Romanticism and Cultures of Print
Series Standing Order ISBN 978–1–403–93408–6 hardback
978–1–403–93409–3 paperback
(*outside North America only*)

You can receive future titles in this series as they are published by placing a standing order. Please contact your bookseller or, in case of difficulty, write to us at the address below with your name and address, the title of the series and the ISBN quoted above.

Customer Services Department, Macmillan Distribution Ltd, Houndmills, Basingstoke, Hampshire RG21 6XS, England

---

Literature and Encyclopedism in Enlightenment Britain

The Pursuit of Complete Knowledge

Seth Rudy
Assistant Professor, Rhodes College, USA

First published 2014 by
PALGRAVE MACMILLAN

Palgrave Macmillan in the UK is an imprint of Macmillan Publishers Limited, registered in England, company number 785998, of Houndmills, Basingstoke, Hampshire RG21 6XS.

Palgrave Macmillan in the US is a division of St Martin's Press LLC, 175 Fifth Avenue, New York, NY 10010.

Palgrave Macmillan is the global academic imprint of the above companies and has companies and representatives throughout the world.

Palgrave® and Macmillan® are registered trademarks in the United States, the United Kingdom, Europe and other countries.

ISBN 978–1–137–41153–2

A catalogue record for this book is available from the British Library.

Library of Congress Cataloging-in-Publication Data
Rudy, Seth, 1978–
Literature and encyclopedism in Enlightenment Britain: the pursuit of complete knowledge / by Seth Rudy, Assistant Professor, Rhodes College, USA.
p. cm. – (Palgrave studies in the Enlightenment, romanticism and the cultures of print)
Includes bibliographical references and index.
ISBN 978–1–137–41153–2
1. English literature—18th century—History and criticism.   2. Knowledge, Theory of, in literature.   3. Enlightenment–Great Britain.   4. Epic literature, English—History and criticism.   5. Encyclopedists—Great Britain.   6. Encyclopedias and dictionaries—Great Britain—History and criticism.   7. Learning and scholarship—Great Britain—History—18th century.
I. Title.   II. Title: Encyclopedism in enlightenment Britain: the pursuit of complete knowledge.   III. Title: Pursuit of complete knowledge.
PR448.K56R83 2014
820.9'005–dc23   2014021122

Typeset by MPS Limited, Chennai, India.

Transferred to Digital Printing in 2014

Contents

Acknowledgments

I was first introduced to the study of Enlightenment encyclopedias in a graduate seminar taught by Mary Poovey and Clifford Siskin at New York University's Graduate School of Arts and Sciences in the fall of 2005. That seminar, "Topics in the History of Knowledge Production: Genres of Enlightenment," marked the beginning of an entirely new phase in my education and career. This book has its origins in that class, and any success it enjoys is owed in large measure to the enduring influence its leaders had (and continue to have) on my work. I remain immensely grateful for their candor, wisdom, encouragement, and insistence that I must and could work at a level higher than any I had previously thought possible to attain. I would also like to thank Paula McDowell, Gabrielle Starr, Ernest Gilman, and Dustin Griffin for the insights and opportunities they provided as faculty mentors throughout my time in the extraordinarily challenging intellectual environment of NYU's Department of English and American Literature.

The readiness with which I was welcomed to the English Department at Rhodes College in 2010 and the level of support I have consistently met with from my truly remarkable colleagues have made the transition from graduate student to faculty member improbably smooth. I am now not only a better scholar but also a much better teacher and professional thanks to the guidance they have given me ever since my first visit to campus. Working with Mark Behr, Gordon Bigelow, Marshall Boswell, Jenny Brady, Rebecca Finlayson, Lori Garner, Ernest Gibson, Judy Haas, Mike Leslie, Scott Newstok, Leslie Petty, Jason Richards, Rashna Richards, Brian Shaffer, and Caki Wilkinson has been both a privilege and a pleasure; I cannot thank them enough for the adoptive intellectual home they have built here at Rhodes. I must also extend my thanks to the college for its additional institutional support; the Faculty Development Endowment Grant awarded to me in 2011 and the Early Leave granted in Fall 2012 made it possible to devote time and resources to the project without which it would not now be complete.

I am furthermore indebted to several colleagues and mentors in other institutions, departments, and disciplines who took meetings, answered emails, read materials, and very graciously listened to the ten, five, two, one-minute, and thirty-second long versions of the same book proposal. I would in particular like to offer thanks to Jayne Lewis and Yohei Igarashi for the invaluable feedback and moral support they offered at critical junctures in the life of the project, and to Scott Garner for his help in compiling the index. I also owe significant (though not statistically significant, which I now know is redundant) gratitude to Jeff Hamrick for his assistance with time series analysis. The book would certainly not be what it is without them. The same must also be said for the insightful, straightforward, and constructive criticism I received during the review process at Palgrave. I am extremely grateful to have had the advantage of it in the project's final phases.

I would not have been in a position to benefit from their input, though, had not others given me opportunities to share my work at earlier stages. I have presented portions of this project at conferences organized by the American Society for Eighteenth-Century Studies and the Modern Language Association, and I greatly appreciate the experiences I have had in those forums. I must also extend special thanks to Helge Jordheim, who invited me to present my work at a conference sponsored by the National Library and KULTRANS at the University of Oslo. The trip was intellectually and culturally invigorating, and I am honored to have been among those in attendance. The Re:Enlightenment Project has also been of invaluable importance to the development of this project and to the clarification of my goals and values in the broader context of academic life. I cannot express the full measure of respect and admiration that I have for its members and directors.

Editors and authors often speak of finding the "right home" for a book. As a reader, I have been a very frequent visitor to Palgrave Macmillan, and the depth of my gratitude to Anne Mellor and Clifford Siskin for finding my book a place in their exceptional series of scholarly works is genuinely profound. I must also express my appreciation to commissioning editor Ben Doyle and editorial assistant Sophie Ainscough. Their efficiency and patience have made it even clearer to me how right a home Palgrave is for this book as well as its author. It really is a great place they have here, and I thank them for letting me stay.

Finally, I would like to recognize my family and friends for their seemingly inexhaustible patience and support. Lenora Warren, Rachael Scarborough King, and Claude Willan have offered much-needed sympathy, sarcasm, and gallows bonhomie; I count myself very lucky to have friends and compatriots with such high tolerances for anxious rumination. My parents-in-law, Maureen and Cameron Robertson, are among the kindest and most generous people I have ever known; I thank them for welcoming me into their family and for providing a base of academic operations in Northern California—even, all too often, during holidays. The thanks I owe to my parents—Linda and Ronald Rosenthal, Richard and Debbie Rudy—is beyond measure. Their confidence has always been unwavering; without their counsel and encouragement over the past years I could not have finished this book or much else besides. It now seems entirely possible that they may have been right about other things too. By far the greatest share of gratitude, though, must go to my wife, Maggie Robertson, who has read every word on every page of every draft of every part of this project. Without her love and brilliance, I could not have come this far and would scarce have reason to go farther. She is at once compass, sextant, horizon, and star.

1
Introduction: Concepts of Completeness

In 1710, the author and biographer Richard Ward summarized his thoughts on the limits of human comprehension with a phrase he claimed to have borrowed from antiquity. "When a Man shall be join'd to *Intellect*, or *Understanding*," he wrote, "by a sort of Complete Knowledge of all things, then a God (or, as I would interpret it, an extraordinary Hero) may be said to sojourn in a Human Body."[1] Ward's assessment implies that such a joining is improbable if not impossible—that neither the single human memory nor the single human lifespan is suited to achieving a perfect understanding of all knowledge in all its complexity. The future tense and ancient pedigree of the remark cast the pursuit of complete knowledge as part of a venerable tradition of frustrated ambition; by the early eighteenth century, it seemed, humanity had already sought it for millennia and either altogether failed to achieve it or simply lost what it once supposedly knew.

At a moment when Google seeks "to organize the world's information and make it universally accessible and useful," this book tells the story of long-term aspirations to comprehend, record, and disseminate "complete" knowledge of the world. It explores the persistent failure of these ambitions, their collapse in the third quarter of the eighteenth century, and the subsequent redefinition of completeness in modern literary and disciplinary terms. The pursuit of complete knowledge in ancient epic and then in epics and discursive works of the seventeenth and eighteenth centuries advanced the separation of encyclopedism from epic poetry, epic poems from novels, literature from "Literature," and the sciences from the humanities; the distinctions between "high" and "low," ephemeral and eternal, useful and useless that still persist today all stem from the concepts of completeness that emerged during and as a result of the Enlightenment.

1

The reputation of Homer and Virgil's comprehensive knowledge in antiquity and the Middle Ages—a reputation neither always unchallenged nor entirely defeated, even as late as the early eighteenth century—helped make epic an enduring signifier of great magnitude and longevity, if no longer one of truly universal scope. Now, as new technologies bring with them new modes and forms of knowledge production and transmission, scholars have again begun to look to epic as the ancestor of an emerging genre that has the potential to redefine the standards, value, and possibilities of complete knowledge. Database, as Ed Folsom argues in 'Database as Genre: The Epic Transformation of Archives,' may be gaining recognition as "the genre of the twenty-first century," but in truth it "has been with us all along, in the guises of those literary works we have always had trouble assigning to a genre," and in the phenomenological life of epic.[2] The ancient commonplaces praising Homer and Virgil's more-than-human capacities connect epic and its history to everything from the *Iliad*, *Odyssey*, and *Aeneid* to Francis Bacon's *Great Instauration*, and from the encyclopedias of the Enlightenment to the reputation of Google's PageRank as an "all-knowing" algorithm.[3] This study charts the historical process by which different kinds of completeness came to be associated with such different forms and methods of knowledge production and suggests both how and why those associations continue to inform our understanding of their purposes and value.

Even at its most basic, the concept of completeness carries two contradictory meanings. On the one hand, "complete" indicates comprehensive: a full account of every part of knowledge or every article relevant to a given subject or subjects of inquiry. On the other hand, it also implies cohesion: the connection of all those parts or articles together into a unified whole without defect. As numerous readers and writers of the seventeenth and eighteenth centuries observed, however, the more comprehensive an account became, the more difficult it became for that account to achieve cohesiveness. Thus, what a work gained in one sense of completion it often lost in the other. As the volume and kinds of information in and about the world both changed and proliferated with the emergence of new modes of knowledge production and the expansion of the literary marketplace, these two aspects of completeness tended more and more towards mutual exclusivity. Sacrificing too much detail in the name of overall coherence might leave readers without valuable content, but then again, attempting to render a full and dedicated treatment of even one subject might simply overwhelm. Simply put, too much could present as much an obstacle to understanding as too little.

A vast field of literary potential lay between the extremes. According to the numerous plans, prefaces, dedications, and advertisements written to justify the presence of yet another book in an already overcrowded marketplace, either extreme unacceptably jeopardized the usefulness of the work and any knowledge it contained. Horace, in his *Ars Poetica*, had declared usefulness one of the two characteristics fundamental to successful poetry, and throughout much of the Enlightenment achieving some version of *dulce et utile* remained the aspiration (and self-proclaimed accomplishment) of all kinds of literature, from poems and pamphlets to encyclopedias and enchiridia.[4] Writers of all kinds sought to manage the proliferation of print and the expansion of knowledge; they attempted to establish or reconstitute the utility of their texts as durable mechanisms of literary organization and as effective mediators of complete knowledge as they construed it.

The "experience of overabundance" and the simultaneous attempts to alleviate it via collection, organization, distinction, and abridgment, then, are no more new now than they were in the seventeenth century, when John Milton surrounded his Adam with an entirely new world and found himself surrounded by new ways of knowing it.[5] There has been "too much to know" (to borrow a phrase from historian Ann Blair) for hundreds or perhaps thousands of years, and for just as long there have been thinkers, writers, and readers concerned with the potential as well as the potential danger of accumulating knowledge and texts. The practices of compilation and summary developed in antiquity to stem the tide (or harness its power) were joined in the Middle Ages by a host of supplementary tools including indices, concordances, alphabetical and systematic arrangements, tables of contents, and textual subdivisions. The dictionaries, florilegia, and other compendia that employed these tools remained staple genres throughout the Early Modern period, when print technology and the rapid production of books it enabled made complaints about volume and variety a regular feature of texts beyond the scholarly world.[6] In the seventeenth and eighteenth centuries, as the print market continued to expand, such complaints gained new cultural significance and became influential forces in a broadening swathe of literary as well as scientific, historical, and technical discourses.

Despite their seeming differences, a host of writers and titles made similar attempts to identify, collect, and preserve what they deemed the true and worthwhile parts of human knowledge and literary history even as they changed, added to, and became part of the past they captured. Bacon knew that the limitations of mortality and memory would not permit him to record or comprehend all the phenomena of the universe in his lifetime; John Milton made the origins of those limitations central to the plot of *Paradise Lost*. The authors and editors of universal histories recommended or supplied charts that represented all of human history "at one view" in order to make their narratives more comprehensible; Laurence Sterne suggested that it would take more time to write a complete account of just one life than it would take to live it. Alexander Pope wrote that a full exploration of even so small a part of the universe as "Man" was beyond his power as a poet to complete; William Wordsworth's autobiographical epic simply leaves a great deal out of the record. Dictionary-makers and encyclopedists throughout the century variously relied upon trees, cross-references, indices, alphabetization, supplementation, systemization, and division to help readers manage and make sense of the knowledge they provided. While these and other authors frequently disagreed with one another, both implicitly and explicitly, about the proper pathway to complete knowledge, the best way to represent that knowledge, and even what completeness itself entailed, they are all connected by their involvement in the modeling and mediation of that concept—the realization of which we have sought, if one takes Milton for a guide, since Creation, and which has continued to elude us since the Fall.

According to some, only the mind of a truly gifted poet could forge a picture of the whole world both as it was and as it should be. According to others, the power of a single brain could "go but a little way" when compared to the combined intellectual efforts of a whole country.[7] On the one hand, the synthesized narrative of a poem or novel could theoretically provide the cohesiveness left wanting by mere alphabetization; on the other hand, alphabetization theoretically allowed for the relatively easy incorporation of new material by multiple contributors. Alphabetical encyclopedias and other such compendia could function according to a program of planned obsolescence, with each new edition introducing the latest discoveries while simultaneously carrying forth and re-authorizing whatever their compilers deemed the durable content of earlier versions. When Pope found a new dunce in Colley Cibber, though, he brought forth a *New Dunciad* to accommodate him, and Richardson too continued to expand his "finished" *Clarissa* in subsequent editions.

"Complete" knowledge, then, did not come in a single form. The range and breadth of titles and projects promising some version of completeness have problematized the concept in scholarly and vernacular literatures since at least the early seventeenth century, when their numbers, kinds, and availability began to increase. Specific features responsible for increasing sweetness or entertainment value, especially with respect to what modern readers would more readily recognize as "traditional" reference works, generally went without much explanation beyond authorial assurance and the presumption that learning was a pleasure in itself. Articulations of what made a work more useful, however, frequently went into greater detail and offered a rationale for an author's claim to completeness whatever the scope, subject, or nature of his or her text. No uniform standard of what constitutes a genuinely complete body of knowledge prevailed then or now, and attempts to apply such a standard almost immediately make little sense even within single works.

Thomas Cooper, for example, advertised *The universal pocket-book* (1740) as "the most comprehensive, useful, and compleat book of the kind, ever yet publish'd." It contained just under 300 pages duodecimo of material "designed for the use, benefit, and convenience of all sorts of persons" and included a map of the world, an account of all the stage coaches and carriers in England and Scotland, a list of members of the House of Peers, and a treatise on gardening. Somewhat less practically, it also provided readers with a table of "remarkable events" from the creation of the world to the time of Julius Caesar, brief descriptions of the Seven Wonders of the World, a truncated history of England, and "short definitions of all the arts and sciences."[8] The fifth and final edition of the book appeared in 1745, a year after the publication of *A supplement to Dr. Harris's Dictionary of arts and sciences*, the full title of which deployed several similar terms but nevertheless operated according to very different standards of completeness. Its title page declared it "more copious and extensive than any Work of this Kind" and insisted that, when joined with Harris's earlier volumes, it would "make the most useful Set of Books, and compleat Body of Arts and Sciences yet extant."[9] Given that Harris's volumes collectively comprised roughly 2600 pages and plates, the thousand pages of the folio supplement represented a significant step towards comprehensive completeness that, at least in terms of size, must have made Cooper's pocket-book seem somewhat less than truly universal.

That any two works of such radically disproportionate lengths should equally trumpet their completeness might simply appear to evacuate the word of any substantive meaning. Like their Early Modern and Enlightenment antecedents, modern authors and booksellers still offer thousands of "complete" histories, narratives, guides, dictionaries, encyclopedias, and other compendia covering every category from Business and Investing to Literature and Fiction to Religion and Spirituality.[10] In many, if not most, the presence of the word "complete" in their titles is always already ironic and typically indicative of a mass-market rather than scholarly appeal. It seems improbable, for instance, that *The Times Complete History of the World* (2010), a 432-page book that supposedly "has all the answers" and covers everything "from cavemen to the Cold War, from Alexander the Great to global warming, from warfare through the ages to the great voyages of exploration" is in fact "the most comprehensive, authoritative and accessible work on world history available today"—especially given that Sir Walter Raleigh's widely read *The history of the world* (1614) had 400 fewer years to cover but still ran to nearly 800 pages in half-folio.[11] Raleigh's unfinished history in fact never made it past the second century BC, and that despite his having had all the free time afforded by a prolonged stay in the Tower.

The ambiguity and perceived ubiquity of the term "complete," then, somewhat justly occasioned cynical responses to it less than twenty years after its first English-title appearance in Henry Peacham's *The compleat gentleman* (1622). As Peter de Bolla points out, however, a distinction must be made between a "concept" and merely "the use of a word."[12] The frequent appearance and casual use of "complete" and its variants in the titles and prefaces of seventeenth-century guidebooks for example—a subject I will examine further in Chapter 2—helped to establish "complete" less as a determinate quality than as a way of thinking about the order, organization, transmission, and progress of human learning—particularly as mediated by literature. The completeness of knowledge in general and the completeness of a "Literary" work in terms of formal structure and generic propriety, moreover, were not always already divided, particularly in the cases of epic and encyclopedic endeavors. The distinction and its naturalization to what became different *kinds* of literature are the results of the historical processes of pursuit, collapse, and reconstitution that this book recovers.

The concept of completeness remained (and remains) part of literature and knowledge production in part because its definition depended not only upon the extent of coverage, but also upon the extent to which that coverage served the designs of the work as well as the needs of its readers. In other words, to be complete, whole, or universal had as much to do with the utility of knowledge as it did with knowledge itself—a concept that also defied (and defies) simple explanation and which term I use throughout this book in a very general sense capable of accommodating its historical and contextual contingency. I share the concern expressed by Alan Rauch in *Useful Knowledge* that "the concept *knowledge* may strike the reader as too sweeping, particularly given the breadth of its meaning," but like Rauch I believe that "no better term exists."[13] There are important distinctions to be made among data, information, and knowledge, but those distinctions were not always precise or stable—Johnson's dictionary, for example, lists "information; power of knowing" as a definition of "knowledge."[14] The substance of what counted as knowledge, I argue, depended in part upon the relationship between completeness and utility.

The unmanageably comprehensive and the superficially concise were both potentially opposite to usefulness. In purely quantitative terms, Cooper's universal pocket-book necessarily contained altogether less content than Harris's universal dictionary, but with respect to mobility, affordability, and comprehensibility, it may well have been more useful to some readers and therefore more complete. Similarly, an architect, artilleryman, midwife, navigator, or lawyer might have had need of all the knowledge about those arts and sciences contained in a multi-volume encyclopedia, but if that encyclopedia allowed alphabetical organization to scatter them across thousands of pages without adequate regard to coherence, then the user could not necessarily come away with a "complete" understanding of his or her chosen subject. Single works often promised to do the work of many: some encyclopedias promised to do the work of entire libraries, and when encyclopedias became too large, at least one, *The new royal encyclopœdia* (1788), promised to do the work of all encyclopedias.[15] If the latter could lay greater claims to completeness because they were larger, then the former could do so because it was smaller.

Descriptions and defenses of plans and methods all designed to digest "valuable" learning and make it useful echoed throughout a range of works intended to supplant proliferating and competing forms of instruction and entertainment. The literary engagement with what we might call "encyclopedic" knowledge extended far beyond what we now recognize as conventional encyclopedias. The relative stability of the features and functions of general encyclopedias over the last two centuries, moreover, has tended to draw critical attention away from other forms of writing once much more closely related to them than they are now, as well as those formal experiments the successes and failures of which helped to define what was until very recently the enduring paradigm. In addition to guidebooks, dictionaries, and encyclopedias, then, epic poems, histories, and novels constitute a central focus of my argument because of their engagement with concepts of completeness and because they too underwent significant and demonstrable changes during this period that produced what have thus far proved relatively stable characteristics.

The juxtapositions of these and other works are as much heuristic as connective or causal. Some relationships are more direct than others, but the still-developing distinction between literary and non-literary works (a distinction that developed in part as a result of the intellectual pursuits under scrutiny in this book) necessitates a broad selection of seemingly disparate texts. As Kevis Goodman writes, late seventeenth-century verse "inhabits a cultural situation in which it has to define itself not only against an array of prose genres, whose material it often usurps, but also in relation to non-written means of perception and communication."[16] An array of prose genres, I submit, had to do the same with respect to verse. Encyclopedias, novels, and epic poems shared, or were widely believed to have shared, a common ancestry: Fielding and Chambers saw themselves as pursuing an epic tradition; so too did Milton and Pope. The concept of completeness provides a way of thinking about these works in concert; this study establishes a new approach to them and uses the points of contact among them to reframe our understanding of British literary history.

By the Numbers

In order to make certain kinds of arguments about even a single species of literature, a more or less misleadingly "complete" theorization is required in order to avoid losing oneself or one's readers in a kind of Borgesian map or Shandean supertask.[17] Clara Reeve acknowledged this much in her own attempt to define the novel in *The Progress of Romance* (1785), and the same could likely be said about any number of other kinds of writing to which authors put their hands and which their hands put to the presses. The question we have for decades had to ask ourselves as literary scholars and historians—and which one of the characters in Reeve's dialogue does ask, albeit somewhat indecorously—is how much of a "genus" one must read in order to speak of any part of it.[18]

As it did to what have become the primary texts of the Romantic period, the volume of texts available for scrutiny has contributed to what Mary Poovey describes as "the lyric features of contemporary criticism." The same trope of "organic unity" associated with Romanticism, Poovey writes, "makes contemporary criticism a romantic lyric and converts its analytic objects into lyriclike organic wholes." The use of embedded quotations from texts under analysis, for instance, "functions to present the literary text in fragments that synecdochically contain the larger whole."[19] A version of this synecdochical representation can and frequently does occur at the level of genre as well: each ode, epic, encyclopedia, essay, history, novel, romance, and so on represents a fragment of a genre (*the* epic, *the* encyclopedia, *the* novel) that in turn constitutes part of a literary system in which all genres can be conceived of (if not completely comprehended) as connected. No single text can speak on behalf of an entire form, especially not given the fluidity or permeability of formal boundaries. Presuming one could read *every* part, the question then becomes how much of every *other* genus one must read in order to discuss the system.

The growing size and accessibility of the web at large, along with that of digital databases like *Early English Books Online* (EEBO), *Eighteenth-Century Collections Online* (ECCO), and Google Books—Reeve's cast of characters, already overwhelmed in 1785, had no idea what they were in for—constitute a kind of re-proliferation of "print" that has again made information management a matter of immediate and historical interest across disciplines, both inside and outside academia. The new kinds of literature and modes of scholarship that have already started to emerge as twenty-first century authors and audiences seek to redefine the standards, value, and possibilities of completeness in the Digital Age, I conclude, are best understood in relation to the earlier chapter in the history of completeness that this study recovers. We are again in the midst of a technological moment that promises (or threatens) to shift our lyric-like construal of wholeness further towards the comprehensive end of the complete. From the perspective of the individual analyst, the number of texts available for literary analysis is practically infinite—depending, that is, on how one understands the practice.[20] Whereas Reeve's characters questioned how *much* one had to read, we are now, though not for the first time, asking ourselves what *kinds* of reading will lead to a greater understanding of literature.

Digital Humanists, cognizant of the profusion of materials available to them, have begun to experiment with methods dependent on a more comprehensive approach to literature than an individual reader could reasonably take. Franco Moretti, co-director of the Stanford Literary Lab, writes that "today, we can replicate in a few minutes investigations that took a giant like Leo Spitzer months and years of work. When it comes to phenomena of language and style, we can do things that previous generations could only dream of."[21] Those things require the quantitative analysis of huge data sets rather than the more traditional examinations of a necessarily small (or smaller) selection of texts. As Moretti argues, "we need distant reading ... because its opposite, close reading, can't uncover the true scope and nature of literature."[22] In this construction, if taken to an extreme, a more complete knowledge of literature can be had without "reading" *any* part of it, and its "nature" inheres in information and relationships exclusive of the familiar, more localized experiences of production and consumption that have defined the basis of literary study for centuries.

The clusters and visualized nodal networks of the Literary Lab, the graphs, maps, and trees of Moretti's *Graphs, Maps, and Trees* (2005), and even the kind of bibliographical data compiled in *The English Novel 1770–1829: A Bibliographical Survey of Prose Fiction Published in the British Isles* (2000) can unquestionably account for a massive number of texts and produce potentially useful knowledge about literature.[23] The usefulness of such accounts, though, still depends upon a measure of abstraction, and that they operate at a larger scale or via different means of abstraction than the synecdochical representations upon which other modes of analysis largely depend does not necessarily make them more complete in a universal sense. They rather reinforce a definition of knowledge, information, or comprehension that privileges one kind of completeness over another.

Simply put, critical studies too must sacrifice some aspect of completeness in the name of utility. As this one will prove no exception, I think it important to acknowledge that in my examination of the links between and among the works I have selected as well as the ways in which, over time, those links were recast or altogether broken, I do not propose to offer a full or definitive explanation for the disappearance or establishment of all those features and functions that since the eighteenth century have become the naturalized conventions of what we now treat as essentially distinct forms. I likewise do not mean to suggest that every article necessarily participated in or reflects the processes of change that this project recovers, nor that they are the only ones involved in that process. I rather seek to supply an additional element to the histories of each without which I believe the histories of all would remain incomplete.

This book, in other words, can no more escape the paradox of completeness than can any other. It too is a response to information overload, and as such it necessarily participates in and to some extent duplicates the phenomena it seeks to describe. While certainly operational in the texts I have selected, the concept of completeness was also at work in and across a much larger body of literature than can be fully accounted for in a single study. Many texts fall thus beyond the scope of this work, and argumentative cohesion takes precedence over a more comprehensively complete examination of all the potentially relevant items. A more complete book would obviously include more texts representative of more kinds of writing. The phrase "more complete," which has already appeared in this introduction and was ubiquitous in the guidebooks, dictionaries, and encyclopedias of the seventeenth and eighteenth centuries, suggests the compromise that the limitations of time and space generally compel us to make—a compromise that treats completeness as a continuum.

Simple searches of the *English Short Title Catalogue* (*ESTC*) suggest the extent to which even those texts the most self-evidently engaged with concepts of completeness might easily overwhelm a single conventional reader. The seventeenth century alone saw the publication of at least a thousand items with the word "complete" in the title, and the eighteenth century added at least another 6742 (Table 1.1, in Appendix). That number, furthermore, does not reflect the entirety of texts that participated in the mediation of "complete" knowledge. The word "universal," for example, often did the same or similar work as "complete." Indeed, the two were often deployed in tandem, as in Henry Curzon's *The universal library: or, compleat summary of science* (1712). The title page of *The new royal encyclopædia* similarly identified it as a "complete modern universal dictionary." Taking that term into account as well increased the total number of potentially relevant titles by a further 3242 (Table 1.1). Beyond simple descriptors, certain kinds of writing too were relatively recognizable for their involvement in the mediation of complete knowledge, albeit at different times and in different ways. In addition to "complete" and its orthographic variants, terms such as "universal" and "whole" frequently modified the still developing categories of dictionaries, encyclopedias, and systems (Table 1.1).

All told, and using only these five terms, the initial number of items that might warrant at least cursory bibliographical examination in a history of complete knowledge and its relationship to literature in the British Enlightenment amounts to approximately 16,000 (plus an additional 597 identified by their titles as "whole arts"). The inclusion in these figures of multiple editions of single titles as well as duplications resulting from dual deployments ("complete system," "universal dictionary," "complete encyclopedia," etc.) would certainly make the real number somewhat lower, but at the same time expansions and reductions from edition to edition are an important part of how authors, editors, and audiences construed completion within distinct properties.

Unless one examines each title individually, the precise usage of the key term or terms in each case cannot be determined. In addition to the theoretically unified account of all knowledge related or relevant to a given subject or subjects, as in *The compleat midwifes practice* (1656) or *A compleat practice of physick* (1656), "complete" might refer to complete histories of individuals, nations, and events (*A compleat history of magick* [1715], *A compleat history of the late war in the Netherlands* [1713]); complete collections (such as an author or authors' corpus, bound volumes of periodicals, jokes, songs, letters, etc.); complete paratextual devices (charts, indices, lists, schedules, tables of contents); and complete states of being distinct from those suggested by mastery of a given art or science ("complete happiness," "complete penury"). Though the boundaries between and among these features and functions often overlapped, many—including almost of all of those in the final category—would be of little or no direct relevance. Semantics would almost undoubtedly reduce the total more significantly than any other factor, but to an auditor the initial number approaches a version of the sublime.

Given the hundreds of thousands of texts readily available via the digital archive, and the still too many thousands of those texts revealed by simple searches as being potentially germane, statistical analysis seems a reasonable and even necessary alternative to conventional investigation. As previously indicated, quantitative data alone can rarely if ever present the whole story, but statistical analysis of title searches requires an additional measure of caution. As Tim Hitchcock has pointed out specifically in regard to such methodology, "what appears on a title page of a book, on the colophon, and on the end papers changed dramatically between the late fifteenth and the eighteenth centuries as the very nature of books changed. For all the heroic efforts of cataloguers and bibliographers to force early modern print objects into a single format ... it is not credible to read the title of a book published in 1520 in the same way as one produced in 1690."[24] The seventeenth-century figures thus likely represent a less comprehensive picture of the complete literary landscape than might otherwise appear, and though the use and substance of title pages became more stable in the eighteenth century, those figures too must be taken as an initial assessment rather than the final count. Neither manuscript works nor texts un-translated from their original languages factor into the account. These figures and the brief analysis below are therefore presented not as the basis of my argument, but rather as one part of its background; they are a starting point for further statistical analysis, and here they primarily suggest the legibility of completeness as a concept in the period and the often unspoken rationale behind modern analytical and compositional methodologies that have (in quantitative terms) left out more than they have comprehended.

At first glance, the data indicate that the numbers of titles featuring one or more of these terms generally increased over the course of the seventeenth and eighteenth centuries. The use of the word "complete," for example, reached an apex in the 1760s, during which decade they constituted 2.35 per cent of all items published before dropping back to 1.7 per cent by 1800.[25] Given that the entire corpus likewise generally continued to expand, those numbers by themselves do not necessarily indicate a verifiable trend; however, statistical analysis suggests that all five trends are significant.[26] The decade-over-decade increases readily seen in the tables, in other words, are not merely keeping pace with general growth. All five keywords (complete, universal, encyclopedia, dictionary, and system) are used with increasing intensity over the twenty decades under consideration. This suggests, in a very preliminary but yet still more than anecdotal way, the presence of a wider literary phenomenon.

Statistical analysis furthermore confirms that the increases in the intensity with which the word "universal" was used are significantly above and beyond the overall positive trend. Statistical spikes occurred in the 1650s, 1720s, and 1750s. Even setting aside the seventeenth-century result as the least reliable for reasons already described, the correlation of these spikes with the publication dates of many of the major texts that constitute the focus of this study lends credence to the possibility of their having been similarly concerned with questions of completeness and universality despite seeming generic differences. Pope's original mock-epic *Dunciad* and the expanded *Dunciad Variorum*, for example, were published in 1728 and 1729, respectively; the first edition of Chambers's *Cyclopædia* appeared in 1728; Richardson's *Clarissa* closely preceded the spike in 1748, as did Fielding's *Tom Jones* in 1749, but the prospectus and first volumes of the French *Encyclopédie*, published in 1751, were timely, as was Richardson's third novel, *Sir Charles Grandison*, in 1753. The first installment of *Tristram Shandy*, a narrative its fictional author refers to as a "cyclopedia of arts and sciences" and which is intimately concerned with completeness—or rather, the impossibility of completeness with respect to compiling a comprehensive account of even a single human life—arrived in London in 1759.

To claim absolutely at this point that these texts' approximate coincidence with an increased intensity in titular uses of "universal" and a rise in the number of works specifically invoking some version of completeness is in fact anything more than just coincidence would overstate the case. If nothing else, though, the data suggest a broad but otherwise invisible context for the concerted comparison of these "literary" texts with other works more explicitly engaged with concepts of completeness. The larger difficulty, however, remains the fact that claims to completeness did not necessarily require *any* of these words to invoke the concept.

The specific examples mentioned above and throughout this book all involve formal features or organizational strategies deployed by individual texts or common to particular forms. Those are the levels most pertinent to my study of completeness, and for that reason this study does not take into account other contemporary projects related to the pursuit of complete knowledge but of a sufficiently different nature to warrant their exclusion. While the histories of libraries, both real and imagined, had some bearing on the production of the many compendia and collections advertised as possible substitutes for them, and though their construction to some extent paralleled (albeit on a much larger scale) the financial, material, spatial, and organizational processes involved in the compilation and publication of such single properties, I have left detailed analyses of their operation to other studies. As Roger Chartier explains, "the dream of a library (in a variety of configurations) that would bring together all accumulated knowledge and all the books ever written can be found throughout the history of Western civilization." By the early seventeenth century, however, the proliferation of print had already "ruined all hope for an exhaustive collection." Various degrees of selectivity were therefore unavoidable, and the resulting "tension between comprehensiveness and essence thus ordered the complex and contradictory relations between the library in its usual spatial and architectural sense and print genres."[27] This work examines the effects of this tension in areas beyond the bounds of the catalogues, collections, and libraries (with or without walls) that Chartier describes.[28]

If on the one hand I have excluded the process by which librarians and other collectors culled essential knowledge from the mass of books available as part of their pursuit of complete knowledge, then I have on the other hand largely excluded a single book that many would have considered essential and complete in its own right. As the quotation with which this introduction began suggests, divine knowledge to many represented the only and ultimate solution to the paradox of completeness, and in Protestant England—particularly during its more rigorous phases of religious governance and practice—the doctrine of *sola scriptura* made the Bible, as an infallible collection of all the knowledge required to achieve salvation, the one truly indispensable book. As an object of study itself, however, the Bible in the seventeenth and eighteenth centuries to some extent underwent the same encyclopedic treatment as the second of God's two books.[29] Scripture may have taught all, the argument went, but without books like *A complete Christian dictionary* its lessons might not be fully comprehended. According to John Bagwell, one of its editors, the book was "more worthily called, The Key to the Treasures hid in holy Scriptures ... A Light for Ministers, wherat they may borrow light; A Lanthorn for the people to direct them in the light."[30] Bagwell's description borrows from Psalm 119:105 and thereby reflects glories upon his own text that the verse reserves for the laws of God.

Neither Bagwell nor I contest the completeness of the Bible. All the parts of the natural world and the part of humanity in it may likewise operate in a still incompletely articulated total harmony. Over the centuries, the question of complete knowledge with respect to Scripture has played out in private worship and on the world stage in ways far beyond the scope of this inquiry. The purpose of this study is not to validate or explode such claims, but rather to examine the literary features put to the purpose of making that presumed completeness intelligible. Though I do not include the Bible itself as part of my study, the theological aspects and spiritual ramifications of pursuing "complete knowledge" constitute key components of many if not all of the texts under examination.

* * *

My analysis of completeness and its relationship to literature begins in the first decades of the seventeenth century. In *The Advancement of Learning* and *The Great Instauration*, Sir Francis Bacon declared that works that claimed or were believed to have brought the arts and sciences to a state of perfection actually left human knowledge woefully *in*complete. Bacon insisted that truly complete knowledge would emerge only from a genuinely comprehensive account of all phenomena—an account that the limitations of human memory and mortality ensured would take lifetimes and legions to compile. Bacon's emphasis on comprehensiveness and long-term collaboration set the new learning in opposition not only to the many whole arts and finished systems attempted in his lifetime, but also to the supposed encyclopedic knowledge in the epics of Homer and Virgil. When John Milton took up the mantle of epic poet nearly a half-century later, he wrote into his depiction of Eden the inadequacy of the single person, poet, or poem to comprehend complete knowledge in a postlapsarian world bereft of Raphael's archangelic mediation. These texts, all published during a period when the number of self-described "compleat bodies" of various arts and sciences was steadily growing, demonstrate how each author approached the matter of completeness of knowledge and the inadequacy of the epic form.

In 1704, John Harris published the first self-described "universal dictionary of arts and sciences" in the English language, thus inaugurating the British part in what has come to be known as the Age of Encyclopedias. The next chapter of my project (Chapter 3) examines how such universal dictionaries took over from epic the work of representing knowledge cohesively and comprehensively. The efficiency of print technology made planned obsolescence and the promise of "more complete" editions critical components of their durability. In 1728, Ephraim Chambers, as I have already noted, explicitly positioned the *Cyclopædia* as the epic's successor. A year later, the pointedly incoherent prose apparatus of Pope's *Dunciad Variorum* parodied the piecemeal construction of encyclopedias, magazines, and miscellanies alike. I argue that Pope advanced the autonomy of poetry by using it to identify both what kinds of knowledge should count in the future and how that knowledge should be understood. Pope attempted to make the discriminating poet rather than the comprehensive poem responsible for mediating complete knowledge. While Pope's projects advanced the autonomy of poetry, however, they also began to define its limitations. New versions of poems do not render their predecessors obsolete; as works of imaginative writing, each has equal purchase on posterity, and each destabilizes the integrity of the others.

Chapter 4 examines how the pursuit of completeness extended beyond poetry and encyclopedias to reshape several of the defining literary forms and texts of the mid-eighteenth century. Select features and functions of the epic and encyclopedia informed the literary experiments of Samuel Richardson and Henry Fielding; the massive and long-lived *An Universal History*; and the periodical and philological projects of Benjamin Martin. These experiments contributed to the ongoing reorganization of the broader system of literature as they both succeeded and (more importantly) failed to function as compendia of "complete" knowledge. Richardson's "writing to the moment" sought to make comprehensive accounts of his characters' lives while Fielding's epic plots emphasized closure and cohesiveness at the expense of detail; the proprietors of *An Universal History* strained to contain the gaps, disagreements, and scope of the documentary record without snapping the thread of a master narrative; magazine editors' intentions to review every publication that appeared became promises to review all those of note; and *Martin's Magazine* attempting to produce a complete body of arts and sciences one half-sheet at a time.

Chapter 5 returns to encyclopedias and epic poems. In 1768, a year after Sterne left *Tristram Shandy* behind, the first *Encyclopædia Britannica* departed from its own predecessors by offering extended individual systems and treatises dedicated to single subjects. The third edition formally (if temporarily) gave up the attempt to represent the unity of all knowledge by sharpening the boundaries among the modern disciplines. Not long after the *Britannica* officially gave up the task that the encyclopedias had taken over from epic earlier in the century, William Wordsworth boldly identified poetry as the last, best mediator of universal knowledge. He spent the rest of his life at work on an epic that recounted the journey of a life remembered not in comprehensive detail but rather through "spots of time." The chapter offers a new way of thinking about these "spots of time" as integrated with Enlightenment concepts of completeness and suggests that the newness of Romantic poetry inheres in its categorization according to other universalities. If by the end of the eighteenth century the concept of completeness had already begun to break up along disciplinary and literary lines, then by the time the last volume of Samuel Taylor Coleridge's *Encyclopædia Metropolitana* appeared in 1845, it had witnessed the final stages in what has been (but need not necessarily remain) a long-lasting separation.

As new technologies fuel the proliferation (or re-proliferation) of old and new materials alike, organizations like Google and Wikipedia have emerged to help manage the mass of knowledge available even as they contribute to its growth. Work likewise continues on developing new coding languages and web-scale reasoning systems that will change the nature of Search and the way knowledge is produced, organized, and consumed by both humans and machines. In the coda, I examine these technologies and the ways in which old and new forms and formal features have already begun to emerge and reemerge from the reinvigorated tension between the comprehensive and the cohesive and the continuing pursuit of complete knowledge. The work they do—or might do—I conclude, stands in the long shadow of the Enlightenment.

2
Complete Bodies, Whole Arts, and the Limits of Epic

In the first decades of the seventeenth century, the English philosopher and statesman Sir Francis Bacon declared in both *The Advancement of Learning* and *The Great Instauration* that any and all works that claimed or were believed to have brought the arts and sciences to a state of perfection actually left human knowledge woefully incomplete. In his plan to advance and achieve complete knowledge, Bacon recognized the need to compile a comprehensive account of all phenomena; he likewise acknowledged that the limitations of human memory and mortality ensured that such an account would take lifetimes and legions to complete. His emphasis on comprehensiveness and long-term collaboration, whether the result of design or necessity, set the new learning in opposition not only to the many self-described whole arts and complete systems attempted before, during, and after his lifetime, but also to traditional (though never uncontested) interpretations and praise of the classical epics.

Epic poetry had long enjoyed a critical association with encyclopedic learning. The reputation of Homer and Virgil's comprehensive knowledge in antiquity and the Middle Ages helped make epic an enduring signifier of great magnitude and longevity throughout the Renaissance. Readers of epic poems, however, no longer expect to find complete knowledge in the form of a unified account of all the arts and sciences as they stood at the time of the poem's composition. The theory of epic encyclopedism remained important into the eighteenth century (particularly, as I will show in Chapter 3, to writers of encyclopedias) but in practice the links had already begun to break by the time Milton took up the mantle of epic poet in the 1660s. *Paradise Lost* marks a legible inflection point in the broader pursuit of complete knowledge that advanced the permanent reduction of epic encyclopedism to poetic

18

synecdoche and divided "literary" completeness from its scientific and "non-literary" counterparts.

Despite the remarkable breadth of knowledge displayed by *Paradise Lost*—and despite the highly conventional accolades the poem received for having displayed it—Milton did not seek to provide a comprehensive account of human learning. He makes complete knowledge a subject rather than the substance of his epic; his depiction of Eden and humanity's fall reflects the inability of the single person, poem, or poet to comprehend complete knowledge in a postlapsarian world. Milton's approach to the questions of completeness and the inadequacies of the epic form in *Paradise Lost* did not inaugurate a formal break with encyclopedic learning so much as justify it to Christian theology and Baconian knowledge production in the context of an expanding knowledge market increasingly crowded with guidebooks, scientific dictionaries, and other reference works. These texts further complicated the concept of completeness by distinguishing between general and essential knowledge even within specific subject areas while simultaneously normalizing the processes of relatively frequent (and often competitive) revision, expansion, and re-publication.

No single sense of completeness emerges from these works, and few if any fit the Baconian ideal. Each fulfills the promise of complete knowledge according to different and changeable standards that err on the side of either comprehensiveness or comprehensibility. Together, however, they reveal a spectrum of authorial approaches to the conceptualization and textual representation of complete knowledge and the inadequacy of the epic form in seventeenth-century Britain.

Bacon's Lament

The defining work of Francis Bacon's life was one he knew he could not finish. In *The Advancement of Learning* (1605), Bacon insisted that "nothing parcel of the world is denied to man's inquiry and invention."[1] He likewise claimed that, when rightly understood, Solomon's warnings against too much reading, Saint Paul's misgivings about the links of philosophy to atheism, and even humanity's fall from grace itself constituted no moral, intellectual, or religious barriers to the human will and capacity to learn. Human knowledge, he believed, "may comprehend all the universal nature of things," and towards that end Bacon set to work on composing a new system of learning. At the time of his death in 1626, however, only *The New Organon*—originally intended as the second section of his six-part *Great Instauration*—was finished. Published at the height of his career and immediately preceding a dramatic decline in fortunes that included public disgrace and a brief stay in the Tower of London, the work that Bacon left to posterity ultimately left posterity to complete the best part of the work.

In addition to the methodological precepts Bacon set down as the basis of new scientific inquiry, he also professed the need for the kind of comprehensive work that the encyclopedists of the eighteenth century later insisted they could, did, or one day would supply. Indeed, he had intended the third part of *The Great Instauration* to record what he called "the *Phenomena of the Universe*; that is, every kind of experience, and a natural history such as can serve as the foundation on which to build philosophy."[2] Bacon offers the following description of the section:

> Now as to how it should be compiled, I arrange it as a history, not only of Nature free and untrammeled ... as is a history of heavenly bodies, of meteors, of the earth and sea, minerals, plants and animals—but much more of Nature constrained and vexed, by which I mean when, by the art and intervention of man, she is forced out of her natural state and is pressured and moulded. I would therefore describe at length all experiments in the mechanical arts, and in the operative part of the liberal arts, and in those practical crafts that have not developed into an art of their own.[3]

This comprehensive compilation would provide the groundwork for the subsequent sections, in which Bacon and his successors would in accordance with the rules of his inductive method determine higher-order axioms and partial explanations that would in turn "be subsumed under the totalising explanatory system of the sixth part."[4] Only then would Bacon's plan and human knowledge be brought to a state of completion.

Whatever that system might ultimately look like and however it might function, it would only emerge from a new and comprehensive foundational text or texts generated by modern methods of knowledge production. The future of human intellectual achievement, Bacon asserted, demanded that the wisdom of "a few received authors," too long viewed as the *ne plus ultra* of learning, be set aside so that humanity might explore uncharted waters.[5] In addition to articulating the flaws and limitations of classical learning—particularly that of Aristotle—Bacon modified the notion of the Homeric encyclopedia to fit his program for the new science. As Gerard Passannante argues, Bacon's assessment of Homer's apparent immortality relied upon a materialist sense of an always-unfixed Homeric corpus continually flowering through the perpetual scattering and recombination of its parts.[6] Instead of valorizing the *Iliad* and *Odyssey* as stable and divinely inspired bodies of universal knowledge, as others had, he numbered the poems among those books that continued to "cast their seeds in the minds of others, provoking and causing infinite actions and opinions in succeeding ages."[7] The seed metaphor recalls Politian's description of Homer as containing the *"semina"* of all disciplines as well as the pseudo-Plutarchan concept of the Homeric encyclopedia from which Politian borrowed, but Bacon borrows his sense of scattering ['*spargere'*] from Lucretius, who understood it as a generative rather than destructive process.[8]

Bacon's conceptual revision thus made the greatest part of Homer's contribution to knowledge production the inspiration of a collective and ongoing effort rather than an already complete and individual achievement. His own plan required the same kind of effort. Bacon's comments on Homer's immortality and the permanence of his words, as Anthony Grafton suggests, are entirely ironic; writing did not confer complete stability on the poems.[9] Writing, however—and more specifically print—would permit the progressive and perpetually self-revising program of learning that Bacon envisioned for the future. He recognized that the "shortness of life, ill conjunction of labours, ill tradition of knowledge over hand to hand, and many other inconveniences" that defined the human condition posed the greatest threat to his vision of humanity's future.[10] The success of that vision therefore depended (and continues to depend) not only upon a massive collaborative endeavor, but also on the efficient handing down of the ongoing achievements of that endeavor to successive generations of knowledge producers, consumers, and transmitters. Books, when properly preserved or given new life in fresh bodies, had already demonstrated their ability to outlast the civilizations that first produced them. Thousands of years after their composition, the Greek and Roman epics to some minds remained compendia of all the arts and sciences, and Homer and Virgil still stood amongst the founding fathers of knowledge. The medium, then, was proven; only the message needed changing.

Bacon, as I have already noted, viewed notions of completeness and the perfection they implied as one of the many inconveniences and ill traditions of knowledge potentially counterproductive to scientific inquiry and progress. In his opinion, the popularly celebrated authors and texts of his day that practiced or evinced some "neat method of summarizing knowledge" actually threatened to stall the advancement of learning either by leaving out important discoveries or by implying that there were none left to be made.[11] He devotes the entirety of Aphorism 86 in Book I to this concern:

> Moreover, the admiration of men for doctrines and arts, of itself rather naïve and almost childish, is increased by the cunning and artifice of those who have practiced and handed down the sciences. For they propound them with such ambition and affectation, and present them to view so shaped and masked, as if they were in all parts complete and finished. And if you look at their method of exposition and their partitions, they will seem to embrace and include every single thing that can fall within that subject. But although these divisions of the subject are badly filled out, and are like empty cases, yet to the common understanding they present the form and plan of a perfect science.
>
> But the first and earliest seekers after truth, with greater frankness and better success, were in the habit of casting the knowledge which they gathered from their study of things and which they intended to keep for use, into *aphorisms*, short and scattered sentences, not linked to each other by a rhetorical method of presentation; nor did they pretend or profess to embrace the entire art. But the way things are done now, it is hardly surprising that men look no further into matters that are handed down to them, as if they were perfect and long since complete in every respect.[12]

Bacon's reference to the first and more successful truth-seekers defines the two fundamental qualities of total completeness and sets them at odds within the context of his program for knowledge production. Collection must precede connection; he implicitly places greater immediate emphasis on comprehensiveness and reaffirms (albeit in a different sense) the utility of "scattered" ['*sparsas*'] rather than artificially "linked" ['*revinctas*'] knowledge.

In theory, the process of collecting, disseminating, and re-collecting knowledge would in time return to all of humanity some version of what Adam had supposedly possessed in himself: knowledge of all the useful arts and dominion over nature. The powers conferred on him by and through his encyclopedic knowledge (evinced in Genesis by his naming of the animals) were dispersed among his progeny and eventually lost. The course charted by Bacon in his *Instauratio Magna*, as Charles Webster writes, was "conceived as a means of completing the restoration of that harmony of nature which was sacrificed at the Fall."[13] The pursuit of complete knowledge was in this respect part of a larger concept of completeness with more than literary, material, or even practical implications. To declare prematurely any part of human knowledge "complete" was to delay or jeopardize an obviously unachieved but still eminently achievable ontological perfection.

Knowledge projects of similarly ambitious scope and equally unattained ends continued to rise and fall throughout the century and across the continent. Robert Burton's *Anatomy of Melancholy* (1621), for example, went through multiple editions that over several decades made the malady far more comprehensive than it had been in the original. As Christopher Grose explains, though, Burton's "emphatic distinction between an historical Democritus, *omnifariam doctus*, and the indefinitely deferred work which the present author sets about to 'complete and finish in this treatise,'" reflects his "doubts about the likely fate of encyclopedic intents."[14] René Descartes too had in common with Bacon a plan to achieve complete knowledge as well as an inability to complete that plan. Ian Maclean's description of *A Discourse on Rational Method* (1637) and its accompanying essays as a substitute for a work "that would have been more comprehensive, more coherent, and more 'scientific' in character" invokes both of the fundamental qualities of completeness.[15] The text itself reveals how Descartes' pursuit of those qualities set his plan at odds with itself: he declares in Part Two of *A Discourse* that in its last part he would "undertake such complete enumerations and such general surveys that [he] would be sure to have left nothing out," but in part six he acknowledges the impossibility of finishing such a task without the assistance of others. Such assistance would threaten conceptual unity, which according to an earlier assertion could only be achieved via single authorship.[16]

John Comenius, a contemporary of Bacon, Burton, and Descartes, similarly failed to see his comprehensive educational program through to fulfillment. He proposed in *Via Lucis* that the members of a projected Universal College should compose a series of sixteen handbooks as the foundation of a new national school system, including (among other things) a call for reforming all schools; an introductory encyclopedia of natural objects; several books on Latin grammar; an encyclopedic survey of natural philosophy, arts, and sciences; and the *Pansophia Opus*, a culminating "digest of human wisdom." As Webster observes, however, "it was ... impossible to follow Comenius's programme exactly," and the scope of the project overwhelmed even its creator.[17] Though Comenius printed parts of the seven-section, six-volume masterwork of his scheme for a Universal College, Universal Language, Universal Schools, and Universal Knowledge—*De Rerum Humanarum Emendatione*

Consultatio Catholica (A General Consultation on the Reform of Human Affairs)—neither he nor his heirs ever published a complete edition. Comenius's other, earlier, and often simpler writings continued to find favor among the puritans who would integrate them and the Baconian empiricism they sanctioned into their eschatological worldview, but his work, like that of Bacon and Descartes, remained unfinished.[18]

The influence of all these authors on Samuel Hartlib did not result in any equivalent single work or single-handed attempt to systematize human knowledge, but collaborations and extensive correspondence with a circle of knowledge producers across mid-century Europe did advance the universalist cause.[19] The Office of Address project based upon the Parisian *Bureau d'adresse* and for which the Hartlib Circle hoped to acquire state funding from the English Parliament involved creating and maintaining comprehensive registers of information.[20] In *The advice of W. P. to Samuel Hartlib. For the advancement of some particular parts of learning* (1647), William Petty writes that the Office would first need "to see what is well and sufficiently done already"; this could be achieved, he continues, by "perusing al Books and taking notice of all Mechanicall Inventions" and then sifting out the real or experimental learning they contained. Out of these books, "one Booke or great Worke may be made, though consisting of many Volumes."[21] The construction of indices and tables should follow, and the whole made the stable basis of continued research and a reformed educational system. In Petty's estimation, then, humanity's practical progress towards universal knowledge and the Office of Address's contribution to it depended not only upon a full assessment of extant learning but also its reduction to a single, extensive reference work.

In other words, an organized and systematic, if not systematized, pursuit of complete knowledge in the modern sense (as described by Bacon, understood by Petty, and recommended to Hartlib) would have to begin with some kind of encyclopedic body of learning. The "one Booke," which did not materialize in their lifetimes, was conceived as a collaborative venture that absolutely required many hands. Even if one reader could survey the entire body of works from which the great work was to be compiled, Petty insisted on multiple readers that would work in tandem to prevent errors and check each other's conformity to the proscribed method. Single agents could imagine Enlightenment and contribute to its progress, but, as Bacon and his successors made clear, they could not execute their plans and programs without aid—no matter how extraordinary their intelligence or extensive their educations. All of their masterworks, whether by design or necessity, evinced or advocated for at most a provisional completeness that placed the absolute at least temporarily out of reach.

The "Compleat" Guidebook

Bacon was not speaking abstractly in his condemnation of self-proclaimed complete arts and sciences designed to appeal to the common understanding. Although Aphorism 86 does not mention any of the offending writers or works by name, it does highlight several of the key phrases they deployed and had been deploying in their titles and prefaces throughout the long "now" of Bacon's experience. Indeed, from his vantage point in 1620, Bacon could look back on at least sixty years' worth of texts that advertised themselves in almost exactly these terms or held out precisely these promises. None, though, achieved the full measure of complete knowledge to which Bacon aspired. New works or new editions of established titles published with expanded or revised content announced that earlier versions had in some way been found wanting, and the very fact of those wants confirmed that the "neat arrangement" (and therefore implicit completeness) of the knowledge they contained had been premature.

Even amongst the "whole arts" and "compleat" bodies of knowledge, the concept of completeness and its relationship to utility lacked consistency. Amongst the earliest examples to refer to a "whole art" is Thomas Hill's 1556 abridged translation of Bartolommeo della Rocca's *Chyromantie ac physionomie anastasi*, which he titled *A brief and most pleasau[n]t epitomye of the whole art of phisiognomie, gathered out of Aristotle, Rasis, Formica, Loxius, Phylemo[n], Palemo[n], Consiliator, Morbeth the Cardinal and others many moe, by that learned chyrurgian Cocles.*[22] The original, published in Bologna in 1503, ran to six folio volumes; Hill's "epitome" condensed those six volumes into only eighty-eight pages in octavo. Setting aside the dubious validity of the science (which along with chiromancy or palmistry had by the mid-sixteenth century passed somewhat into the realm of pseudo-science and charlatanism), the title by itself indicates that the "whole art" was indeed already known and completely contained.[23] While Hill does not openly state that an epitome such as his could replace a full treatment like della Rocca's outright, the publication of such an account created the possibility that it might, and as the first text printed in England dedicated entirely to physiognomy it very probably (if temporarily) did.

This text and its successors, however, destabilize any sense of what wholeness might have meant with respect to the representation of even a single branch of knowledge. Hill at no point recommends reading the original and he does not explain the deficits of his summary. Furthermore, while his title suggests that della Rocca had captured the "whole art," by the end of the work Hill has quietly displaced him. In the final section, "a conclusion or briefe rehearsall of the whole arte of Physiognomie," Hill epitomizes his own epitome: "nowe let us reduce all these matters afore spoken, to a conclusyon: Although these afore rehearsed appeare sufficiente."[24] The conclusion thus becomes the epitome and the epitome, at eighty-eight pages, becomes the whole art. In 1613, a new edition of the work openly gave the whole art to Hill while continuing to worry the matter of apparent sufficiency raised by the old conclusion. The 129 pages of *A pleasant history declaring the whole art of physiognomy* expanded the epitome of 1556 by 47 per cent, but they still came nowhere near the scope of the "whole art" as comprehended by della Rocca's six volumes.

Bacon may or may not have known Hill's work, but he could have pointed to a number of recent texts with similarly suggestive titles. He would almost certainly have been familiar with the works of Gervase Markham (1568–1637), whose books on agrarian, veterinary, and domestic matters shaped the literary landscape of estate management for much of the early seventeenth century. Markham's works were instrumental in defining both a uniquely English national identity as well as the place of an English print market within it, and in 1610 he published the first edition of the work he evidently considered to be his masterpiece.[25] Entitled *Markhams maister-peece*, it promised that within its two books and roughly 500 pages one could find "all possible knowledge whatsoeuer which doth belong to any smith, farrier or horse-leech," including "all cures physicall" and "whatsoeuer belongeth to chirurgerie."[26] The word "possible" connotes precisely the kind of completeness that Bacon thought impeded progress. Markham purported to have captured not only all that was known, but also all that *could* be known, and rather than encourage readers to continue private exploration or experimentation so that the stock of knowledge might continue to grow—as Bacon no doubt would have preferred—a prefatory note insists in its last line that if readers would but follow it, then "the booke will make [them] most perfect."[27]

Whereas Hill's works suggest that the relationship of wholeness to length is at best arbitrary and that with respect to capturing a "whole art" the difference between recording all knowledge and recording all *necessary* knowledge may simply be semantic, Markham's more substantial treatment of farriery and its related arts unabashedly pretends to total coverage. Bacon lived to see a second printing of the *maister-peece* as well as the publication of several other books by Markham that supposedly contained the "whole art of riding great horses," the "whole discipline of war," and "the whole art of fowling."[28] He may also have encountered the whole arts of surgery, husbandry, planting, gardening, arithmetic, hunting, hawking, fishing, handwriting, and gunnery. Only his death in 1626 spared him from the abundance of other whole arts that continued to appear throughout the century.

The genres of completeness, however, went beyond treatments of single subjects. Those that took on more were even more likely to fall short of the Baconian ideal. Though "the original Greek concept of encyclopedia was available" before and during the seventeenth century, "it had become highly unstable, oscillating between the ideas of fundamental training and near universal knowledge."[29] Henry Peacham's *The compleat gentleman* of 1622 and Johann Heinrich Alsted's *Encyclopædia septem tomis distincta* of 1630 represent close contemporaries at opposite ends of that spectrum. Peacham's text divided into sixteen chapters and some 200 pages his argument in favor of genteel education and the circle of learning he deemed crucial to forming the character of an English nobleman. His perfect gentleman came complete with an understanding of style in speaking and writing, of history, cosmography (which in turn "containeth Astronomie, Astrologie, Geography and Chorography"), surveying, geometry, poetry, music, drawing and painting in oil, armory or blazonry, exercise of the body, travel, and the management of one's reputation and carriage in general. A careful reader, moreover, would come away from the text knowing not only *why* he should, for example, paint—"since Aristotle numbreth *Graphice* generally taken ... amongst those his παιδεύματα, or generous practises of youth in a well gouerned Common-wealth"—but to some extent *how*: representing black velvet, for instance, requires a base of lamp-black and verdigris, while a sword-hilt wants umber, red lead, and masticot.[30]

Peacham's is thus somewhat more than a historical or philosophical disquisition on the intellectual value of these subjects and their appropriateness for gentlemanly study. His invocations of the Aristotelian παιδεύματα (*paideumata*) clearly mark his text as participating in a genre that from the sixteenth century had applied the Latinized term for the circle or round of education to their treatments of the seven liberal arts: as Quintilian used and (mis)understood it, that term—*encyclopædia*—derived from ἐγκύκλιος παιδεία (*enkyklios paideia*), or "cyclical" and "education."[31] Peacham did not precisely follow either the classical or medieval curricula, but as a work dedicated to the concept of a "complete" education, *The compleat gentleman* was clearly encyclopedic in all but name.

It was not, however, encyclopedic in the same sense as Alsted's *Encyclopædia*. That work—among the first modern texts to be encyclopedic in name as well as in nature—also looked to ancient models, but Alsted described his compendium in more expansive terms. Its four volumes, Alsted wrote, comprised a "methodical systematization of all things which ought to be learned by men in this life. In short, it is the totality of knowledge."[32] In addition to illustrating the overarching organization of knowledge via multiple diagrams of disciplinary subdivisions and hierarchies, Alsted included sections on philologia and an extended treatment of philosophy before describing "twenty-one mechanical arts (from brewing to playing musical instruments)" and concluding with "a 'farrago of disciplines' comprising forty-one fields of study from Cabala and the physics of Moses to the study of tobacco ('tobacologia')."[33] Though both Alsted and Peacham's texts took a somewhat programmatic approach to the organization and transmission of knowledge—the systematic diagrams and philological information of the *Encyclopædia* are *præcognita* to the disciplinary treatises, and *The compleat gentleman* begins with a general overview of nobility before proceeding to its individuated components—only Alsted's includes a detailed alphabetical index that facilitates its use as a reference work.[34]

The finished *Encyclopædia*, though reprinted for the first and only time nineteen years after its original publication, remained influential for decades: it informed the work of Comenius, who studied under Alsted (and Johannes Piscator) in Herborn; Cotton Mather called it "a North-West Passage to all the Sciences"; and when Samuel Pepys came across a copy in St. Paul's Churchyard in 1660 (thirty years after its completion) he apparently thought it still worth the price of 38 shillings— well over half the £2 10s Pepys budgeted for an entire year's worth of theater-going in 1664.[35] Nevertheless, the fact that Gottfried Wilhelm Leibniz's own (unfinished though thoroughly contemplated) encyclopedic project began as a proposal to modernize and expand it underscores the fact that it was never the totality of knowledge it claimed to be.[36]

Nor, however, was Peacham's. Any gentlemen "completed" by the first edition of 1622 would have found themselves at a two-subject disadvantage to readers of the 1628 edition, and they in turn would have lacked the knowledge of statues and medals possessed by purchasers of the much-enlarged edition of 1634. Indeed, by 1661, *The compleat gentleman* had roughly doubled in length thanks to the addition of these new subjects and several largely self-contained "books" on matters more briefly treated within earlier chapters. The 450 octavo pages of that edition, though—the last to be published in Peacham's name, albeit some seventeen years after his death—could still not (and were likely never meant to) compete with Alsted's 2400 pages in folio.

That edition, moreover, did not include an index, and though chapters in the earlier editions rarely ran beyond fifteen pages (and could therefore be quickly read and re-read in their entirety), the eighty-seven pages on armory and heraldry as well as the three longer books appended to the last edition could not have been so easy to digest.

According to the standards that remain in place today, then, Alsted's *Encyclopædia* was the more "encyclopedic" undertaking. On occasion, though, less could mean just as much as more. Whereas Hill substantially expanded his epitome of physiognomy and Peacham his course of gentlemanly learning, Markham in 1616 did just the reverse with *The maister-peece*. In a note addressed to "the old and new readers," Markham describes how his latest work, *Markhams methode, or epitome*, emerged from the paradoxes of completeness. Though *The maister-peece* did, he insists, contain "euery disease, and euery medicine, so full & so exactly that there is not a Farriere in this Kingdome, which knowes a medicine for any disease ... but I will finde the substance thereof in that booke," some of his friends remained unsatisfied. He explains:

> The greatnesse of the booke and the great price thereof, depriued poore men of the benefit; and that the multiplicity of the medicines, and the cost of the ingredients, were such as poore men stood amazed at, and found that their beasts perished before they could compasse that should cure them: from whence onely I haue with much labor and experience found out the Contents of this Booke, where with twelue medicines, not of twelue-pence cost, and to be got commonly euerywhere, I will cure all the diseases that are in Horses, whatsoever, and they almost 300...[37]

The volume of what Markham initially represented as "all possible knowledge whatsoever" had made that knowledge less useful to those in need of it; in order to maximize its utility he had to reduce its size and scope. He therefore ingeniously (or shrewdly) discovered a way to perform the function of his more comprehensive treatment—granting the ability to cure all the diseases in horses and a host of other animals—with only twelve medicines and in only eighty pages.[38] If we may take him at his word, the reduction did not make the knowledge any less complete.[39] The above passage thus suggests that what constituted complete knowledge might have depended to some extent on what it cost to produce or purchase it.

As the century wore on, the number and kind of supposedly whole arts and complete bodies of knowledge continued to grow, and with each new title or edition the concept of completeness as they deployed it continued to lose any sense of the true finality and permanent perfection that Bacon had fretted over in the *Novum Organon*. Indeed, some accounts indicate that it had been evacuated of any true meaning at all. By 1640, the market for such works was apparently already so well saturated and the terms so much abused that the anonymous compiler of *A Manuall: or, analecta, being a compendious collection out of such as have treated of the office of Justices of the Peace* moved to debunk the notion of complete knowledge as being more advertising ploy than actual achievement. His manual, he writes, was in truth the latest version of a work "formerly (but vain-gloriously, to make it more *saleable*) styled *the Complete Justice*."[40]

Despite this author's objections to the trumping of substantive integrity by effective branding, however, the promise of perfection remained an operational trope of the guidebooks, manuals, and dictionaries that continued to emerge from the presses. These books were aimed at everyone from craftsmen, professionals, soldiers, and gentlemen to gentlewomen, ladies, midwives, and maids. Alsted's large, Latin *Encyclopædia*, for instance, could only have appealed to a well-educated and relatively affluent audience while Markham's shorter, English texts had lower barriers to entry in terms of both literacy and affordability. Some authors assured potential buyers that both the professionally interested as well as the merely curious might benefit from reading them; others insisted that even those of "the meanest capacities" or "weakest memories" might attain to the knowledge they held in store. Many claimed to comprehend greater breadth of knowledge than did their competitors and to have gathered that knowledge from the widest range of the best possible authors, whether foreign, domestic, ancient, or modern. Patrick Gordon's *Geography anatomized* (1693) deployed almost every keyword and catchphrase from the whole art of advertising: the frontispiece gives the full title of the work as *A compleat geographical grammer. Being a short and exact analysis of the whole body of modern geography, after a new, plain and easie method, whereby any person may in a short time attain to the knowledge of that most noble and useful science. Comprehending, a most compendious account of the continents, islands, peninsula's, isthmus, promontories, mountains, oceans, seas, gulphs, straits, lakes, rivers and chief towns of the whole earth.* By the close of the century, there were nearly 200 separate titles dedicated to summarizing and organizing at least fifty branches of knowledge ranging from astronomy, geography, and navigation to stenography, surveying, and trade.

Bacon might have taken some solace in the knowledge that the generality of texts made Markham's wholesale pretensions to completeness the exception rather than the rule. In 1635, for instance, William

Scott wrote in *An essay of drapery: or, the compleate citizen* that "though no knowledge is unfruitful; yet the course of a generall knowledge being too long, the knowledges most pertinent to himself, are to bee chosen, which hee shall hardly end before his course bee ended; so much is there to be known of his trade and about it."[41] Thomas de Grey marked several of the cures included in his *The compleat horseman and expert farrier* (1639) as untested and promised to verify their worthiness pending future trial.[42] Similarly, while a poem prefatory to Richard Elton's *The compleat body of the art military* (1650) applauds the author's ability to marshal his collected knowledge into an extensively and coherently complete work, Elton himself recognized that the work could not actually be counted as such in perpetuity. The poem, written by Captain John Hinde, opens thus:

> To give thee prayse according to thy skill,
> I want both *Virgils* verse and *Homers* quill.
> Experimentall knowledge of thine art,
> Commands my *Muse* to sacrifice her part
> To thy *Compendious* Body: so compleat,
> It may be term'd a *Lezbian* squires feat.
> Such sure defence was ne're in *Ajax* shield,
> As *Mars* and *Pallas* met in *Eltons* field.
> *Heroick art*, indeed, that doth unite
> In one, a number numberlesse to fight
> As if one hand did guide them all; nay more:
> Ne'r were such *Principles* in Print before.[43]

Hinde's appeal to the completeness of ancient knowledge is very much in keeping with a way of thinking that Bacon had wished to unsettle and that Elton implies is faulty. "All the expert and learned in this art have written before, and what succession shall dictate to the ages to come," Elton insists, "will be too little to leave nothing new to perfect it."[44]

The juxtaposition of the poetic conceit with the prosaic concession in Elton's work reflects the contradictions of complete knowledge and the productive indeterminacy of completeness as a literary feature. The most that Elton or indeed anyone else could reasonably claim was that their compendia had achieved a kind of practical perfection circumscribed by the bounds of the present state of learning and complete only inasmuch as their methods of collection and organization rendered that learning coherent. New knowledge would always provide justification for new volumes, but because completeness also depended on the "heroic art" (as Captain Hinde had put it) of uniting multiple facts and facets into a single body, authors and editors could even in the declaimed absence of significant discoveries or advancements tout the superiority of new books that more effectively negotiated the tension between the comprehensive and the coherent. E. R., the gentleman author of *The experienc'd farrier, or, A compleat treatise of horsemanship* (to return once more to a subject itself frequently revisited in the seventeenth century), explains: "these Old Collections are become New, not because they are New Printed, but because they are New Digested and Modelized, and put into a better Form and Method than ever yet before Printed. For let me tell you, there was never any thing in this Nature ever Printed before, but there was something or other wanting to make it a Compleat Book of Faring."[45] Having said that, the author also claims to have added over 150 new recipes and directions along with a table of the virtues and most up-to-date prices of the recommended drugs as sold by the druggists of London. Naturally, the next edition was very much enlarged.

Such assertions were commonplace. *The academie of eloquence* (1653), which contained "a compleat English rhetorique," was supposedly "digested into an easie and methodical way to speak and write fluently, according to the mode of the present times."[46] The prefatory note to *The husbandman, farmer, and grasier's compleat instructor* (1697) insisted that "although this Book, to Appearance, seems little, it contains much more than at first sight can be reasonably imagined, far exceeding what the Title Page sets forth; and indeed much more adapted to the Purpose, than all the books of its kind."[47] Finally, the second edition of John Evelyn's translation of Jean de la Quintinie's *The compleat gard'ner* (1699)—"Now Compendiously Abridg'd, and made of more Use" by George London and Henry Wise—claimed to have "reduc'd into a proper method, that in the which the Original is so prolix and interwoven, that the reader was rather tir'd than inform'd."[48] The ubiquity of these works' claims that more judicious selection, marginal glosses, alphabetization, tables, or even simple word economy could drastically improve the coherence of the knowledge they contained to some extent represents nothing more than the chatter of a crowded marketplace. Though they did deploy different organizational features, actual degrees of difference remain difficult to qualify. Nevertheless, the sense that textual compendia could effectively manage what was perceived or presented as an overabundance of information remained critical to their ongoing production even as their numbers made them part of the problem they had been designed to solve.

Whatever the claims of an individual work with respect to embracing an entire art or science, and despite the application to the many arts and sciences of as many neat methods of summarizing knowledge, when considered as a body of texts with a legible history and a clear *modus operandi*, these self-proclaimed complete works would have made obvious to the generality of mid- and late seventeenth-century readers—even those of the most common understanding—that they did not traffic in perfection so much as perfectibility. They did not, broadly speaking, construe completeness as a binary state. New knowledge and new organizational tactics made them, to borrow a common phrase of the time, "more complete"—a phrase that implicitly allows for the possibility of progress. Francis Gouldman, like many others, wrote that possibility into the title and preface of his *A copious dictionary in three parts* (1664). He describes the work as "the most complete and useful of any in this kind yet extant" before asking "who can fix the time when such works are at the height of all desirable or possible Perfection, where Hercules's Pillars may be placed with a Ne plus Ultra?"[49] Both quotations speak to Gouldman's understanding that just as he had followed in the footsteps of others, so others would follow in his.

If this question recalled to some readers' minds the frontispiece to *The Great Instauration* and Bacon's warnings against so-called "complete" works, then Gouldman's concluding thoughts spoke to another concern that would continue to trouble readers and writers alike for decades to come. "We are not guilty of so much vanity," Gouldman continues, "as to pretend this work Perfect, either in the Whole, as if nothing could be added; or in its Parts, as if nothing might be altered: *Nor can any humane Work lay claim to this priviledg*, much less Dictionaries in which are so great varieties and intricacies."[50] Guilt, vanity, perfectibility, and the possibility (or impossibility) of complete knowledge would be at the heart of another great seventeenth-century work the ancestors of which had conventionally been thought of as the greatest compendia of learning ever composed.

Epic Fail

By 1667, the question of how much and what kinds of knowledge the classical epics truly comprehended had not been definitively answered—despite its having been asked and argued about since antiquity. As early as the sixth century BC, Theagenes of Rhegium, often credited as Homer's first allegorizing exegete, defended Homer from contemporary detractors by finding in the poems' depictions of the Greek pantheon a veiled treatment of natural and moral phenomena: Apollo and Poseidon, for example, stood respectively for fire and water,

Athena and Ares for wisdom and folly.[51] Allegory similarly informed the interpretations of Anaxagoras of Clazomenae and his pupil, Metrodorus of Lampascus, two other readers of the sophistic period. Whereas Anaxagoras seems to have performed a relatively cautious form of moral allegoresis on the texts, his student devised a more radical interpretation that identified the gods and heroes of the *Iliad* as different parts of the universe and human body—possibly in order to justify the poem to his master's model of the macrocosm and microcosm.[52] Conventional wisdom has also marked the Stoics as allegorists, for they too found in Homer's descriptions of certain episodes "a correct understanding of the world—its physical structure and processes, its god(s), its basic causes and purposes."[53] To these readers, amongst others, Homer deliberately crafted his epics as vehicles for the encyclopedic knowledge he apparently possessed.

This view did not go unchallenged. Critics accused the Stoics "of willful misreading and distortion"; Plato "adopted an adversarial position with regard to the 'Homeric encyclopedia,' and the Ionian philosophical tradition before him had been actively hostile."[54] The astronomer, geographer, and mathematician Eratosthenes denigrated the epics as entirely frivolous entertainments, and though Strabo later argued that Homer truly had founded the science of geography and provided much demonstrably accurate information about what had been the known world, he also conceded that a man who attempts "to ascribe all knowledge to Homer" might be one "whose enthusiasm has gone too far."[55] Despite their doubts and derision, however, the belief that Homer's poems contained the complete learning of their time continued to find purchase. The pagan Neoplatonists of the third century, for instance, looked to the epics as texts of wide-ranging authority. Pseudo-Plutarch's extensive essay on Homer's life and verse described him both as a gifted philosopher and as the master of a broad spectrum of practical *technai*; the text painted an enduring portrait of the poet as the father of all of the arts and sciences as well as every subsequent literary genre.[56]

That essay remained "the favourite ancient text on Homer in the Renaissance," and though notable humanists of the fifteenth and sixteenth centuries like Michel de Montaigne and Julius Caesar Scaliger often turned a skeptical eye towards the allegories and syncretism upon which Homer's supposedly universal knowledge depended, the concept of such knowledge nonetheless remained closely associated with epic composition both during and long after their lifetimes.[57] Politian's description of Homer's poems as compendia that contained the seeds of all learning drew much from the image drawn by pseudo-Plutarch;

allegoresis, validated by international consensus, continued to "reveal" the abundance of natural, theological, and moral truths in Homer's poems to students. Even Francis Bacon found some merit in the allegorical tradition that located in the Homeric myths "remnants of a lost Greek cosmology far more profound than those of Plato and Aristotle."[58] The fact that Bacon, in *The Advancement of Learning*, specifically mentions and dismisses as hyperbole the idea that "if all sciences were lost, they might be found in Virgil" furthermore implies the extent to which that poet's reputation as another master of all human knowledge—a commonplace in the Middle Ages—still retained some measure of currency in the early seventeenth century.[59]

Modernity, then, inherited an epic tradition steeped in a complex and still unsettled debate about the relationship of epic poetry to the production, containment, and transmission of encyclopedic knowledge. If Milton "would have considered it the duty of a writer of epic to embrace *all* the learning of his day," as Karen Edwards suggests, then any sense in which he might have done so would not necessarily have been uniformly understood. The practice and theory of epic, as suggested above, were by his time already somewhat divided. Renaissance epicists, though they might often have received the same compliments given to poets of ages past, far less frequently made actual claims to having comprehended all knowledge or were deemed to have failed strictly for want of inclusiveness. Dante had concerned himself more with spiritual than earthly matters, and neither Ariosto nor Tasso explicitly sought to capture the full extent of human learning. Camoens' *The Lusiads* (*Os Lusíadas*) pays homage to Homer and Virgil, but it follows in their footsteps primarily as a national epic focused on the figure and exploits of Vasco da Gama.

The first half of the seventeenth century, though, saw a number of poetic projects that, while they did not pursue universal coverage, still accomplished less than the fully encyclopedic treatments of various subjects that their authors originally intended. Edmund Spenser, for one, had thought that "to fashion a gentleman or noble person in virtuous and gentle discipline" would take twenty-four books, but he left *The Færie Queene* unfinished in twelve.[60] Michael Drayton devoted nearly twenty-five years and 7500 alexandrine couplets to the topographical and quasi-historical survey of Britain that was his *Poly-Olbion*, but by the time the final twelve songs appeared in 1622 he had yet to turn his attention to Scotland.[61] Though Phineas Fletcher's Virgilian epic *The Purple Island* (1633) did display detailed knowledge of human anatomy both in the verse and in the more scientific marginal glosses of its first five cantos, the poem earned its author few accolades and went without revision or new notes for 150 years.[62]

To those who defended the supremacy of ancient learning over modern and deemed the successful epic "the greatest Work Humane Wit is capable of," Homer and Virgil had truly achieved a version of complete knowledge.[63] These words, which belong to the anonymous English translator of René Le Bossu's influential *Traité du poème épique* (1675), express the sentiments of René Rapin, the French Jesuit scholar whose works figured prominently in the *Querelle d'Homère* and "provided the standard neoclassical view of Homer's omniscience."[64] *Paradise Lost* initially received a great deal of praise very much in that tradition. In a poem printed with the 1674 edition, for example, Samuel Barrow called it "the story of everything," and Joseph Addison later described it as a book in which "every Thing that is great in the whole Circle of Being, whether within the Verge of Nature, or out of it, has a proper Part assigned it."[65] Milton's epic, though, actually marks the ancient substance of epic encyclopedism as impracticable in an age of modern knowledge production and opposed to Milton's understanding of the teleology of human learning in its postlapsarian state. The world that lay all before Adam and Eve at the end of the poem and the new work of knowing that they would have to do are external to Eden and the possibility of complete knowledge as it had there existed. So too, Milton suggests, are they beyond the bounds of a literary genre that like Eden had once been a place wherein the mortal most closely approached the divine.

The critics, scholars, and poets who have attempted to codify that divinity had (and have) for more than two thousand years resorted to various concepts of completeness in order to advance their arguments.[66] Despite Bacon's efforts to shift the works of Aristotle from the path of new knowledge production, they remained an authority with respect to the rules of poetic and dramatic composition. To many, the critical history of epic completeness began with his *Poetics*, a work concerned primarily with drama and (ironically) incomplete in its treatment of epic.[67] Like tragedy, the form to which he ultimately gave the highest rank, epic according to Aristotle "should be concerned with a single action which is a whole and complete, with a beginning, middle, and an end, like a single animal, which is a whole."[68] The unity of any beautiful thing—unity being a requirement of beauty and a characteristic of the perfection implied by completeness—consists in the proper ordering of its parts and the appropriateness of its magnitude to the observer.

Tragedy, wrote Aristotle, could accomplish completeness (and most other things) with greater success than epic. The principal advantage epic had over tragedy consisted in the ability of the former to incorporate a greater number of diverse episodes than the latter—a function of its narrative structure, which permitted the poet to represent multiple simultaneously occurring events. What one gained in scope, however, one frequently lost in cohesion. Aristotle's final words on the subject remark upon the lesser unity of epic imitation and deny the status of the *Iliad* and *Odyssey* as perfect unities at all. These poems, he concludes, have many parts of "considerable magnitude" in themselves, and though each poem "is constructed as well as it can be and is, as far as possible, an imitation of a single action," the sheer number of episodes and actions each contains—and which make an epic epic—ultimately negated the possibility of their achieving perfect completeness.[69] Comprehensiveness properly belonged to (if anyone) the historian, who could record series or simultaneities of events without worrying if they led to a single end.[70] The entire Trojan War, Aristotle observed, had too many parts and players to make a fit plot for an epic poem; it could not be "grasped as a whole" and "would have become too complex in its variety of events."[71] Even Homer, with his greater share of divine inspiration, could not manage it.

Aristotle therefore insisted that the primary concern of the poet must be unity. Though the extent to which the *Iliad* and *Odyssey* achieve completeness is necessarily limited, what unity they do possess results from authorial discernment rather than inclusivity. Aristotle identifies the completeness of these works as an effect of selectivity and narrative fictionalization; instead of following the historian, as too many poets did, Homer judiciously selected only a part of the Trojan War and a number of episodes from it in order to create a narrative for the *Iliad* that his audiences would be better able fully to comprehend. The "real" world, according to Aristotle (or even such a relatively small part of it as the Trojan War), with its daunting surplus of information and the lack of apparent connectivity among its parts, could not be represented to or comprehended by an audience with as much unity (and therefore beauty) as a carefully constructed and limited account the whole of which exceeded the sum of its parts. The full beauty of the world was necessarily lost on an individual whose mind and memory were unequal to the task of comprehending how all its parts might lead to some single end. A shade of that beauty, however, could be seen in the fictions and fables that approached unity by leaving enough information out of the picture.

Unfortunately, Aristotle gave no indication of exactly how much information is too much. Debates about what if anything constituted epic unity continued throughout the sixteenth and seventeenth centuries, when the *Poetics* again became a central focus of critical attention. Castelvetro identified the single action of a single hero as the highest form of subject matter, whereas Tasso insisted that the action "does not depend on the individual for cohesion or form," and that "true epic" may incorporate not only numerous incidents but multiple heroes as well.[72] Ben Jonson later pointed out that the classical poets in any case gave only partial accounts of their heroes' lives. Even the action of an individual, he claimed, was too various and complex a matter to comprehend as a cohesive unity. Virgil and Homer included no more about the lives of their heroes than they deemed essential to their respective purposes. Virgil "pretermitted" detailed descriptions of Aeneas's birth, upbringing, and battle with Achilles, and Homer too "laid by many things of Ulysses" that would have added to the length of his poem but diminished its overall coherence.[73] An ideal epic, then, according to Jonson, could contain neither a comprehensive account of an event like the Trojan War nor the whole life of anyone who fought in it. An epic hero could only be complete in the same restricted sense as an epic plot.

Jonson's conclusions about epic, though, ultimately echo those of Aristotle. Every work has its natural bounds and just proportions: a hall may not have the grandeur of a palace, but each can achieve the perfection appropriate to its class. The epic should have greater magnitude than tragedy or comedy, and the poet should seek to extend that magnitude to the greatest extent possible without overwhelming the mental capacities of the audience and thereby forfeiting that unity which makes an action and an epic one and whole. Though Jonson repeats Aristotle's observation that the poet takes some risk in dissatisfying audiences with a subject too small to fill the space, the best part of his commentary and the addition of his observations on the unity of individual action suggest that the greater danger to the skilled poet lay in affrighting readers with overabundance and complexity. The structure of an epic, like a house, might contain "divers materials," but with respect to both the length of its plot and the lives of its protagonists an epic, again like a house, must close out a great deal more than it encompasses if its author hopes to render it appreciably complete.

René Le Bossu revisited these matters only a few decades after Jonson. By the time his *Traité du poem epique* first became available in an English translation (twenty years after its initial publication), it had earned its author significant acclaim and established a new groundwork of critical thought about the genre. In 1701, John Dennis claimed that "none of the Moderns understood the Art of Heroick Poetry, who writ before

Le Bossu took pains to unravel the Mystery."[74] A quarter of a century after that, large sections of it appeared before Pope's translation of *The Odyssey*.[75] Like many of his predecessors, Le Bossu (who favored corporeal rather than architectural metaphors to demonstrate the right relationships of parts to wholes) emphasized the importance of proportion and connectivity to completeness; however, in the seventh chapter of the second book he finally says about the unity of epic action what generations of critics before him must have thought: "The Unity of the Epick Action, as well as the Unity of the Fable, does not consist either in the Unity of the Hero, or in the Unity of Time: This is what we have already taken notice of. But 'tis easier to tell wherein it does not consist, than 'tis to discover wherein it does."[76]

The unity of the epic, Le Bossu then dares to venture, depends not only upon the connectedness of its parts but also the *in*completeness of those parts in and of themselves relative to that whole. "Each Member," Le Bossu writes, "should be no more than a Member; an imperfect Part, and not a finish'd compleat Body."[77] Aristotle had already said as much. Le Bossu, however, advances upon Aristotle's arguments by offering a conception of the complete epic that locates multiple hierarchical orders of completeness operating within the narrative. He contends that an author can complete an action in two ways: with respect to the principal characters and circumstances involved (which destroys unity of action), or with respect to characters and circumstances ancillary to the principals (which preserves unity of action). Homer, Le Bossu explains, leaves the duel between Paris and Menelaus unresolved; this irresolution marks the action of Paris, Menelaus, and Helen—and by extension, the entire Trojan War—as subordinate to the greater action of Achilles' anger, which the subordinate action does not complete. Similarly, the episode of Dido in the *Aeneid* contains an action complete only with respect to Dido; to Aeneas and the action that defines his role as hero, the episode serves as obstacle rather than end. In order to produce a right reading of the incident, Le Bossu contends, the poet must prevent the reader from losing sight of the larger order in which Dido plays only a part, and the reader must maintain the proper perspective as established by the poet.

The ability to integrate and articulate these multiple orders of completeness exemplified one aspect of that near-divinity still attributed to the best poets by Le Bossu and other contemporary critics of like mind. To those readers who looked to Homer and Virgil for an understanding of nature—as many insisted they could and should—the epics offered a functional approximation of an idealized universal order. When correctly understood, Le Bossu insists, the unities of Homer's and Virgil's epics are "exact."[78] Any failure to appreciate the completeness they achieve, he suggests, originates in misreading or misunderstanding rather than the integrity of the material. The right way to read the poems would be to presume their perfection and relegate what might appear as disharmonious or disconnected events to their appropriate, subordinate places within the greater single action. The genius of the epic poets resided in their creation of a narrative that made the unity of this greater single action visible and comprehensible.

Though Le Bossu does not specifically advance a theological argument in his articulation of epic completeness, Milton does, and within the Christian framework of his epic the subordination of parts to wholes that Le Bossu labeled essential to the apprehension of perfect unity in the classical epics becomes integral to Milton's updated and parallel programs of moral instruction and the advancement of knowledge. Convention, as I have already explained, held up the classical epic as a reflection of the divine nature; Christian theology said as much about the natural world. To read one was to read the other, and both should therefore be read the same way: presume their perfection and attribute apparent inconsistencies or disunity to the inescapable limitations of human understanding. Milton, however, problematizes epic completeness by choosing a subject the action of which the narrative of *Paradise Lost* does not and cannot complete.

Rather than offering a text in any way mistakable for a complete body of modern knowledge, Milton directs his readers' attention beyond the boundaries of the epic narrative and towards their own part in the heroic work of knowing that remained to be done in the world. Human learning does not stop at the end of *Paradise Lost* but begins anew under drastically altered conditions—conditions that continued to inhere in the seventeenth century but which had been joined with new standards and modes of knowledge production.[79] Before the Fall, Adam's study of God and the natural world takes place in concert under the direction of Raphael, whom Milton describes "in terms that associate the archangel with the emerging sciences."[80] This association lends those sciences the esteem of divine authorization and adds them to the many other parts of human learning that had a recognizable if idealized presence in the garden as components of a complete body of knowledge. Though Milton's dramatic presentation of these lessons divides several categories of knowledge (theological, historical, moral, and natural) into multiple books and dialogues, Raphael's single-source mediation always implies their ultimate unity.

The sciences retain their importance in the aftermath, but whereas in Eden Adam could fruitfully pursue and comprehend that value via direct individual effort, the Fall necessitated the transformation of his singular endeavor into the kind of long-term collective undertaking described by Bacon in *The Advancement of Learning*. A corollary epistemological change attends the ontological change wrought by disobedience. With Adam and Eve's removal from Eden comes the loss of Raphael as guide and the ability to know the world as they once had.[81] Some degree of the knowledge and quality of comprehension they possessed, however, remains discoverable or retrievable in the world beyond the walls. Michael explains: "in valley and in plain/God is as here and will be found alike/Present, and of his presence many a sign/Still following thee, still compassing thee round."[82] The phrase "compassing thee round" figures the physical universe as a kind of encyclopedic compendium: a Book of Nature that comprehended a "round of education" in itself and the study of which would lead, or lead back, to knowledge of God.[83]

Understanding those many signs absent the prelapsarian state of human perfection requires the descendants of Adam and Eve to take a more comprehensive approach to knowledge production.[84] Disobedience makes distinction rather than unity the principal mode of human comprehension. Satan speaks of the power given him by the tree, the "Mother of Science," to "discern things in their causes," and though he never actually eats of the fruit, in this much at least the devil speaks true: the tree does bestow the power to discern.[85] The first knowledge of humanity's postlapsarian experience comes from understanding difference; Adam and Eve learn to know good and evil.[86] Their new power to discern—from the Latin *discernere*, literally "to separate"—divides one branch of knowledge into two and makes fragmentation the new basis of human epistemology.[87] Discovering truth in the postlapsarian world, as Kathleen Swaim writes, "requires human beings to collect as many as possible fragments towards a total structure. Once fragments have been collected, they must be remembered, or re-collected, as the standard against which future options are measured and to which true additions may be made." This "shift from space to time and from established unity to progressive transcendence of divisions," Swaim continues, "is precisely the difference between the prelapsarian and the postlapsarian."[88]

Milton's Protestantism made the process of gathering fragments of Christian truth a matter of scriptural exegesis performed by the individual, who must struggle to comprehend their unity. This vision of the Fall establishes a course by which the advancement of human knowledge proceeds back to unity not despite division but *through* it. That process aligns

Milton's religious methodology with that of the natural philosophers who likewise sought to undo the damage of the Fall by collecting fragments of knowledge. Bacon had made fragmentary forms such as the essay and aphorism the new basis of knowledge production and progress; in *The Great Instauration*, he specifically declared "compleat" bodies of learning and premature reductions of fragments into supposedly unified systems counterproductive to the search for truth.[89] Nearly half a century later, the Royal Society adopted a similar policy:

> The Society has reduc'd its principal observations, into one common stock; and laid them up in publique Registers, to be nakedly transmitted to the next Generation of Men; and so from them, to their Successors. And as their purpose was, to heap up a mixt Mass of Experiments, without digesting them into any perfect model: so to this end, they confin'd themselves to no order of subjects; and whatever they have recorded, they have done it, not as compleat Schemes of opinions, but as bare unfinish'd Histories.[90]

Sprat's *The history of the Royal-Society* appeared in the same year as the first edition of *Paradise Lost*, and with respect to the methods of mediating completeness they describe or perform, the positions defined by each neatly divide the concept along what they helped to define as the boundaries separating the sciences from the humanities and literature from Literature. Even the greater magnitude of the epic could not contain the whole circle of the arts and sciences as they appeared to readers in the latter half of the seventeenth century, and to those who had redefined the terms of understanding and advancing them any attempt to do so was either bound to fail or likely to be superseded.

Paradise Lost, then, could not offer the comprehensive knowledge valued by the practitioners of the new science while attempting to represent how such knowledge might ultimately cohere, and the unfinished histories and essays of the Royal Society could not provide the coherence of epic while remaining open to the process of correction and expansion. The poem suggests that the mediation of complete knowledge as a function of literary representation finally demanded a division of labor—in essence, an updated version of Aristotle in which the modern epicist prioritized the presentation of a limited, literary unity and left the production and collection of different kinds of knowledge to other writers and literatures unburdened by the other conventions of epic composition and completeness. In short, no book of human knowledge about the world could be the last or the only book one would ever need—regardless of what one believed about Homer and Virgil.

The broader print market of the period, furthermore, was already awash in dozens of "complete" guidebooks, treatises, enchiridia, and scientific dictionaries that devoted hundreds and sometimes thousands of pages to every segment of the circle of arts and sciences. As Edwards argues, "new *kinds* of encyclopedias were reflecting the new interests of the experimental philosophers ... *Paradise Lost*, while not ignoring the learning of the traditional encyclopedias, nonetheless fully acknowledges the new encyclopedias in its depiction of plants and animals."[91] That "acknowledgement" functions as a substitute for the kind of complete inclusivity traditionally associated with the ancient heights of epic composition. No poet could possibly have covered so vast a range of knowledge in equivalent detail. *The compleat chymical dispensatory* (1669), for example, offered over 500 pages of information about "all sorts of metals, precious stones, and minerals, of all vegetables and animals, and things that are taken from them, as musk, civet, &c. how rightly to know them, and how they are to be used in physick."[92] The nearly 200 pages on ordnance, metallurgy, and mathematics comprising *The compleat gunner, in three parts* (1672) likewise made available much more knowledge potentially useful to the aspiring artilleryman than could Milton's descriptions of the cannon deployed during the war in heaven. Moreover, however much information Adam might have possessed about the assorted florae of God's creation, he never makes so full a display of it as does the compiler of *The compleat gardeners practice, directing the exact way of gardening in three parts* (1664).

The scope and number of such works continued to grow throughout the period, and with every new edition, supplement, or competing advertisement came the suggestion that humanity had made some progress towards an even "more complete" account of knowledge. The commonplace phrase furthermore implied continued growth, comprehensibility, or usefulness. For Milton to embrace all the learning of his day meant to embrace the incompleteness of that learning and the limitations of a single human mind. Raphael's conversation with Adam specifically addresses those limits and dramatizes the challenges of epic encyclopedism in the context of modern knowledge production: the same speech in which the angel necessarily avoids giving a definitive answer to the still-unsettled question of heliocentrism discourages Adam from seeking knowledge above his station and emphasizes the pursuit of that which has more "use."[93] *Paradise Lost*, rather than attempting to comprehend all knowledge—knowledge that had changed and would continue to change—signals Milton's assessment of epic completeness. The text remains another kind of fragment: complete as a poem, perhaps, but still just one part of a larger body of knowledge its author could conceive of but not comprehend in its entirety. Milton is no angel; he might notionally embrace all learning, but he does not seek to contain or comprehend it.[94]

In short, *Paradise Lost* could only do its part. As a text interested and invested in the progress of human learning, Milton's epic devotes more energy to advancing new forms of literary and imaginative knowledge production than it does to those parts of knowledge that had largely become the province of other forms of writing. The status of epic as compendium, though, perseveres in Milton's incorporation of "so complete a spectrum of literary forms and genres."[95] His "encyclopedia of literary forms" uses the genre system it comprehends in order to change that system and alert readers to the cultural and moral values embedded within it; major classical and Renaissance paradigms undergo a process of transformation in *Paradise Lost* that runs parallel to the progress of Milton's religious, social, and political educational programs.

The completion of the narrative in turn completes a series of shifts that at once mark the old paradigms as defunct and declare the new ones morally perfected by their marriage to the content of that narrative. This transformation of the system, Barbara Lewalski writes, created "new models which profoundly influenced English and American writers for three centuries."[96] This rejuvenation of literary forms represents the poem's principal contribution to knowledge production: it restored the possibility of advancement in the realm of *imaginative* writing—one of few kinds that could do the work necessary to but left undone by the other genres of Enlightenment. In so doing, however, it would seem to have sacrificed the one greater form in its attempt to restore the rest. As many have observed, Milton's epic, despite its vitality, did not generate a lasting line of like texts. To the extent that he made the redemption of other literary forms part of the work of his epic, then, finishing the former meant finishing off the latter.

3

Worlds Apart:
Epic and Encyclopedia
in the Augustan Age

In the early eighteenth century, a new generation of encyclopedias and encyclopedists began to claim that they could put some version of complete knowledge in hand. John Harris and Ephraim Chambers both believed that some understanding of the relationships between the different branches of knowledge would prove useful not only to the reader but to the continued advancement of knowledge itself. Harris, for example, stressed in 1704 that his *Lexicon technicum*—England's first self-described "Universal Dictionary of Arts and Sciences"—was a book "useful to be *read carefully over*" as well as consulted occasionally, as if by such treatment a reader might come away from it with a sense of knowledge as a totality rather than a mere collection of data.[1] Chambers, editor of the subsequent and far more successful *Cyclopædia* (1728), thought that the ancient divisions of knowledge into discrete parts had severely impeded progress, and he positioned his own work as both the symbol and location of a new mode of knowledge production that embraced connectivity. "I do not know whether it might not be for the more general Interest of Learning," he wrote, "to have all the Inclosures and Partitions thrown down, and the whole laid common again, under one distinguished name."[2] The *Cyclopædia* attempted to do both; it embraced an even greater number of arts and sciences than Harris's *Lexicon* and attempted to demonstrate the relationships of their terms and parts with the help of a genealogical tree of knowledge as well as a detailed system of internal cross-references. Both authors executed their works under the assumption that the whole circle of learning could be textually represented and "grasped by an individual mind."[3]

In attempting to do that work, the eighteenth-century encyclopedists appropriated a function of what had long been considered the highest form of writing: epic. This chapter examines how these "universal" dictionaries along with the continued expansion of the print market and contemporary constructions of literary history both in Britain and beyond created a set of circumstances in which the Augustans' attempts to defend the high status of the poet furthered the division of literary from non-literary writing. Their defense of the Homeric epic required a reconsideration of the nature of Homer's learning not only with respect to the issues of taste, decorum, and morality at the center of the *Querelle d'Homère*, but also with regard to modern knowledge production and the work of epic in general.

The works of Alexander Pope are particularly revealing in this light. His translations of Homer and original projects like *The Dunciad* advanced the autonomy of poetry by using it to identify both what *kinds* of knowledge should count in the future and how that knowledge should be valued. In other words, Pope attempted to make the discriminating poet rather than the comprehensive poem responsible for mediating complete knowledge as he understood it and as he would have it understood by others. His poetry and prose advanced the decoupling of epic from genuinely encyclopedic completeness and promulgated the now conventional understanding of epic as encyclopedia even as others sought to establish a now forgotten sense of encyclopedia as epic.

The classics remained widely praised for the comprehensive knowledge they supposedly contained long after Bacon's disparagement of Virgil in 1605 and Milton's death in 1674. Thomas Hobbes, for example, deployed the ancient commonplace in the preface to his translations of Homer's *Iliad* and *Odyssey* (1677). The two poems, he wrote, contained "the whole learning of his time (which the Greeks call *Cyclopædia*)."[4] Pope sounded a similar note in the prefatory matter to his own translation of the *Iliad* nearly two decades later. Homer, he wrote, possessed "comprehensive Knowledge," and had taken in "the whole Circle of Arts, and the whole Compass of Nature."[5] When Virgil set about writing his own great works, Pope believed, he had but to look to Homer to discover any part of nature. Modern readers, he insisted, could still do the same—provided that they brought to their inquiry taste, discernment, and a correct understanding of the work of the poet.

The Quarrel of the Ancients and Moderns that raged through late seventeenth-century France and defined much of Restoration culture in Britain emerged from already well-established tensions between the humanities and sciences. The Quarrel itself became, as Dan Edelstein writes, "the catalyst that precipitated the Enlightenment narrative. By obliging its participants to consider how the present compared with the distant past, the Quarrel provided both an opportunity for self-reflection ... and a conceptual framework (Ancient versus Modern) around which to structure their comparisons."[6] As Joseph Levine has shown, by 1700 the republic of letters had been divided "into different and hostile camps" reinforced by advances in experimental science and classical philology.[7] To many of antiquity's most stalwart defenders, the modern world, with its effrontery scholarship, questionable morality, and indiscriminate publication, did not merit true epic treatment. To those who saw modern advances in learning as valuable and potentially profitable substitutes for or supplements to established knowledge, enduring literary glory of the kind still enjoyed by the Ancients could yet be achieved—if not with actual epics, then with works of epic proportions.

Harris and Chambers as well as Denis Diderot and Jean le Rond D'Alembert all participated in the structure of comparison Edelstein describes. They suggest in their works that a new and improved Augustan age would more likely result from the imitation of Augustan aspirations as well as artifacts. Their continuing pursuit of complete knowledge in new cultural and epistemic contexts left plenty of room for modernity and the destabilization of traditional literary hierarchies that came with it. Their encyclopedias fulfilled the organizational needs of contemporary knowledge production and continuity in ways formerly associated with epic poetry, and in so doing they positioned their works as the most durable mediators of an Enlightenment narrative and a modern answer to the ancient form. The eighteenth century has since come to be known as the Age of Encyclopedias, for during that period more encyclopedias were produced than ever before, and in its quest to provide both complete and comprehensive knowledge the genre that had existed in one form or another since antiquity took on new features, importance, and purpose.

Just as the new universal dictionaries were rising to prominence, the Ancients' dedication to traditional values and the force of their efforts to secure a place for those values in the present and future debarred the epic poem from playing its traditional part as a container and disseminator of general knowledge. The Quarrel between the Ancients and Moderns—between, as Levine puts it, imitation and accumulation—accelerated a cultural division and the emergence of more specialized forms of completeness.[8] Modern knowledge production, in addition to the explosion of print that followed the lapse of the Licensing Act in 1695, led Pope in particular to define the work of poetry and poets as mechanisms of organization and selective mediators of a literarily "complete" knowledge distinct from modern encyclopedic endeavors.

Epic as Encyclopedia

The Augustan poets writing in Milton's wake did not attempt to keep pace with the rapidly expanding horizons of literary knowledge production by composing epics of their own.[9] To encourage epic generativity with original contributions might have authorized others to publish additional and unwelcome variations that would only further diminish the high status of a genre and tradition already under threat by modernity. Instead, the Augustans largely suspended epic production altogether. Despite Pope's having thoroughly infused his translations of the *Iliad* and *Odyssey* with his very eighteenth-century English sensibilities, they did not technically add to the total number of epics considered by his contemporaries to constitute an already "complete" body of works.[10] They functioned instead as updated versions of the classics that theoretically maintained their purchase on modernity while providing Pope with a means to attach his own fortunes to works of proven durability.[11]

Pope's translations, then, rather than problematically expanding a canon to which his cultural and literary conservatism would scarcely suffer additions, folded the classics into a larger program of literary mediation that attempted to carry on the work of the epic without it. Though poems could not contain the complete knowledge of their time in the sense championed by the Moderns—the apparatus of Pope's *Dunciad Variorum* clearly demonstrates the inelegance and futility of such projects—they could be used to define both what kinds of knowledge should count in the future and how that knowledge should be understood.[12] If in *Paradise Lost* humanity emerged from the garden dependent on their powers of discernment to know good from evil, then under the Augustan conservatorship of taste and judgment discernment became the critical faculty by which the parts of knowledge worth keeping would be separated from those better left to what Harold Weber has described as the "'garbage heap' of memory."[13] Improving, advancing, and demonstrating the powers of discrimination that would define and delimit knowledge of permanent value rather than completely comprehend knowledge in its temporally unstable entirety became in Pope's poetry the new prestigious work of authorship.

As suggested above, the idea that one good epic could render whole libraries unnecessary remained a trope of literary criticism and epic paratexts well into the eighteenth century, and among the highest compliments one could pay a poet whether living or dead was still a remark upon that poet's comprehensive capacities. In 1719, Joseph Addison wrote of *Paradise Lost* that "every Thing that is great in the whole Circle of Being, whether within the Verge of Nature, or out of it, has a proper Part assigned it in this admirable Poem."[14] Even half a century later, John Brown, author of *A dissertation on the rise, union, and power, the progressions, separations, and corruptions, of poetry and music* (1763), remained in awe of Milton's "all-comprehending Mind."[15] The dissertation addresses the separation of music and poetry and opens with a quotation from Milton that emphasizes the natural unity of those arts.

All the best poets of the English language, according to several eighteenth-century critics, supposedly shared with their Greek and Roman predecessors some special comprehensive power or characteristic that separated them from the masses of occasional poets and partisan hacks who wrote without high literary ambition. Dryden, for instance, surmised that Chaucer "must have been a man of a most wonderful comprehensive Nature, because, as it has truly been observed of him, he has taken into the compass of his *Canterbury Tales* the various manners and humors (as we now call them) of the whole English nation, in his age. Not a single character has escaped him."[16] Shakespeare, in his opinion, had the "largest and most comprehensive Soul," for "all the images of Nature were still present to him."[17] Samuel Johnson likewise remarked upon Shakespeare's "comprehensive genius" and bestowed similar praise upon Dryden.[18] Neither Dryden nor Johnson, however, described the comprehensive capacities of these poets as having extended to the encyclopedic knowledge of arts and sciences that had once been considered the province of the epic poets in particular.

Their defenders too had to make concessions. The scope of Homer and Virgil's knowledge was increasingly understood to be relatively narrow in comparison to that collectively possessed by modernity. Even some of those who held the classics in the highest regard had begun to retreat from territories they deemed impossible to hold. In *An essay on poetry* (1682), John Sheffield, Earl of Mulgrave (afterwards the 1st Duke of Buckingham and Normanby, a patron of Dryden, and a friend of Pope), places Homer and Virgil at the very top of Parnassus. To read Homer once, he writes, renders all other things dull; "yet *often* on him look/And you will hardly *need* another book."[19] The praise is utterly conventional, but Mulgrave situates it within a conceptualization of the Homeric encyclopedia that recalls Bacon's use of Politian. Homer, Mulgrave continues, "describ'd the Seeds, and in what order sown,/That have to such a vast proportion grown." The couplet credits Homer as the father of the arts and sciences while acknowledging that he wrote in a time of only nascent learning; the field had since expanded far beyond what his poems actually contained.

Mulgrave's recognition of vast and subsequent growth participates in a modern understanding of Homer's poems as original disseminators of learning and ideas rather than complete and fixed bodies of knowledge. His essay concludes with a series of rhetorical questions leading to a less than optimistic conclusion about the ability of modern poets to achieve in their times what some still believed Homer had achieved in his:

The way is shewn, but who has strength to go?
Who can all the *Sciences* exactly know?
Whose *Fancy* flies beyond weak *Reason's* Sight,
And yet has *Judgment* to direct it *right*?
Whose *just* Discernment, *Virgil like*, is such,
Never to say too little, or too much?
Let such a man begin without delay,
But he must do much more than I can say,
Must above *Cowley*, nay and *Milton* too prevail,
Succeed where great *Torquato*, and our greater *Spencer* fail.[20]

Mulgrave can only gesture towards the scope of a modern epic undertaking; the job itself had gotten so large that even the job description defies concise articulation. The essay places its final focus on the greater work of pure epic, and it literally ends in failure.

A letter written by William Molyneux, the natural philosopher and founder of the Dublin Philosophical Society, similarly reflects what some might have deemed the diminished state of epic composition at the turn of the century. On 27 May 1697, Molyneux described his desire to see the physician and poet Sir Richard Blackmore attempt "a philosophick poem" that would expand upon the many scientific "touches" Molyneux had seen in Blackmore's first two epics, *Prince Arthur* (1695) and *King Arthur* (1697). Molyneux wished his correspondent to inform Sir Richard that, like him, he objected to all philosophical hypotheses as enemies of learning; by proposing a philosophic poem, Molyneux insisted, he meant only that Blackmore should compose "*a natural history of the great and admirable phenomena of the universe.*" He would desire the poem to extend "so far, and no farther."[21]

Molyneux had reason enough to recommend Blackmore for the undertaking. Like many at the turn of the century, Molyneux deemed him a national treasure whose prowess put every other English poet except Milton to shame.[22] Blackmore had already demonstrated his willingness and ability to produce a new epic every few years, as he would undoubtedly have to do if he did not wish to see his work quickly and permanently outdated, and despite whatever knowledge of ancient learning and literature he possessed, in practice his approach to both reflected decidedly modern sensibilities.[23] John Locke, to whom the letter was written, apparently agreed with Molyneux's assessment and promised to discuss the matter with Blackmore upon their next meeting.[24]

Despite the fact that Molyneux still looked for and found in epic poetry elements of natural philosophy, however, he discovered only "touches." Blackmore's poems did not, in his opinion, contain the full circle of arts and science or the complete learning of his time, and Molyneux moreover did not necessarily identify epic as the appropriate genre for a more comprehensive examination. He did not disqualify verse entirely—indeed, he believed natural history might "afford sublime thoughts in a poem"—but rather than specifically request another epic wholly dedicated to the subject, he suggests the "philosophick" poem as a more appropriate alternative.[25] The distinction speaks to what was then the still ongoing separation of epic from its former universality as well as to Blackmore's particular part in its advancement.

The poem proposed by Molyneux never materialized. Rather than a universal natural history, Blackmore's "philosophical poem" took as its subject a didactic unfolding of Locke's philosophy within an extended proof of the existence of God. *Creation. A philosophical poem* (1712) earned its author his most lasting accolades; it remained in print throughout the eighteenth century and was thus the only one of his long poems to survive him. The most enduring work of the most productive epic poet of the day, therefore, was not actually an epic. Those who believed genuine epic poetry had seen its best days in antiquity, moreover, dismissed as soporific duncery the epics that Blackmore did write. Even the praise of Addison, Dennis, and Johnson could not rescue Blackmore's reputation from the damage done to it by works like Pope's *Dunciad*.

Mulgrave's poem and Molyneux's letter both raise the question of precisely what kind of needs could be answered so completely by reading epic poems—even those of Homer—that almost all other books would be rendered superfluous. The space between the supposedly universal utility of the *Iliad* and *Odyssey* and the necessarily limited learning contained by all their descendants implies a decoupling of epic and archival values linked to the likewise interrelated phenomena of progressive knowledge and expanding volume. This decoupling was in turn part of a larger process of differentiation that over the course of the eighteenth century effected the division of what we now think of as the sciences and humanities. As Trevor Ross observes, "several defenders of the Moderns, like Wotton, believed that nature and knowledge were the purview of science, whereas literary works trafficked in mere opinion and were therefore redundant to an understanding of the truth." In order to preserve the cultural value of poetry, Ross continues, "it had to be autonomized as a superior form of knowledge."[26]

Despite their disagreements about manners and morality, Pope and Anne Dacier (whose translations of the *Iliad* and *Odyssey* had already earned her great renown) both had to acknowledge the apparent limits of Homer's breadth of knowledge as reflected in his poems. Dacier, for her part, considered the epic a *corps de doctrine* in all fields but natural philosophy and devoted the bulk of her critical attention to elucidating the complete perfection of Homer's poetic "beauties."[27] Pope, in contrast, specifically resituated Homer's oft-alleged mastery of the arts and sciences within a specialized literary discourse that prioritized original genius and individual achievement over regular method and collaborative enterprise. "His comprehensive Knowledge," Pope writes in the essay on Homer attached to his translation of the *Iliad*, "shews that his Soul was not form'd like a narrow Chanel for a single Stream, but as an Expanse which might receive an Ocean into its Bosom."[28] Homer, as any self-respecting epicist must, took in "the whole Circle of Arts, and the whole Compass of Nature; all the inward Passion and Affections of Mankind to supply his characters, and all the outward Forms and Images of Things for his Descriptions."[29]

By themselves, these claims do not distinguish Pope's commentary from those of other and older celebrants of epic poets and epic magnitude. Later in the essay, however, Pope qualifies his earlier statements in a passage that significantly changes the tenor of his otherwise tropic assessment of Homer's comprehensive capacities:

> But however that we may not mistake the Elogies of those Ancients who call him the Father of Arts and Sciences, and be surpriz'd to find so little of them (as they are now in Perfection) in his Works; we should know that this Character is not to be understood at large, as if he had included the full and regular Systems of every thing: He is to be consider'd professedly *only in Quality of a Poet*; this was his Business, to which, as whatever he knew was to be subservient, so he has not fail'd to introduce those Strokes of Knowledge from the whole Circle of Arts and Sciences, which the Subject demanded either for Necessity or Ornament.[30]

Set against his previous claims, these lines must function either as a limited concession to those who dismissed the completeness of Homer's knowledge or as a suggestion to those readers who still looked to Homer for absolutely everything that for some things they had better look elsewhere.

Though the passage clearly demonstrates an attempt by Pope to promote the autonomy of poetry as a superior form of knowledge, his appeal to readers to make a qualitative distinction between the Poet and other, unnamed kinds of knowledge producers contains language that links it to the burdens of quantity. We find "little" of the arts and sciences in Homer's poems; they do not include "full" systems of "every thing"; he drew from the whole circle only that which served or supplemented the greater inventive power of his poetic imagination. Whatever the actual depth and breadth of Homer's knowledge of the arts and sciences, the poetry took precedence. The "quality of a poet" towards which Pope directed his readers' attention, then, did not entail the obligation to contain in one's poems the complete circle of arts and sciences in what some other discourse of knowledge production might define as a comprehensive sense.[31]

This retroactive limitation of the extent to which Homer's epics established and advanced a program of encyclopedic representation set out a narrower scope for poetry that effectively relieved all poets— including Pope—of what had become far too great a responsibility. Pope's "strokes" recalls Molyneux's "touches" and suggests that, at least with respect to capturing the complete knowledge of his time, Blackmore had perhaps done no worse than Homer. That, however, ceased to be amongst the standards by which past and present poets would be judged. Rather than continuing to defend the indefensible or attempt the unachievable, Pope changed the terms of the debate and declared a victory. The complete knowledge contained by even those poems of the greatest possible magnitude was in his opinion not of a kind with that sought by the unfinished histories of the Royal Society and the ongoing collections of the universal dictionaries, even though the authors and editors of the latter continued to locate in Homer's epics precisely the kind of copious, commodious, comprehensive, and in other ways concise but complete records of knowledge that they now took it upon themselves to provide. When Pope in turn appropriated the genres, terminology, and publishing protocols of those texts or institutions—as he did most appreciably in the *Essay on Man* and the several versions of the *Dunciad*—he tried, albeit with limited success, to adapt them to reflect his conception of what should constitute complete knowledge within a poem as well as within its readers.

Encyclopedia as Epic

In 1729, the same year in which Pope's *Dunciad Variorum* appeared, an anonymous contributor to *The Tribune* alleged that an Irish country gentleman by the name of Richard Marygold, Esq., of Kerry, felt so strongly about the comprehensive capacity of Homer's mind that "he would go near to renounce the Society of any Man, who should deny *Homer* to have been Master of the whole *Cyclopedia* of Arts and Sciences."[32] Marygold (or his erstwhile biographer) may not have had Ephraim Chambers's work specifically in mind when he made (or almost made) this proclamation, but contemporary readers could not have overlooked the connection between Homer's poems and the new encyclopedias. Though the word "encyclopedia" had graced the covers of compendia since the sixteenth century, Chambers's proposal had begun to appropriate the shortened version of the term in 1726, and the *Cyclopædia* itself had enjoyed a successful debut only the year before *The Tribune*'s brief run at the end of the decade.[33] Indeed, few texts published after 1728 used the term to refer to anything other than *the Cyclopædia*.[34]

To some extent, its very title thus presented the "universal dictionary of arts and sciences" as both a step towards Bacon's unrealized comprehensive compendium and a potential eighteenth-century successor to the epics of Homer and Virgil. The encyclopedists took over from the classical poets the kind of work that those like Mr. Marygold maintained had been completed in antiquity but which had been rendered more obviously *in*complete by the advances in knowledge production that followed. As historical records and literary accomplishments, then, the *Iliad, Odyssey,* and *Aeneid* were, like *Paradise Lost*, perhaps complete insofar as they were "perfect" and finished poems; however, only as such could they continue to hold their high literary value.

The encyclopedias of the eighteenth century were therefore in a position to co-opt a conventional function of the epics and execute it via new features better aligned with modern standards of knowledge production. The anonymous compilers of *A new and complete dictionary of arts and sciences* (1763–64), following Aristotle, claimed that "the sovereign perfection of an epic poem ... consists in the just proportion and perfect connection of all the parts."[35] Encyclopedists throughout the eighteenth century consistently spoke of the successes or failures of their own and their competitors' works in precisely these terms. They struggled to contain the right amount of information in each entry and insisted that the plans upon which they constructed their encyclopedias effectively reflected the connection of all the seemingly disparate parts of knowledge that when rightly understood constituted a system of the world. The encyclopedias in this way offered themselves as epics freed from poetry and plot. Poetry and plot went on to have long lives in other kinds of writing, and though authors of some of these—notably, but not exclusively, the novel—for some time aspired to capture varying degrees of comprehensiveness, their efforts ultimately resulted only in intractable problems and the permanent separation of genuinely encyclopedic knowledge from narrative forms of writing. The state of knowledge production in the eighteenth century assured that the complete set of epic features as most generously understood at the time would not again appear in a single work or genre.

The relationships between Augustan authors and their Ancient models had more to them than veneration and imitation. To Pope, Britain was not yet but might one day be better than Virgil's Rome; the classics were perfect in Greek and Latin, but might be made even more so when rendered in English couplets reflective of English values. Chambers seemed to think that a new and improved Augustan age would more likely result from reactivating Ancient aspirations as well as artifacts. Such a philosophy left plenty of room for modernity and the destabilization of traditional literary hierarchies that came with it. Neither Chambers nor any other editor of an eighteenth-century encyclopedia explicitly declared himself the Homer or Virgil of his day, but the plans for and prefaces to their works make clear that several had precisely such pretensions. The authors and editors of the major universal dictionaries of the century specifically positioned themselves and their works within an appropriated mythos of epic completeness.

To Chambers, the title of "Augustan" might more properly have belonged to the Moderns—or at least, to Modern works like the *Cyclopædia*, which while including Ancient knowledge as part of a whole "course of learning" still remained dedicated to recording its latest developments. In the dedication of his work to the king, Chambers writes that the time when Rome would envy England's Augustan age finally seemed to be at hand. As Greece was under Alexander and Rome under Caesar Augustus, he insists, so would Britain be under the newly crowned George Augustus.[36] If the reign of Augustus established new foundations for a stronger Roman Empire than the Emperor himself would live to see, then that of George II would do as much and more for Britain. The first *Cyclopædia*, like the *Aeneid* before it, would mark a starting point for the new age: the initial edition circumscribed the current boundaries of the "Republick of Learning." Later editions would record its continuing expansion.

The forward-looking stance adopted by Chambers and the encyclopedists that followed him constitutes a critical counterpoint to the contemporary neoclassical perspective on literary achievement. A new Augustan period would begin with a work not only destined but also *designed* to be surpassed; an age does not begin at its height, and an enlightened (or Enlightenment) Virgil would welcome the coming of his betters. The epic poem might therefore once have been the pinnacle of the Virgilian triad, and Homer, as Chambers writes, might still have been the best poet in the world, but in his opinion the *Cyclopædia* would eventually become "the best Book in the Universe."[37] Chambers does not qualify the remark with formal distinctions. The *Cyclopædia* would not merely be the best book of its kind, but the best of *all* kinds and for all times.

Other encyclopedists made the same or similar claims about their own texts. Chambers, Jean le Rond D'Alembert, and Denis Diderot (who took the *Cyclopædia* as the starting point for what eventually became the *Encyclopédie*), and many others followed Bacon in debunking some of the specific accolades attached to the classical epics and went on to appropriate others. The preface to Henry Curzon's *The universal library: or, compleat summary of science* (1712), a two-volume, non-alphabetized compendium of treatises covering an array of subjects from theology, philosophy, and ethics to physic, chirurgery, and chemistry, states that "within the Structure of this Work, like Homer's *Iliads* in a Nut-shell, have you Enclosed the Learning, Arts, and Artifices of the Microcosm ... that like the World Mapp'd down in one Sheet of Paper, you have demonstrated together at one View, all Humane, Sciential, Natural and Artificial Rarities."[38] Curzon's preface thus walks the expected line between comprehensiveness and conciseness long associated with a variety of reference texts while also invoking the specifically epic provenance supposedly appropriate to works of "universal" scope.

Chambers went even further. He names Homer five times in his preface, and his discourse on the proper place of poetry in the system of arts and sciences runs throughout the first sixteen of its thirty pages. The most purely inspired and nearest to Heaven, poetry cooperated so closely with Nature that people mistakenly deemed poets the inventors of all subordinate arts, and they thought Homer—in whose works all Nature could supposedly be found—the inventor of poetry. "Thus it is," Chambers explains, that "Homer is often complimented with being the Father of all Arts." He continues:

This has, indeed, an Appearance of Truth; but 'tis only an Appearance: For *Homer* ... has no other Title to the Invention of other Arts than what he derives either from a greater Share of the Spirit whereby they are produc'd, than other people; or from his having communicated that Spirit, by the force of his Poems, thro' other People, where it has generated, and brought forth other Arts.[39]

Chambers's assessment of Homer's actual contribution more closely resembles that of Bacon than Pope: the classical epics, when disseminated amongst the populace, inspired people to build upon their foundation and bring to maturity the "seeds and principles" of the arts and inventions those epics described. A greater share of spirit may have enabled Homer to invent poetry (a supposition Chambers grants only grudgingly), but actual progress in the arts belonged and would continue to belong to those his poems inspired to go further.

Chambers suggests the same might one day be said of the *Cyclopædia*. His delimitation of Homer's accomplishments again positions the encyclopedias as their natural successors. As had been the case with the epics, the principal accomplishment of the *Cyclopædia* and all other universal dictionaries would be the force by which they would communicate and advance existing knowledge. As compendia of both theoretical and practical knowledge, the books had to be both useable and useful; they transmitted knowledge in part for the sake of simply educating readers, but also with the hope and expectation that those readers might generate more knowledge by applying what they had learned. Chambers, for instance, believed that his work "would contribute more to the propagating of useful Knowledge thro' the Body of a People than any, I had almost said all, the Books extant."[40] William Smellie, the compiler of the first *Encyclopedia Britannica* (1768–71), similarly wrote in his preface that, "to diffuse the knowledge of Science is the professed design of the following work."[41] Both prefaces posit the dissemination of useful scientific knowledge as an end in and of itself. Homer, Chambers writes, cast the first seeds over the world; others cultivated them and brought forth new arts and knowledge of the sciences. The encyclopedias then harvested the new knowledge and carried on what Homer started.

The crucial difference is that what Homer only began the encyclopedias could theoretically finish. The encyclopedia scatters knowledge in the same generative sense Bacon adapted from Lucretius and applied to Homer, but it also re-collects the products of its own dissemination in an (ideally) endless cycle of self-reproduction. The new encyclopedias, though perhaps immediately epic in scope, therefore necessarily began in less rather than more complete states. Every advance in the arts or sciences gave (and continues to give) the genre a reason to exist and the opportunity to adapt. "May posterity add their Discoveries to those we have registered," D'Alembert exclaims, "And may the History of the human Mind, and its Productions, be continued from Age to Age, down to the most distant Period of time! May the Encyclopædia remain a Sanctuary, to preserve human Knowledge from the Ravages and Revolutions of distant Ages!"[42] The encyclopedia, both individually and categorically, could respond to changes and thus usurped one more function formerly given to the now ossified epics. "The most glorious moment for a work of this sort," writes Diderot, "would be that which might come immediately in the wake of some catastrophe so great as to suspend the progress of science, interrupt the labors of craftsmen, and plunge a portion of our hemisphere into darkness once again."[43] Whereas according to the old conceit people could supposedly look to Virgil to restore all the sciences should they be lost, they might now look to the latest encyclopedia instead.

The encyclopedists may have hoped that in such an event the glory of the moment would extend back in time to those whose early efforts made such a moment possible. If, however, "the professional work of knowing—whether about the stars or about the arts—became, during the eighteenth century, the newly heroic work," then the encyclopedists of the time did not fully participate in that elevation despite the enduring and widespread cultural impact of their works.[44] They might have undertaken Herculean labors—Chambers boasts in the very first line of his preface that compiling the *Cyclopædia*, which he did single-handedly, "might have employed an Academy"—but most would not be heroes.[45] Whereas, according to Clifford Siskin, "the deep aura of heroism" has obscured the status of some authors as professionals and wielders of "a central form of modern power," the reverse holds true for the vast majority of encyclopedists.[46] Indeed, the temporality of the genre and the nature of its work ultimately returned its epic singers to a new version of the age-old anonymity that other "artists" managed to escape. Ironically, however, that anonymity allowed the encyclopedia to remain the repository of other modern epic values that over the course of the century *transcended* individual heroism. The authoring of eighteenth-century encyclopedias, then, both takes the baton passed by the epic and also forms part of a complex response to the rise of information.

The epic value of comprehensively complete knowledge could not be achieved by completely individual efforts. Homer might have been able to capture, as Hobbes had put it, "the whole learning of his time" in a poem he was thought to have composed single-handedly, but the proliferation of writing about the arts and sciences that took place during the seventeenth and eighteenth centuries increasingly made such a feat a matter of effective mediation and collaboration rather than original composition. Even so, the encyclopedists did wield significant authorial and discursive power, particularly over those inexpert readers who made up the largest part of their audiences. Rather than relying directly on the experts for an understanding of the most groundbreaking and advanced scientific ideas of the day, those readers who had neither the time nor the resources (whether financial or intellectual) to keep abreast of the latest publications had to rely on the understanding of an editor or editors whose own expertise or knowledge did not necessarily match that of the contributing authors. Harris, for example, though he greatly admired the works of Newton and apologized in his preface for not having taken more from the newly published *Opticks* than he did, assured his readers that he inserted all he could and had in all other ways captured "the Substance of what [Newton] had published in the Philosophical Transactions on that most Noble Subject."[47] One might investigate what Harris had left out, but one would never know why he deemed inessential any part of what Newton had bothered to write.

Such editorial choices did not go unnoticed. Competitors were always happy to remark upon a treatment they deemed too slight. They just as readily attacked those they deemed too full. The marketplace made this kind of criticism simply part of the encyclopedia's background noise. The power of the encyclopedists truly stood out when the mirrors they held up to the world also reflected the social, political, or religious biases of their compilers and aroused the unwelcome attention of other parties interested in controlling what counted as knowledge. In France, the entire *Encyclopédie* constituted a potentially dangerous political statement. Not only did it potentially make knowledge available to literate members of the middling classes (thousands of whom may have had indirect access to the work via relatively inexpensive memberships in *cabinets littéraires*), but much of the knowledge it made available flew in the face of established Catholic dogma and government ideology as well.[48] If, as Foucault writes, one purpose of the author-function as it emerged during this time was to indicate to those in power whom they could and probably should punish, then D'Alembert and Diderot were very much authors indeed.[49] The inclusion of potentially seditious articles in the first volume (some of which Diderot wrote himself, some which he and D'Alembert merely edited) led to Diderot's arrest in 1752;

in 1759, a rapidly growing list of subscribers and what they perceived as Diderot's unchecked rabble-rousing compelled the courts to suppress the work by official decree. D'Alembert withdrew from the project shortly thereafter, but Diderot carried on for another thirteen years. He finished the last pages in 1772 only to see the printer strike out the more controversial passages for fear of retribution.

Such actions suggest that for many readers the encyclopedists really did have a hand in determining who and what represented the highest authorities and best knowledge in the world. Nevertheless, the political power and individual identities of the encyclopedists often paled behind those primarily responsible for their source materials. A series of entries by Locke or Newton remain by Locke or Newton no matter how adeptly their editors abridged and arranged them, and even those entries or sections whose authors went without acknowledgment could not necessarily be claimed as the encyclopedist's own work. The "plan" or "method" conceived by this or that encyclopedist might have constituted a genuinely original and individual contribution to knowledge production—certainly the encyclopedists themselves thought as much—but regardless of the strategies undertaken to distinguish one work from another, the goal of every such text remained the most effective possible use of *other* people's original and individual contributions. This does not mean that their efforts were necessarily *un*heroic, but rather that in the panoply of knowledge producers they perhaps resembled Patroclus more than Achilles.

Encyclopedists who sought fame equivalent to that of individual authors therefore had to defend their special brand of authorship and deliberately assert (or rely on others to assert) their professional acumen and the validity of their authorial status. Richard Yeo suggests that such assertions "were rhetorical moves in the debates on literary property, or copyright; but they were also supported by prevailing beliefs about the labour and knowledge involved in the production of dictionaries and encyclopedias."[50] Whether such beliefs actually prevailed among a wide range of readers remains debatable, but the fact remains that the encyclopedists' brand of heroism was categorically different than that of the knowledge producers upon whose works their own depended.[51] Yeo cites as evidence of the importance of individual responsibility to encyclopedic projects the Royal Society's endorsement of Chambers as the "Author" of the *Cyclopædia* and the fact that he remained the nominal author long after others had taken over and largely expanded the property. Chambers, however—who did indeed set the standard for decades—became a notable exception to the rule as it developed along with the genre over the course of the century. While many single "authors" of encyclopedias did receive their own by-lines, they did not usually achieve such extensive longevity. The temporality of the genre necessarily limited their potential to achieve the kind of lasting literary fame now almost exclusively enjoyed by those individual authors who possessed what the late eighteenth and nineteenth centuries styled "original genius." If in the eighteenth century the encyclopedia reemerged as a genre that made the eventual obsolescence of the individual edition not an unavoidable weakness but rather an important part of its diachronic functionality, then those who compiled such editions would also have to be replaced.

Those whose names and reputations did last beyond the grave often became obstacles to the class-wide elevation of encyclopedists to authors and authors to heroes. Harris, for example, to whom Chambers owed so much, died in 1719. New editions of his *Lexicon technicum* continued in his name until 1736; in 1744, though, *A Supplement to Dr. Harris's Dictionary of arts and sciences* appeared. Authored by and printed for "A Society of Gentlemen," the supplement acknowledged the primary authorship of Harris at the expense of those who carried on his work. After that, with the *Cyclopædia* in its ascendancy, the *Lexicon* finally went the way of Harris and took the names of those gentlemen with it. By this time, Chambers himself was already four years into the posthumous phase of his reign. The note to the reader of the 1753 *Supplement to Mr. Chambers's Cyclopædia* insists that, with Chambers dead, "the benefits of his labours would have been entirely lost, had not George Lewis Scott, Esq; F. R. S. a Gentleman of renowned learning ... been prevailed upon to peruse the papers left by Mr. Chambers, to select such articles as were fit for the press, and to supply such others, as seemed to be most wanting."[52] The *Cyclopædia*, it suggests, would not have advanced, adapted, and therefore survived without Scott; nevertheless, Scott's name appears nowhere else in the supplement—including the title page.

Abraham Rees, whose revision and expansion of the *Cyclopædia* in the 1770s produced a work twice as long as and fully integrated with the original, fared little better. Encyclopedism became less and less an individual effort with each passing year and every new advance. Some dozen or so new encyclopedias had come and gone in the time it took Abraham Rees to finish a single edition of his 45-volume *New Cyclopædia* (1819); the *Britannica* alone had run through three new editions and one supplement as well as the three chief editors who saw them through the press.[53] Many of them borrowed fairly freely from encyclopedias past and present, and every recycling of someone else's compilation set original authorship at an additional remove.[54] Thomas Lloyd, who had taken over as chief editor of *The new royal encyclopædia* from William Henry Hall, Esq., claimed in the third edition of 1797 to have "ransacked, as it were, the whole world more fully to enrich the banquet."[55] The "whole world" referred to both new primary sources as well as their predecessors within the genre.

Furthermore, while the massive multi-volume works that had come to define the genre at the beginning of the nineteenth century dwarfed their early eighteenth-century counterparts, the number of additional authors and editors with whom their chief compilers now had to share credit had also substantially increased. Harris and Chambers had taken from numerous primary authors; so had Diderot.[56] William Smellie reportedly claimed to have put together the first edition *Britannica* "with a pair of scissars."[57] During the last half of the century, however, encyclopedists increasingly turned to assistants or associates for help with information management, and during the last quarter of the century they routinely recruited experts to compose new and entirely original materials specifically for inclusion in encyclopedias. The "republick of learning" once single-handedly surveyed by Chambers and reduced to two volumes had grown to so great an extent that a single person could not possibly account for it in its entirety. Therefore, as Yeo observes, "by the close of the eighteenth century the days of the individual compilers such as Chambers or Tytler were over. From this time, there were negotiations between an editor and the experts he recruited to write specialist articles—which they usually signed, and for which they were sometimes granted a separate copyright for later re-publication."[58]

Varying degrees of what must be called collective authorship thus became the standard as encyclopedias expanded both in breadth and depth on their way to comprehensive completeness. As I noted above, "A Society of Gentlemen" shared credit for the first supplement to the *Lexicon technicum* in 1744. The Reverend Temple Henry Croker took responsibility only for the theological, philological, and critical branches of knowledge in *The complete dictionary of arts and sciences* (1764–66); Thomas Williams, M.D., Samuel Clark, and "Several Gentlemen particularly conversant in the arts and sciences they have undertaken to explain" handled the rest.[59] Despite Smellie's singular skill with a forfex, his title page gives authorship of the work to "A Society of Gentlemen in Scotland"; the title page to the second edition announces only that it had been compiled "from the writings of the best authors, in several languages; the most approved dictionaries, as well of general science as of particular branches; the transaction, journals, and memoirs, of learned societies, both at home and abroad; the ms. lectures of eminent professors on different sciences; and a variety of original materials, furnished by an extensive correspondence." Hall and Lloyd likewise had the help of several "gentlemen of scientific knowledge," and they promised that those gentlemen's names and addresses appeared in the book. Even Rees had to acknowledge the assistance of "eminent professional gentlemen" on his title page, and in his preface (which he wrote last) he mentions most of them by subject as well as name.[60]

Though the individuals certainly mattered and deserved credit for the work they did, over the long term the institution mattered more. Great authors could have their due, Bacon wrote, provided that "time, which is the author of authors, be not deprived of his due—which is, further and further to discover truth."[61] The names and identities of the tens, then hundreds, then thousands of compilers, contributors, publishers, printers, and booksellers responsible for bringing forth the encyclopedias of the last two and a half centuries have almost entirely vanished into a sea of similar works or beneath waves of successive improvements. In order to uphold and perpetuate the epic value of comprehensive completeness in the wake of Bacon's *Great Instauration* and the proliferation of writing and knowledge production that followed it, the epic hero—and epic heroism—had to be sacrificed at the level of individual authorship so that something greater could be achieved.

The Small World of *The Dunciad*

When the *Dunciad Variorum* appeared in 1729, one might have expected to find among its revised lines or within its new apparatus some reference to Chambers and his ambitious attempt to organize the world's knowledge. Both Chambers and his universal dictionary, however, are entirely absent from Pope's poems and letters.[62] Indeed, with respect to encyclopedias and scientific dictionaries, Pope was categorically rather than selectively dismissive: the titles and authors of all such reference works published in the first quarter of the eighteenth century are missing. This conspicuous absence and the genre in which Pope chose to work together constitute a continuation of the strategy of differentiation and delimitation that I have already described. The omission of the encyclopedias and encyclopedists from the *Dunciad* reflects the same separation of poetry and the ideal Poet (now represented by the figure of Pope) from certain kinds of knowledge production, and the mock-epic form allows for a necessarily less-than-epic ambition that traffics in an appropriately limited version of Pope's recalibrated epic encyclopedism.

Though many of the same conventions govern both epic and mock-epic, they do not operate at the same scale. As an anonymous contributor to the *Grub-Street Journal* quite fairly observes in 'An essay on *the Dunciad*', "true epic's a vast world, and this a small:/One has its proper beauties, and one all."[63] The same author goes on to acknowledge the need for an "epic" treatment of the literary world and pays Pope a heady compliment by reversing the relationship of parts and wholes as it applied to the knowledge of poetry he believed Pope to have possessed: "Books and the man demand as much, or more/Than he who wander'd to the latian shore:/For here (eternal grief to Duns's soul,/And B—'s thin ghost!) the part contains the whole: Since in mock-epic none succeeds but he/Who tastes the whole of epic poesy."[64] The first couplet anticipates by more than two centuries Marshall McLuhan's declaration that "it is to the *Dunciad* that we must turn for the epic of the printed word."[65]

Pope does not aspire to contain complete knowledge of the world itself. That had supposedly been the work of epic proper, and that again had to be understood in the limited sense appropriate to the quality of a poet. Weber argues that "the *Dunciad* represents Pope's unusual and ungainly attempt to realize the promise of the print revolution and modern library, to create the one (or in Chambers' case, two) volume(s) that represents the key to all knowledge," and while this assessment maintains the functional parallel of epic and encyclopedia, it does not explain the acknowledged lack of explicit connection or entirely account for the nature of mock-epic.[66] Pope restricts the complete knowledge contained by *The Dunciad* to the literary world in which it directly participates. Some of the token phrases of epic praise remain—Scriblerus insists that "the third book, if well consider'd, seemeth to embrace the whole world"—but this embrace amounts only to an account of Dulness's global domination and the means by which the goddess will achieve it.[67] Those means are the progeny of Settle and Theobald: bad authors of scant learning, the producers of "farces, opera's, shows"; weak literary criticism; partisan pamphlets and poor plays; and the destruction of education itself.[68] As William Ayre notes, in this "most compleat Satire ... without the last Mercy (being thereto most scandalously provok'd) [Pope] lashes the whole Body of Dunces."[69] Theirs is the world the *Dunciad* comprehends.

Like many who wrote in response to the proliferation of writing and print in and about the world, Pope sought to mediate media in the only way that was left: he answered the problem of too much with a bit more. As Paula McDowell rightly observes, however, Pope was not anti-print. "It was not print technology, the spread of printing, or print *per se*," she writes, "that was making these authors feel like an epochal shift had occurred. Rather, there was a sense that what we would call a 'technology' was on the brink of being used in profoundly new ways."[70] Indeed, despite the prolific output of authors like Defoe, Haywood, the much maligned Blackmore, and the whole host of braying asses whose words (whether written, spoken, or shouted out loud) in his opinion equally amounted only to so much cultural noise, Pope still embraced print technology as the best medium to carry his work forward through time and secure for it a place in the future.[71] In "Of the Poem," Pope presumes the endurance of his own work. "He lived in those days," Scriblerus writes, "when (after providence had permitted the Invention of Printing as a scourge for the Sins of the Learned) Paper also became so cheap, and printers so numerous, that a deluge of authors cover'd the land."[72] Readers have focused a great deal on the attitude towards print reflected in this oft-quoted passage, but few have given equal attention to the prolepsis of the past-tense construction. Scriblerus writes from a present that places Pope in the past: he implies that the deluge of authors has dried up and that *The Dunciad* has stood the test of time.[73]

Blackmore, according to Pope, was "everlasting" in a different sense. Though he intended with his poems to improve upon the manners and literature of English men and women in the wake of the Restoration—an admirable if less than lofty ambition for epic poetry—he also unabashedly declared himself a stranger to verse, admitted that self-amusement rather than serious engagement guided his hand, and insisted that because he had to compose his works in carriages and coffeehouses while between professional appointments, he could not turn his attention to more "useful" works of literature dedicated wholly to philosophy or physic.[74] These revelations, along with the unseemly political opportunism of Blackmore's epics and the leisurely attitude with which he approached them, would have been more than enough to attract Augustan ire, but Pope leveled an additional charge that went beyond content and character to address the equally important matters of number and length. The first part of a long note to II.268 of the *Dunciad* reduces much of Blackmore's corpus into purely quantitative terms. Its author lists the number of books contained by each of Blackmore's "no less than six Epic poems" (a total of 58) and sneers at the existence of "many more" texts churned out by Blackmore's "indefatigable Muse."[75] This gesture towards the quantitative reflects Pope's general concern with the expansion of the literary marketplace and the volume of literature within it. The Augustans' veneration of the classics proceeded largely from what they perceived as the superiority of ancient learning and the unmatched ability of Homer and Virgil to comprehend a great deal of useful knowledge in only one or two poetic masterworks; these works simultaneously defined the heights of their careers and set the limits of human literary achievement.

Pope's disparaging description of Blackmore and his muse appropriately occurs within a poem the very form of which presented itself as both echo and guardian of a genre that, according to Pope, Blackmore's untowardly mass productions threatened to devalue and destabilize. His comparatively rampant output—by Pope's count, an average of one new epic every five and a half years between 1695 and 1728—at the very least entailed the symbolic implication of the epic and epic poets in precisely the problem that the epic and epic poets were supposed to solve or ameliorate. If a critical part of the work of epic was the selection, organization, and transmission of a society's knowledge, then a single poet publishing multiple epics over a brief span of time had the potential to defeat that purpose by making it just another kind of writing the many examples of which themselves required selection, organization, and transmission by additional literary forms or institutions. The qualitatively "everlasting" epic poets and poems that had formerly distinguished themselves from their inferiors by recording knowledge of truly enduring value would become instead what Pope considered Blackmore and Blackmore's poems to be: quantitatively "everlasting" poets and poems the unending labors of which diminished the prestige of both by exposing them to the cycles of obsolescence and relative ephemerality that Pope in particular associated with hack writing and the proliferation of print in the early eighteenth century.[76]

The Dunciad Variorum moreover literalizes the distinction between quality and quantity by representing both within the same printed text. The apparatus almost doubled the length of the original poem's forty-nine pages in octavo and nearly quadrupled that of the work over-all by adding prolegomena, testimonies, annotations, and appendices out of which no coherent plan or meaning emerges. The information it contains is by turns factual, fictional, reliable, and satirical; most of the notes add nothing useful to the forming of a correct understanding of the poem proper, and those that do are sprinkled indiscriminately among the rest. The apparatus contains many of the comments made by those trivial critics whom Pope set out to pillory; it includes the critiques and attacks of Dennis, Bentley, and Curll, and the very first annotation—a ridiculous digression on the right spelling of "Dunciad"—supposedly belongs to Theobald, the poem's protagonist. Pope in fact wrote many of the notes himself, and he invited his fellow Scriblerians to contribute to the cacophony as well. Swift almost certainly wrote notes in response to Pope's request that he should "make a few in any way you like best, whether dry raillery, upon the style and way of commenting of trivial critics; or humorous, upon the authors in the poem; or historical, on persons, places, times; or explanatory; or collecting the parallel passages of the ancients."[77] The apparatus, in short, represents a scaled-down version of precisely that kind of heterogeneous mixture of suspect attributions, legitimate explanations, and spurious nonsense that flowed indiscriminately through the minds and marketplaces of eighteenth-century Britain.

Aubrey Williams provides an apt summary of the effect that the apparatus creates. "The result of this fretting and corrosion of fact by fancy," he writes, "is a curiously ambiguous realm of half-truth in which the reader wanders, never quite sure as to the validity of what he reads, never certain what is fact, what is make-believe."[78] The apparatus thus produces in miniature what McDowell describes as "the fog of Dulness" created by the spread of print. "For Pope," McDowell continues, "the willingness of literate gentlemen to allow themselves to be caught up in the fog of Dulness is at least as much of a problem as too many bad writers."[79] *The Dunciad Variorum* addresses both by providing such readers with an opportunity to repeat their mistakes while simultaneously offering them a vastly superior alternative.

Pope's close control over the printing and publication of his works allowed him to take full advantage of the possibilities of print in advancing his project. He very likely determined the layout of *The Dunciad Variorum* and oversaw its production into book form from beginning to end.[80] The decisions to precede and follow the poem with roughly the same number of pages (between fifty and sixty), to display a single verse couplet on each of the first two pages of verse, between two and seven couplets on most pages, and never more than eleven on any, were therefore probably Pope's. This typographic layout, as many have observed, visually recreates the contest between Pope's poetry and the commentaries that threaten to overwhelm it. Of course, they never do. The verse literally remains central to the whole text, and even when a single couplet must share space with nearly a full page of remarks, it remains above the fray. The discerning reader—the reader to whom Pope wishes to appeal, or if not to appeal to, then to create—should know or learn better than to duplicate the unsavory games of the dunces in Book II by spending too much time diving down into the notes in a genuine search for truth or a key to unlocking the poem.

As a body of information, the apparatus never amounts to more than a scattershot collection of half-truths. The whole truth—the complete truth—resides in the poem. The verse, Pope would have us believe, is the way out of the fog. Weber suggests that "although the poem's textual apparatus attempts to function like a street map, the ubiquitous A–Z, for instance, that both residents and tourists depend on to make London navigable, finally it recapitulates the effects of Dulness rather than counteracting them."[81] This, however, is precisely the point. The apparatus models the kind of comprehensive but chaotic collection that trapped those who denied the authority of the poetry as poetry and the poet as poet—those who refused, in the words credited to William Cleland but usually attributed to Pope, to "consider the unity of the whole design" and accept that "the Poem was not made for these Authors, but these Authors for the Poem."[82]

Aristotle's notes on the limits of epic magnitude and those of Le Bossu on the importance of maintaining the heroic perspective both echo throughout the poem. To insist upon the "unity of the whole" invokes the ancient codes of epic completeness and the singular power of the poet to produce knowledge by rendering large amounts of information into a coherent model of a coherent universe. Effective knowledge production and management meant more to Pope than just the process of culling and collecting practiced by other mediators of media. Weber quite rightly observes that *The Dunciad* reflects Pope's general concern with the material preservation of all kinds of literature in libraries and private collections as well as his "powerful ambivalence toward the 'storehouse' and 'archive' as the sites of a new collective memory."[83] Though no collection could be entirely indiscriminate—the simple problem of space, if nothing else, prevented anyone from keeping absolutely everything—those collectors who managed to find a place for pamphlets, ballads, and other kinds of literature with no real investment in the codes of cultural prestige ensured that Pope could not even rely on the continued ephemerality of actual ephemera, much less on that of other Grub Street refuse with pretensions to long-term value. This concern extended to the lower orders of para-archival mediation that with every passing week or month promised to supply readers with a selection of the best literature to be found anywhere in England, Britain, Europe, or beyond. Weber notes that while the 1729 edition makes some space for the magazines, journals, and miscellanies that in one way or another aped the practice or claims of works like John Dunton's *The compleat library* (1692–94), the 1743 *Dunciad in Four Books* makes Pope's distaste for such works more explicit. In 1:37 of the *Variorum*, for example, Pope spouts venom at each "weekly Muse," but in the 1743 version he specifically derides "Miscellanies ... Journals, Medleys, Merc'ries, and Magazines."[84] A note explains that such works "were thrown out weekly and monthly by every miserable scribler; or picked up piece-meal and stolen from any body."[85]

The process of picking up piecemeal from anybody defines the nature of the textual apparatus and its lack of integrity as a body of knowledge. Given the means by which Pope gathered the fragments, and the insouciance of his appeal to Swift for contributions, Weber's conclusion that Pope failed to notice that "by 1743 *The Dunciad* itself had become a collection of extracts from a host of other works" seems highly unlikely.[86] As I have already suggested, the variegated conglomeration of the notes stands in contrast to the narrative of the verse; the former participates in Pope's argument on behalf of poetic supremacy by mimicking the manners and effects of the opposition. In the contest to determine who or what should do the work of defining, preserving, and transmitting knowledge to present and future audiences, the magazine and miscellany publishers—like the encyclopedists, whose works offered a different class of knowledge but nevertheless represented a particular mode of knowledge production—necessarily advanced method and collaboration over natural genius and individual authorship. Chambers had declared in the *Cyclopædia* that when compared to that of a whole commonwealth, the product of "a single brain ... would go but a little way."[87] Magazines and miscellanies—the encyclopedias of Pope's world—likewise drew from the breadth of the nation, and while they could perhaps offer more, they could not, according to Pope, necessarily offer better.

Collection without synthesis did not reflect the completeness made possible by the singular intellect and elevated imagination of an individual author. Despite the cross-references and genealogical trees of the *Cyclopædia*, for example, readers (as well as subsequent encyclopedists) remarked upon the difficulty they encountered in piecing back together that which the Chambers's methodical presentation had plucked apart; William Smellie later offered to remedy this problem by personally writing most of the extended treatises and systems of the first *Encyclopædia Britannica*. The piecemeal collections of magazines, miscellanies, and like works similarly presented no coherent picture of the entire literary landscape or even necessarily a single subject. To Pope, such works too tended instead to reproduce division and dullness rather than complete knowledge.[88] As he reveals in the first book of *The Variorum*, "a folio Common-place/Founds the whole pyle" of Tibbald's library and thus forms the basis of his knowledge. In *The Dunciad in Four Books*, Pope transfers the commonplace book to Cibber's ownership, and he secures a place for the magazines and miscellanies in the Cave of Poverty and Poetry, where Dulness sits upon her throne "in clouded Majesty."[89]

All writing entails a degree of collaboration, and the production of books could in no way be understood as entirely individual affairs. Nevertheless, as the century wore on, debates about copyright and authorial ownership—debates in which Pope had personal interest— increasingly involved matters of genius and the ability of the author to produce out of the language something entirely his or her own. Baron James Eyre's opinion on *Donaldson v. Beckett* (1774) made the "unity" of a literary invention a critical component of his argument in favor of authors' rights:

> There is the same Identity of intellectual Substance; the same spiritual Unity. In a mechanic Invention the Corporeation of Parts, the Junction of Powers, tend to produce some one End. A literary Composition is an Assemblage of Ideas so judiciously arranged, as to enforce some one Truth, lay open some one Discovery, or exhibit some one Species of mental Improvement. A mechanic Invention, and a literary Composition, exactly agree in Point of Similarity; the one therefore is no more entitled to be the Object of Common Law Property than the other.[90]

The spiritual unity and advancement of a single end described by Eyre recall (albeit perhaps unwittingly) Aristotle's *Poetics* and the long history of praise reserved for the best poets. *The Dunciad* makes the same case in its purposeful contradistinction of verse and apparatus. The former has an editor, Martinus Scriblerus—himself a composite creation symbolic of inconsistency, Modern scholarship, and sinking in poetry—while the latter has an author.[91] Authors, in turn, have genius, while editors have only method or art.[92]

The comparison of mechanical invention to literary composition has something of an antecedent in *Gulliver's Travels*, the first edition of which Swift completed roughly two years before the first *Dunciad*. Book three comprehends an extended parody of Royal Society projects and projectors, including one that speaks specifically to the pursuit of complete knowledge and the composition of a universal encyclopedia.

For six hours each day, one of the Professors at the Academy of Lagado has a team of forty students manning a giant machine that with every turn of its forty handles generates a new arrangement of the words printed on its many movable blocks. Some of these words inevitably form sentence fragments, which thirty-six of the students dutifully copy down. "The Professor," Gulliver explains, "showed me several Volumes in large Folio already collected, of broken Sentences, which he intended to piece together, and out of those rich Materials to give the World a complete Body of all Arts and Sciences."[93] A further 500 such frames contributing their fragments to the common collection, the Professor insists, would greatly expedite the process.

The students turning the handles, though, are simply spinning their wheels. The project perfectly combines the mindless and the useless; the machine operates by chance, and the snippets of language it produces are therefore entirely nonsensical and bear no intrinsic relation to each other.[94] No actual knowledge is produced by this collaborative project and will not be until the Professor pieces together the fragments. The Professor, with several folios in hand and working towards the production of countless more, will presumably never begin this process (he has not yet) or will gather so much that he cannot complete it. The machine might achieve a unity of parts, then, but its literary output does not. The folios of fragments, to borrow Baron Eyre's words, do not and likely never will reflect that judicious arrangement of ideas necessary to the enforcement of some truth. Gulliver's promise to acknowledge the Professor as the "sole Inventer of this wonderful Machine" and to defend his honor in case of theft by rivals significantly leaves out any mention of the actual folios.[95] The output of the machine—the only part of it that should matter—literally means nothing without an act of authorial invention equivalent to the machine in its unity of design and execution.

Peri Bathous, published the year after *Gulliver's Travels*, skewers the inadequacy of mechanistic collaborative composition both more directly and more specifically with respect to the literary world that would occupy Pope's full attention in *The Dunciad*. Scriblerus, this time in the role of author rather than editor, proposes an association of rhetorical tradesmen that would "incorporate into one Regular Body" and by their labors place the art of writing poetry "upon the same foot with other Arts of this Age." In Scriblerus's scheme, the work of authorship can be divided into branches and conducted piecemeal:

Now each man applying his whole Time and Genius upon his particular Figure, would doubtless attain to Perfection; and when each became incorporated and sworn into the Society, (as hath been propos'd) a Poet or Orator would have no more to do, but to send to the particular Traders in each Kind; to the Metaphorist for this Allegories, to the Simile-maker for his Comparisons, to the Ironist for this Sarcasmes, to the Apothegmatist for his Sentences, &c. whereby a Dedication or Speech would be compos'd in a Moment, the superior Artist having nothing more to do but to put together all the Materials.[96]

That the "Artist" in this case seeks to construct speech and dedications marks this manner of composition as appropriate to lowly Grub Street manufacture, and Scriblerus's embrace of divided labor ironically underscores Pope's insistence that the genuinely superior artist must possess in himself a more comprehensive capacity. A complete poem, in other words, demands a complete poet.

Without the synthesizing mediation of a true author's naturally given judgment, taste, and discernment, these texts suggest, order remains obscured by its own vastness and complexity or prevented by the lack of single unifying mind and perspective. In order to make sense of and improve the world, one must leave a great deal out of the account and carefully connect what remains into a reflection of both what is and what should be. The details of the dunces' lives and the extent to which the portrayals in the verse of *The Dunciad* match up with the realities of life are irrelevant to the poem's greater single action and the one truth it means to enforce: the advancement of polite learning, good writing, and Pope's own brand of cultural perfection. Pope positions himself in *The Dunciad* as a kind of archangel of the fallen world; he attempts to tell his readers what knowledge is truly worth having—whose writing is worth reading, whose words worth listening to—and what amounts to mere distraction. The quality of his opinion is underlined by the completeness of the verse and its contradistinction to the fragmentary representation of knowledge mocked and mimicked by the apparatus. The reader is free to sort through the undifferentiated masses of information in the apparatus as well as in the magazines and miscellanies or even in the entirely un-re-mediated body of works the apparatus severally represents, but with respect to his verse, as Pope would have it, one truth is clear: whatever is, is right.[97]

Not everyone granted that Pope achieved the unity to which he aspired, and the complex history of *The Dunciad* reveals that Pope's experiments in textual extension ultimately exposed his poems to the same criticisms leveled at genuinely encyclopedic texts. They also ironically demonstrated the limits of the form whose utility he was trying to expand. James Ralph, for example, would not allow that with respect to poetic grace the verse accomplished anything more than did the piecemeal collections and commonplace books it disparaged. In the preface to *Sawney*, he calls *The Dunciad* "a strange wild, Linsey-woolsey Composition ... so notoriously full of Pride, Insolence, Beastliness, Malice, Prophaneness, Conceits, Absurdities, and Extravagance, that 'tis almost impossible to form a regular Notion of it."[98] Beyond its suggestion of simple nonsensicalness, "linsey-woolsey" specifically connotes medley or mixture, as does "rhapsody," which term Ralph also deploys in his assault. "One knows not where or How to find Head or Tail," he opines.[99] These attacks on Pope's ability to bring order to his poem and a regular notion of it to his readers denigrate precisely those talents that Pope identified as critical to the work he believed poetry could and should continue to do provided it was done under the aegis of "natural" and gentlemanly genius.

Whatever the veracity of his criticisms, Ralph had reason enough to deride Pope. Ralph, a professional writer who despite Benjamin Franklin's admonitions "continued scribbling Verses, till Pope cur'd him," had gone without notice in the first *Dunciad*, but he nevertheless belonged to that class of Grub Street hacks Pope universally ridiculed.[100] His response to Pope in *Sawney* along with his other poetic efforts eventually earned him Pope's attention and a formal place among the other duncesin the *Variorum*. Ralph did not amount to much either as a poet or a threat, but his inclusion in subsequent versions of *The Dunciad* provides an illustration-in-miniature of the contradictions inherent in Pope's attempt to make a long-term regulatory institution out of a single work of poetry. After 1729, *The Dunciad* was no longer a single work. Dunces come and go, but Dulness is forever; Pope's awareness of this unfortunate reality led to multiple revisions and additions of *The Dunciad* that immediately destabilized the integrity of the poem and continue to problematize any conception of what might constitute a "complete" version.

One can accept that the substitutions and revisions in the verse of the 1729 edition do not substantially undermine Pope's claim that the true names and natures of his duncesmeant relatively little—that one James Ralph, more or less, did not a *Dunciad* make. The addition of *The New Dunciad* of 1742, however, along with the even greater changes entailed by the switch of protagonists in *The Dunciad in Four Books* of 1743, appreciably altered the tenor and scope of the earlier versions. These multiple versions of itself did more to align *The Dunciad* with the magazines and encyclopedias crowding quality poetry out of the bookstalls than did the unwieldy textual apparatus, and when considered together they render Pope's poetic defense of cohesive completeness precisely the kind of linsey-woolsey composition Ralph thought it to have been from the start. The additions and changes to *The Dunciad* evince a strategy of appropriation intended to prolong the life and utility of the poem as well as poetry itself—a demonstration of the ability of poet and poem to perform not only what Pope construed as the work of poetry, but also that of those kinds of literature that could do what poetry did or had not.

Simply put, encyclopedias, magazines, and miscellanies could keep up with the latest developments in their respective areas of interest. Their modes of mediation made the necessity of periodic addition, self-replacement, or planned obsolescence no obstacle to institutional longevity. The "compleat" bodies of knowledge in a given year's crop of encyclopedias always came with the implicit promise that "more compleat" bodies would appear in the future. Readers similarly did not understand the selections comprising this month's *The compleat library* to make it so complete that next month Dunton would not have to select more. The unending supply of new dunces, bad writing, and wrong thinking likewise provided Pope with plenty of reasons to continue his own work—had he lived longer, *The Dunciad in Four Books* might not have been the last—but his efforts to add value to the poem in this way only served to undermine the kind of completeness he identified as a critical component of authorial genius and poetic achievement. As Joseph Warton put it, Pope "was persuaded, unhappily enough, to add a *fourth* book to his *finished* piece, of such a different cast and colour, as to render it at last one of the most motley compositions, that perhaps is any where to be found, in the works of so exact a writer as Pope."[101]

Warton's criticism encapsulates the paradox of what Pope attempted given where he attempted it. "Speaking of the *Dunciad* as a work of art," Warton continues, "I must venture to affirm, that the subject of this fourth book was foreign and heterogeneous; and the addition of it as injudicious, ill-placed, and incongruous, as any of those dissimilar images we meet with in *Pulci* or *Ariosto*."[102] Just as readers and compilers alike complained about the impact of encyclopedic supplements on the unity and wholeness of already "complete" editions, so too did Warton object to that of the *New Dunciad* on an already complete poem. The subsequent change of protagonists and a new wave of revisions wrought further disruptions and finally made *The Dunciad in Four Books* a distinct and separate work that exists alongside the versions of 1728 and 1729.

The new versions did not replace the old or render them obsolete; rather, as works of art, each has equal purchase on posterity. Poetry had achieved some measure of the autonomy that has since preserved its value and place in the panoply of literary forms. The success of *The Dunciad* as a poem prevented its equal participation in the kinds of success enjoyed within other branches of literature. In order to make it more complete in one way, Pope made it less so in another. As a result, no complete *Dunciad* exists. Each version of the poem is one part of an impossible whole.

Epic Alternatives

When Pope temporarily turned his attention away from *The Dunciad* in 1730 so that he might "vindicate the ways of God to man"—a clear reference to the goal Milton had set out for himself in *Paradise Lost*—he chose a genre considered by his contemporaries as second to epic in terms of both heroic ambition and poetic prestige. *An Essay on Man* could trace its heritage through Defoe's *Jure Divino* (1706), which versified much of the second part of Locke's *Two Treatises of Government*; Dryden's *Religio Laici* (1683), in which the author explored matters of faith, church history, and religious politics; and John Davies's *Nosce teipsum* (1599), "one of the first English poems to present a system of philosophy."[103] Like epic, the verse essay depended on the incorporation of multiple genres and styles and therefore demanded an extraordinarily high degree of compositional skill in order to execute successfully. At the same time, however, it called for the subordination of rhetorical beauty to clarity of argument, and it did not seek to contain the whole circle of arts and sciences or approximate the complete learning of its time. Though many of the seventeenth-century poets that followed Davies took *Nosce teipsum* for their model and human knowledge for their subject, they, like Davies, also approached the matter philosophically rather than encyclopedically. Verse essays did not provide an account of all human knowledge of nature in the sense that epic did (or, as Pope would have it, did not), but rather explored the nature of human knowledge itself.

Davies's poem articulates a vision of limited human capacity and defects in human understanding that themselves required more attention than did the worlds beyond their comprehension. "I know my Soul hath Power to know all Things," writes Davies. "Yet is she blind and ignorant to All."[104] Until humans came to know their own souls, the knowledge they sought of rhetoric, law, leech-craft, the causes of the ebbs and flows of the Nile, the geography of the whole terrestrial globe, and the movement of each sphere beyond it could profit them but little.[105] Only an accurate understanding of the soul, that part of humanity most divine in nature and therefore the means by which a more divine understanding of nature might be had, could make a map of all other knowledge readable, and the Fall had placed such a perfect self-understanding out of reach. Like all knowledge, then, a complete understanding of the self had to be reconstituted over time and by degrees.

Davies drew together his map of man in just over 100 quarto pages' worth of quatrains with occasional marginal glosses highlighting specific points or shifts in topic. In the late seventeenth century, however, as part of an ironic effort to make the whole more comprehensible, printers of the poem formally divided the poem into an introduction and thirty-six discrete parts separated from one another by line breaks, section numbers, and subheadings.[106] To an eighteenth-century reader like Pope, then, the table of contents would have illustrated that Davies had disposed of all five senses in only six pages; fantasy and sensitive memory in one page apiece, and wit, reason, understanding, opinion, judgment, and wisdom in one altogether. Pope's new "general map of man," though it follows the conventions and traditions popularized by *Nosce teipsum*—Pope even incorporates the title of that work in the first line of the second epistle—sets out a much larger project.[107] The first epistles, Pope writes, "mark out only the greater parts, their extent, their limits, and their connection, but leaving the particular to be more fully delineated in the charts which are to follow ... I am here only opening the fountains, and clearing the passage. To deduce the rivers, to follow them in their course, and to observe their effects, may be a task more agreeable."[108]

Though Pope continued his defense of poetry as the most functional and therefore highest form of writing by appropriating the weapons of the enemy—the preface to *An Essay on Man* assigns rhymed couplets the power of maxims and verse the grace of conciseness deemed by Bacon most advantageous to the advancement of learning—he did so only in order to rearticulate the impossibility of truly universal human knowledge. Humanity's place in the Chain of Being and the God-given faculties appropriate to that place, he insists, made such a desire futile at best and potentially catastrophic at worst. The language of parts and wholes permeates the entirety of the essay, and Pope emphasizes at every turn that human understanding cannot and should not penetrate beyond its station. "'Tis but a part we see, and not a whole," he writes, and the former cannot contain the latter.[109]

The connection of human limitation to the power of sight underscores his point. Though the power of sight was frequently associated with that of reason, John Locke in his own essay on human understanding had described sight as "the most comprehensive of all our senses."[110] The greatest amount of ideas in and about the world, Locke claimed—light, color, figure, space, and motion—enter the mind via the eye. Even the most comprehensive human sense, Pope thus suggests, was designed to take in neither the vastness of the universe nor the microscopic world of a fly, and even within Locke's system human understanding could therefore do no better.[111] Only God could "see worlds on worlds compose one universe,/Observe how system into system runs,/What other planets circle other suns,/What vary'd being peoples ev'ry star."[112] Complete human knowledge, could such a thing be had, would therefore necessarily be fragmentary because it would still be human. Truly complete knowledge resided in God, through whose power and presence all things were unified; understanding the connection of all parts of art and nature "into one stupendous whole" therefore required faith rather than study. Human study, then, was best applied to humanity.

Pope's study, however, which he intended to complete by mapping out man with respect to the Universal System and with respect to his own, likewise turned out to be too ambitious an undertaking. Pope fell prey to the same fate that Bacon and others before him had identified as one of the major obstacles to gaining complete mastery over the arts, sciences, and nature itself. He died. *An Essay on Man* thus remains a poetic fragment, and while to Pope this outcome was probably unlooked for (though certainly predictable), the fragmentary state of the poem more perfectly reflects the state of human nature and knowledge it sought to describe as well as the conventions of the essay as Bacon and his followers had redefined it. The single poet and poem again proved inadequate to the task of exploring and representing to the fullest possible extent that which it undertook to explicate. The epic could not really contain complete knowledge, and the verse essay could not contain complete knowledge of even that part of the universe most appropriate and open to human inquiry. Pope's poem, like the many essays produced throughout the seventeenth and eighteenth centuries that knowingly embraced their incompleteness, left more work to be done.

"Encyclopedic" poems did not go out of the world simply because Pope and the Augustans declared a moratorium on epic poetry; nor did poets abandon any and all attempts to capture or access the essence of that total connectivity inherent in the concept of completeness. At the same time Pope was placing limitations on the scope of epic knowledge in order to defend the completeness of epic structure and the organizational power of the epic poet, James Thomson was doing precisely the opposite. *The Seasons* (1730), a composite poem the individual parts of which had been separately published since 1726, followed Pope's translations of the classics and largely overlapped with his *Dunciad* and *Dunciad Variorum*. Though Thomson disparaged the contempt many "modern" writers had for poetry and longed for it to "be restored to her antient Truth, and Purity," his own work turned away from ancient models and instead follows a less rigid structure that to this day prevents its easy categorization.[113] John Chalker places Thomson's "long poem" in the Georgic tradition (which tradition Thomson specifically invokes in his preface to the second edition of "Winter"); Ralph Cohen, in contrast, denies its status as Georgic and further claims that despite some featural similarities, it was also "not an epic in any traditional sense."[114] Samuel Johnson more simply observed that *The Seasons* lacked any clear method by which its disparate parts might be brought into a harmonious whole, and for that want he saw no remedy.[115]

This want extends to the poem's rejection of any single set of literary conventions in which a preexisting, well-defined, and therefore perhaps undesirably artificial system of organization might have inhered. In the preface to "Winter," Thomson identifies the *"Works of Nature"* as being full of beautiful, enlarging variety and suggests that there could be no more inspiring subject for poetry than "a calm, wide, survey of them."[116] Additional seasons and subsequent revisions introduced additional subjects and poetic modes that broadened the scope of the whole while remaining within an order more intimated than imposed by seasonal chronology. "Multiple kinds of speech and the ways of seeing or knowing they imply (Newtonian physics, Spenserian romance, Miltonic epic, the nascent science of geology)," Gabrielle Starr writes, "suggest not so much the vision of a single 'I' as the accumulated knowledge of an entire society."[117] That suggestion decidedly locates the poem in the tradition of idealized epic encyclopedism, but Thomson's subordination of an individualized poetic vision and the exclusion of conventional organizational mechanisms shifted the work of the long poem towards the pursuit of a different kind of complete knowledge. *The Seasons* thus effected conceptual and structural alterations of epic encyclopedism at the same moment Pope's poems were contributing to its ossification and universal dictionaries assuming some of its duties.

The Seasons does not depend for its completeness on the comprehensive learning of a single heroic poet, the embedding of accrued knowledge within the limiting structure of a fictional or historical narrative, or the methodized fragmentation of that knowledge into a collection of incongruously alphabetized parts with an implied but unrealizable unity.[118] Within the confines of the single poem and season, Thomson's survey of nature's works achieved what Sandro Jung describes as a "more coherent ... ideational program" insofar as it "limit[ed] its scope to the engagement with and praise of the sublimity of Nature and its creator." The revisions of each individual poem that Thomson undertook in order to composite *The Seasons* of 1730, however, resulted in a "a more complex composition that illustrates the friction, tensions, and continuities of the evolving textual conditions."[119] The expansion of each book in subsequent editions further diminished any clear and authoritative unifying structure. Although, as Starr concludes, "one man has brought these disparate images and kinds of knowledge together ... what filters perception and shapes representation in Thomson is system rather than self—the harmony of creation or the moral music of nature."[120] Thomson acknowledges the inadequacy of the single self and redirects the focus of his new epicist poetry from representing complete knowledge in a classical sense to seeking and evoking the "unifying principle" behind it.

This does not mean that Thomson made no concessions to readers unlikely to detect the connections made across the full poem's 250 pages in quarto. As Jung explains, Thomson realized that the comprehension of an overall structure required more than just seasonal chronology; he therefore composed "Arguments" for each book designed to serve as "explicit structural pointers" towards the links between or among seasons.[121] At the same time, these arguments identify elements in each that the author counts as digressions—material that by definition departs from or does not advance the main subject. Thomson writes of "Spring" that, "This Season is described as it affects the various parts of Nature, ascending from the lower to the higher; and mixed with Digressions arising from the subject." "Autumn," meanwhile, includes (amongst much else) "a description of fogs, frequent in the latter part of Autumn: whence a digression, enquiring into the rise of fountains and rivers."[122] In both cases, Thomson intimates an emergent order inspired by the subject at hand rather than determined by the author in advance.

Instead of arguing (as Le Bossu did with regard to select episodes in the classical epics) that the unity of the entire poem depends upon arriving at an understanding of the subordinate status of the digressions or the ways in which they serve some larger single end, Thomson's Arguments insist upon permanent, albeit slight, structural disjunctions. They announce the presence of digressions in all four seasons and allow them to stand as such; arising as they do from the main subjects (like the fountains and rivers into the origins of which the digression of "Autumn" inquires), the digressions must be connected to those subjects, but as digressions they must also stand somewhat apart. The Arguments thus highlight an overall structural incompleteness following from the poem's brand of specifically poetic encyclopedism; in the composited *Seasons*, Thomson embraces developing rather than fixed knowledge and privileges scope over immediate structural cohesion or permanence.

Where Samuel Johnson saw a lack of order, a later age saw what it might have called organic rather than mechanistic composition. *The Seasons*, as many scholars have observed, marks an important point of departure from the neoclassicism of the Augustans, and it remains a foundational text of modern constructions of eighteenth-century pre-Romanticism.[123] The poem was at its most popular in the mid-1790s, decades after its "invocations of patrons, topical references to politics and empire, and the discourse of the New Science" had, as Jung explains, "lost their currency." Fortunately, "the interpolated episodes could easily be detached or severed from the contexts of actuality" that originally gave them meaning, and the poem's new booksellers "privileged a simplified and less complex reading of *The Seasons* as a poem of action, drama, and sentiment."[124] The success the poem enjoyed at century's end, in other words, depended upon the elevation of ways of reading less concerned with discerning the structural coherence of all its elements—an elevation authorized by *The Seasons* some sixty years earlier and (as I will show in Chapter 4) crucial to the re-conceptualized literary completeness of much Romantic poetry.

The long poems that followed in the wake of *The Seasons*, like Edward Young's *Night Thoughts* (1742–45), Oliver Goldsmith's *The Deserted Village* (1770), and William Cowper's *The Task* (1785), all had in common a lack of apparent method or design. According to the poet John Scott, this want applied to the bulk of modern poetry: "modern poetry has in general one common defect, viz., the want of proper arrangement. There are many poems, whose component parts resemble a number of fine paintings, which have some connexion with each other, but are not placed in any regular series."[125] The absence of an artificial organizing principle, however, along with the resultant lack of formal unity, allowed these poems more readily to comprehend a multitude of diverse elements.[126] If Pope's criticism of Homer advanced the decoupling of epic poetry from encyclopedic completeness, then the long poems of his successors advanced the separation of poetic completeness from encyclopedic connectivity.

The rational methods of works like those of Harris, Chambers, Diderot, and D'Alembert deconstructed nature in order to make the connection of all the parts of knowledge comprehensible to the human mind. While they persisted in their efforts to write the universe small and unite all knowledge through alphabetical arrangement, genealogical trees, and extensive cross-referencing—tactics that met with resistance in the 1730s and rejection in the 1790s—poets like Thomson and Young did not attempt to follow suit. They instead allowed the seemingly incomprehensible connections of the natural world to dictate their methods. Like Thomson, Young imposed order in his poem according to that which "spontaneously arose" in his mind. Their "organic" poems take the order of nature as given; they function not as great mirrors, but as conduits to the immensity of an always already organized world about which their knowledge could only ever be incomplete.

4
Mid-Century Experiments in Encyclopedism

To whatever extent the public perception of the literary marketplace in the early eighteenth century gave new purchase to ancient woes about an overabundance of writing and the difficulty of distinguishing the worthy from the unremarkable, by the 1740s such complaints had again become thoroughly commonplace. As they had for decades, missives about the impossibility (or, at the very least, the inconvenience) of attempting to read and understand everything available in print continued to feature regularly in the hundreds if not thousands of texts published in order to fight the rising tide that supposedly threatened to sink all boats. Descriptions and defenses of extensive plans and methodized programs— all designed to bring some kind of order to what had been or would otherwise be an unmediated and therefore unmanageable chaos—echoed throughout the literary landscape of the mid-eighteenth century in a wide range of works intended to supplant proliferating forms of instruction and entertainment even as they competed with each other to define and control the past, present, and future of British literature.

Epic poems and universal dictionaries, in other words, were not the only forms associated with complete knowledge, and if epic conventions had a life beyond epics, then so too did encyclopedism go beyond encyclopedias. Though the many periodicals partly responsible for the spike in titular occurrences of the word "universal" between 1750 and 1760— properties that neither achieved nor actually set out to achieve anything like genuinely comprehensive coverage or the conceptual unity of what they presented—helped to make "universal," like "compleat" before it, another advertising term of dubious substance, the mid-century also saw the production or expansion of several literary projects that did indeed aspire to some version of universality or completeness in a more encyclopedic sense.[1] A one-volume supplement to Harris's *Lexicon technicum*, for example, finally appeared in 1744; the two-volume supplement to the *Cyclopædia* appeared in 1753. Dennis de Coetlogon designed his *An universal history of arts and sciences* (1745), also a two-volume venture, as an alternative to somewhat more conventional universal dictionaries like *A new and complete dictionary of arts and sciences*.[2] The *Encyclopédie* eclipsed all of these in size as well as scope. The first seventeen of the twenty-eight volumes intended by D'Alembert and Diderot to "collect all the knowledge that now lies scattered over the face of the earth" appeared from 1751 to 1765.[3] Four years into its production, Samuel Johnson finally published his encyclopedic dictionary of the English language—a work that he acknowledged could go on forever and never actually be complete.[4]

The production of these works, in turn, largely overlapped with the conceptualization, composition, and sale of yet more projects that not only continued the pursuit of completeness in other literary forms and fields of knowledge production, but also engaged in a debate about the nature and substance of that pursuit. Samuel Richardson, for instance, made full accounts of his characters' experiences central to the triumvirate of epistolary novels he published between 1741 and 1753. The second of these, *Clarissa, or, the History of a Young Lady* (1748), remains one of the longest in the English language. The "epic" plots of Henry Fielding's *The History of the Adventures of Joseph Andrews* (1742) and *The History of Tom Jones, a Foundling* (1749), in contrast, placed greater emphasis on closure and cohesion, but both nonetheless acknowledged a connection to reference works and universal history as well. In 1755, Benjamin Martin sold the first issues of his *The general magazine of arts and sciences* and spent another decade trying to combine the connectivity and scope of an encyclopedia with the variety and ornament of a periodical magazine. Four years after Martin began his project, the proprietors of the 65-volume *An Universal History* ended their own with the publication of the 44th and final volume of its modern part. All of these texts represent different experiments in encyclopedism that contributed to the ongoing reorganization of the broader system of literature as they both succeeded and (even more importantly) failed to function as compendia of "complete" knowledge.

Concepts of completeness—informed as usual by questions of utility and troubled as ever by the problematic relationship of utility to comprehensiveness and cohesion—shaped and reshaped all of these texts as well as the classes of literature they represented and helped to define. Though the claims to complete knowledge made by the encyclopedists did not depend chiefly on matters of detail, their related claims to utility were often made around promises not to overwhelm readers with too much information, and in this much they were joined not only by numerous magazine editors who made selection and abridgment their first order of business but also by the authors of universal histories and the writers of prose fiction. The contributors to *An Universal History, from the earliest account of time* understood very well that a preponderance of (often contradictory) historical detail could undermine the coherence of the grand narratives they sought to provide, and their pursuit of complete knowledge ironically compelled them to undertake a strategy of organizational division. The "histories" of the mid-century novelists too experimented with the limits of comprehensive but still comprehensible detail, and from the whole worlds they represented in verisimilar miniature emerged an alternative and specifically literary kind of complete knowledge separate from those of the increasingly unmanageable universal histories and dictionaries charged with comprehending the whole record of human civilization or the full account of human learning.

At the time of their publication, such works remained at least tentatively connected by similar concerns and ambitions as well as a number of shared organizational features designed to create the ideal combination of completeness and utility. Some of those features remained regular conventions while others did not. Collectively, these novels, histories, and magazines constitute a series of experiments that contributed to the ongoing differentiation of literary and non-literary works and the eventual emergence of the more stratified system with which we are all familiar. As I will show in this chapter, the functional, critical, and commercial successes or failures they enjoyed as compendia of "complete" knowledge helped to establish the kinds of work their associated literatures would do and the concepts of completeness readers continue to associate with them.

Ravelings of Time: *An Universal History*

By the time the first chapters of *An Universal History, from the earliest account of time* appeared in 1736, Homer's accounts of the arts and sciences had largely been reconceived and compartmentalized as poetic rather than properly encyclopedic accomplishments. Chambers had found room in the preface to the *Cyclopædia* to acknowledge Homer's greatness, but he restricted the extent of his learning and dismissed the ability of any individual to know or account for as much as could a collaborative consortium of modern knowledge producers. Pope had made a similar concession in his translation of the *Iliad* when he insisted that readers should consider Homer "only in quality of a poet."[5] The introduction to the revised twenty-volume edition of *An Universal History* likewise addresses Homeric knowledge, and it too compliments Homer while distinguishing between poetic and other kinds of knowledge production. The authors make no mention of Homer's connection to the arts and sciences but focus instead on historiography and the classics' place in constructing a history of the world.

Homer's *Iliad*, the authors suggest, is both history and poem, and Homer accordingly deserves commendation as both historian and poet. The modern historian, though, had to consider those functions discretely. "Homer, *tho' a Poet*, discovers to us the State of Greece at that Time; he gives us an Account of the Kings and Generals, describes their States, Cities, and Government ... These and a great many other Events are purely historical, and confirmed by creditable Historians."[6] The purity of the historical content, in this construction, exists both separately from and in problematic commixture with those fictions that for the authors of *An Universal History* substantiated a categorical distinction between "Poet" and "Historian." Pure history occurs in the poems *as* poetry, but also, as the phrase "tho' a Poet" suggests, *despite* poetry. The distinction, largely naturalized by the mid-eighteenth century, required the extraction of historical verity from its confusion with poetical improbability. The poems of Homer and the other "first" historians of antiquity, though "interspersed with many fabulous Strokes," might thus furnish "a judicious Historian, that could distinguish between Truth and Fiction, with good Materials for a History."[7]

To Pope—a poet—the "strokes" introduced into Homer's poems had been knowledge of the arts and sciences; the authors of *An Universal History*, in contrast, saw in Homer's histories "strokes" of poetical fiction.[8] None would allow that the ancient epics could do or had ever done the work of all in equal measure. All, however, sought to achieve what they deemed an ideal or at least functional balance between coverage and coherence. In their effort to follow the thread of time from the creation of the world to the present day, and to pursue its course around the entire globe, the proprietors of *An Universal History* produced a work that even within a genre defined by extensive breadth placed greater emphasis on comprehensiveness than had any of its predecessors. The emphasis on scope set in sharp relief the tensions between completeness and utility to which most forms of knowledge production, and all narrative histories, are heir. The struggle to control the collected knowledge of human history within and across the project's two parts highlighted the extent to which the narrative qualities of coherence, integrity, fullness, and closure stood in conflict with the apparently irresolvable complexity of the more comprehensive chronological and historical accounts that the editors set out to provide.[9]

Not all of the challenges faced by *An Universal History* were unique to it or to world history at large. Just as guidebooks and systems dedicated to single arts or sciences offered arguments similar to those made in universal dictionaries, so too did universal histories rehearse the complaints made in any number of more specific accounts of events, nations, or peoples. All made use of similar rhetoric and described methods or features intended to remedy the deficits of their competitors, and where those deficits typically involved the interconnected matters of coverage, coherence, accessibility, and usefulness, so too did the supposed remedies justify conventional claims to greater perfection or completeness.

The seventeenth century offers several examples. Denis Pétau's *The history of the world: or, An account of time* (1659), for instance, charges the length of Sir Walter Raleigh's *The history of the world* (1614) with oppressing its readers' patience and condemns Johannes Sleidanus's *De quatuor summis imperiis* (1557) for passing over numerous worthwhile acts. Pétau predictably supposes himself to have found the happy medium.[10] William Howell, in *An institution of general history* (1661), suggests that the co-mingling of multiple nations' histories in earlier works produces "a strange confusion, like the several ingredients of an Olio in the same Dish ... and he that would read an History by itself, finds it immediately embroyl'd and interwoven with the affairs of other Nations, so that he will not easily form a perfect Idea in his mind of that which is given him but in parcels."[11] Howell therefore separates the nations which he treats into numerous distinct chapters. The Oxford-educated antiquarian Thomas Hearne, author of *Ductor historicus: or, a short system of universal history* (1698), naturally questioned Howell's efficacy. In Hearne's opinion, Howell, Raleigh, Pétau, and most others actually "tell the story of the whole World together," and while this might benefit advanced students, it leaves beginners lost.[12] His arrangement, he explains, more properly follows the precepts of analytic division set down by the French historian and political philosopher Jean Bodin. If Hearne's analysis did not actually lead readers "to a perfect Knowledge of the whole" (he readily admits that Howell's is the more comprehensive treatment), then it at least brought the history of the world into a more manageable and memorable compass.[13]

The plan of *An Universal History*, then, sounded what nearly a century's worth of Latin and vernacular histories had made a familiar note: despite an abundance of titles, the world still wanted a true history of the world.

Earlier efforts either did not move far enough forward in time, as was the case with Raleigh's, or they did not extend much beyond the nations of Europe—the flaw of Howell's.[14] To comprehend the full extent of modern historical knowledge, a modern universal history had to account for improvements in geography, chronology, and the advances in learning that followed from increases in travel and travel writing as well as the recent establishment of modern history professorships at Oxford and Cambridge.[15] "History," the preface begins, "is without all doubt, the most instructive and useful, as well as entertaining, Part of Literature; more especially, when it is not confined within the narrow Bounds of any particular Time or Place, but extends to the Transactions of all Times and Nations."[16] If nothing else, the sixty-five volumes of *An Universal History* succeeded in making the general histories of the previous era seem comparatively miniscule, but they all came with nearly identical assurances regarding prolixity, brevity, and organizational division.[17]

More, however, is different.[18] In the first paragraphs of the first chapter describing the origins of the world—at the moment of creation, as it were—George Sale, the editor-author of the first two volumes of the ancient part, articulates the ironies inherent in the composition of such a massive text. He describes it as "an undertaking of vast extent, and which would, perhaps, be scarce practicable, were the histories of all nations now extant, and their series complete." Such a history is possible, in other words, because a lack of ancient records has "reduced history into a closer compass." At the same time, though, the historian must so frequently rely on "precarious conjectures" and "have recourse to so many shifts, to connect and supply [the frequent interruptions and defects], that his labour seems to be encreased by the scarcity of materials; and he is unable, after all, to give his reader satisfaction."[19] The more histories the work incorporates, the greater the number of gaps and disagreements; as the whole becomes more complete, it also becomes less complete. The authors can only attempt a universal history of antiquity because the records are fragmentary, but because they are fragmentary, the universal history must have recourse to conjecture, and the more fragments they gather, the more conjecture they require. Maintaining the integrity of all those threads that *An Universal History* sought to weave into one general account, then, jeopardized its overall historical integrity.

The difficulties began with the first order of historiography. Sale, like many before him, observed that order (and, by extension, sense) depended in the first place upon "an exact Distribution of Time," without which history "would be only a Chaos of Facts heaped together."[20] Systems of reckoning time, though, had for centuries been highly problematic in and of themselves. Civilizations and faiths beyond and before those of Christian Europe did not follow one or the same thread; the challenge of reconciling multiple, often contradictory records and winding them into the order of a single timeline had troubled western scholars at least since the time of Eusebius of Caesaria.[21] The discovery of the Americas and increased exposure to India, China, and Japan in the Early Modern period brought new and even greater levels of complexity to the construction (or re-construction) of a uniform, universal chronology. The former revealed a whole "new" world whose peoples had no place in the narrative established by biblical history, and the latter—particularly with regard to China—provided substantial documentary evidence of civilizations older than biblical history allowed.[22]

A more expansive view of human history, in other words, required more time in which to arrange it. Joseph Scaliger, whose *De emendatione temporum* (1583) reformed the study of chronology and established new methodological foundations for its advancement, and James Ussher, whose dates for the Creation, Flood, and Resurrection in *Annales Veteris Testamenti* (1650–54) were later enshrined in annotated editions of the King James Bible, both desired to incorporate the historical records of older or other peoples within their chronologies.[23] Their efforts granted those histories legitimacy while maintaining the basic integrity of the biblical historical narrative but at the cost of occasionally compromising or abandoning the accepted Vulgate text in favor of the Septuagint, which, as Rachel Ramsay explains, "in general ... adds fifteen centuries and budgets a 37 per cent increase for the total length of world history."[24] Simply put, chronologists needed more time, and they found it; the necessary adjustments, though, cast doubt on the possibility of compiling a truly comprehensive chronological record that would not stretch or rupture the presumably unified and unifying religious framework into which it had to fit.

The problem, according to *An Universal History*, had no simple solution. Computation alone did not answer; neither did the authority of Scripture. The proliferation of chronological systems—"every Author almost having one of his own"—became another element of modern universal history that threatened its larger goals.[25] Previous chronologers, the text claims, retained or discarded various particulars "just as it suited their Humour of making the Sacred History agree with the Prophane; or otherwise of reducing the Prophane to the Sacred."[26] The charge immediately precedes a table of ninety-eight different computations of the years of the world to the birth of Christ. The figures listed range from 6984 to 3616. Each computation, the preface implies, represents a separate system based on a series of selective judgments driven either by caprice or a deliberate elevation of "agreement" at the expense of truth. The authors of *An Universal History* promise not to duplicate the mistake by forcing facts to fit hypotheses or by imposing uniformity across the profane and sacred chronologies.[27] This does not mean that they forgo the evaluation of sources or fail to devise and defend their own systems of reckoning; it suggests instead that the ancient part of *An Universal History*, at least initially, located historical truth in often irreducible or irresolvable complexity rather than in the fiction of a single unifying system. The first volume invites readers to judge for themselves the merits of no less than ten individual and comparative tables of chronological computations that illustrate the disparities among scriptural variants. The order of Sale's encyclopedic treatment of cosmogony in the first volume further reflects the secularizing pressure placed by modern Pyrrhonic skepticism on antediluvian chronologies derived from Judeo-Christian Scripture. He includes the Mosaic account of creation, which would normally have come first, only after reviewing "every known theory of the earth's creation that he could gather"—Greek, Phoenician, Egyptian, Indian, Persian, Chinese, Siamese, even atheistic.[28]

Chronological tables were fairly typical additions to narrative histories.[29] Publishers likewise often included maps and genealogical charts intended to serve as aids to memory and comprehension. The visual arrangement of simple information (geographical location, orders of familial or royal succession, dates) in theory permitted readers to take in the structural frameworks of history "at one view" and hold the spatiotemporal connections in mind while reading. Thomas Hearne specifically relied on such devices to smooth the way through the main text. The purpose of chronological tables, and more particularly of the single general table Hearne recommended providing to younger students of history, was to minimize the need for "large Digressions" in the main body that would unify the larger history but "too much break the thread" of the discourse in the process. The author, who could relate only one part of one history at a time, relies upon the reader to have consulted the tables and to bring to the text a basic knowledge of the events occurring at the same time in other nations. Only in this way can the reader "comprehend the Story."[30] According to Hearne, the main text and its supplements were thus designed to work in tandem to produce a more coherent understanding of the whole as such.

An Universal History, in addition to tables, maps, charts, plans, illustrations, engravings, and portraits, offers another feature that it identifies as a formal innovation intended to serve a similar function. "It is not usual to publish Histories with Notes," the authors observe, "or at least to crowd them with so great a Number: But tho' no other History, perhaps, has need of them, yet they are necessary to this which we have undertaken."[31] Many notes in *An Universal History* leave little room for the narrative above; some go on for several pages. All of them generally serve two interdependent but seemingly oppositional organizational purposes. On the one hand, the notes allow the main body to offer the version of history constructed by the authors without significant interruption. On the other hand, they disrupt that version by providing evidence of the larger body of documents and disputations upon which it is based.

The first function is typical of conventional paratexts. Had the authors attempted to elucidate within the narrative the meaning of every historical detail or term obscured by the passage of time, "the Thread of the most beautiful Story would have been often broke, and no Point of History would have been brought to its Conclusion, but in a languid Manner."[32] Forming an accurate understanding of ancient nations, faiths, manners, and dress required the observations related into the notes—the history "would have been imperfect" without them—but in order successfully to complete that history they must be separated from the rendering of its "points" into units that strive to achieve the coherent qualities of narrative.[33]

At the same time, the notes create a venue for the presentation and containment of contradiction—without which the history would *also* be incomplete. The preface explains:

> Besides, abundance of Disputes have been raised by learned Men upon several Events, which we are obliged to inform the Public of, in order to make our Work more compleat. But this could not have been, if we had not taken Notice of the Variations of the several Authors, who have transmitted to us the same Facts. Historians often disagree as to the Circumstances, and, on the other hand, the Thread of the History will not admit but of one way of relating the Event. We have therefore placed in the Body of the History what seemed to us most probable, and the rest in the Notes, lest those Readers, who peruse but one Author, should charge us with Falshood, if we differ from his Historian.[34]

The thread metaphor connects the order created by critical evaluation and selection to that imposed by exact chronology. In both cases, pursuing the single "thread of the history" ties the historian's hands. The author must choose one way of relating a point or event from amongst many known alternatives and present it as the most probable historical reality; otherwise, the whole would become an incomprehensible tangle of facts and theories that in presenting the full range of modern historical knowledge would make that knowledge less useful.

Together, these passages reveal how the tension between extensiveness and coherence affects the organization of the text and informs the operational definition of historiographical completeness according to *An Universal History*. Dividing the text into body and notes cuts the Gordian knot; neither the "one way" of the main narrative body nor the "abundance of disputes" addressed in the notes on its own constitutes a "compleat" history. When recounting the history of the Moabites, for example, the main text relates that the angels who visited Lot in Sodom blinded the people who came to his house demanding that he turn the angels over to them. The note, however, offers that the sense of the passage in the Septuagint indicates dizziness rather than actual blindness, and that the author of the Book of Wisdom "supposes some change in the air" rather than in the vision or minds of the assailants.[35] The point is minor but demonstrative: the men were and were not actually blinded; the completeness of the relation inheres in the historical indeterminacy reconstituted by the dynamic of narration and note. Closure is created but also revealed as an authorial choice rather than a purely factual reality.

I do not mean to suggest that previous universal or general world histories concealed disputed facts or omitted contrary findings. The critical evaluation of contradictory documents had long been a component of historical writing. In his chapter on the Egyptian kings in book two of *Histoire du monde* (1698), for example, Urbain Chevreau includes several possible etymological origins of "Egypt."[36] These occupy only a few paragraphs, and many similar instances occur in the main text of *An Universal History* without substantial annotation. A more substantial interruption, though, occurs in Jacques Bossuet's *Discours sur l'histoire universelle* (1686). Bossuet literally halts his narration of the reign of Cyrus the Great to address a point of chronological uncertainty: "Here we ought a little to make a stop, because it is the most entangled place of all the Antient Chronology, by reason of the difficulty in conciliating the Prophane History with the Sacred."[37] The English translation underscores the break with a blank line not present in the French original and proceeds for a further eight pages before resuming the narration. The *Discours* and *An Universal History* both choose to follow the *Cyropædia* of Xenophon rather than the history of Herodotus and explain their reasoning in the main body, but *An Universal History* confines its explanation to less than two pages and relegates to the notes many of the details that would have troubled its otherwise uninterrupted sixteen-page narration of Cyrus' life from birth to death.[38]

Once again, the text prioritizes the integrity of a given "story" while the notes remind readers that the historian's determinations are probably rather than absolutely accurate. The narrative elides complication and the notes restore it; as part of a project that depended upon popular success for its continued survival, the "new" feature of annotation allowed the authors of *An Universal History* to make comprehensible to a general audience what was often a highly fragmented and unfamiliar history while still remaining true to responsible scholarship and the conviction that it would not be "reasonable to confine the Reader to [their] own Sentiments."[39] The text divides what it presents in order to make the whole more complete not just as a series of supposedly coherent prose narratives or a comprehensive collection of disparate facts, opinions, and chronologies, but as a work of history distinguished from either by the presence of both.

The notes, though, engage with only one order of compositional comprehensiveness. The unique ambition of *An Universal History* to write the stories of *all* nations known to Europeans and to bring them all down to the current moment constituted a higher order of completeness that required multiple hands, ample time, and sustained profitability to achieve. In combination, these factors contributed to multiple unresolved stylistic and ideological discontinuities within what would ideally have been a uniform account. To whatever extent the work successfully accommodated the disagreements among those bodies of historical knowledge upon which it drew, the very means by which the work proceeded resulted in the duplication of some of the same kinds of disagreement within and across its two parts.

The first two editors of the ancient part did not share a common outlook. In George Sale, the syndicate found an accomplished Orientalist who brought to the project primary knowledge of Arabic literature and a more accepting attitude towards Islam. When the Grub Street writer and erstwhile impostor known as George Psalmanazar assumed editorial control, his new (and not entirely unsubstantiated) identity as a scholar of Hebrew led him into conflict with the work of his predecessor.[40] Psalmanazar, who amongst much else wrote the better part of the history of the Jews for the fourth folio volume, did not agree with Sale's earlier assessment of the Old Testament. As Tamara Griggs notes, he "was willing to sacrifice the narrative thread of the whole universal history in order to assert his interpretation."[41] When Psalmanazar later asked the publishers to reissue corrected editions of the first volumes, they deemed uniformity not worth the expense, and the disparities were allowed to stand .[42]

The next greatest threat to the coherence of the work, according to Psalmanazar, came from Archibald Bower, a Scottish writer of similarly dubious provenance.[43] Setting aside questions of Bower's acumen as a historian—later critics did not look on his contributions favorably—Psalmanazar fretted the damage done not by philosophical or theological disagreement but solely by Bower's organizational tactics. Like Hearne, Psalmanazar believed that restricting the narration of each nation's history to only those events that transpired within its actual borders would minimize redundancies and clarify the separate parts of history. Clearer parts would contribute to a clearer whole; where histories overlapped, contributors were meant to provide cross-references to the other nations' treatments in prior volumes or indicate what would appear in later ones. These cross-references, like those in the *Cyclopædia*, were meant to aid the reader in putting back together what the text had pulled apart for the sake of clarity.

Bower's six volumes on the Roman Empire, however, swallowed as many countries as did the empire itself. Some readers, Psalmanazar admitted, approved because they created "a more connected history of that nation," but as chief editor he objected. He had to truncate the individuated histories of the Germans, Gauls, and Spaniards to offset Bower's swollen narrative, and neither treatment satisfied. Psalmanazar's repeated in a much smaller compass what Bower had digested, and Bower's left them so "scattered and so interspersed with [the history] of other nations, that it cannot be called a regular and compleat history of them."[44] Furthermore, the unwillingness of other authors to see their own contributions reduced left inadequate room to cover the ancient histories of India, Siam, China, Japan, Russia, Turkey, Tartary, parts of Africa, and America, all of which had been promised and would now have to be taken up in the modern part of the history provided the syndicate still wished to pursue it.[45] Bower's "more connected" history of Rome thus left the other histories he incorporated as well as the entire ancient part of the project *less* complete. It also left Psalmanazar convinced that the design of such a work could not be successfully executed unless given over to "the whole care and revisal" of just one person—a virtual impossibility, given the scale of its ambitions and the fact of its corporate control.[46]

Ironically, then, the integrity of the project had been jeopardized as soon as the proprietors brought on Psalmanazar. When the syndicate in 1758 proposed to proceed with the modern part, however, their particular emphasis on connectivity within the new volumes and across the whole belied an even greater disruption to its overall coherence. The proposal offers "a succinct view of the contents of the first part, and a more copious detail of what may be expected in the second; that the connexion of the whole may appear," but the penultimate paragraph of the new proposal marks a clear shift of focus:

> But the objects most attentively kept in sight, have been the rise and progress of those nations, that supplanting the great empires of antiquity (the histories of which are contained in the first part) ... have necessarily introduced new scenes in respect to policy, religion, and science. By developing these, it appears that the corruption of manners, the introduction of luxury, and the prevalence of tyranny and superstition, chiefly contributed to enervate, and undermine the old, as a wild unpolished spirit of liberty, gave an irresistible impetuosity, to the new. That by the revival of Science, in the western world, these have been tempered and civilized, which has given *Europeans* a superiority to all, and the command over many nations, in other parts of the globe. The distinguishing the real causes of these great events, and pointing at their consequences, make it truly an UNIVERSAL HISTORY.[47]

This represents a crucial revision of the earlier proposal's claim that previous universal histories were not complete because they failed to comprehend enough time or nations. The new proposal suggests that modern European history had actually reorganized the history of the whole world; covering more time and more nations had supposedly revealed that all threads led to the single end of Europe's rise and global impact. The unifying narrative of commercial progress and civilizing influence adopted by the modern part thus reframes (or attempts to reframe) the whole as a more comprehensive version of a coherent Eurocentric universalism; however, because the developments behind this new vision of history did not transpire until after the conception and publication of the original, the two parts do not cohere. The ancient part, necessarily unaware of the events that would inform the writing of the modern, does not anticipate what follows it.[48]

Simply put, the project designed to manage a large body of knowledge became unmanageable in its own right. Though the authors and editors could exert some measure of control over irreconcilable records and disputed facts by dividing the notes from the body, and though they could fill the chasms of history with critical evaluation and probabilistic conjecture, they could not escape the limitations of large-scale and long-term collaborative composition.

In trying to tell the whole story of humanity, the architects of *An Universal History* discovered that they could not achieve or sustain all measures of completeness; despite their plans and promises, the sixty-five volumes finally present a narrative of irresolvable complexity, digression, and disagreement.

Even as the modern part brought the narrative down to the current moment, more condensed universal histories that offered more cohesive philosophical arguments were already beginning to enjoy greater success.[49] In his *Essai sur les mouers* (1756), Voltaire pointedly questions the usefulness of committing chronological data to memory and studying the inconsequential parts of history alongside those of estimable significance. He arrives at the following conclusion: "In this immense collection, all which it is impossible to embrace, you must confine your reading, and make some choice. It is like a great magazine, out of which you may take what will serve your purpose."[50] The rationale for Voltaire's approach and the shift in historiography it advanced, then, stemmed in part from the perceived incomprehensibility of history as a totality and the greater utility of a less inclusive but more synthesizing theorization. The tradition of overarching narrative historiography that reached an apex in *An Universal History* only continued to wane as the more focused analytical works of the next generation of historians established a clear trend towards specialization and the general separation of world history into its component parts.[51]

The Complete Novel

Despite their nearly simultaneous rise to cultural prominence and a mutual connection to epic, the universal knowledge projects of the mid-eighteenth century—including *An Universal History* and the modern encyclopedia—receive relatively little attention in critical studies of the novel.[52] They are, however, an important part of the literary and intellectual context in which the modern novel emerged, and it is in this context that we must reconsider the development of that form as a means of organizing knowledge.[53] The encyclopedists of the period often described their projects in terms appropriated from traditional descriptions of the classical epics, and universal history aspired to tell the tale of civilizational origins in the most comprehensive sense. Fielding's *Joseph Andrews*, a "comic Epic-Poem in Prose" featuring an action "more extended and comprehensive; containing a much larger

Circle of Incidents, and introducing a greater variety of Characters" than could comedy or drama, does the same on behalf of narrative prose fiction, and though Richardson makes no direct claim to an epic inheritance, his novels too—especially when one accounts for their paratexts, supplements, and publishing histories—share several characteristics with contemporary reference texts like the universal dictionaries.[54]

Richardson and Fielding both sought to enlarge the capacity and utility of the novel in the mid-century knowledge economy by reconstituting it as a single-source compendium in which narrative principles organized multiple parts of literature and learning into "complete" systems of cultural knowledge. Their disagreement about how best to embed those systems within the fictional representations of reality upon which their sense depended made the paradox of completeness, though long operational in narrative discourse, the locus of a new debate within and around the form. In trying to do with prose fiction and for imaginative writing alternative versions of what epic poets no longer attempted, what earlier prose fiction narratives had not achieved, and what the "universal" knowledge projects around them sought to accomplish, they defined the limits of those ambitions when brought to prose fiction and further solidified the boundaries between the novel and other forms of literature.

The organizational capaciousness of the novel had specific implications with respect to amatory fiction and the "elevation" of the form in the mid-eighteenth century.[55] The proliferation of novels in the 1730s took place in the presence of a past that continued to weigh heavily on its definition.[56] The success of what became the "new" novel depended in part upon a disavowal of earlier efforts; prose fiction had to be freed from its ties to authors like Aphra Behn, Delariviere Manley, and Eliza Haywood in order to render it a viable medium for different kinds of knowledge projects.[57] That disavowal, though, ironically came in the form of discursive containment rather than exclusion. As William Warner observes, "the incorporation of the novel of amorous intrigue within the elevated novel of the 1740s is one of the means by which old pleasures are disowned and forgotten."[58] *Pamela*, with which Richardson first claimed to have made a definitive and innovative break with the past of prose fiction, may have repackaged the pleasures it meant to reform, but at the very least, the new novels succeeded in transforming the suddenly "old" fictions into limited parts of their supposedly more complete accounts of human nature and its mediating literatures.

Marshall McLuhan provides an apt model for the consideration of what was new about these "new novels": the old or preexisting literary forms became the contents of a new organizational technology.[59] The "masculine" program of annexation and subordination Warner describes further affirms a connection between the new novel and other encyclopedic texts: like the overwhelming majority of epic poems, the universal dictionaries and histories of the period had almost exclusively male authorship and ownership. In subordinating the function of the novel of amorous intrigue within their own fictions, Richardson and Fielding designated the completeness (or exhaustion) of a discrete, "feminine" genre and asserted the "masculine" cultural authority of encyclopedism. Their new novels came to occupy a higher place in the hierarchy of literary forms in part because of their elevated moral *and* utilitarian valences; the form could do more than their predecessors had done with it.

The amatory novel may have posed a specific challenge to new prose fiction projects, but it was just one of many kinds of instruction and entertainment subject to encyclopedic remediation. Richardson and Fielding offered their texts not only as "replacements for novels they characterize as degraded and immoral" but for a wide range of materials.[60] Fielding clearly states his intent to take over the principal subject of several major forms of writing in the introductory chapter to the first book of *Tom Jones*. The narrator announces that human nature, in all its "prodigious variety," will be the provision of the forthcoming feast; "for what else," he asks, "is the Subject of all the Romances, Novels, Plays and Poems, with which the Stalls abound?"[61] The list at once links Fielding's novel to a subset of popular literature and implicates the proliferation of print as a motive for his appropriating intervention.[62] The stalls "abound" with literature devoted to a single, sweeping subject; *Tom Jones*, the narrator implies, could answer all of their purposes entirely by itself. The many kinds and cuts of humanity served up by these and other kinds of writing are all on offer in his single Bill of Fare.

The promise of such universal coverage (and a lasting claim on readers' attention) is literally and figuratively central to both of Fielding's first novels. In the first chapter of the third book of *Joseph Andrews*—halfway through the narrative—the narrator looks beyond even epic to associate his novel with narrative historiography's most comprehensive form. He labels *Don Quixote*, the model for *Joseph Andrews*, as more deserving of the name of history than "even Mariana's [*Historiae de rebus Hispaniae*]: for whereas the latter is confined to a particular Period of Time, and to a particular Nation; the former is the History of the World in general, at least that Part which is polished by Laws, Arts, and Sciences; and of that from the time it was first polished to this day; nay and forwards, as long as it shall so remain."[63] These lines bear a striking similarity to the first sentences of *An Universal History*: history, it begins, is "the most instructive and useful, as well as entertaining, Part of Literature ... *especially, when it is not confined within the narrow Bounds of any particular Time or Place, but extends to the Transactions of all Times and Nations.*"[64] While this likeness may not necessarily have led readers to recall *An Universal History* specifically—the narrator does not name it—the reference to "History of the World in general" would nonetheless have established a connection. The allusion marks *Joseph Andrews* as not only a contribution to the discourse of historiography, but also a direct engagement with a form the most recent example of which might well have been on sale alongside it in Andrew Millar's bookshop in the Strand.[65]

A similar statement of universality occurs at the same place in *Tom Jones*. In the first chapter of its ninth book—again, at the start of the novel's second half—the narrator explains what the writing of such a history demands. Historians of his order must first of all possess genius, which he parses as the capacity of Invention and Judgment to detect the essences of and distinguish the differences among "all things within our Reach and Knowledge."[66] Secondly, a historian's experiential conversation with humanity must be "universal; that is, with all Ranks and Degrees of Men."[67] Discernment precedes systemization; one must have knowledge of "low" and "high life" first in themselves and then in relation to each other.[68] "And though it may be thought," the narrator continues, "that the Knowledge of either may sufficiently enable him to describe at least that in which he hath been conversant; yet he will even here fall greatly short of Perfection: for the Follies of either Rank do in reality illustrate each other."[69] The same might be said of the parts of any other subject, art, science, or history; an understanding of each part leads to a more complete knowledge of the whole. In its particular application of this method to "the true, practical system" of human nature, *Tom Jones*, like *Joseph Andrews*, reproduces a limited form of universal history that claims to perform the same function of corralling all the peoples of the world into a single, theoretically uniform work.[70]

Richardson's novels did not necessarily aspire to comprehend general history, but he was certainly no stranger to it. He was one of the original proprietors and an occasional printer of *An Universal History* from its beginning until his death in 1761.[71] John Osborn and Charles Rivington, who were also part-owners of the history, encouraged Richardson to write the book of familiar letters from which *Pamela* developed; he refers to them as fellow "proprietors" of the novel in the introduction to the second edition.[72] George Psalmanazar, who had corresponded with Richardson about *An Universal History* (and who had more experience with writing prose fiction than he cared to admit), sent him a chapter for a proposed sequel.[73] Millar, yet another shareholder, joined Osborn and Rivington's sons John and James as sellers of *Clarissa*, and all three stocked *Sir Charles Grandison* even as the syndicate put the final touches on the last octavo of the *Universal History*.[74]

The links between the *History* and Richardson's novels involve somewhat more than commercial interest and parallel composition. *An Universal History* and *Clarissa* are by far the largest examples of their respective kinds produced in the eighteenth century. Richardson, moreover, eventually claimed that the roughly one million words of *Clarissa* were just the second part of a tripartite project that with his other two novels comprised eighteen volumes duodecimo. Though he almost certainly conceived of this single extended endeavor well after the fact of *Pamela*, the first words of his preface to *Sir Charles Grandison* nevertheless announce that with its publication he has "completed the Plan, that was the Object of his Wishes, rather than of his Hopes to accomplish."[75] Richardson reaffirmed his sense of their combined purpose in a letter to the Reverend Mr. Hildesley written in 1755: the collection of moral sentiments drawn from all three histories and about to be published in a single pocket volume, he explains, will show "that there are not many of the material articles that may be of use for the conduct of life and manners unattended to in one or the other of them; so that all together they complete one plan, the best I was able to give."[76]

To those who could suspend their disbelief in the goodness of Pamela and survive their impatience with the story of Clarissa long enough to read *Sir Charles Grandison*, Richardson's fictions did indeed contain more than the stuff of any mere novel.[77] Aaron Hill effused that Richardson had contained, "like the new notion of philosophy in vegetation, a whole species in one single kernel."[78] Tobias Smollett (who would spend much of the late 1750s and early 1760s correcting and compiling some 3000 pages of *An Universal History*'s modern part) collectively described the three histories as "a most sublime system of ethics."[79] The Protestant clergyman and writer Philip Skelton too invoked the genre of system: he declared *Clarissa* a "System of Religious and Moral precepts and examples" and *Grandison* a "living system of manners." Others made similar pronouncements. One early reviewer identified *Grandison* as "ye most complete System of life & manners & ye best calculated for ye amendment of head & heart, that ever has been exhibited in Prophane writing." If it could not replace entire libraries, as had been said of epics and encyclopedias, then it at least might (in another reader's words) "supply the place of a Tutor, or boarding school."[80] Such compliments acknowledged Richardson's fictional histories as providers of the same kinds of knowledge generally associated with other forms of literature and instruction, from periodical essays like the *Spectator* to the numerous conduct books published for younger readers of both sexes.[81]

They also resituate the novels as participants in the broader Enlightenment genre of system. Authors and booksellers had for decades digested and organized various branches of natural philosophy, theology, history, art, poetry, and grammar into texts sold under the banner of systematicity. Conduct literature was no exception. In 1740, for example—the same year in which Richardson published *Pamela*—Wetenhall Wilkes printed his *A letter of genteel and moral advice to a young lady*. The book takes the form of a letter written to a "favourite niece" by an unnamed uncle.[82] The "System of Rules and Information" announced in the subtitle, though, clearly takes precedence over the conceit devised to convey it. A table of contents lists in simple terms the subjects to be addressed and precisely where they can be found in the body, the first page of which inverts the literary hierarchy of the title page. "A System of Rules" now takes pride of place in large letters beneath a printer's ornament while "Being a Letter of Advice..." follows in smaller print. The "letter" then begins with a brief confession of the uncle's past sins before proceeding to an extended, unbroken, and amply footnoted explication of the virtues and habits supposedly appropriate to a girl of sixteen. Signs of the "familiar Method" largely recede; the system persists in its self-aggrandizing claim to universal coverage (it will "qualify the Fair Sex to be useful and happy in every State") and in its ability to function as a linear progression of advice as well as a delineated work useful for occasional reference.

Richardson's works much more closely resembled novels than they did Wilkes's supposedly methodized system. Though Richardson eschewed the term "novel" (and only counted *Pamela* a history following the success of *Clarissa*), his readers generally referred to all three of his narratives as novels, and subsequent imitations solidified their status as such after the fact. The references to system in the comments above, however, suggest that Johnson's definition of system as the "complexure of many things acting together" or reduction "of many things to regular dependence or co-operation" obtains in Richardson's novels at levels distinct from (while not necessarily independent of) narrative cohesion.[83] Smollett's words in particular, which describe all three novels as a single contribution to moral philosophy despite their unconnected plots and characters, affirm Richardson's insistence in the advertisement to the second edition of *Clarissa* that "the story is to be principally looked upon as a *Vehicle* to convey the proposed INSTRUCTION."[84] The systematicity detected by his critics and the supposedly single plan of his design primarily refer not to the unity of any individual narrative action, but rather to the schematized knowledge of morals, manners, religion, and ethics that those actions helped to organize.

Narrative serves as another method by which an author or editor attempts to render a system of knowledge appreciably coherent and therefore useful to the reader. When the story creates the opportunity, for example, Grandison neither simply demonstrates the proper mode of conduct in dueling nor merely justifies his actions with respect to contemporary mores. Instead, he delivers a history lesson on the subject that extends from the Roman legend of the Horatii and Curiatii to the challenge offered by the Elector Palatine to Turenne during the Dutch War of 1672. Similarly, when melancholy seizes Clementina, the young Italian who fails to win Grandison in marriage, she experiences the exact sequence of stages (fits and fainting to hallucination and amnesia to the appearance of symptoms consistent with consumption) described by George Cheyne in *The English malady* (1733). The course Grandison recommends—diet and exercise, medicine, diversion, and marriage (to someone else, naturally)—closely follows the prescription set out by Robert James in *A medicinal dictionary* (1743). Richardson had previously printed both texts.[85]

This is not to suggest that narrative unity did not matter to either author. Despite their different approaches to knowledge organization, both Richardson and Fielding depended upon the precision of their narrative systems to establish and clarify the meaning or "value" of the other kinds of knowledge imparted by their novels. Narrative unity, though a conventional aspiration, had additional ramifications in the context of an Enlightenment worldview. Fielding and Richardson tried to construct their novels so that they would work consistently and uniformly—just as a system should, and just as the actual universe was believed to do. Newton's theorization of universal gravity and the laws of motion in *Principia Mathematica* (1687) had by the early part of the century resolved the solar "system" into so much well-ordered clockwork; his improvements on the works of Copernicus and Kepler finally rendered regular and predictable the motions of celestial bodies.[86] Despite resistance from those who viewed the unexplained and invisible force of gravity as a retrogressive appeal to the occult, the idea of a machine-like cosmos in which each part occupied a place within a complete (and completely knowable) whole soon held great sway in other areas of scientific inquiry.[87]

The human body and mind did not escape the pull of Newton's theory. As a result of the analogy made by philosophers between "the natural and the human orders"—an analogy sanctioned by Newton's own tacit anthropomorphizing of the universe—"man became a model of the cosmic clockwork."[88] By the 1740s, the clockwork analogy behind a mechanistic and systematic view of human existence had also become a trope of probabilistic representations of "real" life. As Ian Donaldson observes in his examination of "the clockwork novel," Samuel Johnson expressed his preference for Richardson's fictions over those of Fielding in just such terms: "the difference was 'as between a man who knew how a watch was made, and a man who could tell the hour by looking on the dial-plate.'"[89] Fielding uses similar language to describe the operation of the universe and the actions of his characters in *Tom Jones*. "The world may indeed be considered as a vast machine," the narrator explains, "in which the great wheels are originally set in motion by those which are very minute, and almost imperceptible to any but the strongest eyes."[90] Donaldson interprets this as Fielding's warning to the reader "to attend to the importance of such apparently trifling incidents as Sophia's concern over the scorching of her muff. Sophia ... like the world itself, is 'set in motion' by such minute 'wheels' as these."[91]

The internal mechanisms of Fielding and Richardson's novels may differ, but both authors encode the moral laws of their novels within the "natural" laws that supposedly governed the real world. The novels have the appearance of natural truth and empirical credibility despite having come from artificial sources because of their probabilistic verisimilitude and the separation of a necessarily subjective authorial voice from the events of their narratives. *Clarissa* and *Tom Jones*, John Bender notes, offer "virtually evidentiary accounts of the physical and mental circumstances that actuate their characters and motivate the causal sequences of their plots, but they also attempt to frame the subjectivity of their characters within editorial objectivity ... or narratorial objectivity."[92] Richardson and Fielding, in other words, attempt to recreate the world in miniature and in a laboratory setting; their authors set the specific conditions of their experiments, but the universal laws of human nature drive the action. Ideally, they would seem simply to have put all the pieces in place and set the novels in motion.

The completeness of the clockwork novel, though, depends on duplicating an appreciably cohesive, mechanistic systematicity representative of a modern understanding of the universe and human nature. In order for those novels and the higher order knowledge conveyed by them to qualify as truth, every piece of "objectively" presented evidence from each account had to bear a discernible and meaningful relation to every other piece. These novels therefore had in common with universal dictionaries and histories the goals of strategically systematizing multiple parts of knowledge into a coherent whole. "In the Universal Mapp," Jacques Bossuet writes in *A discourse on the history of the whole world*, "you learn how to situate those parts of the World in the whole: You see what Paris, or the Isle of France is in the Kingdom, what the Kingdom is in Europe, and what Europe is in the Universe ... to understand the whole clearly, you must know what relation every History can have to others, which is done by such a way as this is, in short, where at one glance of your Eye, as it were, you may see all the order of time."[93] Universal historians provided chronological charts and maps as aids to memory and spatial organization, and (as in the case of *An Universal History*) experimented with ways of dividing national histories in order artificially to separate into discrete elements a body of knowledge they understood to be necessarily interconnected.

Universal dictionaries, though they did not (yet) generally traffic in historiography, also pursued a systematic completeness with respect to the circle of arts and sciences.[94] Chambers explains:

> It seems more natural to consider knowledge in its proper parts ... than to consider the whole Assemblage of it in its utmost Composition: which is a thing merely artificial and imaginary. And yet the latter Way must be allowed to have many and real Advantages over the former; which in truth is only of use and significance as it partakes thereof: For this Reason, that all writing is in its own Nature artificial; and that the Imagination is really the Faculty it immediately applies to. Hence it should follow, that the most advantageous way, is to make use of both Methods: To consider every Point both as a Part; to help the Imagination to the Whole: and as a Whole, to help it to every Part.—Which is the View of the present Work.[95]

Chambers guides the reading of his book in accordance with this objective: cross-references and annotations ideally lead the reader to and from the various entries and allow that reader conceptually to reconstitute any given subsystem. Those subsystems in turn comprise a cognitively comprehensible total system and order of "knowledge."

In both cases, however, the challenge of rendering the knowledge they contained genuinely cohesive remained difficult if not impossible entirely to overcome. The cross-references of the encyclopedias—first those of Chambers, then those of the *Encyclopédie*—though capable of generating useful and productive connections among the parts of knowledge, also generated frustration and resistance. Advances in learning likewise problematized coherence as the need for periodic supplements disrupted the systematicity of individual editions. The complexity of and gaps in the documentary record, as I have already shown, unavoidably strained the unity of *An Universal History* from its inception, and the disagreements of its multiple contributors broke the single thread of the narrative almost as soon as they began to unwind it. These books could not uniformly and clearly represent the knowledge of the world they comprehended in such a way that reflected their understanding of how the world implicitly operated.

Narrative fiction offered the possibility of solving some of these problems. Fielding's novels (to say nothing of *Don Quixote*) do not actually subsume the entirety of world history in the style of Hearne, Howell, Sale, or Psalmanazar any more than Homer's epics comprehended the full circle of arts and sciences as represented by the encyclopedias of Chambers, Rees, Diderot, and D'Alembert. Just as Pope reduced the scope of his epic to mock only the whole body of dunces, so does Fielding restrict the province of *Joseph Andrews* to the ridiculous. Likewise, when the narrator of *Tom Jones* praises Homer and Milton as "Masters of all the Learning of their Times," he does so within the context of a defense of his and their capacities as historians and observers of human nature.[96] His references to physic, law, farming, planting, and gardening in the same passage treat them simply as additional branches of knowledge that require empirical experience to understand.

Instead of an incomprehensibly massive collection of information with which any author (to say nothing of any reader) would struggle to negotiate, Fielding's novels offer specialized versions of historical writing that rely more fully on probabilistic verisimilitude and synecdochical inclusivity in order to achieve the comprehensible completeness and "higher truths" with which more strictly factual accounts of human events were typically incompatible.[97] Fielding's emphasis on invention in *Tom Jones*, John Tinkler argues, invokes and follows a humanist rather than an antiquarian conception of historiography— a conception that granted rhetoricians license to distort or augment the historical record in pursuit of more meaningful arguments. To the humanists, "'not factual completeness or accuracy, but moral guidance was expected from a true historian.'"[98] Humanist historiography was still pinioned to actual people and events, but its writers had license to enhance their stories with what later readers might identify as (illuminating) fictions.[99] The Fieldian novel evinces an even greater separation from that kind of factual completeness in pursuit of a different order of complete knowledge.

Freed from any strict correlation with literal historical truth, *Joseph Andrews* can provide what the narrator describes as a kind of general world history or universal system of human nature precisely because it does not have to accommodate an all but unmanageable body of knowledge or conform to a set of practices that would either undermine or overwhelm it. As fictional histories, Fielding's novels neither have to defend a disputable universal chronology nor include, acknowledge, reconcile, or bridge the many gaps and disagreements across the historical records upon which they might otherwise rely.[100] These exercises made *An Universal History* more complete, according to its authors, but they also threatened its coherence, swelled its length, and jeopardized any claims it could make to absolute truth. The narrator of *Tom Jones* may have had "no publick Notoriety, no concurrent Testimony, no Records to support and corroborate" the story, but then again the story could not be contradicted on the basis of such evidence, and he did not have to justify his use or interpretation of it.[101]

Probabilistic verisimilitude, in short, allowed Fielding to create historical truth without historical documentation.[102] In the context of historiography in general and of universal history in particular, which had already abundantly demonstrated the extent to which the written records of history were cumbersome, subject to contradictory interpretations, and in any case always already incomplete, fiction emerges in Fielding's first novels as an alternative mode of knowledge management—a means of creating and providing in a much smaller compass what Fielding deemed the knowledge of human nature lost or corrupted by the "Topographers and Chorographers" of the world.[103] By writing of manners rather than men, or of a species rather than individuals, Fielding escapes the more unwieldy elements of modern historiography and can present a more cohesive, if highly satirical, picture of the whole. The figure of the Lawyer in the stagecoach, immediately recognizable but unattached to any single living person, represents multitudes; his name is legion. Alive "these 4000 Years ... he hath not indeed confined himself to one Profession, one Religion, or one Country."[104] The comparison of *Don Quixote* (and by extension, *Joseph Andrews*) to a history of the world in general suggests that, according to the narrator, Fielding's "little volumes" could comprehend at least as much if not more of the world—provided one did not fixate upon the niceties of literal historical reality.[105]

The introductory chapter of Book II, however, hints that the book might still have taken on too much. The sole subject of Fielding's inquiry in *Joseph Andrews*—the Ridiculous—may have emerged from the single spring of affectation, but that spring in turn branched into such "infinite streams" that scarcely a person did not deserve a place in his account.[106] As *Joseph Andrews* seeks to capture some sense of that infinitude, the narrator posits the division of the text into chapters and books as a guard against fatigue and a boon to the book's utility. "Many notable Uses," he claims, arise to the reader from this method. The spaces between chapters, first of all, "may be looked upon as an Inn or Resting-Place" suitable for taking refreshment, and the blank pages between books are in turn "to be regarded as those Stages, where, in long Journeys, the Traveller stays some time to repose himself, and consider of what he hath seen in the Parts he hath already past through." Fielding's language again bears a striking resemblance to that of a contemporaneously popular universal history. Periods memorable for great events and actions, Bossuet explains in his *Discourse*, are called *Epocha* "from a Greek word that signifies to pause upon, because we stay our selves there to consider, as at a place of rest, whatsoever hath happened both before and since, and by that means to avoid the Anachronisms, that is to say, that sort of Error which makes the confusion of time."[107] Division in both cases aids the understanding of a complex whole.

The irony characteristic of Fielding's narrative interludes, it must be acknowledged, does threaten to render the defense of divisions endlessly ambiguous. Contextual references to the division of Homer and Virgil's poems into multiple books and an aside on the practice of publishing dictionaries by numbers worry the novel's concept of completeness as a matter of deliberate composition and comprehensible unity. The narrator's claim that "a chapter or two ... may be often pass'd over without any injury to the whole" creates an obvious contradiction: if chapters can be safely skipped, then the text must be whole without those chapters; however, those chapters are by definition parts of the whole. The passage, then, suggests two simultaneously operating modes of completeness in the novel: in one, the integrity of the "whole" inheres in the text itself, independent of and perhaps beyond the reader's comprehension. In the other, the wholeness of the text is the product of a process of selective reading and cognitive reconstruction (dubiously) encouraged by the chapter summaries and narrative pauses that divide the whole into manageable parts.[108] Either option may be said to more accurately reflect the truth about the individual's actual relationship to the system of the world.

In some respects, Richardson's novels addressed similar issues by means directly opposite to those subsequently adopted by Fielding. Fiction allowed Richardson to provide a version of what real history rarely if ever did: a comprehensive record of events and experiences written in extraordinary detail and largely by a single hand. His histories were not wholly individual accomplishments, for Richardson sought criticism and contributions from numerous friends and acquaintances. One of these, though, initially declined. Charged with reviewing letters XI and XII of *Clarissa*, Aaron Hill returned them unchanged, and following his assurance that Richardson could not make the novel "too tall, though [he] should stretch her out to as much vastness as the same of Virgil," he explains his reasoning:

If there is any place that can be shortened, without maiming this delightful composition, you, who have created it, and have its whole proportion and connexion in your eye at once, are better justified in doing it, than it is possible for any other man to be, who, seeing it in parts, divided, and at distant times, would use, methinks, a boldness too unpardonable in advising to retrench the smallest piece of any of its pages, till he has revised and re-considered it in its conclusive and accomplished fullness.[109]

Single authorship, Hill indicates, has its advantages; he presumes that Richardson has a unified vision and can hold in his mind's eye the complete novel in the most complete sense. The sole author sees at once the whole proportion and connection of his work—the system of its world. In retrospect, the reasoning behind Hill's reluctance seems to presage Richardson's discontent with the abridgment he invited Hill to attempt in 1746.[110]

Though Richardson occasionally insisted that he was far too irregular a writer to proceed according to any plan at all, he nevertheless wrote in the second edition of *Clarissa* that the table of contents appended to it would "shew the Connexion of the whole."[111] That assertion, regardless of its accuracy, demonstrates Richardson's insistence that the text achieved the total connectivity described by Hill despite the narrative conceit that its contents came from multiple authors whose various perspectives and motivations generated the kinds of disagreements and distortions one would expect from any actual history. Unlike an actual history, however, the novel by and in its conclusion could systematically resolve those disagreements in accordance with the author's supposedly unifying moral purpose without necessarily jeopardizing its claim to historical veracity.

The need to illustrate the connection of the whole through an appended paratext, though, suggests the difficulty audiences had in perceiving that connectivity with only the narrative to reveal it. If to recreate a true system of life or the human experience requires the reconciliation of all its parts, then fiction again allowed for what reality did not: the creation of a full and "to the moment" account of that experience.[112] Richardson presented each collection of letters as a history the higher truths and moral guidance of which depended upon their exhaustive documentation; the psychological realism of his characters— particularly that of his heroines—and the value of the texts as instruction followed in part from the extent and nature of the records they kept. Hill acknowledges that Richardson does "crowd" his work with observations and reflections, but then asks "is not that the very life, and soul, and fire, that makes the use and beauty of it impressive and so striking?"[113] "Use" in this case might equally refer to the reading of the text or to the usefulness of the knowledge embedded within it when applied in the real world. In either case, the letter hints at the paradox of completeness and its relationship to utility in the context of Richardson's epistolary style. "Use and beauty" followed from crowding, but crowding, as several readers remarked, threatened use.

Anna Laetitia Barbauld, writing just after the turn of the century, offered a more direct assessment of the epistolary form's strengths and weaknesses in her introduction to Richardson's collected correspondence. "It is incompatible with a rapid stile," she notes, "but it gives room for the graceful introduction of any remark and sentiment, or any kind, almost, of digressive matter. But, on the other hand, it is highly fictitious; it is the most natural and least probable way of telling a story. That letters should be written at all times, and upon every occasion in life, that those letters should be preserved, and altogether form a connected story, it requires much art to render specious."[114] Other authors of prose fiction frequently introduced subplots or remarked upon events only to dismiss the details as being of little interest or potentially harmful to the integrity of their central narratives. The claim to historicity with which Aphra Behn opens *Oroonoko*, though problematic in the context of the narrative that follows, entails an assurance that "a thousand little accidents of his life" have been omitted despite the hero having provided "the whole transactions of his youth."[115] Defoe's *Roxana* reduces two years' worth of adventures on her "Grand Tour"—the full relation of which "would almost fill up a Volume of itself"—to just a few pages; she declines to write more, she claims, because "it would be too full of Variety."[116] *Moll Flanders* similarly deems it "enough to tell" of her husband's history that "in about two years and a quarter he broke" and was subsequently arrested.[117] Such references to events beyond the immediate concerns of the story in these cases serve as markers of verisimilitude; characters and narrators refer to larger worlds in which much of what occurs cannot or need not be connected to the matters at hand.

Barbauld's description of the epistolary style sets its encyclopedic capacity at odds with cohesion as well as reality. Though the nature of Richardson's first two plots in some sense enables him to *limit* their scope—Clarissa, for instance, spends a substantial part of her time confined to this room or that with little to do apart from write—the literally incredible prolixity of all three novels reveals them as improbable fictions while simultaneously emphasizing their function as storehouses of knowledge separate (but not easily separated) from story. Richardson acknowledged as much himself in both *Clarissa* and *Sir Charles Grandison*. In the former, he recalls the advice of an unnamed gentleman who recommended that he "give a narrative turn to the letters" and strike out all those entries not of immediate relevance to the heroine. Richardson finally determined, however, to follow the course authorized by other unnamed gentlemen who "insisted that the story could not be reduced to a dramatic unity ... without divesting it of its warmth and a great part of its efficacy."[118] When faced with the paradox of completeness, Richardson too had to prioritize. The more he attempted to include in his novels, the less able they became to reflect the presumed systematicity of the world and the more they taxed the patience as well as the credulity of their readers.

He ultimately chose comprehensiveness, and the anti-*Pamelists* quickly seized upon the improbability of Pamela's thorough recordkeeping. Fielding's *Shamela* openly mocks Pamela's "to the moment" composition and critiques the epistolary experiment in general by filling in the gaps created by her one-sided presentation. Fielding provides not an alternative but a supplemental history that disrupts the ideological and meaning-making system of the original by discovering "new" information about the world it creates but for which it did not account and could not accommodate. *Joseph Andrews*, though tangential to the events of *Pamela*, represents a still greater expansion and alteration of its universe with events and characters connected to but never mentioned by its heroine. Both of Fielding's literary responses imply that *Pamela* was both too complete and not complete enough to be true to life.

The even more comprehensive completeness of *Clarissa* theoretically closes the discursive circle that *Pamela* left open. Readers could locate and verify the truth of the new novel by constelling all the points contained within its field; each of the characters' letters could (again, in theory) be connected to or cross-referenced against the others without direct authorial imposition. Many, however, found in the parallel correspondences another conglomeration the sheer size of which threatened to obscure what it meant to reveal. As Leah Price observes, "the impossibility of fitting all eight volumes of *Clarissa* or seven of *Grandison* into the human mind at once turns readers into editors."[119] Readers compelled by story or sentiment could skip or skim in search of what they most desired, and their work became even easier with texts like *A collection of the moral and instructive sentiments, Maxims, Cautions, and Reflections, Contained in the Histories of Pamela, Clarissa, and Sir Charles Grandison* (1755) and *The paths of virtue delineated: or the history in miniature of the celebrated Pamela, Clarissa Harlowe, and Sir Charles Grandison* (1756). These alphabetized collections and narrative abridgments at least superficially seemed to divide the contents of the epistolary behemoths back into two familiar preexisting forms: the reference work that "stretched encyclopedically from the advantages of Absence to the dangers of Zeal" and the novel that unified the story "by stripping discontinuous digressions away from linear plot."[120] Each treatment functioned as a more efficient provider of the different kinds of knowledge and experiences held sometimes in mixture and sometimes in solution by the original.

Richardson did not necessarily intend such texts to serve as total substitutes for reading his novels. In *Sir Charles Grandison*—his final encyclo-novelistic experiment—he devised dual indices that divided "similes and allusions" from "historical and characteristical" references in order to enable multiple ways of reading. Writing to Thomas Edwards of the 1755 *Collection*, he insisted that the anthology of excerpts would counter the inclinations of those who read only for story by providing "at one View ye Pith & Marrow of what they had been reading ... in order to revive in their Minds ye *Occasions* on which ye Things were supposed to be said & done, and ye better to assist them in ye Application of ye Moral."[121] Though the shift suggests that Richardson located greater immediate utility in an encyclopedic rendition, Price points out that the emphasis on memory indicates a sense "that the Collection set out not to divorce generalizable 'sentiments' from particular 'story,' but to anchor one to the other."[122] In this respect, the collection bears approximately the same relation to the novel as chronological tables do to the body of universal history and genealogical trees do to the dictionary of arts and sciences: all serve to present "at one view" a skeletal version of a body of knowledge too large or complex to be understood at once in its entirety.

Neither Richardson nor Fielding achieved the combination of comprehensive and cohesive completeness upon which a truly complete understanding of all things supposedly depended. The idea that one could—an idea perhaps most directly debunked by Barbauld's critique of Richardson's epistolary style and the "violence" Fielding knowingly did to probability in order to conclude the many plots and subplots introduced to accommodate the prodigious variety of Human Nature—became part of the "manifest fictionality" towards which the genre increasingly turned at mid-century.[123] The novels that followed borrowed heavily from both, but the same features responsible for some of the success of their predecessors were subsequently implicated as potential threats to the durability of the genre. As Siskin argues, "Fielding and Richardson largely function as dead ends ... their 'programs' for the novel had, in important ways, to be written off before the novel as we know it rose up."[124] Their novels produced countless imitations, but their experiments with encyclopedic knowledge were seldom precisely duplicated.

Martin's Magazine: A Periodical Encyclopedia

Other and now far less well-known efforts to produce encyclopedic, universal, or in other ways "complete" bodies of knowledge were neither duplicated nor even widely imitated. Long-term projects like Benjamin Martin's *The general magazine of arts and sciences* and short-lived ventures such as Dennis de Coetlogon's *An universal history of arts and sciences* either did not set new standards of functionality or failed to find audiences large enough to sustain them as individual properties. The titles of both contain fairly commonplace markers of the mid-eighteenth century: relatively few "universal histories" before 1745 offered anything other than histories of the church or the more general overviews of human events associated with Hearne, Howell, Bossuet, and Sale, and by the time the first issue of Martin's magazine appeared a decade later, Edward Cave's *The Gentleman's Magazine* and its imitators had already defined the basic conventions associated with the term for a generation.[125] While both Martin and de Coetlogon proclaimed the novelty of their experiments, then, they did not completely dissociate them from already established categories of literature. They instead attempted to expand the horizons of the increasingly familiar and abundant universal dictionaries to other modes and models of knowledge distribution. In so doing, they contributed to the further sharpening of formal boundaries and the ongoing differentiation of literary kinds.

Cave may have been the first to popularize the term "magazine" in its modern sense, but many of the periodical publications before, during, and after his time similarly offered a wide range of content in the name of providing and preserving the kinds of knowledge their editors deemed worthy. The suggestion of universal coverage became so widespread that the *OED* specifically notes the frequency with which the word formerly appeared in magazine titles. The entry offers *The fashionable magazine* of 1786—"being a compleat universal repository of taste, elegance, and novelty, for both sexes"—as one of many possible examples.[126] Content could vary wildly in scope, and none that traded in nominal universality could be said to have delivered as much as it promised. They generally defined the "universal" as a matter of widespread appeal rather than material inclusivity or as the inclusion of only that which their editors and contributors deemed worthy of attention given particular tastes, politics, print schedules, or production costs. Nevertheless, many periodicals claimed for themselves a version of the same usefulness often promised by many reference works and once conventionally ascribed to the "encyclopedic" epics of antiquity: any one of these texts, the story went, could render a great many others unnecessary. Readers without enough time or money to traverse the entire breadth of the literary world or even the bounds of their own particular interests merely had to select the best works available and let the rest fall into oblivion.

Abstract serials, often aided by absent or unenforced copyright laws that permitted them to abridge or heavily excerpt the works of others (particularly those from abroad) with impunity, could in some circumstances save their purchasers the cost and bother of reading the whole of even those books that they identified as being worthy of notice in the first place. Other journals that combined a variety of features similarly insisted that all the demands of instruction and entertainment could be met within their pages. Even newspaper editors occasionally invoked the trope of overabundance: an advertisement announcing the first issue of *The Evening advertiser and Universal correspondent* (1754), for example, wondered "that when One Paper was published, any more should have been thought necessary; for ONE PAPER, properly conducted, is sufficient for the Circulation of Intelligence throughout the Kingdom."[127] The authors, editors, printers, and sellers of these periodicals represented them as being capable of serving the same function as the other "best" books of their day—albeit at different levels of literary or cultural discourse and with respect to different orders of time.

Amongst the first to achieve relatively widespread popularity in England was John Dunton's *Athenian Mercury*. First published in 1690, the journal departed from the more rarefied intellectual positions of its predecessors by soliciting and answering questions about any topic its readers—both men and women—cared to submit, from points of religious doctrine to medical inquiries to matters of natural philosophy. Urmi Bhowmik has argued that in "treating cases of conscience and questions about nature as if they were equally susceptible to the same processes of collective inquiry and consensual interpretation ... the *Mercury* asserted the unity of social, moral, and natural realms."[128] This assertion, Bhowmik suggests, situates the *Mercury* within what Michael McKeon has called a "synthesizing countermovement" of the Enlightenment that "sought to establish all the different branches of knowledge on a common foundation."[129] The unity asserted, however, was in the *Mercury* more philosophical than functional, for despite "the encyclopedic aspects of the journal" highlighted by its bound, alphabetically indexed collections and the eventual cessation of weekly numbers in favor of single, reference work-like volumes, the knowledge comprehended by the journal necessarily remained miscellaneous.[130]

Dunton's *Mercury* may have addressed a wide variety of subjects, then, but whatever "encyclopedic" completeness the journal achieved followed from its editors' exercise and advancement of an abstract intellectual or ideological position rather than any methodological system of knowledge organization. The *Mercury*, in other words, did not seek directly to demonstrate the cohesion of what it contained in any ways remotely similar to those devised by the major universal dictionaries of the following decades—even though both presumed a common foundation and the ultimate unity of all knowledge. A similar emphasis on a sense of universality exclusive of any necessary or direct appeal to connective completeness continued to define the bulk of periodical literatures as they grew in number over the next half-century.

Complete coverage in the magazines and journals also necessarily meant somewhat less than it did in works of greater physical size and endurance. Dunton claimed in his *The compleat library* (1692)—in essence an abstract serial and continuation of *The young-students-library* (1691)—that "nothing shall pass in Europe worthy of Consideration of the Learned World that shall not be within this journal... So at length our undertaking may fully answer the Title, and be a Compleat Library."[131] The "Learned World" at the end of the seventeenth century, as Robert Mayo points out, did not comprehend fiction or imaginative writing, and so, like the *Philosophical collections* and the *Weekly memorials for the ingenious* before it, Dunton's *The compleat library* disregarded them in favor of "new books of an historical, antiquarian, or scientific character."[132]

Even within that narrowed field, however, Dunton's initial plan soon foundered. He saw the potential of the journal as a venue in which to advertise more of his own wares and at the same time determined to increase circulation by cutting the length, and therefore the price, of each issue. In December of 1692, only months into its run, he announced that he lacked the space to accommodate all of the worthy books from abroad. The following February, he practically gave up continental literature altogether. The *Library* from then on, he wrote, would be "filled up only with Select Books, and those mostly of writers of our owne Little World, Great Brittain, without troubling [readers] with any Extracts of forein Books but what shall very well deserve it."[133] The "compleat library" that month comprehended only six titles.

The promise of Dunton's *The post-angel, or Universal entertainment* (1701) to "omit nothing" that would help it live up to its name clearly echoes that of his earlier *Library*, but he takes a far bolder position with respect to breadth of coverage.[134] "Always ambitious to provide a full record of everything," J. Paul Hunter observes, Dunton intended *The post-angel* to include not only the expected collection of *Mercury*-like questions-and-answers, poems, news, and essays, but also descriptions of the lives "of everyone who had died during the past month."[135] These biographies, often drawn from or supplemented with private documents, were part of his plan to create what he called "*a Compleat History of modern Lives.*"[136] Such a history would naturally have to include modern literature, and Dunton accordingly envisioned a review section that would greatly expand upon those of competing and prior journals. The fifth part of *The post-angel*, he writes, would "give an Account of the Books lately publish'd, and now going to the Press; and here I shan't be so partial (as some have been) to insert some, and omit others, but shall give an exact Account of all the Books that are publish'd Monthly." Dunton's desire to make the "universal" truly comprehensive represented a departure from the already established conventions of literary and learned journals. As his own publications had previously revealed, however, success in this regard was at the very least highly improbable. Even in 1701, modern life, to say nothing of literature, comprehended far too much.

A half-century later, such plans were plainly impracticable. The paradoxically selective universality at work in any materially and temporally-bound venture, whether financially self-serving or not, becomes more acute as the universe it purports to comprehend expands. The generality of periodicals published after the *The post-angel* unsurprisingly did not share its stated ambitions. *The Literary magazine: or the History of the works of the learned* (1737–43), for example—for which Ephraim

Chambers was an erstwhile editor—reviewed only the "most valuable Books publish'd in Great Britain and Foreign Parts." "Most valuable" also appeared on the title page of *The Present state of the republick of letters* (1728–36). *The museum: or, the Literary and historical register* (1746–47) hoped to leave out nothing notable. Similar gestures could be found in a host of "universal" properties, including *The Weekly amusement: or, The Universal magazine* (1735), *The Universal magazine of knowledge and pleasure* (1747–1803), *The magazine of magazines* (1751), *The Grand magazine of magazines* (1750), *The Universal museum* (1762–70), and *The Complete magazine of knowledge and pleasure, containing the greatest variety of original pieces on the most curious and useful subjects in every branch of polite literature trade and commerce; and various parts of science and philosophy ... formed on the most extensive plan of public utility* (1764).[137]

One of the clearest mid-century statements on behalf of a circumscribed universality, however, comes from William Fadden, editor of *The Literary magazine: or, Universal review* (1756–58). "It is not to be expected," he writes in the magazine's inaugural issue, "that we can insert extensive extracts or critical Examinations of all the writings which this age of writers may offer to our notice. A few only will deserve the distinction of criticism, and a few only will obtain it."[138] The statement speaks simultaneously to concerns of quantity and quality and to the role of the reviewer as a barrier between the reader and the flood. In "an age of writers," the kind of complete or universal coverage imagined by the *Post-Angel* is simply unfeasible; Fadden flatly denies such completeness a place within the horizon of expectations of a self-described universal review. In fact, he suggests a sense of the universal that signifies even less than the greatest possible number of the most worthy items. Fadden narrows the definition of the universal to "only a few," and the cleft sentence elides the agency of critical judgment in favor of treating limited coverage as an ontological absolute of the format.

Fadden addresses the other characteristic of completeness in similarly absolute terms. "Our design is to give the history political and literary of every month, and our Pamphlets *must consist*, like other Collections, of many Articles unconnected and independent of each other."[139] He makes the magazine's lack of internal cohesion a matter of convention; he cites other collections as precedent and insists that the operation of the magazine as such necessarily precludes total systematicity. It "*must*" consist of unrelated articles. Unlike other kinds of literature that explicitly located value in the unity of the whole, and in which that unity depended on the demonstrable, presumed, or intended interconnectedness of numerous parts, the literary magazine according to Fadden by definition offered variety without the burden of pursuing any conceptual unity beyond the accidental links of topical similarity or temporal coincidence. The distinction generally held true across the magazines of the period.

Benjamin Martin's *The general magazine of arts and sciences* represents a notable exception. It appeared in monthly installments from 1755 to 1765, at roughly the same time that Fadden affirmed the separation of the "universal" magazine from total coverage and connectivity. As a periodical encyclopedia, *Martin's Magazine*, as it was popularly known, attempted to combine the features and functions of those forms into something "intirely new." As Martin explains in his account of the plan and design, "a Body of *Arts and Sciences* has never yet been attempted in any monthly periodical Publication, under the Title of a MAGAZINE."[140] While the decade he spent in that effort suggests a successful outcome— ten years is a respectable lifetime for a magazine, though somewhat less so for an encyclopedia—Martin's experiment was not widely imitated, and in its last months the magazine's new proprietors abandoned most of the features that made it unique.[141] The project as envisioned by Martin was and remains something of an anomaly, and as an anomaly it indicates the boundaries of the forms it tried to unite.

Martin had a long history with encyclopedic projects. A scientific instrument-maker and itinerant lecturer, he had by 1740 already composed numerous textbooks, systems, and compendia of knowledge. In the space of five years, he published *A new and compleat and universal system or body of decimal arithmetick* (1735), *The young trigonometer's compleat guide* (1736), *Pangeometria; or the elements of all geometry* (1739), and *Logarithmologia, or the whole doctrine of logarithms* (1739/40). He embraced the same terms of art deployed by a myriad other reference works and emphasized in familiar language the importance of method and organization to forming a more perfect understanding. In his *Bibliotheca technologica: or, a philological library of literary arts and sciences* (1737), for instance, Martin insisted that all of the subjects within it "do, in regard of Quality, Connection, Dependence, &c. make a compendious System of Philological Literature."[142] The whole of his *Logarithmologia* too comprised a "compleat system," and he justified his *Philosophia Britannica* (1747) with the conventional complaint that none of the extant "Commentaries, Courses, Essays, Elements, Systems, &c ... could be justly esteem'd a TRUE SYSTEM, or COMPLEAT BODY" of the Newtonian philosophy, astronomy, and geography.[143]

Most of these books were intended primarily for inexpert rather than scholarly audiences, and their promises of completeness naturally invite skepticism. As introductions to a wide range of subjects, though, they did encourage a popular appreciation of the rudiments of science and advanced Martin's reputation as a self-taught author and polymath.[144] "His aim," as one early reviewer put it, "is an universal acquaintance with nature, as far as it falls within the compass of human understanding."[145] *Martin's Magazine* aimed to expand that acquaintanceship to an even broader audience over time and by degrees. "A whole Body of Arts and Sciences poured out on the Public at once," Martin explains, "might not perhaps be quite so pleasing and acceptable, as when retained out in monthly Portions; for now a Person cannot think one Half-sheet upon a Science in a Month too much, as he will have Time enough to read and digest that before another come to hand."[146] Rather than overwhelm them with a "simultaneous view of the whole" that would confuse rather than instruct, Martin planned to bring readers along gradually and at the affordable price of sixpence a month. A devoted subscriber, he wrote, would "be allowed to make a great Proficiency, if he can make himself Master of the useful Arts and Sciences in the Compass of Ten Years."[147]

The plan to produce a whole body of arts and sciences in periodical form distinguished Martin's project from contemporary encyclopedias as well as the majority of magazines purely on the basis of temporality. While the former might take just as many or even more years to proceed from A to Z—publication of the *Encyclopédie* had by this point already been underway for four years, with another four to go before its official suspension—such schedules were typically a function of practical necessity rather than pedagogical design. Magazines, in contrast, did not usually envision totalizing outcomes that could only unfold over great lengths of time. Martin had to operate in accordance with both short-term and long-term goals: his magazine needed to generate enough interest and instruction synchronically in order to enable a diachronic accumulation of still fully systematized knowledge.

This dual temporality produced an unconventional organization and eclectic mixture of materials. Martin initially divided each issue into five parts: (1) "A General Survey of the Worlds of Nature and Art"; (2) "An Entire System of the Natural History of the World"; (3) "A Compleat Body of Arts and Sciences which are not Mathematical"; (4) "A Continued Series of Mathematical and Mechanical Institutes or Principles of Geometrical Science"; and (5) "Miscellaneous Correspondence in Prose and Verse." Later issues added or substituted sections dedicated to ethics, religion, geography, and the biographies of eminent figures. In June 1758, for example, the magazine included (1) two narrative dialogues, the first concluding a discourse on thermometers and the second continuing an explanation of hygrometers from the previous issue; (2) a continuation of the natural history of Gloucestershire; (3) chapters XV and XVI of a Church history, both on the state of Christianity in the fourth century; (4) a chapter (XIL) demonstrating the properties of conic sections; (5) a biography of Regiomontanus, the fifteenth-century German mathematician and astronomer; and (6) a miscellaneous collection of typical magazine fare, including an account of the western coast of Africa, a number of mathematical questions and answers, and a proof predicting a lunar eclipse in January 1759; a selection of poems; and finally news, stock prices, bills of mortality, and observations on the weather.[148]

By itself, this assortment would not seem to too much distinguish *Martin's Magazine* from other general interest periodicals or serialized essay publications—even if his placed a greater emphasis on the arts and sciences. The use of dialogue as the vehicle for knowledge has ancient precedents, and Martin's choice of a genteel brother and sister for that purpose indicates both his desired market and a belief in the appropriateness of a rounded education for the youth of both sexes.[149] Like other magazine editors, he printed contributions from readers across the country, both in his miscellaneous collection and in order to facilitate his natural history of England for section two. He furthermore included "the most beautiful Descriptions, Allusions, and Similes that can be found in the most celebrated antient and modern Poets" in order to "embellish" the natural philosophy of the first section and "to render the Whole as compleat as possible."[150] The poetic excerpts introduced the variety and entertainment expected of a popular periodical into what might otherwise have been an unpalatably dry body of knowledge.

They also reveal both the lingering connection and the widening rift between alternative modes of literary knowledge production and dissemination. On the one hand, Martin suggests that his survey of all the works of nature would be incomplete without selections of poetry to enhance its beauty and value; on the other hand, Martin identifies the excerpts he provides as ancillary embellishments to rather than primary vehicles for the knowledge it is his main purpose to transmit. This conceptualization reverses the understanding Pope had of Homer's poems as including only those "strokes of Knowledge from the whole Circle of Arts and Sciences, which the Subject demanded either for Necessity or Ornament."[151] Martin proposed to provide the very "full and regular systems of every thing" that Pope dismissed from Homer, and in his magazine it is strokes of poetry that become ornament to the arts and sciences. In both cases, each author recognizes the connection of the two literary kinds, but each also inverts the hierarchical order of the other and in so doing affirms an epistemic and generic distinction. Epic poems are not primarily encyclopedic, and encyclopedic texts are not primarily poetic.

Unlike the major encyclopedias of the period, however, Martin's magazine did not rely on maps or cross-references to achieve or at least suggest the possibility of unity. Considered in isolation, each issue presents a body of articles with no apparent connection to each other; in some respects, *Martin's Magazine* was actually more fragmented than those periodicals in which the majority of pieces were discrete parts of a discrete whole. The simultaneous parceling out of what were in effect four books in a fixed space occasionally produced very abrupt changes of subject and unfinished thoughts. The chapter on Church history in the June 1758 issue, for instance, stops midway through the ninth item in a list of tactics used by Julian to restore Paganism to the Roman Empire. The natural history of Gloucestershire actually breaks off two words into a sentence presumably completed by the next number.

The fragmentary nature of each section or issue, however, was merely the short-term manifestation of Martin's long-term goal. Martin explains:

> Though the press has long groaned under the Weight of Magazines of various Complexions, not one of them has appeared with any Pretensions of this Kind, most of them being calculated for Amusement only; and as to the rest, if the Words Arts and Sciences are found in their Title-Pages, you seek in vain for the things themselves, in the Body of the Work; or if in any Thing of that Sort appears, it is only Peace-meal, in Bits and Scraps, disjointed and mangled, without Order and Connection, and therefore of no Use to any one. On the contrary, in our Magazine, we propose a compleat Body of *real* Arts and Sciences...[152]

The insistence that this latest offering would fulfill a need somehow left unmet by an already overburdened press was thoroughly conventional. The emphasis on order and connection, however, departs from the norms of periodicals and is all the more remarkable for its placement within the first of five points outlining *The general magazine's* method and purpose. Martin links encyclopedic coverage *and* connectivity to usefulness on the first page of his plan, and he defines the completeness of his magazine in terms of both.

Cohesion, though, would only be realized with the fulfillment of Martin's overarching plan. He designed every issue to facilitate its eventual rebinding into a single collection organized by each of the major subjects.

Each of the first four sections in the June 1758 issue, for example, begins at page 347; the life of Regiomontanus at 153; and the miscellaneous correspondence at 813. This more than anything, Millburn remarks, made *Martin's Magazine* "different from a true periodical, in which the numbers are meant to be collected and bound serially as issued."[153] When reorganized, the thousands of pages printed over ten years amounted to a thirteen-volume body of knowledge including an extended miscellany; there are ninety-one sequential dialogues between Cleonicus the undergraduate and his sister Euphrosine; fifty-four chapters on the natural history of England and Wales; just over a volume on theology, ethics, and religion; another on the geography and natural history of Europe, Asia, Africa, and the Americas; two on mathematics; one of biography; and three of miscellaneous ephemera. Though internally un-alphabetized and therefore not useable in the same manner as conventional encyclopedias, these volumes constituted "complete" extended treatises on or treatments of multiple diverse subjects. The tables of contents and indices provided with each volume saved the whole from total organizational inutility and recreated the long journey through each of those subjects as a large reference work suitable for occasional consultation.

They did not, however, remedy all of the difficulties introduced by the original plan. The introduction to the fourteenth, final, and longest volume of *Martin's Magazine*, completed in 1765, acknowledges its weaknesses and restates the "new" plan adopted by the proprietors. That plan answers the one objection they believed the public had to the magazine in its original incarnation: the printing of each science in separate half-sheets every month resulted in "disagreeable Interruption and Suspension to the Reader's Curiosity and Attention." They would therefore endeavor "to render each Number compleat in itself, and independent of the preceding or subsequent ones."[154] The contents of the volume reflect the change: a year's worth of single numbers are bound serially in the order issued, just as one would expect of any other periodical collection. Though the elements of Martin's original categorical divisions remain, the brother and sister have been done away with, each article begins and ends within the confines of the issue, and "a Candid Review of Interesting Books" now divides the miscellaneous correspondence from the news of the month.

In essence, Martin's experiment ended a year before the magazine did. Its final numbers far more closely resembled the larger body of contemporary periodicals than they did the innovative periodical encyclopedia its author had set out to create. *Martin's Magazine*, then, failed to change the course or substance of magazine or encyclopedia conventions; instead, the conventions changed *Martin's Magazine.* Even conformity, however, could not save it. A final note to the public announces its suspension and recommends *The Universal museum and complete magazine* as a substitute. The project thus ended without having achieved the kind of complete knowledge Martin desired and having rejected the methods by which he hoped to achieve it. His coverage of natural history, ethics and religion, and the arts and sciences was never as comprehensive as promised, and his successors' assurance that they would enlarge the magazine to address the "many Parts of the general Plan [that] have not yet been introduced"—including particulars of "metaphysics, mechanics, botany, chemistry; history natural, civil, and military; Grammar, Rhetoric, Logic, Agriculture, Mineralogy, Zoology, Architecture, Manufactures, &c. &c."—reveals how much was still left undone at the time of its cancellation.[155] If they believed, even temporarily, that broader coverage remained possible, then the fact that the overall systemization of that knowledge was no longer a part of their plan demonstrates their understanding of the magazine's limitations as a vehicle for the distribution of truly encyclopedic learning.

5
Collapse and Reconstitution: Epic and Encyclopedia Revisited

By the middle of the century, the progress of learning and the continued attempts by encyclopedists and encyclopedic works to provide a record of that progress had revealed the irreconcilability inherent in the pursuit of complete knowledge in the fullest sense of the phrase. Full comprehensiveness and total connectivity, while perhaps perfectly united in divine omniscience and still the final objective of Enlightenment, continued to pose tremendous challenges given the limitations of the human intellect. In January 1760, Samuel Johnson insisted in an issue of *The Idler* that the amount of knowledge in and about the world was simply and absolutely beyond the capacity of the single mind to comprehend completely:

> To fix deeply in the mind the principles of science, to settle their limitations, and deduce the long succession of their consequences; to comprehend the whole compass of complicated systems, with all the arguments, objections, and solutions, and to reposite in the intel-lectual treasury the numberless facts, experiments, apophthegms, and positions which must stand single in the memory, and of which none has any perceptible connection with the rest, is a task which, tho' undertaken with ardour and pursued with diligence, must at last be left unfinished by the frailty of our nature.[1]

The multiple series and clauses of this single sentence reflect the over-abundance they describe; they come quickly and without cessation until at last our frail nature is left buried beneath the avalanche. Though Johnson's words distantly echo the laments of Francis Bacon, who likewise recognized mortality as an obstacle in the pathway to complete knowledge, they lack an equivalent sense that such an obstacle might one day be overcome. Human nature, he suggests, defines the limits of human learning, and in the experience of the individual knowledge would always be incomplete.

Johnson's primary concern in the above passage is the human rather than the text—the limits of the mind rather than those of the book. The book, though, also showed similar signs of strain. As discussed in the previous chapter, attempts to facilitate readers' more complete understanding of large bodies of knowledge resulted in the experimental and ultimately unsuccessful organizational tactics of long-lived projects like *Martin's Magazine* and *An Universal History*. They also produced generic anomalies such as *A new and complete dictionary of arts and sciences* (1754), the editors of which determined that article length should be proportional to physical size within categorical subdivisions. "The smallest insects and plants find a place," the preface promises, "only a less one than those allotted for the description of the elephant and oak."[2] "Line" therefore takes up more column inches than "point," and "epic" more pages than "lyric," even though "atom" runs longer than "acorn." Considerations of neither space occupied nor time taken, however, explain why the editors deemed five pages and two plates the appropriate amount to devote to "electricity." The dictionary predictably did not see a second edition.

Just over fifty years after Henry Curzon's *The universal library: or, compleat summary of science* (1712) confidently trumpeted that it had, "like Homer's *Iliads* in a Nut-shell ... Enclosed the Learning, Arts, and Artifices of the Microcosm" and "demonstrated together at one View, all Humane, Sciential, Natural and Artificial Rarities," the author-editors of the *Encyclopædia Britannica* in essence declared an end to conventional claims to encyclopedic completeness. In their estimation, such a view of knowledge could not in fact be composed, and its complete structure could not be appreciably represented in any space whatsoever.[3] Even the most successful encyclopedias of the age, they insisted, left true knowledge (along with the reader) lost in a tangle of organizational inefficiencies. The *Britannica*, conceived in part as a nationalistic answer to the *Encyclopédie* and as a successor to Chambers's by then outdated *Cyclopædia*, therefore planned to do away with what had been the defining features of the Enlightenment encyclopedia.

Neither cross-references nor the old genealogical trees of knowledge, explains the *Britannica* proposal, enabled readers to reconstruct complete systems of knowledge. In previous universal dictionaries, the authors insist, "every art and science lies scattered under a variety of words; by which means, besides the labour of hunting for science through such a labyrinth, it is absolutely impossible for the reader, after all, to obtain a distinct view of any subject."[4] Whereas Bacon had attempted to recuperate the scattering [*spargere*] of knowledge as a generative phenomenon—a sense once applied to Homer and embraced by eighteenth-century encyclopedists, often in terms of dissemination or propagation—the *Britannica* proposal invokes the more usual sense of scattering as an act of destruction or loss.[5] Perhaps unsurprisingly, no mention of Homer's name or poems occurs in any eighteenth-century *Britannica*'s plans or prefaces.

The new plan, devised to aid those unable to reconstruct in their minds the knowledge scattered by alphabetical categorization, changed the nature of completeness as a feature and function of the modern encyclopedia. William Smellie, the editor charged by owners Colin Macfarquhar and Andrew Bell with compiling the first edition, wrote extended and largely self-contained "Systems" and "Treatises" of or about individual arts and sciences. These systems and treatises emphasized the importance of cohesiveness, but they did so only within the bounds of given subject areas; the completion of these parts, the new plan suggested, would have to precede the completion of any larger whole. By adding this stage of delimited completeness to the advancement of knowledge, Smellie's systems and treatises set the stage for the long-standing (but perhaps nevertheless temporary) elevation of general and textual comprehensiveness over total connectivity.

Confrontations with the practical limits of encyclopedic representation and the collapse of claims to maximal completeness in the last decades of the eighteenth century were not restricted to actual encyclopedias. Aaron Hill's suggestion that Samuel Richardson could have "the whole proportion and connexion" of *Clarissa* "in [his] eye at once" implied that the perfect comprehension needed to divide and organize great bodies knowledge belonged to, if anyone, the creators of smaller worlds.[6] In *The Life and Opinions of Tristram Shandy, Gentleman* (1759–67), however, the "small hero" of Laurence Sterne's semiannually-expanded, highly variegated, ostensibly unfinishable and perhaps actually unfinished narrative explores the limit of complete knowledge within the far narrower framework of a single life and arrives at much the same conclusion as Johnson did only months after Sterne published its first volumes.

By referring to the disordered recollection of his life and opinions as a "cyclopædia of arts and sciences," Tristram invites categorical comparison.[7] Sterne saw the same phenomenon that would later influence Smellie's formal revision of the encyclopedia proper—a phenomenon that went beyond any single field of inquiry or literary endeavor. The fictional author's life-as-encyclopedia conflates the two literary kinds and renders the experience of life lived an exercise in encyclopedic knowledge production and information management. They also condense the broad spectrum of literary kinds between personal memoir and universal dictionary into a single amalgamation that illustrates how absurd the claim to completeness had become across that spectrum. As a self-reflexive compendium that terribly (albeit entertainingly) malfunctions, *Tristram Shandy* constitutes another collapse of claims to complete knowledge and highlights the points of fracture among the genres of completeness it contains. Novels made for poor encyclopedias; encyclopedias could not be comprehensibly novelized; magazines resisted systemization; and systems strained under the weight of variety.

At the turn of the nineteenth century, the editors of the third edition *Britannica*, overwhelmed to an even greater extent by the amount of the learning they and their contributors had collected, recognized the necessity of specialization and formally established a new disciplinarity. With that edition, the *Britannica* determinedly freed the encyclopedia from the burden of seeking total connective completeness and announced that the continued progress of learning once again demanded categorical division. To know more, encyclopedically speaking, meant to know apart. At virtually the same moment, the first edition of the *Lyrical Ballads* appeared and proposed to continue the pursuit of completeness on very different terms.[8] Wordsworth's preface to the second edition, published in 1802, used the language of connectivity and universality to describe what he understood as the special power of verse. "Poetry," he wrote, "is the breath and finer spirit of all knowledge ... the poet binds together by passion and knowledge the vast empire of human society, as it is spread over the whole earth, and over all time. The objects of the poet's thoughts are everywhere ... Poetry is the first and last of all knowledge—it is as immortal as the heart of man."[9] Poetry, in Wordsworth's estimation, achieved completeness not because the single poem or poet could comprehend everything, but rather because the poet and poem could comprehend *anything*, and all human beings joined with the poet in singing his song.

Throughout the last quarter of the eighteenth century, the already fraught concept of completeness continued to break up along the lines that have since come to define an enduring (but not necessarily permanent) separation of these kinds of writing. As the next century began, the new model of encyclopedic composition made comprehensive knowledge the primary ambition of the *Britannica* and its successors, which continue to pursue completeness down the long road of knowledge production first charted by Francis Bacon. At the same time, the standards of "Literary" achievement became such that genres of lesser breadth and greater depth came to occupy its heights. The complete knowledge of the poet existed increasingly within the bounds of artistic or imaginative enterprise and without the broadening circle of arts and sciences as defined and represented by the universal dictionaries; the elevation of new forms such as the fragment poem as well as the reconstitution of epic that took place during this period depended in part on the valuation and pursuit of a completeness defined by the essential rather than the comprehensive—another kind of delimited completeness that embraced the limitations of human understanding and made the human experience a window to a world too immense for any single written work to comprehend in its entirety.

The Shandean Assessment

Shortly before he published the first two volumes of *The Life and Opinions of Tristram Shandy, Gentleman*, Laurence Sterne sent a letter to his London bookseller and publisher Robert Dodsley. In it, he offered Dodsley the publishing rights to his book as well as a brief outline of its project. "The plan," Sterne writes, "as you will perceive, is a most extensive one,— taking in, not only, the Weak part of the Sciences, in which the true point of the Ridicule lies—but every Thing else, which I find Laugh-at-able in my way."[10] Following the success of the volumes in both York and London, Dodsley purchased the rights, and Sterne spent the next seven years writing his list of laughable matters into a work that for the last two-and-a-half centuries has defied its readers' attempts to categorize or fully comprehend it. "The Book will sell," he assures Dodsley in his letter. "What other Merit it has, does not become me either to think or say ... the World however will fix the Value for us both."

The "World"—by which Sterne presumably meant his anticipated readership in both the immediate and more distant futures—might have fixed the value of the book in terms of the number of copies sold, but in almost every other sense the "value" of the book remains *un*fixed. The genre of *Tristram Shandy* has been the subject of debate since its publication. Some readers, though, did not hesitate in labeling (or libeling) it. A dialogue supposedly recorded at the Smyrna coffeehouse in Pall Mall and transmitted to the editor of *The Grand magazine* in June 1760, for instance, very clearly identifies it as a novel—albeit an obscene and indelicate one.[11] At about the same time, a Methodist preacher warned Sterne that he "never yet heard of a saint's writing a bawdy novel" (he goes on to call *Tristram Shandy* an anti-gospel and its author the anti-Christ).[12] A report on a copyright trial in *The Weekly entertainer* for August 1794 puts the book in the same category as *Tom Jones* and casts no moral judgments at all.[13] Other readers, however, were more circumspect. The author of the "Character of Laurence Sterne" in the *North British Intelligencer* for January 1777, for example, offered that *Tristram Shandy* "might be called a novel, if it admitted of any determinate name."[14] The compilers of the *General Biography* similarly refer to it only as "a kind of novel of a very peculiar character."[15] Clara Reeve's fictional proxy Euphrasia in *The Progress of Romance*, finally, claims to have left it half unread and leaves it altogether unclassified. Reeve's history of prose fiction refers to Sterne only as a writer and *Tristram Shandy* simply as a "book."

The uncertainty has persisted in modern literary criticism. Ian Watt, after identifying it as Sterne's "only novel," writes that in fact it "is not so much a novel as a parody of a novel."[16] Northrop Frye states that "nearly everyone would say yes" when asked if *Tristram Shandy* is a novel, but then goes on to identify a host of features that mark it as something else.[17] William Warner obliquely categorizes it as "a certain type of novelistic entertainment," and Michael McKeon, who notes that after its appearance "the young genre settles down," avoids calling it anything at all.[18] Patricia Meyer Spacks, in contrast, exuberantly insists in her general overview of eighteenth-century prose fiction that *Tristram Shandy* "not only works brilliantly as a novel; it also comments brilliantly on the novel as a genre." She furthermore reminds readers that Viktor Shklovsky once declared it "'the most typical novel in world literature.'"[19]

If nothing else, both sets of comments unquestionably designate the novel as the form to which *Tristram* bore and bears the greatest resemblance. The disparities, though, on the one hand indicate the taxonomic instability that *Tristram* helped to introduce or maintain in the first place, and on the other hand suggest a reasonably stable body of conventions according to which it can be included or disqualified. One of those conventions—the ability of the novel to adapt and combine other literary forms and to comprehend multiple kinds of information—has allowed the novel to overshadow other points of comparison that no longer seem to bear any relation to it. Even the prominent displays of erudition that have led some to cast *Tristram Shandy* as a "belated exercise in Renaissance learned wit" do not, as Thomas Keymer points out, call for critics "to deny the deliberacy of its engagement with modern forms."[20] By "modern forms" Keymer once again means the novel. The reference in Sterne's letter to a "most extensive" plan, however, hearkens to the language of encyclopedias, histories, magazines, systems, and *all* those other bodies of knowledge defined by breadth or variety of coverage—the mid-century novel included.

Sterne's satire proceeds by extending the pursuit of complete knowledge to an extreme but still logical end: the creation of a meaningfully comprehensive account of a single life. The world of *Tristram Shandy* seemingly starts small. Its title restricts the scope of his book to just the life and opinions of its fictional author; the second chapter introduces Tristram via the miniature but nonetheless already complete body of the homunculus; chapter five laments the many misfortunes of its "small Hero"; and chapter seven defines "the world" as no more than his village and the gifted midwife supposedly at the center of it—"a small circle circumscribed upon the circle of the great world, of four *English* miles diameter, or thereabouts."[21] The emphasis on smallness in the passages outlined above suggests a project of manageably limited proportions; for one man to walk the full round of education in a world with a circumference of only twelve and a half miles should take hours rather than the years required to compose or comprehend those bodies of knowledge with more explicitly universal ambitions.

In practice, however, the plan almost immediately fails. The boundaries between parts and wholes in *Tristram Shandy* all but vanish, and smallness does not equate to simplicity. Each homunculus might have another within it; the *reductio ad absurdum* of the model postulates an infinite series of fully formed and self-similar bodies complete in themselves but parts of larger wholes. If the nature of the individual is already set as a homunculus, then, as Dirk Vanderbeke observes, "it is necessary for a complete description of his hero's life 'to go on tracing everything in it, as Horace says, *ab Ovo*,' and to look into all the causes and the causes of the causes of the causes, etc. Everything contributes to the ultimate result that is our hero."[22] Even before his life begins, *everything* is of potential relevance to it: Tristram's troubles, Sir Walter remarks, "began nine months before he ever came into the world."[23] The smallness of any circles that Tristram might draw around himself is no barrier against the larger world for which he must account in order to complete the description of his life and opinions.

Whether or not Sterne (or Tristram) actually subscribed to the theory of the homunculus—a minority view by the 1760s—its appearance in the second chapter foreshadows what inevitably becomes a seriocomic challenge to the integrity of the text. The minute matters; to strike anything from the record on the grounds of seeming irrelevance is to presume the end or purpose to which it might be relevant before the fact. Whereas in Aphra Behn's *Oroonoko*, perhaps the "first" English novel, the narrator promises on page one "to omit, for brevity's sake, a thousand little accidents of [Oroonoko's] life," Tristram promises to capture as many such accidents as possible.[24] Truth, his father explains, "was kept down at the bottom of her well as inevitably by a mistake in the dust of a butterfly's wing,—as in the disk of the sun, the moon, and all the stars of heaven put together."[25] Critics have occasionally cited this passage as linked to or even anticipating the trope of chaos theory made familiar two centuries later by Edward Lorenz's "butterfly effect"; Sir Walter's systems of geniture, names, and noses seemingly follow from his own understanding of sensitivity to initial conditions and the deterministic universe that he believed made those conditions critical to long-term and large-scale outcomes. While the apparently chaotic structure of Tristram's account rejects the kind of order sought by his father, both make ample room in their philosophies for the supposedly miniscule details that constitute such a large part of life.

Those details, though potentially crucial to forming a complete understanding of the world, at the same time threaten to obscure any coherent systematicity that might emerge from them or flummox any attempt to exert control over the system presumed to be in operation. Sir Walter's claim that the "great, the established points of [the whole circle of the sciences], are not to be broke in upon"—in short, that "the laws of nature will defend themselves"—informs his close reasoning upon small matters and warning that error "creeps in thro' the minute holes, and small crevices, which human nature leaves unguarded."[26] Concerned that Mrs. Shandy will squeeze the "net-work" of his son's mind out of its natural working order during birth, he appeals to her to submit to a caesarian section; she refuses, and he looks to Dr Slop to preserve Tristram's skull; Dr Slop crushes Tristram's nose with the forceps, and Sir Walter names him Trismegistus to make up for the loss; the parson christens him Tristram, and Sir Walter composes the *Tristrapœdia* to compensate for the name; by the time he completes the first part of the book, Tristram has outgrown it and rendered its contents useless. At each step, Sir Walter tries and fails to regain control of the system by counteracting each small accident of Tristram's birth with an equal and opposite reaction of his own design, but he cannot balance the equation. Sir Walter forgets to wind the clock; "error" creeps in where a fundamental drive of human nature meets the clearest emblem of a perfectly ordered universe. The earth proceeds on its course through the heavens without interruption, but Sir Walter fails to set in motion the series of events that will produce a clockwork child.

That Sir Walter's animal spirits should be "scattered and dispersed" at the moment of Tristram's conception faintly echoes Politian's well-known description of Homer as containing the *"semina"* of all disciplines as well as Bacon's subsequent revision of Homer's status as the father of the arts and sciences.[27] When considered in conjunction with Chambers's repetition of the seed metaphor and concurrent description of Homer as a poet possessed of a "greater Share of that Spirit whereby [the Arts] are produced," the description of scattered animal spirits at the very opening of *Tristram Shandy* locates the long process of civilizational knowledge production and transmission associated with the epic and encyclopedia entirely within two generations of a single family.[28] Sir Walter scatters and Tristram collects, and what Tristram collects the book itself again disperses.

Tristram, though, is a different kind of completist. Sterne, John Freeman writes, creates a dynamic system based on "life's temporal flow" and a universal tendency towards entropy—the gradual dissolution of order, or in informational terms, the decay of signal and the increase of noise. Tristram, Freeman explains, "realizes the way to keep the system of the novel from emptying out into the void is to keep feeding information into it as well as generating information from it." Writing produces more writing, and each recaptured memory, opinion, or fact introduces a new network of associations that provide additional information. If Tristram can recover all the information related to the circumstances of his birth, then the disorder of his life can theoretically be recuperated.[29] The process of recovery naturally proceeds by a Lockean association of ideas (the same principle that from Mrs. Shandy's perspective necessitated the winding of the clock in the first place) rather than the stricter order of Newtonian rationalism disrupted by Sir Walter's oversight, and the result, though it aspires to a kind of completeness, is not an organized narrative history, a clockwork novel, or a body of arts and sciences in any conventional sense. Its associative inclusion of minor points and major idiosyncrasies distinguishes it from the "universal" knowledge projects it critiques by keeping what most of those works displaced or discarded in order to achieve some measure of coherence.

Sterne's extension of the general to the individual—the macro to the micro—illuminates a degree of self-similarity across the scales but offers no clear way of comprehending the connections between them. It is an account of a specific life and a compendium of learning the fullness and disorder of which reveal the incompleteness of those other more formally recognizable kinds of literature. Scholars have paid ample attention, for example, to the relationship of *Tristram Shandy* to the universal dictionary of arts and sciences. John Ferriar's *Illustration of Sterne* (1798) addressed Sterne's habitual borrowing from encyclopedic sources, and Sir Toby's extensive knowledge of fortifications and artillery can be traced directly to Chambers's *Cyclopædia*.³⁰ Sterne, though, borrowed more than just content. "In its mock learning," Christopher Fanning writes, "its digressions, cross-references to its own earlier and future chapters, its editorial annotations ... *Tristram Shandy* offers itself as a parodic version of the encyclopædia."³¹ Those features function not to parody the encyclopedia per se, though, but rather the misapplication of Enlightenment methods of systemization to the particular human experience.

Tristram orders his entries according to tangential relevance rather than by alphabetical order. Pagination and chapter order fail. Cross-references refer to previous or subsequently treated ideas or anecdotes, but they do not identify where the reader can find them. Even Tristram cannot always remember where he put things, and he does not always give the information he promises. "I think," he writes, "I said, I would write two volumes every year ... and in another place—(but where, I can't recollect now) speaking of my book as *a machine* ... I swore it should be kept a going at that rate these forty years." Writing of Jenny, he assures the reader that he will reveal her identity "in the next chapter but one to my chapter of Button-holes."³² He never writes the chapter. As an encyclopedia, *Tristram Shandy* fails by design; the author's implication that the organization and operation of his novelized cyclopedia of arts and sciences depends on the vagaries of memory and what from the outside seems like an arbitrary thought process highlights the disjunctions between a universal body of knowledge designed for general utility and the hobbyhorsical situating of one's self in relation to that knowledge. Tristram, like the encyclopedia, can account for a great deal—everything from noses to Namur—but the encyclopedia cannot account for Tristram.

The same holds true for history. Locke's *An Essay Concerning Human Understanding*, Tristram explains to his would-be critics, is a "a history-book ... of what passes in a man's own mind," and such knowledge is necessary to forming a right understanding of and sympathy with the story of Toby's wounding in Flanders. Toby's recreation of the siege of Namur constitutes an effort to place himself in a history all his own but at the same time much larger than his particular part in it. The meeting of micro- and macro-histories at Namur makes it an exemplary site of informational complexity the substance and significance of which depend upon the perspective of the individual observer rather than any universal, authoritative record. Toby expresses certainty that given adequate information he could "stick a pin upon the identical spot of ground where he was standing when the stone struck him"; the notion eventually leads to the reproduction of the entire town and its environs on the grounds of Shandy Hall.[33] The part thus comes to contain the whole: the model inverts the scale of history by literally and figuratively making the man and his mind much larger than the battle in which he participated. Toby's wound and hobbyhorse become the new origin and conceptual center of the siege.

Both of these elements, in the life and opinions of Tristram Shandy, have outsized importance relative to the nature of the events outlined in the first chapter of the second volume. Tristram reminds the reader that one of the most memorable attacks of the siege (about which the reader may or may not have read in the history of King William's wars) "was that which was made by the *English* and *Dutch* upon the point of the advanced counterscarp, before the gate of *St. Nicholas*, which inclosed the great sluice or water-stop, where the *English* were terribly exposed to the shot of the counter-guard and demi-bastion of *St. Roch.*" Tristram summarizes the issue of the attack in a euphemistic "three words" and gives no further space to the immediate ramifications of the conflict or its significance in the larger context of the Nine Years' War. The history he describes in this the second paragraph of the new book is largely abstract; it proceeds from the fact of the wars to the importance of the siege to the allied forces involved to the location of the exchange to the architecture of the relevant fortifications. In the first paragraph, though, Tristram announces that he has begun the book for a more specific purpose: to "have room enough to explain the nature of the perplexities in which my Uncle Toby was involved, from the many discourses and interrogations about the siege of Namur, where he received his wound."[34] The third paragraph returns to Toby's perspective as an eyewitness, thereby enclosing the general history within the particular. Tristram needs more space for the history of Toby's mind.

The individual experience of even a single event comprehends vast amounts of information all in itself, and the general history cannot reasonably accommodate it. The phenomenon predictably becomes more pronounced as the scope of a given work increases, and genre again becomes a mechanism of information management. Just as the universal dictionaries of the early and mid-eighteenth century were not typically intended for experts in need of more in-depth knowledge, the authors of universal history too did not pretend to provide details of events or lives beyond what they deemed crucial to painting the larger picture. The plan for *An Universal History* included with the 1746 proposal to reprint it in twenty volumes draws a clear line: "the Authors, throughout this Work, have avoided introducing long Descriptions of Battles and Sieges, Harangues, Speeches, and Letters, and, in short, all other Digressions, which, though they may be excusable in Particular Histories, ought to be omitted in General ones, where nothing but the Essentials should find a Place."[35] Volumes 25 and 30 of the modern part of the history reference Namur less than a dozen times and name only the principal leaders of the military actions involving the siege; the former volume takes all of thirty lines to bring the siege from the opening of the trenches on 11 July 1695 to the final capitulation of the French under Louis François de Boufflers on 1 September.[36] *Tristram Shandy* and *An Universal History* therefore occupy opposite extremes; the latter excludes lengthy harangues, speeches, letters, and digressions while the former consists of little else.

The history book of what goes on in a man's mind is perhaps the most particular human history possible, though it is no less complicated for its particularity. Tristram describes his book (and life, for they are one) as a machine—one in which he has "so complicated and involved the digressive and progressive movements, one wheel within another, that the whole machine, in general, has been kept a-going;—and, what's more, it shall be kept a-going these forty years."[37] He later describes his family unit in similar terms: its few wheels "were set in motion by so many different springs and acted one upon the other from such a variety of strange principles and impulses—that though it was a simple machine, it had all the honour and advantages of a complex one."[38] Tristram is thus a machine within a machine; both are connected to each other and to the world at large. Toby's hobbyhorse, for instance, connects him and his entire family to a major event in world history and also to several interrelated branches of knowledge from the circle of arts and sciences. The links, as Judith Hawley argues, are not merely expressions of Shandean eccentricity. Fortification "combines mechanical, mathematical, and technical knowledge" as well as Newtonian mechanics; Toby's particular part in the battle, moreover, additionally introduces the subjects of anatomy and physic.[39] That Tristram should suffer a similar injury wrought by a similar force as a result of a similar siege (all scaled down to the small world of Shandy Hall) once again suggests close and complex connections between microcosm and macrocosm—connections perhaps presumed by Enlightenment philosophy to exist but rarely if ever completely described.

Tristram Shandy explores those connections in ways and to a degree not naturalized to the genres from which it borrows. In the process,

Sterne implicitly suggests the incompleteness of all encyclopedic bodies of knowledge and the extent to which the pursuit of complete knowledge would likely never reach its utmost end. The nature of "real" life, contradistinguished from the heavily directed and controlled experimental re-creations of life and the compendia of knowledge that defined so many literary efforts of the mid-eighteenth century, is such that the total amount of knowledge produced simply by the process of living must inevitably overwhelm the ability of the individual to keep a complete and coherent record. Tristram sees this as a mathematical certainty:

> I am this month one whole year older than I was this time twelve-month; and having got ... no farther than to my first day's life—'tis demonstrative that I have three hundred and sixty-four days more life to write just now, than when I first set out ... at this rate I should just live 364 times faster than I should write—It must follow, an' please your worships, that the more I write, the more I shall have to write—and consequently, the more your worships read, the more your worships will have to read.[40]

Tristram cannot, like Pamela and Clarissa are supposed to have done, write to the moment; he cannot recount every detail of his life before death stops his pen. Without a comprehensive record of all phenomena, a fully realized system of all knowledge cannot emerge. Any coherent sense that does or is made must be based on a selection of data rather than its entirety.

Sterne strips away from his machine the fiction of a dial-plate and leaves the unified purpose of his assembly of gears, springs, and wheels undetermined. This is not to suggest that the text or the life it represents is a meaningless chaos. Its value is simply based upon a different system of meaning-making than those of clockwork novels, reference works, general histories, and epic poems. Like Tristram, Sterne too inherits literary forms and conventions that he adopts and adapts to achieve his own objective. Sir Walter's *Tristrapædia* attempts to do the work of the clockwork novel in a more obviously encyclopedic form; he locates a first cause for his system in the sex-urge that drives the action of the Richardsonian and Fieldian novels and selectively orders the rest according to his didactic objective.[41] His failure to complete the *Tristrapædia* reflects the inability of the clockwork novel and the encyclopedia to account for all of the knowledge relevant to the world that it represents as a complete system. Tristram, who refuses to follow "any man's rules that ever lived," takes the work of the previous generation and rewrites it to represent life as individualistic, incomprehensible, and impossible to reduce to a set of inducible laws or consistent structural relationships.[42]

If the genealogical tree represents the overarching organization of complete knowledge in the universal dictionary (as it does in the *Cyclopædia* from which Sterne borrowed so much) then its corollary in *Tristram Shandy* is the marbled page—the "motley emblem" of the work that visualizes the chaotic overabundance of Tristram's life even as it illustrates the impossibility of a systematically uniform reading of it.[43] The branches of the genealogical tree that divide the arts and sciences into neat and rigid lines of text perfectly perpendicular to the braces separating each subgroup stand in stark opposition to the circles and swirls of the marbling that interact in incredibly complex ways but still form a single image framed by the page's marginal whitespace.[44] Despite the unity imposed by the frame, however, the page obviously does not function as a map or chart according to which the contents of the book can be consistently intellectually reordered. While the universal forces that shape the patterns on each marbled page might always be the same, no two marbled pages are alike; this expression of uniqueness in each copy of the book reflects the individuality of each of those readers who will have a similar but necessarily non-identical experience of it. Neither the marbled pages nor the work they emblematize authorize a universal interpretation; each reader must make the book into his or her own version of a whole that, like the marbled page, achieves a kind of completeness only via idiosyncratic abstraction.

Tristram, in other words, does not complete *Tristram Shandy*; the reader does. Absent the predetermined schema and systematic modes of reading structured into the encyclopedia or the unifying moral and historical frameworks typically embedded within narrative teleology, *Tristram Shandy* includes no clear and automatic means of imposing a coherent order on the whole that establishes or fixes its meaning.[45] Tristram's invocation of "the knowledge of the great saint Paraleipomenon" and insistence that without much reading (by which he means much knowledge) the reader will not be able to penetrate the moral of the marbled page acknowledges the inadequacies of the book and the reader's part in completing it.[46] "Paraleipomenon" refers to "material omitted from the body of a text, and appended as a supplement."[47] The reader—all readers—here become supplemental bodies of knowledge not comprehended by *Tristram Shandy*, which is not complete without them. Each reader brings to the text another world of associations (and another hobbyhorse) that have the potential to change the significance of any given part. The blank page—the last in the book's series of three pages entirely devoid of text—makes perhaps the most direct appeal to the strategy of collaborative completion. Even though no extant copies from the period reveal their purchasers' sketched-in Widows Wadman, the blank page nevertheless invites an imaginative contribution that transcends the material limits of the book as well as Tristram's inability to account for the lives and opinions of every reader.

The interpretive acts provoked throughout the whole of the text and particularly by those graphic experiments in which text has no place have the potential to produce meaningful coherence despite the unavoidable gaps and inconsistencies of Tristram's primary account. What in a history, dictionary, or conventional novel of the period might seem an actual omission or deficit becomes in *Tristram Shandy* additional fodder for generative thought; the ten-page chasm of a "torn out" chapter is only an absence if deemed so by the reader. Sterne, though, gives every reason to consider that absence a presence; the reader endows the space with substance that informs an understanding of the whole, however unstable. The constant reference to a spectrum of different readers in the book calls attention to the creative work of reading and connects the singular text back to the larger world of thought and opinion that it could strive to engage but not hope to contain.

The deployment of quintessential Enlightenment tropes and structural mechanisms in *Tristram Shandy* results not in its readers' gaining knowledge of the "fixed" laws governing the novel or the reality it purports to represent, but rather in as many different interpretations of those laws as there are readers to observe the phenomena. Sterne offers an openly open-ended alternative to those works that promised but ultimately failed to deliver complete systems of human nature or knowledge. In their attempts to create such systems, *Tristram Shandy* suggests, they failed to capture a true sense of the human experience. Despite its incredible extensiveness, the book finally externalizes the possibility of complete knowledge as beyond the capacity of text. Sterne even associates the urge to compose self-contained complete accounts and systems with death.[48] Such efforts, as Tristram learns, are not sustainable; his implied inability to reproduce suggests that his life and book might be the end of the Shandean line. While indeed Sterne's text did not and perhaps was not meant to become the prototype of a durable paradigm in its own right—its immense and immediate popularity did not recast the novel in its own image—*Tristram Shandy* did anticipate the productive fragmentation of knowledge and a new phase in the history of literary completeness.

Upon a New Plan: *Encyclopædia Britannica*

Many of the encyclopedias that appeared after the first edition of Chambers's *Cyclopædia* continued to give the concept of completeness a prominent place in their title pages and prefaces. John Barrow's *A new and universal dictionary of arts and sciences* of 1751, for example, advertised itself as a "Compleat Body of Arts and Sciences." *A new and complete dictionary of arts and sciences* made a similar gesture in 1754. Temple Henry Croker and his associates redoubled the promise of completeness in 1764 with *The complete dictionary of arts and sciences. In which the whole circle of human learning is explained.* The two-volume *A new royal and universal dictionary of arts and sciences* that followed in 1772 supposedly comprehended a "complete system of human knowledge." In 1778, a decade after the first *Britannica*, another new and purportedly complete dictionary of arts and sciences—this one entitled *The new complete dictionary of arts and sciences*—appeared, and ten years after that, William Henry Hall's *The new royal encyclopædia* made the most ostentatious display of such terminology to date. Its full title describes the work as a "Complete Modern Universal Dictionary" that contained "complete systems" of the sciences, the "Whole Theory and Practice of the Liberal and Mechanickal Arts" and "the most Comprehensive Library of Universal Knowledge, That was ever published in the English Language."

All of these encyclopedias promised rather more than they could provide, and many of their titles would likely have had Francis Bacon aphorizing in his grave. He warned against premature systematization and the mistaking of old knowledge newly methodized for actual advances.[49] Encyclopedias, however, did not exist in a vacuum. Had their proprietors simply compiled knowledge without simultaneously attempting to organize, summarize, or systematize it, they would have sacrificed the immediate utility of that knowledge to contemporary users, which sacrifice in turn would likely have concluded the profitable life of the form. Fortunately, however, the producers of reference works had sought to capitalize on the commercial appeal of the complete for over a century, and their tactics had inspired cynical responses for almost as long.[50] As a result, any suggestions of completeness would by the mid-eighteenth century have been widely understood as provisional rather than absolute.

Indeed, many encyclopedists of the period readily acknowledged that none of their works would be the last of its kind. John Harris had placed perfection out of reach upon compiling volume two of the *Lexicon technicum*. "It is easie to see," he wrote, "that new Matter will continually occur in a Design of this Nature, and consequently, that there can be no such thing as a *Perfect Book* of this Kind."[51] Chambers too expected that future editions of the *Cyclopædia* would improve upon his original, and D'Alembert remarked that "the ultimate Perfection of an Encyclopedia is the Work of Ages."[52] Even Barrow's encyclopedia qualifies its literally large and boldfaced promise of a "complete body of arts and sciences" by adding "as they are at present cultivated." These qualifications made abundantly clear that the truly universal knowledge they sought to capture was, to borrow a phrase from Wordsworth, "something ever more about to be."[53]

Ironically, none of the most acclaimed, longest, or longest-lived encyclopedias of the eighteenth century made direct claims to completeness. The word "complete" does not occur on any of their title pages, and only the *Cyclopædia* makes use of "universal." Smellie does not even use "complete" in his preface; it occurs for the first time in the *Britannica* beneath the main title printed above the first entries of the body proper—after the title page, preface, and list of authors.[54] The absence of such highly conventional words and phrases from the major encyclopedias of the mid- and late century might reflect a process of stratification wherein the proprietors of more extensive and more expensive properties attempted to dissociate their products from works of lesser quality by eschewing the terms so many of them used without discrimination. It might also suggest the extent to which a qualified completeness or universality had become so naturalized as to need no articulation.

Responsible for presenting human knowledge of the arts and sciences as it stood in relation to its readers as well as to itself, for promoting further knowledge production, and upon the moment of publication becoming part of the history of knowledge that it represented, each edition, volume, and entry of an encyclopedia served as a milestone in the progress of learning. The function of the individual edition mirrors that of the entire form: at the micro level, the content of each edition constituted the compendium of knowledge called an encyclopedia. At the macro level, the "encyclopedia" was itself a feature with a function inseparable from but different than that of its specific content. As James Creech writes, "an encyclopedia must fix the totality of knowledge in one moment, like an image of the national mind that will itself become a stable measure by which future progress can be gauged."[55] That larger function, however, emerges only with the publication of successive and updated editions.[56] Complete knowledge always belonged to the future; the progressive nature of Enlightenment renders each instance of publication a synchronic feature of a genre—itself a feature of Enlightenment—that in turn has a diachronic function.

The success of the encyclopedia at the individual and categorical levels depended (and continues to depend) upon the temporal dynamics that define and direct their operation. The progress towards encyclopedic completeness and maximum utility involved multiple and sometimes contradictory factors. The usefulness of any given article could degrade slowly, suddenly, or partially, and in any combination. While many definitional entries from the first edition continue to hold their value— "acanthus," for instance, means much the same thing now as it did in the eighteenth century—other articles have become half-truths: New Jersey, New York, and Maryland still border Pennsylvania in the east and southwest, but the "five nations of the Iroquois" no longer bound it in the north.[57] Some entries were never useful at all. Smellie might have been uncertain "whether [California] be a peninsula or island," but to the Spanish (and probably to much of Europe) the matter had been decided since 1747, when King Ferdinand declared by royal edict the connection of the territory to the North American mainland.[58]

The length of time required to produce an edition—whether due to financial difficulties, political considerations, technological constraints, or simply the scope of the project—could also problematize usefulness as well as uniformity. In the twenty years separating the first volume of the *Encyclopédie*'s articles from the last of its plates, Halley's comet reappeared (as predicted); Francis Home inoculated his first patient against the measles; James Hargreave invented the spinning jenny, and observations of the first transit of Venus since 1631 helped astronomers refine calculations of the astronomical unit. The French Revolution and Napoleonic wars helped make the successor of the *Encyclopédie*, the *Encyclopédie Méthodique*, as much an accomplishment of the nineteenth century as the eighteenth; by the time Thérèse-Charlotte Agasse, daughter of the original publisher Charles-Josephe Panckoucke and wife of his successor, Henri Agasse, completed the work in 1832, the revolution, the wars, and the lives of both men had ended. Serial publication, moreover, meant that earlier entries might be out of phase with later ones in the same edition. Whereas the article "Colonies" in the second *Britannica* notes the "present revolt" in America, that on "Virginia" acknowledges its statehood. Similarly, when it came time to write the article on "phlogiston" in the third edition, the growing acceptance of Antoine Lavoisier's claim that it did not exist compelled Tytler to write it in the past tense—even though it had been an integral part of the earlier treatise on chemistry.[59]

To remedy some of the inevitable errors, oversights and asynchronies, encyclopedists typically produced occasional single or multi-volume supplements between full editions. While such additions may have made those editions more complete in one sense, though, they simultaneously jeopardized their completeness in another. The "double alphabet" of the encyclopedia and supplement, as the editors of *The complete dictionary of arts and sciences* observed, inconvenienced the reader and encumbered the work by destroying whatever coherence the principal text had managed to achieve. Supplements, then, once again set completeness at odds with utility, and for that reason Croker and his associates assured purchasers that, as care had been taken "to render the work complete of itself, no *Supplement* will be necessary."[60] They do not suggest that no further *edition* will be necessary (though they never managed a second), but rather that the current edition had achieved sufficient synchronic completeness to satisfy the readers' needs until an entirely new one was warranted.

The provisional completeness of any given edition always implied a more complete edition to follow that could address the systemic problems of print encyclopedia production. A new edition would ideally render earlier editions and their supplements entirely obsolete by accounting for the new knowledge produced during the interim *and* by re-presenting the useful knowledge of its own past. The first edition *Britannica* offered relatively little knowledge that did not previously exist or that its readers could not have found elsewhere. The second edition carried over much of the material from the first, as did the third. Indeed, each edition of the *Britannica* carried over a greater amount of preexisting material than did the last until the ninth edition of 1875.[61] Without this process of re-presentation, the new knowledge collected would remain disconnected from any tangible standard of growth.

It also reaffirms the value of that content as knowledge and the value of the property or of encyclopedias as a whole. Purchasers of successive editions of encyclopedias pay multiple times for much of the same content, but repeating the "old" in new editions confers the added value of confirmation or at least greater certitude. Bruno Latour explains the process in a broader sense:

> By itself, a given sentence is neither a fact nor a fiction; it is made so by others, later on. You make it more of a fact if you insert it as a closed, obvious, firm and packaged premise leading to some other less closed, less obvious, less firm and less united consequence ... the status of a statement depends on later statements. It is made more of a certainty or less of a certainty depending on the next sentence that takes it up; this retrospective attribution is repeated for this next new

sentence, which in turn might be made more of a fact or more of a fiction by a third, and so on...[62]

Readers of encyclopedias could observe this process take place entirely within a single property. Numerous statements about the arts and sciences constitute the content of a given encyclopedia. The encyclopedia organizes those statements into a collective statement about the present state of knowledge. The next edition builds upon the statements made by its predecessor, which statements it renders more factual by repeating them as part of the new collective statement or reveals as "fictions" by leaving them out of the new account. Given a long enough life and deep enough pockets, an eighteenth-century encyclopedia enthusiast could chart the course of Lockean metaphysics or Newtonian optics by following the relevant entries through encyclopedias from the *Lexicon technicum* to the *Cyclopædia* to the *Britannica*. Their treatment in the latter would indicate to what extent the knowledge contained by the others had been "permanent" and therefore complete. The disappearance of phlogiston and other outmoded ideas would demonstrate the opposite.

A similar process operates at the level of genre. Just as a new encyclopedia constitutes a statement about previous statements about the arts and sciences, so too does it constitute a statement about previous encyclopedias. All eighteenth-century encyclopedias in essence faced the same challenges, had similar goals, and worked in similar ways. The *Britannica* followed in a long tradition of universal dictionaries and other compendia that struggled to balance completeness and utility. Harris had written usefulness into the modern encyclopedia at its inception; when Smellie took up the pen he put utility above all else. "Utility" is the first word of his preface, and he insists that it "ought to be the principal intention of every publication. Wherever this intention does not plainly appear, neither the books nor their authors have the smallest claim to the approbation of mankind."[63] The full title of the work, though, announces a departure from tradition that Smellie believed would better serve that intention: *Encyclopedia Britannica; or, a dictionary of arts and sciences, compiled upon a new plan. In which the different Sciences and Arts are digested into distinct Treatises or Systems and the various Technical Terms, &c. are explained as they occur in the order of the Alphabet.*

The *Britannica* did not take up all of the statements made by its predecessors about the organization of knowledge. Instead, it made or attempted to make certain conventions less closed and firm by not repeating them or by adapting them to its own ends. Though some obstacles to encyclopedic completeness could not be redressed by any available means, the new plan of the *Britannica* identifies two defining features of the form as hindrances capable of redress. Previous universal dictionaries organized all the terms of knowledge under their own headings and left readers at the mercy of their ability to discover and hold in memory all the relevant parts of a subject as they came across them: the *Encyclopédie*, like the *Cyclopædia* before it, relied upon extensive cross-references and a complex tree of knowledge to help guide users through the field.[64] Though the former was something of an innovation in the late 1720s, the roots of the latter could be traced back to the Bible, and scholars had used similar devices to represent the organization of all knowledge since at least the late Middle Ages. The defining encyclopedias of the mid-century, then, on the one hand made use of an important new organizational tool (cross-references) but on the other hand still appealed to a centuries-old model of overall connectivity. Encyclopedias on both sides of the channel continued to make use of one or both conventions for a further forty years.

The first edition of the *Britannica*, in contrast, boldly—or brashly—did away with both. Smellie objected in particular to the "lack of intrinsic logic" in alphabetical arrangement. The *Cyclopædia*, in the words of the preface of the third edition, was nothing more than "a book of threads and patches, rather than a scientific dictionary of arts and sciences; and considering the letters of the alphabet as the categories, the arrangement was certainly inconvenient as well as antiphilosophical."[65] The fabric topos speaks to a familiar concern with a lack of cohesion or uniformity. To the editors of the *Britannica*, the simple alphabetic deconstruction of learning that had been the defining feature of the encyclopedia for most of the century (and of other compendia for much longer) actually *dis*qualified the *Cyclopædia* as a useful scientific dictionary. Smellie composed his systems and treatises in order to counteract its lack of logic by gathering beneath the banners of individual arts and sciences all those terms that would otherwise be unproductively and incoherently scattered across the whole.[66] His article on astronomy, for example, occurs (as it should) between brief definitions of "astronomicals" and "Astrop-Wells" but separates them by some sixty-six pages. Its two-page counterpart in the *Cyclopædia*, in contrast, refers readers to nearly forty other entries across both volumes.

The proprietors of both encyclopedias made distinctions between their projects and the periodically published records of recent discoveries, Royal Society papers, and collections of "unconnected miscellanies, and detached essays" that constituted the fragments out of which they hoped to fashion a more complete understanding of the universe.[67] In both cases, those distinctions depended upon reflecting the presumed connectivity or systematicity of learning. In order to facilitate the transmission of true and complete knowledge, Chambers enlarged the categorical scope of the universal dictionary and deployed new features designed to demonstrate such connectivity. Smellie elected to perform part of that work primarily; rather than leave reconstruction to the reader, he wrote the systems and treatises to present a printed record and demonstrate a paused moment of the sort of mental activity that would with continued effort achieve what the *Cyclopædia* allegedly failed to facilitate.

When the full set of the first edition went on sale in 1771, the approximately 2400 pages of its three quarto volumes did not approach the size of the *Encyclopédie*.[68] That, however, soon changed. Under Tytler's editorial supervision, the second edition grew to ten quartos and 8595 pages. The eighteen quartos of the third edition (1788–97) made it the largest British encyclopedia of the century. This shift towards comprehensiveness involved a redefinition of literary boundaries as well as a specific and not uncontroversial program of appropriation. In addition to including several new systems and treatises on the arts and sciences as well as a wealth of new independent entries (including one on "Novelty, or Newness"), the second edition *Britannica* also made biography and history part of its province. The expansion was not without precedent: Dennis de Coetlogon included historical content in his *An universal history of arts and sciences* (1745), and *Martin's Magazine* published brief biographies of notable mathematicians and philosophers along with its collections of scientific knowledge, natural history, and conventional magazine fare. Even the *Encyclopédie* included a limited amount of biographical content. Smellie, however, despite his embrace of other innovations, believed such subjects had no place in a true dictionary of arts and sciences. Historical and biographical dictionaries predated the modern encyclopedias by several decades, and the two had remained essentially separate for most of the eighteenth century. These, in Smellie's opinion, remained the appropriate homes for such material, and the owners' decision to include them in the *Britannica* contributed to his departure from their employ.

Whether driven by Bell and Macfarquhar's desire to capture more market share by subsuming those encyclopedic subgenres or by swelling the work to make it appear more valuable to potential customers, the decision had a lasting effect on both the specific and categorical durability of the *Britannica*. Historical and historicized knowledge create a sense of certitude despite practical obsolescence. Discovery might quickly render knowledge of the arts and sciences out-of-date, but publishers and readers alike could to some extent rely on the biographies of the notable dead not to change or require constant revision. Robert Ainsworth, for instance, will always have been born at Woodyale in Lancashire, and he will always have published a Latin and English Dictionary in quarto in 1736.[69] No part of his life or the entry on it should have to change unless proven factually incorrect or insufficiently detailed.[70] While possible, such eventualities were certainly less likely to occur in brief biographical accounts than in entries related to arts and sciences even of equal or lesser length. By adding biography, the publishers dramatically increased the ratio of durable-to-changeable knowledge in the edition. This gave it a tremendous advantage as a knowledge commodity over both its prior incarnation as well as its contemporary competitors.

Tytler offers a substantial defense for the integration of these parts of knowledge into the whole by appealing to the *Britannica*'s established concern with maximizing utility and unity. "After surveying any particular science," Tytler proclaims, "it will be found equally useful and entertaining to acquire some notion of the private history of such eminent persons as have either invented, cultivated, or improved the particular art or science in which our attention has recently been engaged."[71] He applied similar logic to the inclusion of expanded geographical coverage. The preface repeatedly stresses conceptual unity and highlights the means by which it at once reflects the connections made by the human mind and aids that mind in pursuing those connections. An interest in a given art or science begins the journey; the art or science leads to biographies of its notable practitioners; biography refers the reader to geography; geography returns the reader to a science the study of which might lead elsewhere and begin the cycle anew. All inform a more complete understanding of the whole.

Time, "a succession of phenomena in the universe," links everything to everything else.[72] The relationships are not always causal; they are even less frequently clear. According to the concept of time held by the publishers of the *Britannica*, however, it was inextricably linked to a sense of progress. The histories appended to each science give a profound impression of both human intellectual development in the arts and sciences and the implicit possibility of continued achievement. The treatise on war—a new and lengthy addition to the second edition—contains the following assessment of the other sciences: "of most other sciences the principles are fixed, or at least they may be ascertained by the assistance of experience; there needs nothing but diligence to learn them, or a particular turn of mind to practice them. Philosophy, mathematics, architecture, and many others, are all founded upon invariable combinations."[73] Newton had revealed a universe governed by laws; the assumption that all laws could be discerned and comprehended permitted the encyclopedists to organize their works around that basis with the understanding that time and effort would discover all secrets and make each edition more complete than the last. Eventually the encyclopedia would catch up to the universe it represented.

The addition of history to the second edition enabled the encyclopedia to tell the story of knowledge so far. "Air," for example, merited only three lines in the first *Britannica*. The second introduced the subject with essentially the same basic definition: "that invisible fluid which every where surrounds the globe." The entry goes on to recount the history of knowledge regarding the substance from that period during which "the component parts ... were beyond the reach of man's wisdom to discover" through the times and experiments of Galileo, Bacon, Otto de Guerick, Boyle, and Joseph Black—Tytler's contemporary and later one of his consulting experts.[74] "Air," like several other detached parts of knowledge as well as some fully treated systems, also outlines controversies regarding its nature that were still ongoing at or about the time of publication. In this way, the *Britannica* unified itself with the history and progress of knowledge. Time had led up to modernity and tremendous intellectual advances, but to the immediate user, time had also led up to the latest encyclopedia. More time and more advances would logically lead up to another.

In addition to accounting for the latest discoveries, however, the next edition also brought with it another revision that departed from its own established conventions. The third *Britannica* (1788–97) retained biography, history, systems, and treatises, but its editors entirely "jettisoned the earlier concerns about the relations between sciences."[75] The preface to this latest edition, like those of its predecessors, espouses the value of systematic reading and the importance of thinking in method while at the same specifically warning against attempts, whether ancient or modern, "to contract the furniture of the human mind into the compass of a nut-shell, and to give at once a complete chart of knowledge." A quotation from Thomas Reid's "A Brief Account of Aristotle's Logic" (1774) explains the new reasoning: "to make a perfect division (says Dr. Reid) a man must have a perfect comprehension of the whole subject at one view. When our knowledge of the subject is imperfect, any division we can make must be like the first sketch of a painter, to be extended, contracted, or mended, as the subject shall be bound to require."[76] No completely accurate rendition or deconstruction of the relationships among all the parts of knowledge could precede perfect knowledge of the whole as such; the divisions of the *Britannica* into separate systems, treatises, and detached terms and definitions were therefore best understood as aids to immediate comprehension and continued knowledge production rather than the reconstruction of a master system.

The first and second editions of the *Britannica* had perpetuated the encyclopedia's attachment to representing the order of all knowledge; they brought more of its terms together into large treatises on the sciences, and further attempted to relate those sciences to each other. The third *Britannica*, in contrast, wrote that part of the pursuit of complete knowledge out of its mission statement. To the encyclopedists, the already abundant but still incomplete knowledge of the arts and sciences necessarily left any conceptual whole in a state of fragmentation. That fragmentation, however, was not necessarily adverse to the long-term success of the encyclopedic project or to the process of Enlightenment. In *The Wealth of Nations* (which beat the first number of the second *Britannica* to the presses by just over a year), Adam Smith linked the development of the knowledge economy to the division of labor and the progress of society in general:

All the improvements in machinery, however, have by no means been the inventions of those who had occasion to use the machines. Many improvements have been made by the ingenuity of the makers of the machines, when to make them became the business of a peculiar trade; and some by that of those who are called philosophers or men of speculation, whose trade it is not to do anything, but to observe every thing; and who, upon that account, are often capable of combining together the powers of the most distant and dissimilar objects. In the progress of society, philosophy or speculation becomes, like every other employment, the principal or sole trade and occupation of a particular class of citizens. Like every other employment too, it is subdivided into a great number of different branches ... and this subdivision of employment in philosophy, as well as in every other business, improves dexterity, and saves time. Each individual becomes more expert in his own peculiar branch, more work is done upon the whole, and the quantity of science is considerably increased by it.[77]

Progress, Smith writes, entails specialization in all employments, and it is specialization that advances the course of learning. The "whole" in this case refers not to a comprehensibly unified circle of arts and sciences but rather to the simple fact of its many parts, knowledge of which may and eventually must be increased independently of one another.

The third edition of the *Britannica* in essence pursued precisely this philosophy. The encyclopedic project was collapsing under its own weight; progress had made older methods of organization unsustainable and the encyclopedia less useful both to its own ends and to those of its readers. If in 1728 Chambers wondered if the enclosures and partitions between the arts and sciences might be thrown down so that learning could advance without restrictions, then sixty years later, it seemed that learning could no longer advance without them. The new *Britannica* embraced specialization and created a literary workspace wherein and from which the advancement of learning could continue unburdened by one aspect of general completeness. The emphasis on expert contributions and the sharpening of disciplinary boundaries established the course by which the *Britannica* became, according to the preface of the eleventh edition of 1910, a "pre-eminent" reference work—"not merely a register but an instrument of research."[78] In order to remain useful, the encyclopedia had to adapt. In doing so, it changed the face of Enlightenment.

In 1796, months before the last volume of the third *Britannica* appeared, the first number of another Scottish encyclopedia emerged from the presses of Perth. The twenty-three volumes of the *Encyclopædia Perthensis* (1796–1806), its title page announced, were specifically "intended to supersede the use of all other English books of reference." The first page of its preface offered readers the following neat, albeit reductive, history of the form:

> In all the affairs of man, nothing contributes so much to his comfort as ARRANGEMENT. It is the saviour of much time, trouble and expence; and the author of much ease and convenience. The application of such remarks to literature, is obvious and natural; but for the arrangement of Geography into Gazetteers, or of Biography into Dictionaries, how many days might be occupied in ascertaining the site of a city, or the æra of a name? Such books being found absolutely necessary therefore, every Art and Science gradually obtained its Dictionary; and, still improving, they collected under alphabetical arrangement in ONE book—this book, at first a little volume, gradually improved and enlarged into the Encyclopædiae of the present day; and the incredible number of copies of the different works bearing this title which have been sold, and are daily selling,

affords a better proof of the utility of such laborious compilations than any reasoning.[79]

The difficulty of locating, acquiring, and comprehending knowledge of the individual arts and sciences, according to the *Perthensis*, led to the creation of specific dictionaries; their continued advancement in turn led to the creation of the modern encyclopedia. The size of encyclopedias then began to increase until the problematic proliferation of writing about the arts and sciences took place wholly within the encyclopedias themselves. Now, the editors claimed, readers once again needed rescuing. This, unsurprisingly, was best accomplished by yet one more encyclopedia. The *Perthensis* thus took its place as the latest in a long line of attempts by writers of all kinds to save readers from the proliferation of print—whether beyond the bounds of encyclopedias or between their covers. The greatest debt the *Perthensis* acknowledges, however, is to the plan of the *Britannica*.

Once More, with Feeling: Romantic Universalities

In the space of four years at the end of the eighteenth century, Friedrich Wolf's *Prolegomena ad Homerum* (1795) made ancient allegorical readings of Homer's epics entirely the province of history and pronounced any unity they evinced the accomplishment of other minds after the fact; the proprietors of the third *Britannica* (1788–97) advanced the course of specialist knowledge production and disciplinary division by completing the last volumes of their longest and most successful encyclopedia to date; and William Wordsworth and Samuel Taylor Coleridge published the first edition of the *Lyrical Ballads* (1798), which later scholars would mark as an inaugural text of English Romanticism.[80] All three works departed from the established practices or conventional wisdom of previous ages. At the same moment that the first two, albeit in very different ways, formalized new limits on the scope or powers of even the most celebrated individual minds, however, the authors of the third boldly identified themselves and their craft as the last, best mediators of a new kind of complete knowledge.

The language of parts and wholes as well as a strong emphasis on the concept of completeness permeates much of Romantic discourse. In *Biographia Literaria* (1817), Coleridge, who contributed to and did much to codify that discourse, described the poetic creation of an "organic unity" that comprehended the formal characteristics and imagery of the verse as well as the animating passion of the poet (of which the verse was evidence) and the passionate response of the reader. The poet, according to Coleridge, organized the poem according to a naturally possessed instinct as opposed to an artificially imposed plan. The "pre-Romantic" long poems of Thomson and Young supposedly operated on this basis, although, as I have already noted, the popularity they enjoyed did not come without criticism regarding what some perceived as their structural incoherence.

Coleridge's re-conceptualization of poetic unity around principles of instinct and imagination framed the completeness of poetry in terms similar to those articulated by Le Bossu in his *Traité du poème épique* and by Pope in the preface to his translation of the *Iliad*. According to Coleridge, the poem achieves a particular kind of unity that engages what he calls the "high spiritual instinct of the human being compelling us to seek unity by harmonious adjustment." This instinct, he writes, establishes "the principle, that all the parts of an organized whole must be assimilated to the more important and essential parts."[81] In the late seventeenth century, Le Bossu insisted that detecting the unity of an epic required the reader accurately to identify the main action and form an appropriate understanding of the subordinate status of events and information ancillary or in service to that action; Pope wrote in the early eighteenth century that Homer introduced to his poems only those "strokes" of knowledge from the circle of arts and sciences that he deemed necessary to his subject. All three authors claim that the unity of the poems they describe depends upon a structural hierarchy in which all elements are connected but some are more important than others.

Coleridge, however, assigns the creation, detection, and completion of that unity to a common human instinct that he also describes in hierarchical terms suggestive of progressive and transcendent spirituality. The old and highly conventional praise of Homer and Virgil once held that their comprehensive knowledge and unifying power brought them and their poems closer to divinity; Coleridge's new understanding of completeness allowed poets and readers alike to conceive of themselves as sharing in that power without necessarily having to possess that knowledge. He was not writing of epic poems when he wrote of this instinct. The passage occurs in one of many chapters in *Biographia Literaria* devoted to the *Lyrical Ballads*—the text that introduced the "historical phenomenon" of the Romantic fragment poem.[82] As the designation suggests, the fragment poem represents the opposite of the epic in conventional terms of length, scope, and completeness. Fragments, though, could achieve the same "organic" unity as epics because as poems they too, as Mary Poovey notes, "brought together the poet and the reader to relish the most elevated human capacities: 'passion' and 'the imagination.'"[83] The high status granted to these capacities by the Romantic poets set them not apart from but rather above those capacities of intellect and memory that had yet to achieve the kind of fully complete knowledge envisioned by Bacon, once ascribed to Homer, and recently abandoned by the *Britannica*.

The Romantic elevation of these capacities effectively served as another strategy of information management that set poetry in seeming opposition to other kinds of modern knowledge production. Poovey explains:

> The romantic poets' emphasis on the poet's imaginative engagement with the phenomenal world, which initiated the passion that became the reader-engaging poem, paradoxically stripped the trope of the organic whole of any literal connection to natural history. Whereas natural history, like the biological study of life processes that eventually supplanted it, privileged the observer's literal vision—his ability to see and catalogue the physical features of organic creatures—romantic criticism and poetry effaced the details of the physical world through a process of imaginative vision that surpassed and subsumed the literal act of seeing.[84]

The imaginative vision makes connections not between the numberless details of the physical world but through or perhaps even in spite of them; it operates beyond the capacity of physical vision—the most comprehensive human sense, according to Locke—and unifies what separately appeared before the microscopic, telescopic, and unaided eye.

One of the most popular poems of the late eighteenth century sought to maintain a connection between scientific and poetic modes of composition that would transcend what either mode could accomplish alone. Coleridge, in a letter to John Thewall, claimed to have disliked Erasmus Darwin's *The Botanic Garden* (1791) in unequivocal terms.[85] According to Alan Bewell, however, "in the absence of Darwin's verse, Coleridge might not have cherished the idea of a 'philosophical poem,' nor is it likely that Robert Southey's encyclopedic epics, with their heavy load of prose notes, would ever have taken cumbersome flight. With Darwin's *The Loves of the Plants*, a new nature swam into romanticism's ken."[86] The existence at the turn of the century of long philosophical poems and what critics remain content to call "encyclopedic epics" suggests that the links between or among the forms remained in place. While Darwin's desire to "enlist Imagination under the banner of Science, and to lead her votaries from the looser analogies, which dress out the imagery of poetry, to the stricter ones, which form the ratiocination of philosophy" characterizes poetry and science neither as outright adversaries nor as complete strangers, it does suggest the extent to which he viewed them as already parted by methodological or conceptual standards of knowledge production and dissemination.[87]

The actual text, moreover, proceeds not by eliding or collapsing the distinction but by reifying it in the stylistic distinctions and graphical divisions between the verse and the annotation. Darwin, for example, matches the call of the anthropomorphized (and deified) Spring to her "nymphs of primeval fire" with a footnoted explication of "the fluid matter of heat" that goes on for more than half a column and refers the reader to two additional notes in the canto.[88] Another note on "the dread Gymnotus" explores how *Gymnotus electrocus*—the electric eel—produces its charge; over the course of a full half-page, the note introduces the anatomy of the relevant aquatic organs, the operation of the Leyden jar, the principles of attraction and the inverse square law, and a suggestion as to why no land animal possesses the same power.[89] Philosophical notes such as these constitute the bulk of the work.

Whereas Pope had deployed overwhelming documentation in the *Dunciad Variorum* as part of his program to advance the autonomy of poetry, Darwin does the same in order to accomplish the reverse. The science was not made for the poem, but the poem for the science. His argument in defense of those references to ancient mythology and the presence of Gnomes, Sylphs, and Salamanders throughout the verse further underscores the limits of its ability to do the work it once did or was thought to have done:

> Many of the important operations of nature were shadowed or allegorized in the heathen mythology, as the first Cupid springing from the egg of Night, the marriage of Cupid and rape of Proserpine, the congress of Jupiter and Juno, the death and resuscitation of Adonis, &c. many of which are ingeniously explained in the works of Bacon... Allusions to those fables were therefore thought proper ornaments to a philosophical poem, and are occasionally introduced either as represented by the poets, or preserved on the numerous gems and medallions of antiquity.[90]

The representations that by themselves had, according to ancient allegoresis, served to describe the operations of nature become in Darwin's modern poem (and via Bacon's decoding) mere ornaments requiring the support of unadorned and extensive prose treatments distinct from those representations.

The presence of both verse and notes implies the inadequacy of either to render the knowledge it contains comprehensible to the reader as a whole. On one hand, the notes by themselves suffer from the same complexity and organizational disjunctions that stymied true encyclopedic unity; on the other hand, the verse by itself lacks the detail of the notes and can only be considered encyclopedic in the synecdochical sense suggested by Pope in his preface to the *Iliad*. Darwin, Michael Page writes, "in a sense sought to do for Linnaeus and his system of taxonomy what Pope had done for Newton and celestial mechanics in the *Essay on Man*, except that Darwin engaged the system of Linnaeus from the viewpoint of a man of science first and a poet second, rather than simply that of a keen cultural observer."[91] Pope may have prefaced his essay with a prose justification for presenting his system in verse, but he otherwise allowed that verse to stand largely on its own. Page's assessment of Darwin, meanwhile, reaffirms that while Darwin may have believed that the poet and the man of science could occupy the same mind and body, he did not necessarily allow that they could operate at the same time. One came before the other.[92] The same holds true for Darwin's text: with respect to representing human knowledge of the natural world, the two kinds of writing—verse and annotation, poetry and science—remain apart. If that knowledge somehow could or does cohere into a whole, it does not do so on the page or in the book.

Darwin undoubtedly did recall Pope's *Essay* during the composition of the two works that constitute *The Botanic Garden*. The known universe, however, had changed a great deal in the time gone by, and rather than limit the scope of his inquiry to what humanity *could* know, he acknowledged the limitations of his poem and its inability to keep pace with and account for what humanity might know in the future. Darwin's embrace of change and openness to the inevitable obsolescence or supersession of some part of his own poem and understanding of nature constitute a critical component of the work's Romantic turn. Pope gave to God alone the power to "see worlds on worlds compose one universe,/observe how system into system runs / What other planets circle others suns."[93] Humanity, however, had by 1791 seen more and further than Pope would have hoped or likely anticipated—perhaps even to the ends of time and the universe:

> Flowers of the sky! Ye to age must yield,
> Frail as your silver sisters of the field!

Star after star from Heaven's high arch shall rush,
Sun sink on suns, and systems systems crush,
Headlong extinct, to one dark center fall,
And death and night and chaos mingle all!

The note to the passage credits the astronomer William Herschel's observations of "the vacant spaces in some parts of the heavens, and the correspondent clusters in their vicinity" for leading him to believe that the universe might one day contract and "coalesce in one mass."[94] Only a decade earlier, Herschel's discovery of the planet later dubbed Uranus had effectively doubled the size of the solar system.

In the face of such dramatic changes to the structure and fixity of the heavens, the permanence of a poem dedicated to the study of natural history must have seemed scarcely worth considering except inasmuch as it advanced and became part of that history. This is precisely the end and fate Darwin hoped to achieve with *The Botanic Garden*—a hope perhaps signified by its title. In the sixteenth and seventeenth centuries, Bewell writes, botanic gardens were "conceived as recreated Edens, as attempts to recover or recollect the original unity of a Creation that had once existed in a single location before being dispersed by the Fall of Man. They sought to recreate this lost nature, John Prest observes, by gathering 'the scattered pieces of the jigsaw together in one place into an epitome or encyclopaedia of creation.'" In the second half of the eighteenth century, however, they "were more prospective than retrospective ... less about the recovery of a lost order of nature than about making something new."[95] In his Apology, Darwin posts a sign to that effect before the entrance to his own garden:

> It may be proper here to apologize for many of the subsequent conjectures on some articles of natural philosophy, as not being supported by accurate investigate or conclusive experiments. Extravagant theories however in those parts of philosophy, where our knowledge is yet imperfect, are not without their use; as they encourage the execution of laborious experiments, or the investigation of ingenious deductions, to confirm or refute them.[96]

As I have already demonstrated, by the end of the eighteenth century encyclopedias like the *Britannica* operated according to similar principles, but they did so on the other side of a formal divide that would not admit of versification or even the total abandonment of alphabetical order as an organizational method.

The natural philosophers responsible for producing the knowledge and in many cases the actual articles of the *Britannica* did not, in William Wordsworth's opinion, share in the passion of the poet. Indeed, as Maureen McLane writes, "Wordsworth's 'Poet,' allied with a generalized human pleasure-project, is implicitly an enemy both of professionalization and of specialization."[97] Just as the scope and volume of human learning as well as the growing number of its producers began to accelerate the process of division within the fields of knowledge production, Wordsworth began a project that made the poet and poetry a means by which such divisions could be transcended. If the pursuit of comprehensively complete knowledge had finally left the "Man of Science" engaged in an isolated and individual endeavor that entailed no "habitual and direct sympathy" connecting him to his fellow human beings, as Wordsworth believed, then the Poet could re-forge the connections by appealing to what he construed as the essential knowledge of human experience.[98] Just as Pope had circumscribed the bounds of what Homer knew, and by extension what the poet had to know, Wordsworth further narrowed the scope of the learning required to write poetry. "The Poet writes under one restriction only," Wordsworth claimed in the revised *Preface* to the *Lyrical Ballads* (1802). "Namely, that of the necessity of giving immediate pleasure to a human Being possessed of that information which may be expected from him, not as a lawyer, a physician, a mariner, an astronomer, or a natural philosopher, but as a Man."[99] None of these different kinds of readers needed to possess the all of the particular knowledge of the others, and perhaps more importantly, neither did the poet who wrote for them.

For nearly 200 years, the progress of learning in each of those areas had threatened any attempt to address or capture them in writing with the likelihood of eventual obsolescence, and for nearly a century the work of comprehending in a single work all human knowledge about them had been the province of a species of composition to which obsolescence was really no threat at all. With the *Lyrical Ballads*, Wordsworth set out to produce a class of poetry "well adapted to interest mankind permanently," and throughout the career that followed he eschewed the defining features of "encyclopedic" poems like *The Botanic Garden* and embraced the possibilities of perpetual incompleteness.[100] Wordsworth's belief that the knowledge of the Poet constituted a "generalizable, imperial, transhistorical human 'inheritance,'" McLane claims, both reversed "the already established fields of connotation of 'poetry' and 'science'" and revivified the arguments made by Aristotle and Sidney on behalf of the former.[101] It also allowed a previously marginalized form of literature to reemerge with new features and functions not aligned with older modes of durability.

Wordsworth's inability to complete all three parts of *The Recluse* before his death put him in admirable company. Bacon did not see through to its end his plan to compile a comprehensive account of the "Phenomena of the Universe" and "every kind of experience"; nor did Pope live long enough to finish his "general map of man." Richardson had hoped to continue adding new letters to new editions of the novels that constituted his system of ethics, and Sterne may or may not have finished *Tristram Shandy* at all.[102] In some respects, the autobiographical epic that after Wordsworth's death became *The Prelude* rehearses (and offers to solve) a very Shandean problem. Like Tristram's struggle to arrive at the moment of his birth so that he might write the memoirs of his life, Wordsworth's "history of the Author's mind to the point where he was emboldened to hope that his faculties were sufficiently mature for entering the arduous labour which he had proposed for himself" became a substantial part of the work in its own right.[103] What Wordsworth and his executors labeled the "preparatory poem" turned out to be the magnum opus.

The Prelude represents both an endpoint and a new beginning for epic poetry as a functional account of complete knowledge. Wordsworth contemplated a work that would succeed and surpass Milton's *Paradise Lost*; the result was "the first example of what has since become a major genre: the account of the growth of an individual mind to artistic maturity, and of the sources of its creative powers."[104] Milton, according to his contemporary celebrants, supposedly told the story of all things and assigned a proper part in his poem to all objects in the whole circle of Being. As its autobiographical allusions suggest, Milton assigned himself a part in that circle as well. *The Prelude*, in contrast, makes autobiography its principal subject. Wordsworth draws the circle of Being around himself and attempts to achieve a sense of the universal through his own individual experience.

His repurposing of epic to account for his own origins as a poet instead of those of an entire civilization—a traditional epic subject—participates in a broader post-Enlightenment program of literary reform and to some extent reflects a more particular effort to shift the focus of historiography. Wordsworth, Jon Klancher writes, shared with authors such as Coleridge, Joanna Baillie, and William Godwin a sense that genre could be "used to produce, as Shelley put it, 'the seeds at once of its own and of social renovation.'" In 'Of History and Romance' (1797), Godwin, for example, promotes a "biographically focused historicism" ranged against the sweeping and abstract conjectural histories of the

Enlightenment.[105] His critique of such histories proceeds in part from their failure to engage readers via the emotional elements he claims are more conducive to holding interest and in part from their overarching incoherence. The history of nations abstracted from the "passions and peculiarities" of individuals, Godwin asserts, supply the reader with no clear ideas; "the mass, as fast as he endeavours to cement and unite it, crumbles from his grasp, like a lump of sand."[106] Godwin posits the human connections more readily made via biographical study as an alternative means of creating the sense of unity, and therefore understanding, that large-scale narrative historiography either failed adequately to facilitate or (more to the political point) forcefully imposed and thus distorted.

The authors of general histories, cognizant of the importance as well as the difficulty of managing so great a subject, typically insisted that their organizational methods would aid readers in comprehending the whole of human history as such. As *An Universal History* made clear, however, the scope of such projects could quickly overwhelm not only the readers but also the authors and editors responsible for them.[107] Godwin's call for a reformative inversion of the Enlightenment historiographical hierarchy, however, was actually predicated upon the implicit *in*completeness of the general. The histories supporting the hegemonic perspectives to which he objected—and which the modern part of *An Universal History* evinced in its account of an ascendant Europe—were inherently and critically flawed not because they contained too much but because, in some sense, they contained too little. A new form of historiography concerned with the individual rather than the general could place greater emphasis on details and discontinuities within the larger historical patterns represented (or misrepresented) by works that could not accommodate or simply did not have access to the particulars of all those events, actions, and actors around which they built their necessarily reductive unifying narratives.[108]

Godwin specifically references *An Universal History* as the antithesis of that for which he advocates. "I believe I should be better employed in studying one man," he writes, "than in perusing the abridgment of Universal History in sixty volumes. I would rather be acquainted with a few trivial particulars of the actions and disposition of Virgil and Horace, than with the lives of many men, and the history of many nations."[109] Even the "sixty volumes" of *An Universal History* (there were in fact sixty-five) constituted only an abridgment of *actual* history, and abridgments were in Godwin's opinion a prodigious waste of time. They could reveal historical patterns, but only the study of precisely that which they excluded could help humanity escape them. The "materials" of history required analysis in order to understand society as a mass; therefore, Godwin explains, we must "regard the knowledge of the individual, as that which can alone give energy and utility to the records of our social existence."[110] Godwin favorably weighs the study of "one man" against that of "sixty volumes" and knowledge of a "few" particulars against that of "many" men and nations because a more complete knowledge of human history—and by extension the power to direct its course in the future—begins in his philosophy with a more complete knowledge of the passions that drive human actions.

The rhetoric of his essay unsurprisingly reveals continuities with well-established tropes, methods, and challenges of knowledge production. The focus on the individual is in some sense simply an extension of the analytical process of subdivision applied by Jean Bodin to the study of history in the mid-sixteenth century; utility remains of paramount importance; and a reference to the "machine of society" perpetuates a mechanistic view of human existence characteristic of Enlightenment thought. His elevation of romance writers as the writers of "real history," moreover, likewise proceeds from the same pursuit of complete knowledge that had advanced the processes of innovation, differentiation, and recombination throughout the seventeenth and eighteenth centuries. Conventional historians could never resolve contradiction and (at least in the case of *An Universal History*) consequently made the acknowledgment of disagreements and the annotative inclusion of contradictory records parts of what made their works as complete as possible. They furthermore had to rely on precarious conjecture even in the contemplation of human character. Indeed, Godwin explains, so too did everyone else, for we have no unmediated access to other interiorities. The author of romance, in contrast, "must be permitted, we should naturally suppose, to understand the character which is the creature of his own fancy."[111] In other words, as Mark Phillips puts it, "the fiction writer ... has complete knowledge of his own creation."[112]

Authorial omniscience should allow the romance writer to achieve the analysis of individual passions essential to a fuller understanding of human history at large. The theory, though, ultimately fails in practice, and in the end Godwin stages a marginal retreat:

> There is, however, after all, a deduction to be made from this eulogium of the romance writer. To write romance is a task too great for the powers of man, and under which he must be expected to totter. No

man can hold the rod so even, but that it will tremble and vary from its course. To sketch a few bold outlines of character is no desperate undertaking; but to tell precisely how such a person would act in a given situation, requires sagacity scarcely less than divine. We never conceive a situation, or those minute shades in a character that would modify its conduct. Naturalists tell us that a single grain of sand more or less on the surface of the earth, would have altered its motion, and, in the process of ages, have diversified its events. We have no reason to suppose in this respect, that what is true in matter, is false in morals.[113]

Godwin's single grain of sand on the surface of the earth echoes Sterne's mistake in the dust of a butterfly's wing; there is too much in the mind as well as in the world to completely account for either. Romance writers could sketch outlines of human character just as epic poets introduced strokes of knowledge from the whole circle of arts and sciences—both might approach divinity, but neither could actually achieve it. Godwin suggests that when an individual possesses complete knowledge of just one person—even one created in his or her own imagination—then a god may be said to sojourn in a human body.

Wordsworth's poetry takes for its subject the potential of that impossibility. Compelled "either to lay up / New stores, or rescue from decay the old/By timely interference," Wordsworth fashions the *Prelude* into an encyclopedic body of self-knowledge that pursues a completeness entirely dependent upon a provisional coherence rather than a comprehensive collection of all data.[114] Wordsworth cannot completely know himself, nor lead the reader to complete knowledge of him, via a perfect recollection of all his thoughts, emotions, and experiences; the human memory does not under normal circumstances permit total recall, and when it does—an exceedingly rare occurrence—the results can leave the mind "overwhelmed by a chaos of impressions."[115] The condition, known as hyperthymestic syndrome, hyperthymesia, or "highly superior autobiographical memory," reveals the tension between completeness and utility at the level of cognitive neuropsychology: hyperthymestics often lack control over their extensive memories and suffer significant disruption as the past perpetually intrudes upon and dominates their experience of the present.[116]

The limitations of human memory become in Wordsworth's philosophy central to the creative power and the developmental progress of a poetic mind. "Remembering, for Wordsworth," Siskin observes, "is not a passive and arbitrary act of recollection; rather, it becomes an active and highly selective process by engendering its opposite. The poet forges a sense of identity in Books I and II of *The Prelude* not through perfect recall of childhood events and emotions, but by remembering *and* forgetting."[117] Priority attaches to certain images rather than others, and these images—these essential "spots of time"—form the foundation of self-knowledge even as their significance and substance change with additional time and conscious reflection.[118] These spots of time, altered by the poet's mind but also linked to physical locations and hence imbued with empirical validity, thus become the basis of a new and deliberate method of organizing knowledge that attempts to create the conditions under which that knowledge might finally be comprehended by both author and reader as organically complete. In short, Wordsworth made the end of his epic the development and exercise of a "mental power" capable of creating a whole despite—or perhaps thanks to—the seeming impossibility of recalling, recording, and comprehending comprehensive knowledge.[119]

* * *

In the previous century, Milton had made the unifying end of *Paradise Lost* the pursuit of such knowledge that would elevate the human condition—a pursuit that neither he nor his poem could complete and that in the postlapsarian world necessitated all of humanity to collect fragments towards a whole. By the 1770s, humanity had compiled volumes upon volumes of such fragments, but no whole had yet emerged. *Tristram Shandy* and *Encyclopædia Britannica* represent the collapse of claims to a kind of complete knowledge that was more and more self-evidently unachievable: the exploded view of a single life in *Tristram Shandy* satirized the will to systematize, and the "Systems" of the *Britannica* stepped away from the totalizing vision of earlier encyclopedias and onto the long path of disciplinary division. In the early nineteenth century, progress in knowledge production entailed division even at the institutional level; in 1818, Joseph Banks, the long-serving President of the Royal Society, communicated to John Barrow his fear that specialized groups like the Linnaean Society and the Geological Society of London would weaken the standing of the institution from whence they originated. "I see plainly," Banks told him, "that all these new-fangled Associations will finally dismantle the Royal Society, and not leave the Old Lady a rag to cover her."[120] The establishment of the Royal Astronomical Society quickly followed in 1820; Banks died the same year.

Coleridge, for his part, was somewhat less willing than other post-Enlightenment authors to give up the pursuit of complete knowledge in an encyclopedic sense. Even as he extolled the possibilities of poetic transcendence, he remained devoted to the idea that the whole circle of arts and sciences could be united and possessed by an individual mind—provided that mind was trained to "contemplate not *things* only, or for their own sake alone, but likewise and chiefly the *relations* of things, either their relations to each other, or to the observer, or to the state and apprehension of the hearers."[121] To his mind, the attainment of universal knowledge required a similar power to that deployed by Wordsworth in his poetry, for, as Pope's *Dunciad* implied and the encyclopedias of the eighteenth century made clear, it could not emerge from a simple catalogue of information or from the application to that catalogue of arbitrary organizational methods like alphabetization and cross-referencing. Coleridge attempted to make the progressive succession of intuitive or instinctive ideas that unified in the mind the objects of the senses the foundational method of the *Encyclopædia Metropolitana* (1817), the first volumes of which eschewed alphabetization in favor of "exhibiting the arts and sciences in their philosophical harmony."[122] The general map of the encyclopedia resembled the ten-year plan to study universal science Coleridge had set out for himself in 1796.[123]

The concept of completeness, then, remained very much a part of encyclopedic discourse at the turn of the century. Coleridge's section on the science of method in the *Metropolitana* insists that, "it is only in the union of these two branches [external Nature and intellectual existence] of one and the same Method, that a complete and Modern genuine Philosophy can be said to exist."[124] He had hoped to achieve that union. As an encyclopedia, however, the *Metropolitana* proved a commercial failure. Readers accustomed to the encyclopedias of Rees and the *Britannica* found its lack of alphabetization too great a hindrance to utility, and by the time the 59th and final part of the work appeared in 1845 (thirteen years after Coleridge died), the *Metropolitana* could no longer hope to overcome entrenched conventions or to reverse the momentum of disciplinarity. The alphabetical arrangement of "miscellaneous and lexicographical" information in the fourth and final division of the work comprises twelve of its thirty volumes and amounts to a massive editorial concession regarding Coleridge's original projection. The claim of the encyclopedia to lead its readers to complete knowledge in the fullest sense of the phrase collapsed in the midst of production.[125]

According to the British mathematician and logician Augustus De Morgan—himself the author of two major articles (the Calculus of Functions and the Theory of Probability) for the *Metropolitana* as well as hundreds more for the *Penny Cyclopædia*—no encyclopedia had or likely could achieve that kind of completeness. In an 1861 "Review of Cyclopædias" occasioned by the recent publication of the 21-volume eighth edition of the *Britannica* and Charles Knight's 22-volume *The English Cyclopædia*—two works that stood "at the head of the two great branches into which pantological undertakings are divided"—De Morgan names Johann Heinrich Alsted's *Scientiarum Omnium Encyclopædia* (1629) as "the true parent of all the Encyclopædias, or collections of treatises, or works in which that character predominates." *Encyclopædia Britannica* had followed in the footsteps of Alsted by advancing the model of self-contained systems and treatises, but it also persisted in supplementing those treatises with shorter articles and dictionary-like definitions of the detached parts of knowledge.

De Morgan saw the attempt to combine these two organizational tactics as inimical to the grandest aspirations of the encyclopedic project. Systems and treatises, he suggests, are the qualifying features of a true encyclopedia; Chambers's *Cyclopædia*, therefore, could at best lay claim to being "the first great *dictionary*."[126] Maximal utility, however, demanded both, and though it stood in seeming opposition to completeness editors regularly and necessarily gave usefulness priority. "It is true," De Morgan explains, "that the treatises are intended to do a good deal; and that the Index, if it be good, knits the treatises and the dictionary into one whole of reference. Still there are two stools, and between them a great deal will fall to the ground."[127] The conditional and tentative statements of the first sentence clash with the definitive and fatalistic assessment of the second. The dictionary part of the *Britannica*, like the Lexicographical and Miscellaneous portion of the *Metropolitana*—a "great failure," in De Morgan's view—could not compare with the treatises, and the gaps between them left the whole irredeemably flawed. The "defect" of the dictionary, he writes, "is incompleteness"; the systems contained more than the dictionary part could be relied upon fully to deconstruct and offer back to readers in isolated articles. "Practically," he concludes, "we believe this defect cannot be avoided: two plans of essentially different structure cannot be associated on the condition of each or either being allowed to abbreviate the other."[128]

The brief history of encyclopedias that De Morgan offers looks back on the form from nearly a hundred years into the long life of the *Encyclopædia Britannica*. In that history, the organizational methods intended by Chambers, Diderot, and D'Alembert to facilitate the comprehension of complete knowledge across the whole circle of arts and sciences become historical anomalies or outliers; rather than finally making complete knowledge possible, the universal dictionaries of the eighteenth century seem to have interrupted a tradition of encyclopedic works that emphasized systematic and programmatic learning. The *Britannica* offered a compromise that helped secure its longevity but that also compelled the reader, in De Morgan's words, "to regard the *Britannica* as a splendid body of treatises on all that can be called heads of knowledge, both greater and smaller; with help from the accompanying dictionary, but not of the most complete character." Incompleteness, in other words, "is in the casting of the work," and in terms of encyclopedic practices—the practices of compiling, organizing, and actually using an encyclopedia—it would have to remain so.[129]

As to the *Metropolitana*, an anonymous contributor to the *Quarterly Review* in 1863 characterized the flaws of the original plan in terms that speak to the persistent separation of literary kinds and intellectual endeavors that followed from the pursuit of complete knowledge in the seventeenth and eighteenth centuries. "The plan," explains the author, "was the proposal of the poet Coleridge, and it had at least enough of a poetical character to be eminently unpractical."[130] The concepts of completeness championed by early Romantic authors such as Wordsworth and Coleridge had in essence offered a set of solutions to the challenges of knowledge production and management that drove the collapse of claims to complete knowledge over the course of the Enlightenment. By the mid-nineteenth century, if we take the *Quarterly Review* as a guide, those solutions had become markers of specifically "literary" endeavors and achievements distinct from the non-literary and evidently "practical." Complete knowledge—if only for the time being—apparently belonged to the poets.

The modern disciplines into which the historical Enlightenment reorganized knowledge and which have been the dominant platforms of institutional knowledge production for two centuries continue to operate in general according to the logic of divided intellectual labor. The "narrow but deep" knowledge privileged by disciplinarity proceeds largely, though not exclusively, via specialization: "expert" and "expertise" almost always come with qualifying prepositions that reify the separateness of different kinds of learning. One is an expert "of," "at," "with," or "in," but to be an expert at everything is oxymoronic. Ideally, disciplinary divisions enable or result in the reconstitution of limited but more manageable wholes better suited to the continued production of more (and more expert) knowledge. "To invoke the authority of a discipline," as Robert Post writes, is "to appeal to what Kant might call the regulative idea of a unitary and 'formalized method of knowing and expressing the knowledge of a given subject-matter.'"[131] If the body of knowledge produced within any given discipline cannot be entirely known to any given practitioner, then at least the codified methods and discourse of that discipline should allow any part of it to be ascertained by the initiated member and put to the purpose of further knowledge production. The turning of the key implies the completeness of the lock.

This unity, however, typically fails to inhere. Julie Klein has argued that the notion of disciplinary unity is in fact "triply false: minimizing or denying differences that exist across the plurality of specialties grouped loosely under a single disciplinary label, undervaluing connections across specialties of separate disciplines, and discounting the frequency and impact of cross-disciplinary influences."[132] In practice, then, modern disciplinarity begins and ends as incomplete knowledge: it presupposes the necessary fragmentation of some greater whole, its parts tend to reproduce division within themselves, and every productive foray beyond any of its partitions reveals the inadequacy or arbitrariness of circumscription. Such forays, moreover, are often made more difficult by the methodological and discursive differences that distinguish disciplines and define what counts as "knowledge" within each one.

Smellie composed the protodisciplinary systems and treatises of the first *Britannica* in the name of greater utility; the experts who wrote those of later editions expanded the work of the encyclopedia from register to research tool. The modern practices, programs, and goals of transdisciplinarity, multidisciplinarity, crossdisciplinarity, interdisciplinarity, and dedisciplinarity, however, all indicate the limited utility of the base as a platform for the production of more complete knowledge. My purpose here is neither to recount the history of disciplinarity as it unfolded in the nineteenth and twentieth centuries nor to examine how it currently functions (or malfunctions) in the colleges, universities, or other institutions wherein it has become entrenched. I rather introduce it as an example of an Enlightenment epiphenomenon that has in some respects outlived its usefulness but not yet been wholly replaced by a new set of models or protocols. If the pursuit of complete knowledge is to continue in a new phase or extension of Enlightenment, then the movement away from disciplines and the limits they impose on the conditions and substance of knowledge production requires that old structures and organizational models, however necessary or useful they once were, not reassert themselves—that new interdisciplinarity does not become old discipline writ large.

Coda: The Angel and the Algorithm

Though by the early eighteenth century it had largely become the province of charlatans and mountebanks, magic—according to Daniel Defoe—once signified great wisdom. Its earliest practitioners, he writes, were "Men of Knowledge" who observed the motions of the stars, searched into the Arcana of Nature, and seemed to possess a greater understanding of the universe than those around them. "A *Magician*," he claims, "was no more or less in the ancient Chaldean Times, than a *Mathematician*, a Man of Science, who stor'd with Knowledge and Learning, as Learning went in those Days, was a kind of walking Dictionary to other People, and instructed the rest of Mankind in any Niceties and Difficulties which occur'd to them."[1]

The state of learning in antiquity, Defoe observes, was but slight when compared to knowledge in its current condition. Nevertheless, a century after Bacon's *Great Instauration*, seventy years into the life of the Royal Society, and even as Defoe published *A compleat system of magick* (1729), encyclopedists like Ephraim Chambers still believed that the right store of knowledge and an efficient method of presenting it could keep these "dictionaries" on their feet. If readers would but observe the connections suggested by the genealogical trees and follow the paths set out by the systems of cross-references, then they might be able to comprehend the whole circle of arts and sciences in its entirety. Seventy years after the first *Cyclopædia* appeared, however, the eighteen volumes of the third *Britannica* gave up the attempt to represent knowledge as a comprehensible totality and made it clear once more that to possess complete knowledge in its fullest sense required something beyond the capacities of both the individual mind and the printed book.

New technologies and methods have already transcended or transformed some of the processes that shaped the features and functions of

164

the historical Enlightenment, but at the same time and in some of those same areas the same dynamics remain operational. The Age of Print may have given ground to the Digital Age, but the potential for new kinds of knowledge production that has come with increased connectivity, cloud computing, and the expansion of the digital archive has brought with it a number of features, tropes, and conflicts characteristic of "new" knowledge production in the seventeenth and eighteenth centuries. While some of the connections between this moment and that are perhaps happy accidents of metaphor, others are more significant similarities involving technology, literature, and the ways in which changes in both spheres continue to revolve around the problems of knowledge management and the limits of the human intellect.

More is different, in other words, but it is not *completely* different. Mark Horowitz, in an interview with mathematician and computer scientist Martin Wattenberg, notes that "the biggest problem of the Petabyte Age won't be storing all that data, it'll be figuring out how to make sense of it." Wattenberg then describes the purpose of his work and the usefulness of visualizing large data sets:

> You can talk about terabytes and exabytes and zettabytes, and at a certain point it becomes dizzying. The real yardstick to me is how it compares with a natural human limit, like the sum total of all the words you'll hear in your lifetime. That's surely less than a terabyte of text. Any more than that and it becomes incomprehensible by a single person, so we have to turn to other means of analysis.[2]

Wattenberg describes a relationship between data and comprehension in which, as ever, extensiveness and utility do not necessarily correlate. The "natural" limits of human comprehension have informed the development of alternative analytical, organizational, and representational methods for centuries. Wattenberg's words are thus reminiscent of many of the arguments made in the poems, novels, histories, magazines, and encyclopedias that have been the focus of this study.

Indeed, some encyclopedias continue to pursue complete knowledge in much the same way they did at the end of the historical Enlightenment. Over the course of its long life, the *Britannica* has by a kind of metonymy become the hero of an epic narrative that began in 1768:

> In a world where questionable information is rampant, we provide products that inspire confidence, with content people can trust. We do this, as we have for many years, by collaborating with experts,

scholars, educators, instructional designers, and user-experience specialists; by subjecting their work to rigorous editorial review; and by combining it all into learning products that are useful, reliable, and enjoyable.[3]

The opening phrase recalls countless movie trailers featuring the thunderous voice of the late Don LaFontaine. The threat of rampant, questionable information is akin to the "overwhelming mass of writing" fretted by authors and critics in the eighteenth century—a mass in which, as David McKitterick writes, "choice was difficult, and where the poor, the shoddy and the immoral were granted status equal to the best in writing, content, or morals."[4] In the modern face of that threat, the trustworthy, confidence-inspiring *Britannica* somewhat appropriately carries on its quest as it has *for many years.*

This is not to suggest that the *Britannica* or users' experience of it has gone unaltered by technological change. Digitization saves subscribers roughly 3.4 cubic feet of space in their homes and some 143 pounds on their bookshelves; it also eliminates the need for indices and alphabetical arrangement—previously perhaps the defining feature of reference works. An RSS feed will even send weekly news of updated and revised articles, including current events. Having said that, the online *Britannica* remains relatively expensive to access, a number of professional editors still supervise the production of the work, and they continue to rely largely upon experts and specialists. As of 2008, users can generate content and offer editorial suggestions, but a strict editorial hierarchy remains in place, and according to the submission guidelines, relatively few user contributions will meet the institutional standards—standards that apply to subject as well as content. The *Britannica* is thus more open now than in the past, but it continues in general to follow the agenda set by Tytler and Macfarquhar at the end of the eighteenth century: professionals and experts ultimately decide what does and does not constitute what Theodore Pappas, *Britannica's* current Chief Development Officer and Executive Editor, calls the "core knowledge" needed "to understand the world around us, past and present." The scale of the venture has changed, but the principles remain the same.

Wikipedia unquestionably constitutes a new paradigm of encyclopedic knowledge production, but it too has failed to escape all of the issues that rose to prominence in the first Age of Encyclopedias. As of January 2014, Wikipedia comprehends over 22 million articles, nearly 4.5 million of which are in English. As suggested by its own statistics page, the sheer size and perpetual alteration of the database make any attempt to read it in its entirety another kind of Shandean supertask: reading at the rate of 600 words per minute for sixteen hours a day would still take readers more than seven years to finish it—by which point, "so much would have changed with the parts they had already read that they would have to start over."[5] The more one reads of Wikipedia, the more one shall have to read.

Lack of paper makes it possible. The first entry in a long list of what Wikipedia is not—a paper encyclopedia—acknowledges that there is no practical limit to what can be covered. Wikipedia can allot "space" to more subjects that typically fall outside *Britannica*'s purview; comprehensive coverage is thus possible to an extent unimaginable to the likes of Chambers, Smellie, and their collaborators. Synopses of contemporary films that disappear from the theaters in a week, for example, might appear in the database within hours of their release and remain in place for years; the *Britannica*, meanwhile, takes only scattershot notice of even the largest critical and box office triumphs.[6] Likewise, individuals of whom the experts at *Britannica* have never heard might very well have a Wikipedia entry thanks to equally unknown users who thought they merited it. The technology potentially allows anyone and anything to have its fifteen kilobytes of fame.

Nevertheless, some of Wikipedia's own contributors have raised, or rather re-raised, fundamental questions about their role as encyclopedists and the purpose of a form they are in the process of redefining. There is, the site tells us, "an important distinction between what *can* be done, and what *should* be done."[7] The ongoing contest between Wikipedia's associations of Deletionists and Inclusionists in essence hinges upon the potential and the potential dangers of the technological change. Each side has a page on the Wikimedia Foundation's Meta-Wiki site in which they can discuss the matter and (in true encyclopedist fashion) point out the flawed thinking of the opposition. The Deletionists' Meta-Wiki page states two goals: to (1) "outpace rampant inclusionism" and (2) "further our goal of a quality encyclopedia containing as little junk as possible."[8] The Inclusionists' page—ironically somewhat shorter— advocates changing Wikipedia "only when no knowledge would be lost" and states the group's agenda as "building the world's largest and most complete professional encyclopedia."[9] The phrase "most complete" has seen use in encyclopedias, dictionaries, guidebooks, and other reference works for centuries; the Inclusionists' use is therefore as much an echo as it is a clarion call.

This fight about the proper purview of an encyclopedia, while perhaps refreshed by technological change, was not born by it. As I mentioned in Chapter 5, history and biography had no place in the universal dictionaries of arts and sciences for most of the eighteenth century. When Colin Macfarquhar and Andrew Bell, the owners of the *Britannica*, decided that the second edition would include them, William Smellie disagreed strongly enough to leave their employ. Now, such content is completely naturalized to the general encyclopedia, but for some editors of Wikipedia, the same issue—how the encyclopedia will define completeness for itself and for its users—remains contested. The *Britannica's* version of encyclopedic knowledge, as long as it remains subject to review and reliant upon expert contributors, will likely never achieve the same degree of comprehensiveness as Wikipedia, but then again *Britannica* will also likely not have to face occasional affronts to its credibility in the form of misinformation, poor writing, unreliable sourcing, or evidence of interested interference.

Though for Wikipedia the debate between inclusivity and exclusivity is largely a philosophical one, the site also remains subject to certain practical considerations related to the technical limitations of the web browsers used to access content and (as ever) the perceived intellectual capacities of its human users. These issues, among others, have led Wikipedia to publish guidelines on acceptable article length that can impact the conceptualization, composition, and organization of the information contained by a given article. The democratization of knowledge and free access to it that have supposedly upended Enlightenment encyclopedism may not in all instances extend to those with slower internet connections or outdated web browsers that have difficulty rendering large files.[10] In Wikipedia's earlier days, the guidelines strongly recommended a maximum page size of 32 KB, which corresponds to just over 6000 words; such a ceiling would necessarily entail a degree of editorial selectivity and therefore a less than comprehensive single-article treatment of some if not most subjects. At 310 pages, the longest *Britannica* article (in print) would easily have surpassed this limit and faced a series of revisions, subdivisions, and splits designed to make it more manageable—albeit at an unquantifiable cost to its coherence.

This guideline, though, is not strictly technodeterministic. The Wikipedia article on article size states that, "readers may tire of reading a page much longer than about 30 to 50 KB." The suggestion that the contents of substantially longer entries be reorganized or redistributed into other articles recalls the worries of Sale, Psalmanazar, Martin, and Smellie as well as the words of countless other authors and editors who promised that their methods would at last make useful the material that "in the Original"—to borrow a phrase from George London and

Henry Wise's abridgment of *The compleat gard'ner*—"is so prolix and interwoven, that the reader was rather tir'd than inform'd."[11] Most of the longest Wikipedia articles are therefore lists, glossaries, and tables exempt from the standards of prose readability. The longest non-list article as of December 2013, "Richard Helms," is 308 KB, and what was once the longest biographical entry, "Larry Norman," was 280 KB. Until a 94 KB reduction in June 2013, the latter was flagged with the following notices: (1) "This article may contain an excessive amount of intricate detail that may only interest a specific audience" and (2) "This article may be too long to read and navigate comfortably."[12] If an editor or group of editors performs the splits and summations, then the reader in search of an equivalently detailed treatment will have to reconstruct the whole by following the links between and among the main and sub-articles in an exercise that goes back to the *renvois* of Chambers and Diderot. The page on article size offers a very neat, if not entirely helpful, summary of itself and the problem it describes: "This page in a nutshell: Articles should not be either too big or too small."[13] This latest experiment in encyclopedic knowledge production, then, has not yet resolved all of those tensions between completeness and utility that shaped the encyclopedic experiments of the eighteenth century.

Encyclopedias constitute a relatively small proportion of the content available via the World Wide Web. The pursuit of complete knowledge now involves trillions more bytes of data than the 32–50 KB that tire the average reader of Wikipedia and billions more again than the mere terabyte of text that Wattenberg claims would account for every word heard by a single person over the course of a lifetime. Google's mission "to organize the world's information and make it universally accessible and useful" applies the ethos of Enlightenment encyclopedism to the entirety of the internet—or rather, as much of the internet as it can index. Google's servers now process over one petabyte of data every 72 minutes; information management at that scale, Chris Anderson writes, "is not a matter of simple three- and four-dimensional taxonomy and order but of dimensionally agnostic statistics. It calls for an entirely different approach, one that requires us to lose the tether of data as something that can be visualized in its totality."[14] In other words, human modes and methods of comprehending the "completeness" of the internet have become obsolete.

Humans, however, have not. Google has vowed to make the world's information *useful*, and the corporation maintains that for this reason "Search" remains at the core of its efforts to digitize and catalogue as much of that information as possible.[15] From the front end of the World

Wide Web, search engine technology often constitutes the first order of mediation between the user and the vastness of the internet. When the user enters a query, the search engine identifies and (ideally) returns the most relevant information or the address at which that information can be found. The results of this process take the form of the Search Engine Results Page (SERP), a text representative of what is surely one of our time's most common new genres.[16] SERPs allow (or, more problematically, encourage) users to dispense with the overwhelming majority of available data as irrelevant or inferior without having to evaluate that data themselves. The discrete pages of ranked lists generated from a massive and in human terms unknowable archive constitute a medium of information management that serves a function similar to that performed by all those texts from the seventeenth and eighteenth centuries that promised to render unwieldy treatises, multiple tomes, or even entire libraries unnecessary.

The authors of those works theoretically did the required research themselves or drew on the expertise of others in determining the value of what they kept or discarded. Internet searches likewise used to rely primarily upon human resources and judgment. Into the mid-1990s, Yahoo (which name suggests another, though more serendipitous, eighteenth-century connection as well as an initially appropriate degree of technical refinement) provided a two-stage search. Yahoo's software matched search queries against an existing directory of websites compiled by a group of human editors. These editors surveyed the breadth of the web—a task at that time not yet impossible but already fast approaching it—and selected what they deemed the best sites or sources. Their directory was widely regarded as the most authoritative for this reason. The directory effectively created a web-within-the-web wherein all of the information available to registered users was supposedly worth having. Software engineers refer to such closed ecosystems that contain only authorized applications and content as "walled gardens." Beyond their walls is chaos—an unmediated, disorganized, or at the very least undesirable collection of websites and pages in which the work of discerning the useful from the useless, the reliable from the specious, the good from the bad must be done by the user.

The problem, as the owners and editors of companies like Yahoo and AOL quickly discovered, is that human mediation of the kind that had made their walled gardens such safe and reliable places does not efficiently scale. In 1998, Yahoo employed forty people responsible for maintaining their directory of sites, at which point editorial staff director Srinija Srinivasan reported that even with "unlimited resources," the company would no longer be able to keep pace with the growth of the web.[17] Once the amount of information through which Yahoo's editors had to crawl in search of value became too large, they could no longer provide the same quality of service. "A need had arisen," Randall Stross writes, "for a search engine that could do more than simply match the text of the search term with that of the web pages that contained the phrase." In the words of Craig Silverstein, the first employee hired by Google founders Larry Page and Sergei Brin, it also had to "'discriminate between good results and not-so-good results.'"[18] The question for software engineers thus became how best to teach a search engine the art of discrimination.

The modern search now depends upon three main components: the crawl, the index, and the query processor. The crawl relies upon software "spiders" that follow every link they can find and gather information about every page on the web. They return that information to the index, an enormous database "similar to the index in the back of a book," where it undergoes a variable process of statistical analysis.[19] The larger the index, the more effective the analysis of that index will be; the more effective the analysis, the more relevant the results of the search. The compilation of a comprehensively complete index has therefore been a critical part of search technology since its inception. A single spider, however, would never be able to "read" the entire internet for the same reason a single reader would never be able to finish reading all of Wikipedia: crawlers proceed linearly; therefore, by the time a spider finished a full sweep of the web, the number of sites would have grown. The task requires multiple crawlers working in tandem—a breakthrough achieved in 1994, when Louis Monier, a researcher and engineer at a now-defunct computer hardware company, conceived of a way to release a thousand crawlers at once. By the following year, his software had gathered "the closest thing to a complete index the young Web had ever seen—10 million documents comprising billions of words."[20] Three years after that, the Google index included more than 26 million pages. By 2000, the number had grown to 1 billion.

The public indexable web currently contains some 14 billion pages and over a trillion unique URLs. Making sense of that index—yet another part of the work formerly performed by human readers—now belongs to a set of algorithms the exact operations of which differ from engine to engine and remain closely guarded company secrets. No matter what engine a user looks to for guidance, though, the list of sites produced and the rank of those sites on that list result from the ways in which they interpret the index. Google draws on both the connective and quantitative aspects of the "complete" web; its engine determines the rank of a page by taking into account the number of links into that page and the number of links into each of the linking pages.[21] The more connected a page is to other pages, and the more connected those other pages are to other pages, the higher the rank of that page in the search results. The algorithm fragments the web into lists of relevant pages in order to make it useable to the front-end users who never see the full extent of the data, and the rank of each fragment depends on its relationship to a whole that the user cannot know.

Search, then, acts as a kind of Digital Age answer to Milton's Raphael. For four books in the middle of *Paradise Lost*, the archangel patiently answers Adam's questions about matters theological, historical, moral, and natural. Adam's knowledge, while always already encyclopedic in some sense (as evidenced by his ability to name the animals in Eden) is also apparently incomplete.[22] He naturally seeks to know more, and within the first of all walled gardens, Raphael functions as a kind of ideal reference source: an entity with a more complete knowledge of the universe who renders how and what he knows more useful to the seeker. Through Raphael, Adam receives only that knowledge deemed necessary to the progress of human learning in its prelapsarian state. The archangel, in other words, returns only perfectly relevant results.

Though somewhat less than divine and without the benefit of supernatural discernment, modern search engine algorithms serve or strive to serve essentially the same purpose. The web now contains far more pages and URLs than mortal users can comprehend or curate without assistance.[23] The task has simply grown too large; the whole has become, to borrow a phrase from technologist David Weinberger, "too big to know."[24] Human modes of comprehending the "completeness" of the web have become obsolete, and in response to obsolescence we have developed new tools with which to manage and make useful what we perceive as superabundance.

No search engine algorithm, unfortunately, comes complete with Raphael's divine ordination and inherent benevolence. Google's system relies to a great extent upon mass consensus rather than individual expertise, and knowledgeable users or groups of users can turn the "democratic" process by which the algorithm produces its much-vaunted results to their own ends. I in no way mean to suggest that Google or any other organization that shares its ambitions is not subject to various forms and degrees of bias, corruption, or failure, whether from within or without. The relationship of Search to knowledge production, organization, and consumption puts a great deal of power in the hands of those who create and control the mediating technologies; Google's mission to organize *all* human knowledge naturally raises questions about privacy, private interest, and the unanticipated outcomes and discoveries of such an endeavor.

Users should also remain cognizant of the simple but easily disregarded fact that until the index is actually complete, it actually is not. The algorithm is only as good as the archive, and the knowledge that emerges from a partial collection of data will necessarily reflect its imperfections. At an Association of National Advertisers convention in October 2005, Google chairman and CEO Eric Schmidt estimated that only 2 or 3 per cent of the world's information was indexed and searchable.[25] Google engineers calculated that at their then-current pace of acquisition and digitization, making the rest available for indexing and searching would take about 300 years. As Jean-Noël Jeanneney, president of France's Bibliothèque Nationale, has observed, the long-term pursuit of complete knowledge has potentially troubling short-term implications regarding how the archive represents (or misrepresents) that knowledge at any given point along the way. The very process of selection that determines what knowledge becomes available when can have undesirable or simply unforeseen effects.[26] Bacon would likely have instructed Google's engineers to forgo algorithmic analysis until the very last byte had a place in the index. That ship, however, has sailed; users must instead try to make the best possible use of an archive perpetually and problematically becoming more complete.

Whatever their virtues and flaws, the search engine algorithms designed to rescue internet users from information overload are greatly constrained by the fact that most of the web is currently written for human readers. According to some computer scientists, however, today's tools are merely the predecessors of advanced machine intelligences that will be better able to marry completeness and utility. The "Semantic Web," which would in theory evolve out of the web we know now, would rely on new programming languages that allow machines to process far more metadata far more efficiently.[27] This will in turn enable those machines to interpret and manipulate data in more sophisticated ways. The Semantic Web, in other words, will operate less like the relatively simple register with which we are familiar—one that displays data without "understanding" it—and more like an intelligent agent capable of organizing knowledge according to its *meaning*.[28]

Tim Berners-Lee, who coined the term and works to develop web standards as director of the World Wide Web Consortium (W3C), describes the future of the web in language evocative of seventeenth- and eighteenth-century knowledge projects. "If properly designed," he writes, "the Semantic Web can assist the evolution of human knowledge as a whole ... its unifying logical language will enable [new] concepts to be progressively linked into a universal Web." Searching this web, as Larry Page put it, will be like consulting "a reference librarian with complete mastery of the entire corpus of human knowledge."[29] Wolfram|Alpha likewise works towards a future in which what we know as the Search engine is replaced by something infinitely smarter. The creators of a "computational knowledge engine" that aims "to collect and curate all objective data; implement every known model, method, and algorithm; and make it possible to compute whatever can be computed about anything," Wolfram|Alpha's long-term goal echoes the grandest aspirations of the pursuit of complete knowledge in the historical Enlightenment: they wish "to build on the achievements of science and other systematizations of knowledge to provide a single source that can be relied on by everyone for definitive answers to factual queries."[30] Samuel Hartlib might have likened it to visiting the Office of Address.

For the moment, that kind of mastery remains beyond the reach of human as well as machine intelligence. The language and protocols of semantic reasoning continue to encounter conceptual and practical obstacles, and plans for their large-scale implementation have met in some quarters with a substantial degree of skepticism regarding feasibility and the likelihood of unintended and undesirable consequences. The future course of the continuing pursuit of complete knowledge, then, remains unclear, and its outcomes uncertain. When asked what will happen if and when we finally do have digital access to everything, though, Martin Wattenberg—whose mind like most others' boggles at the thought of so much data—responded in terms reminiscent of Defoe's description of the "walking dictionaries" of antiquity. "There's something about completeness," he said, "that's magical."[31]

Appendix

Table 1.1 English Short Title Catalogue (ESTC) title searches*

Date range	No. of items	% change	ESTC total	% change	Date range	No. of items	% change	ESTC total	% change
(A) Terms: "complete," "compleat," "compleate"†									
1601–1610	0	—	4,062	—	1701–1710	308	11.2	23,223	12.4
1611–1620	6	—	5,040	24.1	1711–1720	358	16.2	24,571	5.8
1621–1630	7	16.7	5,823	15.5	1721–1730	402	12.3	21,548	(14)
1631–1640	37	428.6	6,601	13.4	1731–1740	472	17.4	21,785	1.1
1641–1650	49	32.4	20,222	206.3	1741–1750	507	7.4	24,947	14.5
1651–1660	124	153.1	14,989	(25.9)	1751–1760	529	4.3	27,460	10.1
1661–1670	167	34.7	10,922	(27.1)	1761–1770	780	47.4	33,142	20.1
1671–1680	157	(6)	14,346	31.3	1771–1780	915	17.3	41,405	24.9
1681–1690	206	32.1	20,940	46	1781–1790	1,129	23.4	50,844	22.8
1691–1700	277	34.5	20,353	(2.8)	1791–1800	1,342	18.9	78,531	54.5
(B) Term: "universal"									
1601–1610	2	—	4,062	—	1701–1710	101	9.8	23,223	12.4
1611–1620	1	(50)	5,040	24.1	1711–1720	90	(10.9)	24,571	5.8
1621–1630	2	100	5,823	15.5	1721–1730	153	70	21,548	(14)
1631–1640	2	0	6,601	13.4	1731–1740	183	19.6	21,785	1.1
1641–1650	14	600	20,222	206.3	1741–1750	189	3.3	24,947	14.5
1651–1660	60	328.6	14,989	(25.9)	1751–1760	302	59.8	27,460	10.1
1661–1670	46	(23.3)	10,922	(27.1)	1761–1770	311	3	33,142	20.1

(continued)

Table 1.1 Continued

Date range	No. of items	% change	ESTC total	% change	Date range	No. of items	% change	ESTC total	% change	ESTC total	% change
1671–1680	47	2.2	14,346	31.3	1771–1780	368	18.3	41,405	24.9	41,405	24.9
1681–1690	62	31.9	20,940	46	1781–1790	515	39.9	50,844	22.8	50,844	22.8
1691–1700	92	48.4	20,353	(2.8)	1791–1800	702	36.3	78,531	54.5	78,531	54.5
(C) Terms: "cyclopædia," "encyclopædia," "cyclopedia," "encyclopedia"											
1601–1610	2	—	4,062	—	1701–1710	0	0	23,223	12.4	23,223	12.4
1611–1620	0	(100)	5,040	24.1	1711–1720	0	0	24,571	5.8	24,571	5.8
1621–1630	0	0	5,823	15.5	1721–1730	2	0	21,548	(14)	21,548	(14)
1631–1640	1	—	6,601	13.4	1731–1740	4	100	21,785	1.1	21,785	1.1
1641–1650	1	0	20,222	206.3	1741–1750	5	25	24,947	14.5	24,947	14.5
1651–1660	0	(100)	14,989	(25.9)	1751–1760	6	20	27,460	10.1	27,460	10.1
1661–1670	1	—	10,922	(27.1)	1761–1770	2	(66.7)	33,142	20.1	33,142	20.1
1671–1680	0	0	14,346	31.3	1771–1780	11	450	41,405	24.9	41,405	24.9
1681–1690	0	0	20,940	46	1781–1790	36	227.3	50,844	22.8	50,844	22.8
1691–1700	0	0	20,353	(2.8)	1791–1800	49	36.1	78,531	54.5	78,531	54.5
(D) Term: "dictionary"											
1601–1610	0	—	4,062	—	1701–1710	98	55.6	23,223	12.4	23,223	12.4
1611–1620	5	—	5,040	24.1	1711–1720	53	(45.9)	24,571	5.8	24,571	5.8
1621–1630	11	120	5,823	15.5	1721–1730	80	50.9	21,548	(14)	21,548	(14)
1631–1640	9	(18.2)	6,601	13.4	1731–1740	115	43.8	21,785	1.1	21,785	1.1
1641–1650	17	88.9	20,222	206.3	1741–1750	125	8.7	24,947	14.5	24,947	14.5
1651–1660	29	70.1	14,989	(25.9)	1751–1760	176	40.8	27,460	10.1	27,460	10.1
1661–1670	31	6.9	10,922	(27.1)	1761–1770	234	33	33,142	20.1	33,142	20.1
1671–1680	47	51.6	14,346	31.3	1771–1780	287	22.6	41,405	24.9	41,405	24.9
1681–1690	37	(21.3)	20,940	46	1781–1790	297	3.5	50,844	22.8	50,844	22.8
1691–1700	63	70.3	20,353	(2.8)	1791–1800	479	61.3	78,531	54.5	78,531	54.5

(E) Term: "system"

	"system"	% growth	ESTC total	% growth
1601–1610	0	—	4,062	—
1611–1620	0	0	5,040	24.1
1621–1630	0	0	5,823	15.5
1631–1640	0	0	6,601	13.4
1641–1650	0	0	20,222	206.3
1651–1660	4	0	14,989	(25.9)
1661–1670	2	(50)	10,922	(27.1)
1671–1680	6	200	14,346	31.3
1681–1690	12	100	20,940	46
1691–1700	19	58.3	20,353	(2.8)
1701–1710	42	121.1	23,223	12.4
1711–1720	67	59.5	24,571	5.8
1721–1730	81	20.9	21,548	(14)
1731–1740	103	27.2	21,785	1.1
1741–1750	123	19.4	24,947	14.5
1751–1760	165	34.1	27,460	10.1
1761–1770	215	30.3	33,142	20.1
1771–1780	293	36.3	41,405	24.9
1781–1790	459	56.7	50,844	22.8
1791–1800	795	73.2	78,531	54.5

* "ESTC total" refers to the total number of all titles cataloged in the database. Parentheses indicate negative growth. All searches are for the exact phrase in title, in all countries and languages.

† Data suggest that "compleat" was in fact the favored form until the 1760s, the first decade during which more "completes" than "compleats" were printed—possibly due to the influence of Johnson's dictionary. "Compleate" had largely dropped out of use by the mid-seventeenth century. The data in all of these tables reflect ESTC catalog holdings as of August 2011 and will likely be out of date by the time they appear in print.

Table 1.2.A   The Complete "X": 1600–1699

This table includes English-language works that specifically advertised themselves as "complete" bodies of knowledge in themselves or as the means by which an individual's knowledge or self might be made "complete" or perfect. Most were designed to appeal to those wishing to learn or advance in a single art or trade; others (such as the *Compleat Gentleman* and *Wits Interpreter*) comprehend multiple subjects. The texts listed represent a wide and seemingly disparate array of subjects as well as great differences in length, philosophy, credibility, and compositional strategy, but all traffic in the concepts and promise of completeness or complete knowledge.

The list includes only (where possible) first editions of distinct titles and excludes "complete" collections of authors' poems, prose, or correspondence. The 120 titles below come from electronic searches of the *ESTC* and *EEBO*. The list is in itself not complete if for no other reason than that it does not account for texts that made the same promises as the rest but did not use any version of the word "complete" in their titles.

An asterisk appearing by a title indicates duplication in Table 1.2.B.

1622	*The compleat gentleman*
1628	*The complete souldier*
1630	*A compleat parson*
1631	*The English house-wife. Containing the inward and outward vertues which ought to be in a compleate woman*
1635	*An essay of drapery: or, the compleate citizen*
1636	*The complete justice*
1637	*The compleat cannoniere*
1639	*The compleat horseman and expert farrier*
1639	*The compleat woman*
1640	*The Italian tutor or a new and most compleat Italian grammer*
1642	*The boate swaines art, or, The compleat boat swain*
1642	*A compleat schoole of warre*
1643	*The compleat Christian, and compleat armour and armoury of a Christian*
1643	*The compleate copy-holder*
1650	*The compleat bell-man*
1650	*The compleat body of the art military*
1650	*The compleat lawyer*
1652	*Horometria: or the compleat diallist*
1653	*The compleat angler*
1653	*The compleat surveyor*
1653	*The English physitian ... containing a compleat method of physique*
1654	*The academie of eloquence, Containing a compleat English rhetorique*
1655	*The Christian in compleat armour*
1655	*The compleat ambassador*

(*continued*)

Table 1.2.A   Continued

1655	*The compleat clark, and scriveners guide*
1655	*The compleat cook*
1655	*Vignola: or the compleat architect*
1655	*Wits Interpreter, The English Parnassus. Or, A sure guide to those admirable accomplishments that compleat our English gentry*
1656	*Englands compleat law-judge, and lawyer*
1656	*The compleat midwifes practice*
1656	*The compleat trades-man*
1656	*A compleat practice of physick*
1656	*The Compleat politician*
1656	*The compleat doctoress*
1657	*Naturall experiments … being a compleat method of physick*
1657	*The compleat bone-setter*
1658	*The compleat swimmer*
1659	*The compleat school-master*
1659	*The compleat husband-man*
1659	*Pambotanologia… Or a compleat herbal*
1664	*The compleat gardeners practice*
1664	*The compleat ship-wright*
1664	*A compleat body of chymistry*
1665	*Flora: sue De florum cultura. Or, A complete florilege*
1665	*The compleat vineyard*
1666	*The compleat sollicitor performing his duty*
1667	*Poor Robin's jests: or, The compleat jester*
1669	*The compleat measurer*
1669	*The compleate chymical dispensatory, in five books*
1670	*The voyage of Italy, or a compleat journey through Italy in two parts*
1670	*The exact politician, or, Compleat statesman*
1671	*The compleat excise-man*
1672	*The compleat gunner in three parts*
1672	*The compleat academy, or a drawing book*
1673	*The English horseman and complete farrier*
1674	*A complete treatise of chirurgery*
1674	*The compleat English schoolmaster*
1674	*The compleat gamester*
1675	*Every woman her own midwife, or a Compleat cabinet opened for child-bearing women*
1676	*The compleat modellist*
1677	*The compleat chymist*
1677	*The compleat servant-maid*

(continued)

Table 1.2.A   Continued

1678	The complete gauger
1678	A compleat discourse of wounds
1678	A compleat treatise of preternatural tumours
1678	The compleat gentleman
1678	The compleat comptinghouse
1680	The compleat English-scholar
1680	The character of a compleat physician, or naturalist
1681	A compleat treatise of the muscles
1681	Rara avis in terris: or the compleat miner
1681	The compleat soldier, or expert artillery-man
1682	The compleat troller
1683	The compleat courtier: or, Cupid's academy
1683	The compleat academy, the newest nursery of compliments
1684	The compleat conformist
1684	The compleat cookmaid
1684	The compleat tradesman
1685	A compleat guide of justices of peace
1685	The compleat planter and cyderist
1685	The complete English-man
1686	Systema medicinale, a compleat system of physick
1687	Agnliae notitia: or The present state of England compleat
1687	The Scots fencing-master, or, Compleat small-sword-man
1688	A new, plain, short, and compleat French and English grammar
1688	A compleat discourse of the nature, use, and right managing of that wonderful instrument, the baroscope
1689	Compleat guide to the English tongue
1690	A compleat system of grammar
1690	The compleat English and French cook
1691	The experience'd: or, A compleat treatise of horsemanship
1691	The compleat fencing-master
1691	The compleat arithmetician, or, The whole art of arithmetick*
1691	The art of catechising: or, The compleat catechist
1692	The compleat writing master
1692	A new guide for constables … being the most compleat of any work of this nature
1692	The compleat constable
1693	Geography anatomized: or, A compleat geographical grammar
1693	The compleat gard'ner
1694	The compleat French-master

(continued)

Table 1.2.A Continued

1694	*The compleat herbal of physical plants*
1694	*The compleat captain*
1694	*The compleat method of curing almost all diseases*
1694	*The compleat cook: or, the whole art of cookery**
1695	*Every man his own gauger ... together with the compleat coffee-man*
1695	*The compleat mother*
1695	*The compleat statesman*
1695	*Dr. Syndenham's compleat method of curing almost all diseases*
1696	*The gentleman's compleat jockey*
1696	*The compleat surgeon: or, The whole art of surgery**
1696	*The compleat horseman*
1696	*The compleat sheriff*
1697	*The husbandman, farmer, and grassier's compleat instructor*
1697	*Cursus osteologicus: being a compleat doctrine of the bones*
1698	*The compleat bee-master*
1698	*A compleat course of chymistry*
1698	*The compleat book of knowledge*
1699	*Etmullerus abridg'd: or, A compleat system of the theory and practice of physick*
1699	*The golden treasure: or, The compleat miner*
1699	*A compleat body of chirurgical operations, containing the whole practice of surgery*

Table 1.2.B "Whole Arts": 1556–1699

This table includes English-language works that specifically advertised themselves as containing or introducing readers to "whole arts." As with the above, most were designed to appeal to those wishing to learn or advance in a single art or trade ("physick" and "chirurgery" being the most common). The texts listed represent a wide and seemingly disparate array of subjects as well as great differences in length, philosophy, credibility, and compositional strategy. Some, like *Lavernæ, or the Spanish gipsy*—a piece of rogue literature that supposedly included the whole art of thieving—suggest that the phrase "whole art," like "complete," had by the middle of the seventeenth century become a marketing trope.

The list includes only (where possible) first editions of distinct titles. The seventy-seven titles below come from electronic searches of the *ESTC* and *EEBO*. An asterisk appearing by a title indicates duplication in Table 1.2.A.

1556	*A brief and most pleanau[nt] epitomye of the whole art of physiognomie*
1560	*The fower chiefest offices belonging to horsemanship... Conteyninge the whole art of ryding lately set foorth*
1585	*Tables of surgerie, brieflie comprehending the whole art and practice thereof*

(*continued*)

Table 1.2.B Continued

1586	*Foure bookes of husbandrie ... contaning the whole art and trade of husbandrie, gardening, graffing, and planting*
1612	*A discourse of the whole art of chyrurgerie*
1613	*A pleasant history: declaring the whole art of physiognomy*
1613	*The path-way to knowledge; containing the whole art of arithmeticke*
1615	*Country contentments in two bookes: the first, containing the whole art of riding great horses in very short time*
1617	*A daily exercise for ladies and gentlewomen. Whereby they may learne and practice the whole art of making pastes, preserues, marmalades, conserues, tarstuffes, gellies, breads, sucket candies, cordiall vvwater, conceits in suger-vvorkes of seuerall kindes*
1627	*An abbreviation of writing by character. Wherein is summarily contained, a table, which is an abstract of the whole art*
1628	*The complete souldier. Containing the whole art of gunnery**
1637	*The vvhole art of chyrurgery*
1637	*The compleat cannoniere; or, The Gunner's guide. Wherein are set forth exactly the chiefe grounds and principals of the whole art**
1647	*Christian astrology modestly treated of in three books ... with a most easie introduction to the whole art of astrology*
1649	*A new art of short-vvriting... This whole art being every word framed out of the 24 letters*
1650	*Lavernæ, or the Spanish gipsy: the whole art, mystery, antiquity, company, noblenesse, and excellency of theeves and theeving*
1650	*Planometria: or, the whole art of surveying of land*
1651	*Polypharmakos kai chymistes: or, The English unparalell'd physitian and chyrurgian... In which is explained, the whole art and secresy of physick and chyrurgery*
1653	*Dariotus redivivus: or a brief introduction conducing to the judgement of the stars. Where n the whole art of judiciall astrologie is briefly and plainly delivered*
1653	*The compleat surveyor: containing the whole art of surveying of land**
1653	*Astrologia restaurata; or, Astrologie restored ... being a most necessary introduction to the whole art*
1654	*The exact surveyor: or, The whole art of surveying of land*
1654	*Short-writing shorned [sic]; or the art of short-writing reduced to a method more speedy, plain, exact, and easie ... the whole art so disposed, that all usual words may be written with aptnesse and brevity*
1655	*Hungers prevention: or, The whole art of fovvling by water and land*
1656	*The compleat midwifes practice... A work so plain, that the weakest capacity may easily attain the knowledge of the whole art**
1656	*The perfect cook... As also the perfect English cook, or the right method of the whole art of cookery*

(continued)

Table 1.2.B Continued

1656	*The institutions or fundamentals of the whole art, both of physick and chirurgery, divided into five books. Plainly discovering all that is to be known in both*
1657	*A tutor to astrologie: or astrology made easie: being a plain introduction to the whole art of astrology*
1657	*Guzman, Hinde, and Hannam outstript: being a discovery of the whole art, mistery and antiquity of theeves and theeving*
1657	*The perfect husbandman, or the art of husbandry ... with the whole art (according to these last times) of breeding*
1657	*The expert doctors dispensatory. The whole art of physick restored to practice*
1657	*Division of the whole art of navigation*
1658	*An epitome of stenographie; or, An abridgement and contraction, of the art of swift and secret writing... Being a brief, yet plain and full discovery of all the grounds of the whole art*
1658	*Genethlialogia; Or, the doctrine of nativities, containing the whole art of directions, and annual revolutions*
1658	*The whole art of reflex dialling*
1659	*Culpeper's school of physick. Or The experimental practice of the whole art*
1659	*The compleat husband-man: or, a discourse of the whole art of husbandry**
1660	*The whole art of drawing, painting, limning, and etching*
1660	*The accomplisht cook, or The art and mystery of cookery. Wherein the whole art is revealed in a more easie and perfect method*
1662	*Oriatrike or, Physick refined. The common errors therein refuted, and the whole art reformed and rectified*
1669	*Clavis astrologiae; or, A key to the whole art of astrologie*
1669	*Practical navigation; or, An introduction to that whole art*
1671	*The midwives book. Or the whole art of midwifery discovered*
1676	*The anglers delight: containing the whole art of neat and clean angling*
1676	*The art of painting. Wherein is included the whole art of vulgar painting*
1678	*Pharmacopoeia Londinensis. Or, the new London dispensatory ... fitted to the whole art of healing*
1678	*Decimal arithmetick; wherein the whole art is made easie*
1679	*Practical astrology. In two parts. The first part containeth an easie introduction to the whole of astrologie*
1679	*Mikropanastron: or an astrological vade mecum: Briefly teaching the whole art of astrology*
1680	*The whole art of palmestry*
1680	*A key to famous Mr. Rich's short-hand-table... Faithfully discovering the whole art*
1682	*The young angler's companion. Containing the whole art of neat and clean angling*

(continued)

Table 1.2.B Continued

1682	*A perfect school of instructions for the officers of the mouth: shewing the whole art of a master of the houshold* [sic]*, a master carver, a master butler, a master confectioner, a master cook, a master pastryman... Along with pictures curiously ingraven, displaying the whole arts*
1683	*The whole art of converse*
1684	*The whole art of the stage*
1684	*Enchiridion medicum: or A manual of physick. Being a compendium of the whole art*
1684	*The compleat tradesman, or, The exact dealers daily companion instructin[g] [h]im throughly in all things absolutely n[ecessar]y to be known by all those who would thrive in the world and in the whole art and mystery of trade and traffick*
1684	*A pocket companion for seamen... To which is added the whole art of gunnery, and gauging of vessels, measuring of board and timber...*
1684	*Wits cabinet or A companion for young men and ladies; containing I. The whole art of wooing and making love... II. The school of Bacchus, or the whole art of drinking...*
1685	*Military discipline; or The art of war ... with all sorts of instructions and other observations belonging to the whole art of war*
1685	*The whole art of navigation*
1685	*Norwood's system of navigation: teaching the whole art*
1686	*The true fortune-teller, or, Guide to knowledge. Discovering the whole art of chyromancy, physiognomy, metoposcopy, and astrology*
1687	*The triumph of wit, or Ingenuity display'd in its perfection... Part II. Containing the whole art and mystery of love in all its nicest intreagues and curious particulars*
1689	*Chirurgus methodicus; or, the young chirurgion's conductor through the labyrinth of the most difficult cures occuring in this whole art; and whereby he is distinguished from empiricks and quack-salvers*
1691	*The compleat arithmetician, or The whole art of arithmetick, vulgar and decimal**
1692	*The measurer's guide: or the whole art of measuring made short, plain, and easie*
1692	*An epitome of the whole art of war. In two parts. The first of military discipline, containing the whole exercise of the pike and musquet*
1692	*Introitus apertus ad artem distillationis; or The whole art of distillation practically stated ... being the epitomy and marrow of the whole art; supplying all that is omitted in the London distiller, French and baker &c.*
1693	*Seplasium. The compleat English physician; or, the druggist's shop opened... Shewing their various names and natures, their several preparations, virtues, uses, and doses, as they are applicable to the whole art of physick*

(continued)

Table 1.2.B   Continued

1695	*The whole duty of a woman; or a guide to the female sex ... with the whole art of love, &c ... 3. The whole duty of a wife. 4. The whole duty of a widow, &c. Also choice receipts in physick, and chirurgery. With the whole art of cookery, preserving, candying, beautifying, &c. Written by a lady*
1696	*The compleat surgeon: or, the whole art of surgery**
1696	*Practical arithmetick an introduction to ye whole art where in the most necessary rules are fairly describ'd*
1697	*England's happiness improved: or, An infallible way to get riches, encrease plenty, and promote pleasure. Containing ... the whole art and mistery of distilling brandy, strong waters, cordial waters, &c.... The whole art and mistery of a confectioner. The compleat market-man, or woman, to know all sorts of provisions; ... and all other matters relating to marketing.*
1697	*The mystery of husbandry; or, arable, pasture, and wood-land improved. Containing the whole art and mystery of agriculture or husbandry*
1698	*The true fortune-teller, or, Guide to knowledge. Discovering the whole art of chiromancy, physiognomy, metoposcopy, and astrology*
1698	*Wisdom's better than money: or, The whole art of knowledge, and the art to know men*

Notes

1 Introduction: Concepts of Completeness

1. Richard Ward, *The life of the learned and pious Dr. Henry More*, 1710, p.224. Ward offers the Latin (*"Cum Homo copulatus fuerit Intellectui per Scientiam omnium Rerum complete, tunc est Deus in Humano Corpore hospitatus"*) but does not cite the source of the quotation.
2. Ed Folsom, 'Database as Genre: The Epic Transformation of Archives', *PMLA*, 122.5, October 2007, pp.1571–9, 1577. See also Wai Chee Dimock, *Through Other Continents: American Literature across Deep Time*, Princeton, Princeton University Press, 2006, esp. pp.73–106.
3. The efficacy and accuracy of the PageRank algorithm are embellished, but its "omniscience" has become a feature of popular treatments and descriptions of Google's technology and success in Search as well as of algorithms more generally. See, for example, John Battelle, *The Search: How Google and Its Rivals Rewrote the Rules of Business and Transformed Our Culture*, New York, 2005.
4. Niall Rudd translates Horace's Latin phrase, *"omni tulit punctum qui miscuit utile dulci,"* as "every vote is won by the man who mixes beneficial with sweet," where "beneficial" indicates moral improvement and "sweet" emotional attraction. "The combination of *dulce* and *utile*," Rudd writes, "is by no means a bland, superficial formula. If *dulce* is taken as including every delight, and *utile* as embracing everything that helps us to understand and cope with our human condition, then the terms are capable of illuminating the whole of art." Horace, *Horace: Epistles Book II and Ars Poetica*, Niall Rudd (ed.), Cambridge, Cambridge University Press, 1990, pp.343, 232, 206.
5. The phrase "experience of overabundance" comes from Ann Blair, 'Reading Strategies for Coping with Information Overload Ca. 1550–1700', *Journal of the History of Ideas*, 64.1, January 2003, pp.11–28.
6. See Mary Franklin-Brown, *Reading the World: Encyclopedic Writing in the Scholastic Age*, Chicago, Chicago University Press, 2012, and Ann Blair, 'Information Management in Comparative Perspective', in *Too Much to Know: Managing Scholarly Information before the Modern Age*, New Haven, Yale University Press, 2010, esp. pp.11, 20–2, 33–5, 55–61.
7. Ephraim Chambers, 'Preface', in *Cyclopædia*, London, 1728, p.xxi.
8. Thomas Cooper, *The universal pocket-book*, London, 1740.
9. Society of Gentlemen (eds), *A Supplement to Dr. Harris's Dictionary of arts and sciences*, London, 1744.
10. These categories, from Amazon.com, are broken down into numerous subcategories.
11. Formerly known as *The Times Atlas of World History*, the eighth and most recent edition introduced the new title and brought the historical span of the work up to the twenty-first century from its original endpoint of 1975.

The book description is available at http://amzn.com/0007889321 (accessed 13 April 2013).

12. Peter de Bolla, 'Mediation and the Division of Labor', in *This is Enlightenment*, Clifford Siskin and William Warner (eds), Chicago, University of Chicago Press, 2010, p.89.

13. Alan Rauch, *Useful Knowledge: The Victorians, Morality, and the March of Intellect*, Durham, Duke University Press, 2001, p.7; see also pp.12–13.

14. Samuel Johnson, 'Knowledge', in *A Dictionary of the English Language*, London, 1755.

15. The title page of the second edition claimed to comprehend "all the material information that is contained in Chambers's *Cyclopædia*, the *Encyclopædia Britannica*, and the French *Encyclopedie*." William Henry Hall, *The new royal encyclopædia*, Thomas Lloyd (ed.), 2nd ed., 3 vols., London, 1791.

16. Kevis Goodman, *Georgic Modernity and British Romanticism: Poetry and the Mediation of History*, Cambridge Studies in Romanticism, New York, Cambridge University Press, 2004, p.9.

17. Borges' description of the map as large as the territory occurs in 'On Exactitude in Science' (*'Del rigor en la ciencia'*). Philosopher and logician James F. Thomson coined the term "supertask" (or "super-task") in 1954, but articulations of the problem it describes go back to Zeno of Elea. Thomson defines a supertask as one in which "to complete a journey you must do something that is impossible and hence you can't complete the journey." The task, in other words, involves completing an infinite number of steps in a finite amount of time. If it takes Tristram Shandy a year to record the events of a single day, for example, he will never finish writing. James Thomson, 'Tasks and Super-Tasks', *Analysis*, 15.1, 1954, p.1.

18. "What, is it necessary to read all the trash contained in this Genus, as it pleases you to call it, in order to speak of any part of it?" Clara Reeve, *The Progress of Romance*, Colchester, 1785, pp.6–7.

19. Mary Poovey, 'The Model System of Contemporary Literary Criticism', *Critical Inquiry*, 27.3, 2001, pp.432–3.

20. These kinds of contingent conditions and operational definitions are behind the philosophical debate about the actual possibility or impossibility of so-called supertasks (see note 17).

21. Franco Moretti, *Pamphlet 2: Network Theory, Plot Analysis*, Stanford, Stanford Literary Lab, 2011, p.1, available at http://litlab.stanford.edu/LiteraryLabPamphlet2A.Tex.pdf (accessed 9 January 2014).

22. Kathryn Schulz, 'What is Distant Reading?', *The New York Times*, 24 June 2011, available at http://www.nytimes.com/2011/06/26/books/review/the-mechanic-muse-what-is-distant-reading.html?pagewanted=all (accessed 25 June 2011). See also Franco Moretti, *Distant Reading*, London, Verso, 2013, esp. pp.43–62.

23. Oxford University Press describes *The English Novel 1770–1829* as "the first *complete* and copy-based record of the production of new English fiction in the period" (italics added). According to a review of the work in the *Times Literary Supplement* and excerpted by Oxford University Press, the completeness of that record "reminds one forcibly of the insecure base on which literary criticism rests." In an unknowing nod to an old association

with heroism, the same review calls the work (which was ten years in the making) "nobly undertaken."

24. Tim Hitchcock, review of *Society in Early Modern England: The Vernacular Origins of Some Powerful Ideas*, by Phil Withington, *The Economic History Review*, 64.3, August 2011, p.1027.

25. Titles specifically featuring some version of "complete" saw a small overall percentage decline between 1741 and 1760 (dropping from 2.17 per cent to 1.93 per cent) before the "spike" of the 1760s resumed a pattern of growth that (with the exceptions of an off-trend decline in the 1640s and an anomalous decade of negative growth in the 1670s) went all but uninterrupted from 1601 to 1740.

26. According to autoregressive models of order one from the field of statistical time series analysis.

27. Roger Chartier, *The Order of Books*, Stanford, Stanford University Press, 1994, pp.62–3, 69.

28. See Chartier, 'Libraries without Walls', in *The Order of Books*, pp.61–88.

29. Following Cardinal Ximenes's Complutesian Polyglot Bible of 1517 (the sixth and final volume of which consisted of a Greek dictionary, a Hebrew and Chaldaic dictionary, and a Hebrew grammar) and Jean Archer's *Dictionarium Theologicum*, William Patten's *The calender of Scripture* (1575) set in alphabetical order English versions of the "nations, countreys, men, weemen, idols, cities, hills, rivers and of oother places in the holly Byble mentioned." The revised Bishops' Bible had appeared not long before, and having finally acquired a copy, Patten thought it his part "redyly fyrst in this small volume to impart it." The translated names from that bible came with their originals, their Latin derivations, and very brief explanatory notes that Patten claimed would serve as a bulwark against linguistic corruption as well as an aid to memory. His words mark the calendar as a companion piece that promised to make the intrinsically complete Bible somehow *more* complete to vernacular readers. Similar texts followed, and they made similar claims. William Patten, *The calender of Scripture*, London, 1575, p.a3r. Archer's *Dictionarium* is not to be confused with Thomas Gascoigne's better-known fifteenth-century work of the same title.

30. Thomas Wilson, *A complete Christian dictionary*, John Bagwell (ed.), London, 1654, p.a10r. The book was first published in 1612 as *A Christian dictionarie*; it remained in print throughout the first three quarters of the seventeenth century, though from the sixth edition of 1654 to the last of 1678 it appeared as *A complete Christian dictionary*.

2 Complete Bodies, Whole Arts, and the Limits of Epic

1. Bacon acknowledges that human knowledge was indeed circumscribed, but with respect to its proper sphere and rightful application rather than by religious dogma or intellectual limitation.

2. Francis Bacon, *Novum Organum*, Peter Urbach and John Gibson (trans. and eds), Chicago and La Salle, Open Court, 1994, p.24.

3. Bacon, *Novum Organum*, pp.25–6.

4. Lisa Jardine, 'Introduction', in *The New Organon*, Lisa Jardine and Michael Silverthorne (eds), New York, Cambridge University Press, 2000, p.xiii.
5. Francis Bacon, *The Advancement of Learning*, in *Francis Bacon: The Major Works*, Brian Vickers (ed.), New York, Oxford University Press, 2002, p.169.
6. Gerard Passannante, 'Homer Atomized', in *The Lucretian Renaissance: Philology and the Afterlife of Tradition*, Chicago, University of Chicago Press, 2011, esp. pp.128–38.
7. Quoted by Passannante, 'Homer Atomized', p.131.
8. "In *De rerum natura*, the scattering of fire is likened to the dissemination of knowledge, a casting of syllables through deep atomic space and through the minds of men. Bacon's own use of the word '*spargere*' for 'cast' powerfully evokes this generative sense we find in Lucretius, and shifts us again from the language of humanistic despair and skepticism to a language of hope." Passannante, 'Homer Atomized', p.137.
9. Anthony Grafton, 'Renaissance Readers of Homer's Ancient Readers', in *Homer's Ancient Readers: The Hermeneutics of Greek Epic's Earliest Exegetes*, Robert Lamberton and John J. Keany (eds), Princeton, Princeton University Press, 1992, p.150.
10. Bacon, *The Advancement of Learning*, p.123.
11. Bacon, *The Great Instauration*, in *Novum Organum*, p.9.
12. Bacon, *Novum Organum*, p.96.
13. Charles Webster, *The Great Instauration: Science, Medicine, and Reform 1626–1660*, London, Gerald Duckworth & Co., 1975, p.26.
14. Christopher Grose, '*Theatrum Libri*: Burton's *Anatomy of Melcholoy* and the Failure of Encyclopedic Form', in *Books and Readers in Early Modern England: Material Studies*, Jennifer Andersen and Elizabeth Sauer (eds), Philadelphia, University of Pennsylvania Press, 2002, p.82. See also Samuel G. Wong, 'Encyclopædism in *Anatomy of Melancholy*', *Renaissance and Reformation/ Renaissance et Réforme*, 22.1, 1998, pp.5–22.
15. Ian Maclean, 'Introduction', in *A Discourse on the Method of Correctly Conducting One's Reason and Seeking Truth in the Sciences*, by René Descartes, New York, Oxford University Press, 2006, p.xxiii.
16. René Descartes, *A Discourse on the Method of Correctly Conducting One's Reason and Seeking Truth in the Sciences*, Ian Maclean (trans.), pp.17, 12.
17. Webster, *The Great Instauration*, p.113.
18. Webster, *The Great Instauration*, p.114. The first complete edition of the *Consultatio* (in two volumes folio) did not appear until 1966.
19. See *Samuel Hartlib and Universal Reformation: Studies in Intellectual Communication*, Mark Greengrass, Michael Leslie, and Timothy Raylor (eds), Cambridge, Cambridge University Press, 1994.
20. See Webster, *The Great Instauration*, pp.67–77.
21. William Petty, *The advice of W. P. to Samuel Hartlib. For the advancement of some particular parts of learning*, London, 1647, p.3.
22. According to the *ESTC*, Hill's epitome is the earliest English-language text to contain the phrase "whole art" in its title. See Table 1.2 in the Appendix for a catalog of sixteenth- and seventeenth-century "whole arts" and "complete" bodies of knowledge.
23. The practice of physiognomy and of related arts or sciences like palmistry were outlawed in England throughout the Early Modern period, but

manuscripts on the subjects continued to be read and produced. See Martin Porter, *Windows of the Soul: The Art of Physiognomy in European Culture 1470–1780*, Oxford Historical Monographs, New York, Oxford University Press, 2005, esp. pp.94–6, 120–2, and 160–1. Physiognomy enjoyed renewed attention in the third quarter of the eighteenth century thanks in part to the works of the Swiss poet and pastor Johann Lavater.

24. Bartolommeo della Rocca Cocles, *A brief and most pleasaunt epitomye of the whole art of phisiognomie*, Thomas Hill (trans.), London, 1556, p.84.

25. See Wendy Wall, 'Renaissance National Husbandry: Gervase Markham and the Publication of England', *The Sixteenth Century Journal*, 27.3, Autumn 1996, pp.767–85.

26. Gervase Markham, *Markhams maister-peece*, London, 1610.

27. Markham, *Markhams maister-peece*, p.a4r.

28. *Countrey contentments, in two books, the first, containing the whole art of riding great horses in very short time* (1615), *A schoole for young souldiers containing in breife the whole discipline of warre* (1615), and *Hungers preuention: or, The whole arte of fowling by water and land* (1621), respectively. In the 1615 edition of *Markhams maister-peece* (as in all subsequent editions), the phrase "all possible knowledge whatsoever" is replaced with the only slightly less ambitious "all knowledge."

29. Yeo, 'Lost Encyclopedias: Before and After the Enlightenment', *Book History*, 10.1, 2007, p.49.

30. Henry Peacham, *The compleat gentleman*, London, 1622, pp.104, 112–13, 115.

31. Peacham, *The compleat gentleman*, p.104.

32. Percival Cole, *A Neglected Educator: J. H. Alsted*, Sydney, William Applegate, 1910, p.23.

33. Blair, 'Organizations of Knowledge', in *The Cambridge Companion to Renaissance Philosophy*, James Hankins (ed.), New York, Cambridge University Press, 2007, p.292.

34. Blair, *Too Much to Know*, pp.166, 170–1.

35. Samuel Morison, *Harvard College in the Seventeenth Century*, Cambridge, Harvard University Press, 1936, p.158; Samuel Pepys, '27 October, 1660', in *The Diary of Samuel Pepys*, Robert Latham and William Matthews (eds), 9 vols., Berkeley, University of California Press, 2000, 1.275; Robert Hume, 'The Economics of Culture in London 1660–1740', *The Huntington Library Quarterly*, 69.4, pp.497–9.

36. For Leibniz's plan, see Daniel Selcer, *Philosophy and the Book: Early Modern Figures of Material Inscription*, New York, Continuum, 2010, p.68.

37. Markham, *Markhams methode, or epitome*, London, 1616, p.a6r.

38. I have been unable to determine the prices of either book and therefore can speak only in terms of relative expense. The note from the epitome that I have quoted clearly indicates that the *maister-peece* cost significantly more than the *Methode*.

39. I do not mean to suggest that the book could actually have fulfilled its promises; one presumes that many horses, goats, sheep, and so on succumbed to disease despite (or indeed owing to) the application of Markham's medicines.

40. *A manuall: or, analecta, being a compendious collection out of such as have treated of the office of Justices of the Peace, but principally out of Mr Lambert, Mr Crompton, & Mr Dalton*, London, 1641, p.a3r.

41. William Scott, *An essay of drapery: or, the compleate citizen*, London, 1639, p.4.
42. Should "God permit me to reprint," he wrote, the results would appear in an appropriately updated edition. Thomas de Grey, *The compleat horseman and expert farrier*, London, 1639, p.c2r.
43. John Hinde, 'To the Worthy Author His Honor'd Friend Serjeant Major Richard Elton', in *The compleat body of the art military*, London, 1650, ll.1–12. Hinde contributed the fourth and fifth of the sixteen prefatory poems; these lines are from the former. The comparison of Elton's book to the feat of a "Lezbian squire" probably refers to Greek mythology: Homer refers to Odysseus's defeat of King Philomelides in the *Odyssey* and to Achilles conquering the Lesbos citadel in the *Iliad*.
44. Richard Elton, 'To the impartiall and judicious reader', in *The compleat body of the art military*, n.p.
45. E. R., *The experienc'd farrier, or, a compleat treatise of horsemanship in Two Books*, London, 1691, p.a2r.
46. Thomas Blount, *The academic of eloquence*, London, 1653.
47. A. S., Gent., *The husbandman, farmer and grasier's compleat instructor*, London, 1697, p.a2r.
48. George London and Henry Wise, 'An Advertisement to the Nobility and Gentry', in *The compleat gard'ner*, by Jean de la Quintinie, John Evelyn (trans.), George London and Henry Wise (eds), 2nd ed., London, 1699, p.i.
49. Francis Gouldman, *A copious dictionary in three parts*, London, 1664, p.a3r.
50. Gouldman, *A Copious Dictionary*, p.a4r (italics added).
51. Gerard Naddaf, 'Allegory and the Origins of Philosophy', in *Logos and Muthos: Philosophical Essays in Greek Literature*, William Wians (ed.), Albany, SUNY Press, 2009, p.108. All of Theagenes's original writings are lost; the examples of his method come from a scholium to the Venetus B manuscript attributed to the Neoplatonist philosopher Porphyry (which Naddaf provides in translation).
52. N. J. Richardson, 'Aristotle's Reading of Homer and Its Background', in *Homer's Ancient Readers*, p.33; Naddaf, 'Allegory and the Origins', p.117.
53. A. A. Long, 'Stoic Readings of Homer', in *Homer's Ancient Readers*, p.42. Long contests the received opinion of the Stoics as allegorists and argues in favor of the greater importance of etymology to their interpretations. In either case, the poems contain (or were believed to contain) more knowledge than their narratives superficially suggest.
54. Robert Lamberton, 'Introduction', in *Homer's Ancient Readers*, p.xvi. Lamberton notes the Pythagoreans as a possible exception.
55. Strabo, *Geographica* 1.2.3; quoted by Richard Hunter, *Plato and the Traditions of Ancient Literature: The Silent Stream*, New York, Cambridge University Press, 2012, p.101.
56. Robin Sowerby, 'Early Humanist Failure with Homer (II)', *International Journal of the Classical Tradition*, 4.2, Fall 1997, p.171.
57. Sowerby identifies the essay as a Renaissance favorite; it was often appended to both manuscript and printed editions of the poems. Sowerby, 'Early Humanist Failure', p.171. Scaliger reacted negatively to the allegories of his former teacher, Jean Dorat: "the man's begun to debase himself and amuse himself by finding the whole Bible in Homer." Julius Scaliger, *Scaligerana*,

P. Desmaizeaux (ed.), Amsterdam, 1740, p.20; quoted by Grafton, 'Renaissance Readers of Homer's Ancient Readers', p.150. Montaigne too questioned the legitimacy of the Homeric encyclopedia: "is it possible that Homer wanted to say everything he has been made to say, and that he used as many and as varied figures as the theologians, legislators, captains, philosophers, every sort of people who treat sciences ... attribute to him, and cite from him: general master of all offices, works, and artisans, general counselor for all enterprises?" Michel de Montaigne, *Apology for Raymond Sebond*, Roger Ariew and Marjorie Grene (trans.), Indianapolis, Hackett Publishing, 2003, p.147.

58. Grafton, 'Renaissance Readers of Homer's Ancient Readers', pp.153–7.
59. Bacon, *The Advancement of Learning*, p.161. According to Robert Schuler, "Bacon ... to an extent at least, participates in the ancient tradition of reading Virgil as one of the learned poets whose works are compendia of all kinds of knowledge." That is not to say, however, "that he naively attributes to him the kind of universal knowledge (including magic and prophecy) ... still being claimed for Homer, Ovid, and Virgil by some Renaissance syncretists and allegorists. Schuler, 'Francis Bacon and Scientific Poetry', *Transactions of the American Philosophical Society*, 82.2, 1992, pp.43, 47.
60. Edmund Spenser, *Spenser: The Faerie Queene*, A. C. Hamilton, Hiroshi Yamashita, Toshiyuku Suzuki, and Shohachi Fukuda (eds), New York, Longman, 2006, p.1.
61. John Selden supplied the first eighteen cantos of Drayton's verse with historical and philological notes. Drayton's other epics, *Matilda* (1594) and *The Barons' Wars* (1603), did not attempt the scale of either the *Fœrie Queene* or *Poly-Olbion*.
62. See Eric Langley, 'Anatomising the Eye in Phineas Fletcher's *The Purple Island*', *Renaissance Studies*, 20.3, 2006, pp.341–52; also Peter Mitchell, *The Purple Island and Anatomy in Early Seventeenth Century Literature, Philosophy, and Theology*, Madison, Fairleigh Dickinson University Press, 2007. The notes to the poem, Yvette Koepke explains, "approach modern science in their empirical style and content," and go some length to explain why the poem "has long been read as a bizarre transitional text caught between paradigms." Koepke, 'Allegory as Historical and Theoretical Model of Scientific Medicine: Sex and the Making of the Modern Body in Phineas Fletcher's *The Purple Island*', *Literature and Medicine*, 27.2, 2008, pp.179–80. A new edition of the poem, corrected and with additional editorial notes, was printed in 1783.
63. W. J., 'The Preface of the Translator', in *Monsieur Bossu's treatise of the epick poem containing many curious reflections, very useful and necessary for the right understanding and judging of the excellencies of Homer and Virgil*, W. J. (trans.), London, 1695, p.a5r.
64. Kirsti Simonsuuri, *Homer's Original Genius: Eighteenth-Century Notions of the Early Greek Epic (1688–1798)*, Cambridge, Cambridge University Press, 1973, p.150.
65. Joseph Addison, *Notes upon the twelve books of Paradise lost. Collected from the Spectator*, London, 1719, p.7. The English translation of Barrow's prefatory poem is included with Kastan's edition of *Paradise Lost*.
66. "Complete" and its cognates still feature prominently in analyses of the epic form. Bakhtin deployed it to describe the lack of indeterminacy that distinguished the epic world from that of the novel. Howard Weinbrot has

described the treatment of Milton and *Paradise Lost* in the Cibber-Shiels *Lives of the Poets* (1753) as part of a "self-conscious attempt to complete a line of excellence that equals the classics." Bakhtin, *The Dialogic Imagination: Four Essays*, Michael Holquist (ed.), University of Texas Press Slavic Series, Austin, University of Texas Press, 1981, pp.14–17; Weinbrot, *Britannia's Issue: The Rise of British Literature from Dryden to Ossian*, New York, Cambridge University Press, 1993, p.119.

67. Joel E. Spingarn describes Renaissance critics' turn to the works of Virgil for a fuller definition of the laws of epic as the (ironic) result of "the incompleteness of the treatment accorded to epic poetry in Aristotle's *Poetics*." Spingarn, *A History of Literary Criticism in the Renaissance*, 2nd ed., Westport, CT, Greenwood Press, 1976, p.108.

68. Aristotle, *Aristotle's Poetics*, Elizabeth A. Dobbs (trans.), Peripatetic Press, 1990, p.29. "*Hoti dei tous muthous kathaper en tais tragôidiais sunistanai dramatikous kai peri mian praxin holên kai teleian echousan archên kai mesa kai telos, hin' hôsper zôion hen holon poiêi tên oikeian...*"

69. Aristotle, *Aristotle's Poetics*, p.37.

70. Aristotle notes that the historian too *may* be selective in covering a given subject or subjects, but still need not necessarily pursue unity of action, which in some cases might simply not exist. Aristotle, *Aristotle's Poetics*, pp.86–7.

71. Aristotle, *Aristotle's Poetics*, p.29.

72. D. C. Feeney, 'Epic Hero and Epic Fable', *Comparative Literature*, 38.2, Spring 1986, pp.151–2. Feeney quotes from *Opere di Torquato Tasso*, Florence, 1724.

73. "So many there be of old that have thought the action of one man to be one ... which is both foolish and false, since by one and the same person many things may be severally done which cannot fitly be referred or joined to the same end." Ben Jonson, 'Timber, or Discoveries Made Upon Men and Matter', in *The Works of Ben Jonson*, London, 1756, pp.159–60.

74. John Dennis, *The advancement and reformation of modern poetry. A critical discourse*, London, 1701, p.201.

75. James McLaverty writes that Pope had a more complex relationship to the ideas of Le Bossu than that suggested by the inclusion of excerpts from *Traité* with *The Odyssey*. Scriblerus gets in the way of a clear understanding of Pope's purpose, but in McLaverty's opinion Pope's "far from consistently positive" treatment of Le Bossu in the apparatus of the *Dunciad Variorum* at least somewhat counters his earlier "act of deference." James McLaverty, *Pope, Print, and Meaning*, New York, Oxford University Press, 2001, p.100.

76. René Le Bossu, *Monsieur Bossu's treatise of the epick poem*, W. J. (trans.), 2nd ed., 2 vols., London, 1719, 1:137.

77. Le Bossu, *Monsieur Bossu's treatise of the epick poem*, 1:143.

78. Le Bossu, *Monsieur Bossu's treatise of the epick poem*, 1:147.

79. Recent scholarship has provided insight into the influence of Baconianism on Milton's thought and the place of the new natural philosophy in his Eden. See, for example, Karen Edwards, *Milton and the Natural World: Science and Poetry in Paradise Lost*; Angelica Duran, *The Age of Milton and the Scientific Revolution*, Pittsburgh University Press, 2007; Picciotto, 'Reforming the Garden: The Experimentalist Eden and Paradise Lost', *ELH*, 72.1, 2005, pp.23–78.

80. Duran, *The Age of Milton and the Scientific Revolution*, pp.96–7.
81. Kathleen Crowther, *Adam and Eve in the Protestant Reformation*, New York, Cambridge University Press, 2010, p.97.
82. John Milton, *Paradise Lost*, 11.349–52.
83. How and what it meant to "read" that book were likewise subject to interpretation. See Crowther, 'The Book of Nature', in *Adam and Eve in the Protestant Reformation*, pp.184–225.
84. To seventeenth-century audiences, Joanna Picciotto observes, Adam and Eve signified not only the perfect prelapsarian originals of humanity but also the imperfect collective that followed them. "To restore Adam," she writes, "was to reconsolidate humanity as the single subject it once was: redescribed as an intellectual goal, the restoration of Adam defines knowledge production as a collective investment of human energy in a necessarily imperfect activity." Picciotto, 'Reforming the Garden', p.32.
85. Milton, *Paradise Lost*, 9.681–2. Satan speaks in the language of division from the outset: discernment, disdain, and dislike appear in his first speech. The prefix "dis-", which occurs frequently in his rhetoric, reflects the Satan's state of separation from God and adumbrates the division he will visit upon Eve and Adam. See Neil Forsyth, 'Of Man's First Dis', in *Milton in Italy: Contexts, Images, Contradictions*, Mario A. Di Cesare (ed.), Binghamton, NY, 1991, pp.345–69.
86. "It was called the tree of knowledge of good and evil from the event; for since Adam tasted it, we not only know evil, but we know good only by means of evil." John Milton, 'The Christian Doctrine', in *The Complete Poems and Major Prose*, Merritt Hughes (ed.), Indianapolis, 2003, pp.900–1020, 993.
87. "discern, v." *OED Online*. June 2012. Oxford University Press. http://www.oed.com/view/Entry/53685?result=2&rskey=elSa7w& (accessed 13 August 2012).
88. Kathleen Swaim, *Before and After the Fall: Contrasting Modes in Paradise Lost*, Amherst, MA, University of Massachusetts Press, 1986, p.23.
89. Bacon, *Novum Organum*, p.9.
90. Thomas Sprat, *The history of the Royal-Society of London*, London, 1667, p.115.
91. Karen Edwards, *Milton and the Natural World*, pp.9–10.
92. John Schroeder, *The compleat chymical dispensatory, in five books,* William Rowland (trans.), London, 1669. Schroeder composed the original in Latin as *Pharmacopoea Schrödero-Hoffmanniana illustrata et aucta*. He died five years before Rowland's "Englished" version appeared.
93. Milton, *Paradise Lost*, 8.92.
94. The problem of heroism in *Paradise Lost* has long been the subject of critical attention and formed the basis of entire schools of thought; when understood in conjunction with Le Bossu's articulation of epic completeness and in the context of both Milton's piety as well as his relationship to Enlightenment knowledge production, however, the indeterminacy of heroic identity within the poem becomes another critical strategy for directing the readers' attention towards themselves.
95. Barbara Lewalski, 'The Genres of *Paradise Lost*', in *The Cambridge Companion to Milton*, Dennis Richard Danielson (ed.), New York, Cambridge University Press, 1999, p.115.
96. Lewalski, 'The Genres of *Paradise Lost*', p.126.

3 Worlds Apart: Epic and Encyclopedia in the Augustan Age

1. John Harris, 'Preface', in *Lexicon Technicum: or, an universal English dictionary of arts and sciences: explaining not only the terms of art, but the arts themselves*, 2 vols., London, 1704, 1.a5r.
2. Chambers, *Cyclopædia*, 1:vii.
3. Yeo, *Encyclopedic Visions*, p.60.
4. Thomas Hobbes, 'Preface', in *Translations of Homer*, Eric Nelson (ed.), New York, Clarendon Press, 2008, p.6. The word "encyclopedia" did not exist in Ancient Greek; it most likely derives from the misreading of Greek texts by Quintilian and Pliny the Elder. Quintilian's "encyclopædia" is the Latinized form of the Greek ἐγκύκλιος παιδεια ('enkyklios paideia'). See Robert Shackleton, 'The Encyclopædic Spirit', in *Greene Centennial Studies: Essays Presented to Donald Greene*, Paul J. Korshin and Robert R. Allen (eds), Charlottesville, University of Virginia Press, 1984, p.377.
5. Alexander Pope, *The Iliad of Homer*, in vol. 7 of *The Twickenham Edition of the Poems of Alexander Pope*, John Butt (ed.), 11 vols., New Haven, Methuen, 1967, pp.50, 5.
6. Dan Edelstein, *The Enlightenment: A Genealogy*, Chicago, University of Chicago Press, 2010, p.45.
7. Joseph Levine, *Between the Ancients and Moderns: Baroque Culture in Restoration England*, New Haven, Yale University Press, 1999, pp.ix–x.
8. Levine, *Between the Ancients and Moderns*, p.30.
9. Dryden had contemplated a poem on Arthur and the Black Prince but never undertook it, and Pope destroyed all but a few fragments of his adolescent effort on Alexander. At the end of his life, he thought of Brutus for a subject but did not live long enough to put the thought into verse. See, for example, Walter Jackson Bate, *The Burden of the Past and the English Poet*, Cambridge, MA, Harvard University Press, 1970; Harold Bloom, *The Anxiety of Influence*, New York, Oxford University Press, 1973; Alistair Fowler, 'The Life and Death of Literary Forms', *New Literary History*, 2, 1971, pp.199–216; and Dustin Griffin, 'Milton and the Decline of Epic in the Eighteenth Century', *New Literary History*, 14.1, 1982, pp.143–54.
10. In *The Dunciad in Four Books*, William Warburton (writing as Bentley/ Aristarchus) ponders if "we may not be excused, if for the future we consider the Epics of Homer, Virgil, and Milton, together with this our poem, as a complete *Tetralogy*, in which the last worthily holdeth the place or station of the *satyric* piece?" Aristarchus, though, is not to be trusted, and the *Dunciad* does not really qualify as epic. Pope, *The Dunciad in Four Books*, Valerie Rumbold (ed.), New York, Pearson Education, Inc., 1999, pp.77–8.
11. Pope's effort to maintain Homer's permanence ironically came at the cost of changing his poems in order to better align classical epic values with "the superior human values of [Pope's] own age and its preference for a culture united by the bonds of an at least tentatively rational society." Weinbrot, *Britannia's Issue*, p.303. As a result, several critics of the time pointed out, Pope's Homer contained at least as much of the former as the latter, if not more. Richard Bentley (perhaps apocryphally) objected to Pope's calling it

Homer at all. See Roger Lonsdale, *Lives of the Most Eminent English Poets*, New
York, Oxford University Press, 2006, 4:314, 285n.

12. Weber directly compares what he describes as the "archival impulses" of
Chambers's *Cyclopædia* and Pope's *Dunciad Variorum* as well as their authors'
apparent attitudes towards the distillation of knowledge and the culture of
collection out of which their works emerged. *Memory, Print, and Gender*, p.120.

13. Weber, 'The "Garbage Heap" of Memory: At Play in Pope's Archives of
Dulness', in *Eighteenth-Century Studies*, 33.1, 1999, pp.1–19.

14. Addison, *Notes upon the twelve books of Paradise lost. Collected from the
Spectator*, London, 1719, p.7.

15. John Brown, *A dissertation on the rise, union, and power, the progressions, separa-
tions, and corruptions, of poetry and music. To which is prefixed, the cure of Saul.
A sacred ode*, London, 1763, p.104. Brown quotes from the opening lines of
Milton's 'At a Solemn Music': "Blest Pair of Syrens, Pledges of Heaven's Joy, /
Sphere-born harmonious Sisters, Voice and Verse. / Wed your divine Sounds,
and mix'd Pow'r employ!" John Milton, 'At a Solemn Music', in *The Student's
Milton*, Frank Allen Patterson (ed.), New York, Appleton-Century-Crofts,
Inc., 1933, ll.1–3. "So said the sublime Milton," Brown explains, "who
knew and felt their Force: But Those whom Nature has thus joined together,
Man, by his false Refinements, hath most unnaturally put asunder." Brown,
A Dissertation, p.25.

16. John Dryden, *Fables Ancient and Modern*, in *John Dryden: Selected Poems*, Steven
Zwicker and David Bywaters (eds), London, Penguin Books, 2001, p.410.

17. Dryden, 'Of Dramatick Poesy, an Essay', London, 1735, p.lxxii.

18. Johnson also observes that, "the notions of Dryden were formed by comprehensive speculation; and those of Pope by minute attention." The knife,
however, cut both ways. The mind of William Shenstone, Johnson writes,
"was not very comprehensive, nor his curiosity active." Johnson continues:
"his general defect is want of comprehension and variety. Had his mind
been better stored with knowledge, whether he could have been great,
I know not." Samuel Johnson, *The lives of the most eminent English poets.
With critical observations on their works*, 4 vols., London, 1794, 2:129, 4:309,
4:159, 4:314.

19. John Sheffield, Duke of Buckingham, *An essay on poetry*, London, 1682, p.20.

20. Sheffield, *An essay on poetry*, p.21.

21. 'Molyneux to Locke, 20 July 1697', in *Some familiar letters between Mr.
Locke, and several of his friends*, London, 1708, p.219. In a subsequent letter,
Molyneux identified one of those philosophic "touches" that he thought
would bear a fuller treatment in a natural history. He quotes from Book IX
of *King Arthur*:

The constellations shine at his command,
He form'd their radiant orbs, and with his hand
He weigh'd, and put them off with such a force,
As might preserve an everlasting course.

I doubt not but Sir *R. Blackmore*, in these lines, had a regard to the propor-
tionment of the projective motion to the *vis centripeta*, that keeps the planets
in their continued courses ('20 July 1697', p.230).

22. "All our *English* poets (except *Milton*) have been meer ballad-makers, in comparison to him." 'Molyneux to Locke, 20 July 1697', pp.218–19.
23. Milton had sidestepped the problem of potential obsolescence or inaccuracy with respect to the still unsettled issue of heliocentrism by having Raphael declare the answer to Adam's question irrelevant to forming a better understanding of God.
24. 'Locke to Molyneux, 15 June 1697', in *Some familiar letters*, p.223.
25. 'Molyneux to Locke, 20 July 1697', p.219.
26. Trevor Ross, *The Making of the English Literary Canon: From the Middle Ages to the Late Eighteenth Century*, Montreal, McGill-Queen's University Press, 1998, p.158.
27. See Douglas Patey, 'Ancients and Moderns', in *The Cambridge History of Literary Criticism: The Eighteenth Century*, H. B. Nisbet and Claude Rawson (eds), New York, Cambridge University Press, 2005, p.54.
28. Pope, *The Iliad of Homer*, 7.50.
29. Pope, *The Iliad of Homer*, 7.5.
30. Pope, *The Iliad of Homer*, 7.56.
31. Hugh Blair did not list encyclopedic knowledge as a convention of epic, and his definition opened the category to numerous lesser poems admittedly not as "regular and complete" as those of Homer and Virgil. "They are, undoubtedly, all Epic; that is, poetical recitals of great adventures; which is all that is meant by this denomination of Poetry." Supernatural machinery, Blair allows, makes it possible for the epic poet to comprehend the "whole circle of the universe," but the phrase "arts and sciences" does not occur in any part of his treatise on epic. Hugh Blair, *Lectures on rhetoric and belles lettres*, 3 vols., Dublin, 1783, 3:220, 3:237.
32. 'No. 2', in *The Tribune*, Dublin, 1729, 2:12. *The Tribune* ran to twenty-one numbers at the end of 1729. Its first issue questions whether the recent increase in authors had been more help or harm to humanity; it did not last long enough to become too much a part of the problem.
33. See Yeo, *Encyclopaedic Visions*, p.6. Shackleton's list of texts with some variant of "encyclopedia" in their titles suggests that the earliest is a 1536 edition of a twelfth-century text by Alan of Lille. In this case, he notes, the Greek "κυκλοπαιδεια" in the title was most likely added by the editor. Chambers was the first to use the abridged "cyclopædia" as a title. See Shackleton, 'The Encyclopædic Spirit', pp.377–90.
34. Based on full-text searches of *ECCO* and *Eighteenth Century Journals*. By the early nineteenth century, the term referred more frequently to the genre rather than a specific literary property. The earliest use of "cyclopædia" in English occurs in Sir Henry Blount's *A voyage into the Levant* (1636).
35. Society of Gentlemen (eds), 'Epic, or Heroic Poem', in *A new and complete dictionary of arts and sciences*, 4 vols., London, 1763–64, 2:1099.
36. Chambers, 'Dedication', in *Cyclopædia*, n.p.
37. Chambers, 'Some considerations offered to the publick, preparatory to a second edition of Cyclopædia or, an universal dictionary of arts and sciences', London, 1735, p.4.
38. Henry Curzon, 'Preface', in *The universal library: or, compleat summary of science*, 2 vols., London, 1712, 1:a2r.
39. Chambers, 'Preface', in *Cyclopædia*, 1:x.

40. Chambers, 'Preface', in *Cyclopædia*, 1:ii.
41. William Smellie, 'Preface', in *Encyclopædia Britannica*, 3 vols., Edinburgh, 1771, 1:v.
42. Jean le Rond D'Alembert, *The plan of the French Encyclopædia*, London, 1752, p.130.
43. Denis Diderot, 'The Encyclopædia', in *Rameau's Nephew and Other Works*, Indianapolis, Hackett Publishing, 2001, p.290.
44. See Clifford Siskin, *The Work of Writing: Literature and Social Change in Britain, 1700–1830*, Baltimore, Johns Hopkins University Press, 1998, p.125.
45. Chambers, 'Preface', in *Cyclopædia*, 1:i. He goes on to say that the "bare Vocabulary of the Academy *della Crusca* was above forty Years in compiling, and the Dictionary of the *French* Academy much longer; and yet the present Work is as much more extensive than either of them in its Nature and Subject, as it falls short of 'em in number of Years, or of Persons employ'd." The *Accademia della Crusca*, a linguistically conservative society founded in Florence in 1582, began to publish their official dictionary, the *Vocabolario degli Accademici della Crusca*, in 1612. Chambers does not specify to which edition he refers. The first was a single volume in folio; the most recent edition he might have had access to or known of was the third, published in Florence in 1691 and by then expanded to three volumes in folio. See Clarence King Moore, 'L'accademia Della Crusca: Some Historical References', *Italica*, 12.2, June 1935, pp.128–9. Two editions of the *Dictionnaire de l'Académie française* were available in 1728: the first of 1694 and the second of 1718. The current ninth edition, first published in 1992, contains just over 35,000 words.
46. Siskin, *The Work of Writing*, p.129.
47. Harris, 'Preface', in *Lexicon technicum*, 1:a4r.
48. Subscription was cost-prohibitive, but reading clubs offered unlimited reading for "as little as one and a half livres a month." Though access seems to have diminished in relation to economic status, "it is impossible to know where the downward penetration of the book stopped." Elites, then, were certainly the primary audience, but "one cannot exclude the possibility that the *Encyclopédie* reached a great many readers in the lower middle classes." Robert Darnton, *The Business of Enlightenment: A Publishing History of the Encyclopédie, 1775–1800*, Cambridge, MA, Belknap Press, 1979, pp.297–9.
49. See Foucault, 'What Is an Author?' in *The Foucault Reader*, Paul Rabinow (ed.), New York, Pantheon Books, 1984, pp.101–20.
50. Yeo, *Encyclopedic Visions*, p.213.
51. Marjorie Swann has argued that in the seventeenth century, "English writers created what Foucault would term 'author-functions' that were rooted in activities of collecting and cataloguing." Swann, '*The Compleat Angler* and the Early Modern Culture of Collecting', *English Literary Renaissance*, 37.1, 2007, p.101. The eighteenth-century encyclopedists would have shared in a version of this author-function.
52. George Lewis Scott (ed.), 'To the Reader', in *A Supplement to Mr. Chambers's Cyclopædia*, 2 vols., London, 1753, 1:a1r.
53. James Millar oversaw the fourth and fifth editions (1801–09, 1817); Macvey Napier the nearly 5000-page supplement to the latter (1816–24); and Charles Maclaren the sixth (1820–23).

54. Encyclopedists, Yeo writes, appealed "to a notion of public service reinforced by the conviction that scientific knowledge ... should be widely disseminated." Even after the passage of the copyright acts of 1774, encyclopedists continued to "borrow" from primary sources as well as each other. Some, like Colin Macfarquhar and George Gleig (editors of the third edition *Britannica*), gave some credit where it was due but also left without attribution a great mass of articles that contained supposedly common knowledge and hence "belonged to no man." Yeo, *Encyclopedic Visions*, pp.216–20.

55. Thomas Lloyd (ed.), 'Preface', in *The new royal encyclopædia*, 3rd ed., 3 vols., London, 1791, 1:iii.

56. Collective credit was difficult to distribute evenly. Diderot, the abbé Mallet, and Boucher d'Argis composed the best part of the *Encyclopédie*; the chevalier de Jaucourt wrote about a quarter of it. Roughly one-third of the authors wrote only one article. Robert Darnton, *The Business of Enlightenment: A Publishing History of the Encyclopédie, 1775–1800*, Cambridge, MA, Belknap Press, 1979, p.15.

57. Robert Kerr, *Memoirs of the Life, Writings, & Correspondence of William Smellie, F. R. S. & F. A. S.*, Edinburgh, 1811, p.362.

58. Yeo, *Encyclopedic Visions*, p.214.

59. Temple Henry Croker, Thomas Williams, and Samuel Clark (eds), *The complete dictionary of arts and sciences*, 3 vols., London, 1764.

60. The authorship of encyclopedias and dictionaries was incredibly one-sided with respect to gender. Loose enforcement of copyright and attitudes about authority in the arts and sciences largely prevented women from contributing to the genre, having their contributions accepted, or receiving credit for contributions. There are no female contributors acknowledged by name in any of the major encyclopedias of the period. This by no means indicates that women did not participate in professional encyclopedic activities. *The Accomplish'd lady's delight in preserving, physick, beautifying, and cookery* (1675), a 380-page duodecimo compilation, is widely attributed to Hannah Woolley, though this attribution is not unquestioned. *The ladies dictionary*, though compiled and published by men, does acknowledge the contributions of women: "I do not pretend thereby to lessen my Obligations, to those Ladies, who by their generous imparting to me their Manuscripts, have furnisht me with several hundred Experiments and Secrets in domestick affairs, Beautifying, Preserving, Candying, Physick, Chirurgery, &c." H. N., 'Dedication', in *The ladies dictionary*, London, 1694, p.a3r. These contributors, though, are not named and likely received no financial remuneration.

61. Bacon, *The Advancement of Learning*, p.144.

62. Weber, *Memory, Print, and Gender*, p.123.

63. 'Grubstreet Journal No. 24, An Essay on *The Dunciad*', in *Faithful memoirs of the Grubstreet Society*, London, 1732, p.15. Pope is known to have contributed to this journal, but the author here is anonymous. The poem constitutes the bulk of the issue but appears with three other minor poems, including 'Mr. J. M. S—e. catechized on his Epistle to Mr. Pope'. James Moore Smythe was one of Pope's targets in *The Dunciad*, and here as there he is denounced as a thief or plagiarist.

64. 'Grubstreet Journal No. 24', p.16.

65. Marshall McLuhan, *The Gutenberg Galaxy: The Making of Typographic Man*, Toronto, University of Toronto Press, 1966, p.255.
66. Weber, *Memory, Print, and Gender*, p.136.
67. Pope, *The Dunciad Variorum*, in *The Poems of Alexander Pope*, John Butt (ed.), Methuen, 1965, p.51.
68. Though his own Tory affinities cannot be ignored, Pope prided himself on securing the integrity of his verses and character from accusations of party interest. Age and Walpole's regime helped him somewhat to overcome his resistance; the *New Dunciad* and *Dunciad in Four Books* are both more overtly condemnatory of Whig corruption and commercialism than were their predecessors.
69. William Ayre, *Memoirs of the life and writings of Alexander Pope, Esq.*, 2 vols., London, 1745, 1:246.
70. Paula McDowell, 'Mediating Media Past and Present: Towards a Genealogy of "Print Culture" Past and Present', in *This is Enlightenment*, p.235.
71. Kevis Goodman connects the notion of "noise" to Thomson's *The Seasons* and through *The Seasons* to twentieth-century information theory: "'Let us call noise the set of these phenomena of interference that become obstacles to communication,' writes Michel Serres. For Serres, if not for Thomson, such instances of static in the flow of 'information' are not entirely evils to be overcome. They are marks, vital residues, of an observer's awareness of his or her participation in a larger system of forces." Goodman, *Georgic Modernity and British Romanticism: Poetry and the Mediation of History*, New York, Cambridge University Press, 2004, p.64. Though Goodman focuses on history, this description of "noise" applies equally well to Pope's representation of both the written and oral "obstacles to communication" produced by the dunces, which are described in the verse and reproduced in the apparatus. Goodman quotes from Serres's *Hermes: Literature, Science, Philosophy*, Lawrence R. Schehr (trans.), Josué V. Harari and David F. Bell (eds), Baltimore, Johns Hopkins University Press, 1982, p.66.
72. Pope, *The Dunciad Variorum*, p.49.
73. Seth Rudy, 'Pope, Swift, and the Poetics of Posterity', *Eighteenth-Century Life*, 35.1, 2011, p.10.
74. Blackmore offers to excuse these and other faults in the preface to *King Arthur* (1697); see esp. pp.v, vii–ix.
75. Valerie Rumbold points out that, "as described by Blackmore in their titles, only *Prince Arthur, King Arthur, Eliza*, and *Alfred* qualify as epics." Rumbold, 'Note to 2.268', in *The Dunciad in Four Books*.
76. Pope, *The Dunciad in Four Books*, 2:302.
77. 'Pope to Swift, 28 June 1728', in *The Correspondence of Alexander Pope*, George Sherburn (ed.), 5 vols., Oxford, Clarendon, 1956, 2:503.
78. Aubrey Williams, *Pope's Dunciad: A Study of Its Meaning*, London, Methuen, 1955, p.62.
79. McDowell, 'Mediating Media Past and Present', p.236.
80. See James McLaverty, *Pope, Print, and Meaning*, p.109.
81. Weber, *Memory, Print, and Gender*, p.136.
82. Pope, *The Dunciad Variorum*, p.205.
83. Weber, *Memory, Print, and Gender*, p.106.

84. Pope, *The Dunciad Variorum*, 1.39; *The Dunciad in Four Books*, 1.42.
85. Pope, *The Dunciad in Four Books*, n.42.
86. Weber, *Memory, Print, and Gender*, p.123.
87. Chambers, 'Preface', in *Cyclopædia*, 1:xxi.
88. Conradus Crambe, the educational companion of Martinus Scriblerus in his fictional memoirs and a figure of Scriblerian ridicule, claims that his life is as orderly as his dictionary, for by his dictionary he orders his life. "I have made a Kalendar of radical words for all the seasons, months, and days of the year," he tells Scriblerus. "Every day I am under the dominion of a certain Word." Alexander Pope, *Memoirs of the Extraordinary Life, Works and Discoveries of Martinus Scriblerus*, Charles Kerby-Miller (ed.), New York, Oxford University Press, 1988, p.128.
89. Pope, *The Dunciad in Four Books*, 1.45.
90. Alexander Donaldson, *The cases of the appellants and respondents in the cause of literary property*, London, 1774, p.34. Mark Rose cites this passage in *Authors and Owners: The Invention of Copyright*, Cambridge, MA, Harvard University Press, 1993, p.88.
91. The apparatus represents another example of the Scriblerians coming together to compose a single work that demonstrates the opposite of their values. Their collaborations also produced *Peri Bathous* and *The Memoirs of the Extraordinary Life, Works, and Discoveries of Martinus Scriblerus*. Critics will object that the Scriblerians also collaborated on satiric (but short-lived) journals of their own and that they likewise contributed to journals and magazines when it served their purposes. Like Scriblerus, Bickerstaff too had many hands behind him. That their single, extended pieces should critique duncery by reproducing rather than directly correcting it, however, remains significant.
92. Ann Blair and Peter Stallybrass write that, "genre, in emphasizing the conventions within which texts are produced, places limits on the unbounded genius of the individual author." Blair and Stallybrass, 'Mediating Information 1450–1800', in *This is Enlightenment*, p.160. The transformation in the eighteenth century of the author into hero and the continued emphasis on genius, however, overlapped with the continued fragmentation of the generic continuum. The limits of the unbounded genius of the individual author had as much an impact on genre conventions as vice-versa; to some extent the two were mutually constitutive.
93. Jonathan Swift, *Gulliver's Travels*, New York, Penguin Books, 2003, p.171.
94. Martin Gierl, 'Science, Projects, Computers, and the State: Swift's Lagadian and Leibniz's Prussian Academy', in *The Age of Projects*, Maximillian E. Novak (ed.), Toronto, University of Toronto Press, 2008, pp.304–6.
95. Swift, *Gulliver's Travels*, p.172.
96. Pope, *Peri Bathous; or, the Art of Sinking in Poetry*, in *The Poetry and Prose of Alexander Pope*, Aubrey Williams (ed.), Boston, Houghton Mifflin Company, 1969, pp.428–9.
97. The phrase comes from the first epistle of Pope's *Essay on Man*.
98. James Ralph, 'Preface', in *Sawney. An heroic poem. Occasion'd by the Dunciad. Together with a critique on that poem address'd to Mr. T–D, Mr. M–R, Mr. Eu–N, &C.*, London, 1728, pp.ii–iii.
99. James Ralph, 'Preface', p.vi.

100. Benjamin Franklin, *The Autobiography of Benjamin Franklin*, Leonard Labaree, Ralph Ketcham and Helen Boatfield (eds), 2nd ed., New Haven, Yale University Press, 2003, p.91.
101. Joseph Warton, *An Essay on the Genius and Writing of Pope*, 5th ed., 2 vols., London, 1806, 2:369.
102. Warton, *An Essay*, 2:370–1.
103. Paula Backscheider, 'The Verse Essay, John Locke, and Defoe's Jure Divino', *ELH*, 55.1, 1988, p.101. The origins of the verse essay, Backscheider writes, go back to Persius, Juvenal, and Lucretius. Davies's poem remained in print (in Latin and English) throughout the first half of the eighteenth century; it gave rise to several like poems many or all of which Dryden, Defoe, and Pope would have known.
104. John Davies, *The origin, nature, and immortality of the soul. A poem*, 3rd ed., London, 1715, p.12. This re-titled edition of *Nosce teipsum* is one of several that would have been available to Pope.
105. Davies, *The Origin*, p.7.
106. The 1697 edition printed for W. Rogers appears to be the first to appear with these changes as well as a Table of Contents. The third edition of 1715 duplicates all of these features.
107. "Know then thyself, presume not God to scan/The proper study of Mankind is Man." Pope, *Essay on Man*, in *The Poems of Alexander Pope*, 2.1–2.
108. Pope, *Essay on Man*, p.502.
109. Pope, *Essay on Man*, 1.60, 31.
110. John Locke, *An Essay Concerning Human Understanding*, Roger Woolhouse (ed.), 2nd ed., London, Penguin Books, 1997, p.89.
111. Locke had already said as much: "For our Faculties being suited not to the full extent of Being, nor to a perfect, clear, comprehensive Knowledge of Things free from all Doubt and Scruple; but to the Preservation of us, in whom they are; and accommodated to the use of Life: they serve to our Purpose well enough..." Locke, *An Essay Concerning Human Understanding*, 4:540.
112. Pope, *Essay on Man*, 2.24–7.
113. James Thomson, *Winter*, London, 1726, pp.9, 12.
114. Sandro Jung, 'Epic, Ode, or Something New: The Blending of Genres in Thomson's Spring', *Papers on Language and Literature*, 43.2, Spring 2007, p.146. Jung refers to Chalker's *The English Georgic: A Study in the Development of a Form*, London, Routledge, 1969, pp.90–132, and Cohen's *The Unfolding of The Seasons*, Baltimore, Johns Hopkins University Press, 1970, p.92.
115. "The great defect of the 'Seasons' is want of method, but for this I know not that there was any remedy ... the memory wants the help of order, and the curiosity is not excited by suspense or expectation." Samuel Johnson, *The lives of the most eminent English poets*, 4:291–2.
116. James Thomson, *Winter*, p.15.
117. Gabrielle Starr, *Lyric Generations: Poetry and the Novel in the Long Eighteenth Century*, Baltimore, Johns Hopkins University Press, 2004, p.76.
118. The original version of the "complete" poem, published in 1730, has gaps between long verse paragraphs suggestive of shifts in subject matter, but later editions (as had been the case with Davies's *Nosce teipsum*) added section headers that in effect further disrupt the "organic" structure of the seasonal cycle.

119. Jung, 'Thomson's *Winter*, the Ur-text, and the Revision of *The Seasons*', *Papers on Language and Literature*, 45.1, Winter 2009, p.62.
120. Starr, *Lyric Generations*, p.79.
121. Jung, 'Thomson's *Winter*', pp.71–2.
122. Thomson, *The Seasons*, London, 1730, n.p.
123. Starr offers as a principal example Russel Noyes (ed.), *English Romantic Poetry and Prose*, New York, Oxford University Press, 1956, p.76.
124. Jung, 'Print Culture, High Cultural Consumption, and Thomson's *The Seasons*, 1780–1797', *Eighteenth-Century Studies*, 44.4, Summer 2011, pp.497–8.
125. John Scott and John Hoole, *Critical essays on some of the poems, of several English poets*, London, 1785, p.251; quoted by John Barrell, *Poetry, Language, and Politics*, Manchester, Manchester University Press, 1988, p.79.
126. "It was perhaps Young's own willingness to point out the absence of an organising principle in his poem that led Johnson to represent its lack of unity as a magnificent 'diversity' and 'copiousness.'" Barrell, *Poetry, Language, and Politics*, p.80.

4 Mid-Century Experiments in Encyclopedism

1. *ESTC* title search data subjected to autoregressive models of order one from the field of statistical time series analysis reveal a significant increase in this decade. See the introduction to this work and Table 1.1 in the Appendix.
2. See Jeff Loveland, *An Alternative Encyclopedia?: Dennis de Coetlogon's* An Universal History of Arts and Sciences (1745), Oxford, Voltaire Foundation, University of Oxford, 2010, esp. chapters three and four.
3. Denis Diderot, *Rameau's Nephew and Other Works*, p.277.
4. "It may repress the triumph of malignant criticism," Samuel Johnson writes, "to observe that if our language is not here fully displayed, I have only failed in an attempt which no human powers have hitherto completed." *A Dictionary of the English Language*, in *Samuel Johnson: The Major Works*, Donald Greene (ed.), New York, Oxford University Press, 2000, p.328. Robert DeMaria, Jr. has argued that Johnson's extensive use of quotations makes his dictionary an encyclopedic body of knowledge; Jack Lynch similarly claims that Johnson's dictionary "was more encyclopedic than any earlier general dictionary" and that the definitions themselves often bore a strong resemblance in quality and quantity to encyclopedia entries. See Robert DeMaria, *Johnson's 'Dictionary' and the Language of Learning*, Chapel Hill, University of North Carolina Press, 1986, and Jack Lynch, 'Johnson's Encyclopedia', in *Anniversary Essays on Johnson's* Dictionary, Jack Lynch and Anne McDermott (eds), New York, Cambridge University Press, 2005, p.134.
5. See Chapter 3.
6. George Sale, *An Universal History, from the earliest account of time*, 20 vols., Dublin, 1744, 1:xxxv–xxxvi (italics added).
7. Sale, *An Universal History*, 1:xxi.
8. "The known rules of epic poetry suppose the truth of the history, though they admit of its being embellished with poetical fictions." Sale, *An*

Universal History, 5:183. This suggestion of historical accuracy with poetic "embellishment" further affirms a parallel inversion of Pope's earlier claim that knowledge of the arts and sciences (as opposed to factual history or poetic fictions) were added as "necessity or ornament."

9. Hayden White lists these as the idealized qualities of modern narrative historiography. See White, 'Narrative in the Representation of Reality', in *The Content of the Form*, Baltimore, Johns Hopkins University Press, 1987, p.24. Narrative has remained a prevalent (though not uncontroversial) mode of organizing historical knowledge and thus creating historical "realities" in and for modernity; see also pp.1–25, esp. pp.20–5.

10. Denis Pétau (Dionysius Petavius), 'To the Reader', in *The history of the world, or an account of time*, London, 1659, n.p. See also Johannes Sleidanus, *A briefe chronicle of the foure principall empyres. To witte, of Babilon, Persia, Grecia, and Rome. Wherein, is compendiouslye conteyned the whole discourse of histories*, Stephan Wythers (trans.), London, 1563.

11. William Howell, *An instition of general history, from the beginning of the world to the monarcy of Constantine the Great. Composed in such method and manner as never yet was extant*, London, 1661, p.a1v.

12. Thomas Hearne, *Ductor historicus: or, a short system of universal history, and an introduction to the study of it*, 2 vols., London, 1704–05, 1:a3r. The last version of this system, a reprint of the fourth edition of 1723, appeared in London in 1724. Hearne's work as a scholarly editor of English chronicles led Pope to include him as the "Wormius" of *The Dunciad*.

13. Hearne, *Ductor Historicus*, 1:a2v. Bodin's *Methodus ad facilem historiarum cognitionem (Method for the easy comprehension of histroy)* (1566) contributed to Early Modern European *Ars historica* a distinctive emphasis on political theory and the systematic organization of historical knowledge. Bodin calls analysis "'that pre-eminent guide to the teaching of the arts [...] in order that understanding of history (*historiarum scientia*) shall be complete and facile'" (*Methodus*, [Re] 20; Latin [Me] 116). Through analysis, according to Bodin, "one is able to divide universals into parts, and to divide each part into subsections without losing the coherence of the whole." Mario Turchetti, 'Jean Bodin', in *The Stanford Encyclopedia of Philosophy*, Edward N. Zalta (ed.), 2010. <http://plato.stanford.edu/archives/sum2010/entries/bodin/>. Turchetti quotes from Jean Bodin, *Methodus ad facilem historiarum cognitionem*, Parisiis, 1566. Text and French trans. in [Me] 104–269; English translation in [Re].

14. 'Proposals (by the proprietors of the work) for printing by subscription, in Twenty Volumes Octavo, *an Universal History*', London, 1746, p.8. The proprietors identify Howell's as "the most General History extant in English" before their own. That assessment likely comprehends both parts one and two of Howell's history, first published in 1661 and expanded in 1680, as well as the second section of part two, *An instition of general history: or, the history of the ecclesiastical affairs of the world* (1685). Most of the popular English histories did not extend beyond two volumes in any size, regardless of how many centuries or civilizations they covered. Urbain Chevreau's *The history of the world, ecclesiastical and civil: from the creation to this present time* (1703) spanned some 2300 pages over five volumes octavo, but only

one edition appeared in English and the authors of *An Universal History* make no mention of it.

15. 'Proposals', p.8. George I established the Regius Modern History Professorships in 1724.
16. *An Universal History*, 1:v.
17. 'Proposals', p.9. The proprietors' proposal to reprint the ancient part in twenty volumes octavo refers to nine original volumes in folio rather than seven. Volumes one and seven of that edition each contain two parts with separate title pages but continuous pagination.
18. I borrow the phrase from P. W. Anderson's article describing scientific hierarchies and the advancement of knowledge. See P. W. Anderson, 'More is Different', *Science*, 177.4047, 4 August 1972, pp.393–6.
19. *An Universal History*, 1:1.
20. He compared an exact chronology to "Ariadne's Clue, which conducts our Steps through the Windings of the Labyrinth."*An Universal History*, 1:xxxviii. A similar passage appears in Hearne's *Ductor historicus*: "...being a Chronological Account of Events, which we commonly term *The Thread of History*; without which we might soon be at a loss in the Labyrinth of so many Ages that have been from the beginning of the World." *An Universal History*, 1:126.
21. The two parts of Eusebius's *Chronicle* provide, respectively, epitomized histories of the Chaldeans, Assyrians, Hebrews, Egyptians, Greeks, and Romans and "a table of dates arranged in columns so that contemporary events in the histories of different nations would be on the same line." The original text, most of which is lost, was probably compiled in the early fourth century. Andrew Louth, 'Eusebius and the Birth of Church History', in *The Cambridge History of Early Christian Literature*, Frances Young, Lewis Ayres, and Andrew Louth (eds), New York, Cambridge University Press, 2004, p.270.
22. See David Mungello, 'The Proto-Sinological Assimilation of China's History and Geography in the Works of Martini', in *Curious Land: Jesuit Accommodation and the Origins of Sinology*, Honolulu, University of Hawaii Press, 1989, esp. pp.124–33; James Barr, 'Pre-Scientific Chronology: The Bible and the Origin of the World', in *Proceedings of the American Philosophical Society*, 143.3, September 1999, pp.379–87; and Anthony Grafton, 'Dating History: the Renaissance & the Reformation of Chronology', *Daedalus*, 132.2, Spring 2003, pp.74–85.
23. See Grafton, 'Joseph Scaliger and Historical Chronology: The Rise and Fall of a Discipline', *History and Theory*, 14.2, May 1975, pp.156–85, and *Joseph Scaliger: A Study in the History of Classical Scholarship*, New York, Oxford University Press, 1983.
24. Rachel Ramsay, 'China and the Ideal of Order in John Webb', *Journal of the History of Ideas*, 62.3, July 2001, p.491.
25. *An Universal History*, 1:lxxviii.
26. *An Universal History*, 1:lxvi.
27. "In adjusting our Periods, we have strained nothing to any Hypothesis of our own, or to force the Sacred History to agree with any Part of the Prophane, as too many unreasonably have done." *An Universal History*, 1:lxxiv.
28. Though Sale includes a "brief orthodox refutation" of Spinoza and proclaims the Mosaic record the only authentic version, "he had already set

up his reader to perceive the Mosaic account as simply one among many by crowding it in with a series of other more exotic cosmogonies." Tamara Griggs, 'Universal History from Counter-Reformation to Enlightenment', *Modern Intellectual History*, 4.2, 2007, p.234.

29. See Daniel Rosenberg and Anthony Grafton, *Cartographies of Time: A History of the Timeline*, New York, Princeton Architectural Press, 2010.
30. Hearne, *Ductor historicus*, 1:44.
31. *An Universal History*, 1:xxxix.
32. *An Universal History*, 1:xxxv.
33. As Peter Gay put it, "historical narration without analysis is trivial, historical analysis without narration is incomplete." Gay, *Style in History*, New York, W. W. Norton & Company, 1991, p.183.
34. *An Universal History*, 1:xl.
35. *An Universal History*, 2:76–7.
36. The text was published in English in 1703. See Urbain Chevreau, *The history of the world, ecclesiastical and civil: from the creation to this present time*, London, 1703, pp.284–5.
37. Jacques Bénigne Bossuet, *A discourse on the history of the whole world*, London, 1703, p.34. The first English edition appeared in 1686. New English editions and translations, with different titles and publishers, appeared with fair regularity from 1728 to 1785. All quotations are from the second edition unless otherwise specified.
38. *An Universal History*, 4:532–47.
39. *An Universal History*, 1:xxxix.
40. See Michael Keevak, *The Pretended Asian: George Psalmanazar's Eighteenth-Century Formosan Hoax*, Detroit, Wayne State University Press, 2004, pp.9–10, 61–88. Psalmanazar is also the cannibalistic "Salmanaazor" of Swift's *A Modest Proposal*.
41. Griggs, 'Universal History from Counter-Reformation to Enlightenment', pp.234–5.
42. Psalmanazar brought the matter before Henry Herbert, ninth Earl of Pembroke and a major supporter of the work. He agreed with Psalmanazar in principle but thought the problem "past remedying." The publishers claimed to be "so much out of pocket already, that they could not afford to destroy so great a number of copies for the sake of uniformity." George Psalmanazar, *Memoirs of****. Commonly known by the name of George Psalmanazar; a reputed native of Formosa*, London, 1764, pp.252–3.
43. Questions about Bower's character persisted throughout much of the 1750s. In *A faithful account of Mr. A–ch-b-ld B-w-r's motives for leaving his office of secretary to the Court of Inquisition* (1750), Bower asserted that he had been a Jesuit and Inquisitorial counselor in Italy before converting to Protestantism and escaping to England. Alban Butler attacked these assertions, along with Bower's *The History of the Popes* (1748–66), in a pamphlet, *Remarks on the two first volumes of the lives of the Popes*, printed in Douay in 1754. John Douglas carried on the assault in *Six letters from A—d B—r to Father Sheldon, Provincial of the Jesuits in England; illustrated with several remarkable facts, tending to ascertain the authenticity of the said letters, and the true character of the writer* (1756). Bower responded, and the two (amongst others) continued to trade proofs and pamphlets until 1758.

44. Psalmanazar, *Memoirs*, p.263.
45. The other authors of the ancient part included John Swinton, a celebrated antiquary; John Campbell, LL.D.; and George Shelvocke. (George, who journeyed with his father around the world, may have witnessed the shooting of an albatross by the ship's second mate as recorded by his father in *A voyage round the world by way of the Great South Sea* [1723]; Wordsworth was reading *A Voyage* in the spring of 1798.)
46. Psalmanazar, *Memoirs*, p.270.
47. *Proposals for publishing the modern part of the Universal history*, London, 1758, pp.15–16.
48. Griggs cites the Seven Years' War (1756–63), well underway when the proprietors published the proposal for the modern part of the history, as a defining part of the context in which the history became "the perfect vehicle" for championing commercial enterprises. Griggs, 'Universal History from Counter-Reformation to Enlightenment', p.237.
49. Karen O'Brien, 'The History Market in Eighteenth-Century England', in *Books and Their Readers in Eighteenth-Century England: New Essays*, Isabel Rivers (ed.), London, Continuum, 2001, p.117.
50. Voltaire, 'Introduction', in *An essay on universal history, the manners, and spirit of nations, from the reign of Charlemaign to the age of Lewis XIV*, Mr. Nugent (trans.), 4 vols., 2nd ed., London, 1759, 1:2.
51. O'Brien cites the particular influence of Scottish historians such as Lord Kames, Adam Ferguson, James Dunbar, and John Millar on the "disaggregation of the past." O'Brien, 'The History Market', pp.123–4.
52. For the link between novel and epic, see, for example, E. M. W. Tillyard, *The Epic Strain in the English Novel*, London, Chatto & Windus, 1958; Mikhail Bakhtin, 'Epic and Novel', in *The Dialogic Imagination: Four Essays*, pp.3–40.
53. I follow Hunter's assertion that "popular thought and materials of everyday print—journalism, didactic materials with all kinds of religious and ideological directions, and private papers and histories—need to be seen as contributors to the social and intellectual world in which the novel emerged" and add to that list the encyclopedia and encyclopedic projects as materials of particular importance. J. Paul Hunter, *Before Novels*, New York, W. W. Norton and Company, 1990, p.5.
54. Henry Fielding, *Joseph Andrews*, in *Joseph Andrews and Shamela*, Judith Hawley (ed.), New York, Penguin Books, 1999, p.51.
55. See William Warner, *Licensing Entertainment: The Elevation of Novel Reading in Britain, 1684–1750*, Berkeley, University of California Press, 1998.
56. Sellers continued to back new editions of works first published nearer the turn of the century, and before 1740 much of the space given to fiction in magazines, journals, and newspapers was dedicated to reprints of "classic" English novels of proven popularity. See Robert Mayo, *The English Novel in the Magazines, 1740–1815*, London, Oxford University Press, 1962, p.233.
57. Richardson and Fielding both took care to distinguish what they wrote from what they knew in their time as "the novel." Defoe and Sterne also avoided the term. Only Smollett seems to have been content to refer to his novels as such. He likewise refers to Fielding's novels as novels in the fourth volume of his, though the same text labels Richardson's fictions a "species of writing equally new and extraordinary." Tobias Smollett, *Continuation of the Complete*

history of England, 5 vols., London, 1760–65, 4:127–8. An earlier critic had similarly described Fielding's novels in 'An essay on the new species of writing founded by Mr. Fielding: with a word or two upon the modern state of criticism, London, 1751, p.14.

58. Warner, *Licensing Entertainment*, p.42 (italics added).
59. See Marshall McLuhan, *Understanding Media*.
60. Warner, *Licensing Entertainment*, p.42.
61. Fielding, *Tom Jones*, p.26.
62. Fielding specifically derided romances and novels and had been forced to abandon the stage to reproductions and writers less willing or able to offend the Walpole regime.
63. Fielding, *Joseph Andrews*, pp.202–3. Mariana finished the first version of his *Historiae* in 1592 and added another ten books in 1605. He translated them into Spanish as *Historia General de España* (part one in 1601; part two in 1609). Richard Sare published Captain John Stevens's English translation in 1699 as *The General History of Spain*.
64. *An Universal History*, 1:v (italics added).
65. The sixth volume of *An Universal History* was published in 1742, the same year in which Millar (spurred by the success of *Pamela*) published *Joseph Andrews*. Millar's name appears as one of its publishers only on the title page of volume six.
66. Fielding, *Tom Jones*, p.316.
67. Fielding, *Tom Jones*, p.317.
68. Fielding's narrator counts the power of discernment, which Milton identified as an epistemological outcome of sin in *Paradise Lost* (see Chapter 2), amongst the "gifts" of nature with which people enter the world.
69. Fielding, *Tom Jones*, p.317.
70. Fielding, *Tom Jones*, p.327. Barbara Benedict offers several other practices of producing and organizing knowledge that Fielding's novel might be said to borrow from or duplicate. Fielding's novels, she writes, supply readers with "collectible portraits" and a "scientific anatomy" of human specimens with which to "furnish their mental cabinets." Benedict, *Curiosity: A Cultural History of Early Modern Inquiry*, Chicago, University of Chicago Press, 2001, p.187.
71. William Sale, Jr., *Samuel Richardson: Master Printer*, Ithaca, Cornell University Press, 1950, pp.101–4.
72. Samuel Richardson, 'Appendix I: Introduction to the Second Edition', in *Pamela: Or, Virtue Rewarded*, Thomas Keymer and Alice Wakely (eds), New York, Oxford University Press, 2001, p.517.
73. Psalmanazar's *An historical and geographical description of Formosa* (1704), which he falsely claimed to have written from personal experience, came under attack soon after its publication, but Psalmanazar did not admit to the deceit until asked to write a section on Formosa for *A Complete system of geography* (1744), published by (among others) Millar, Rivington, and Thomas Osborne—another proprietor of *An Universal History*. There is some question as to whether the continuation of *Pamela* he wrote for Richardson was invited or unsolicited; Robert Day suggests the former. In any case, Richardson roundly rejected it. See Day, 'Psalmanazar's "Formosa" and the

British Reader (including Samuel Johnson)', in *Exoticism in the Enlightenment,* George Sebastian Rousseau and Roy Porter (eds), Manchester, Manchester University Press, 1990, p.201; Thomas Eaves and Ben Kimpel, *Samuel Richardson: A Biography,* Oxford, Clarendon Press, 1971, pp.144–5; and Frederick Foley, *The Great Formosan Imposter,* St. Louis, St. Louis University Press, 1968, pp.52–4.

74. Millar also published *Joseph Andrews, Tom Jones,* and *Amelia.*
75. Richardson, *The History of Sir Charles Grandison,* London, 1753, p.iii.
76. Richardson, 'To the Reverend Mr Hildesley, 21 February 1755', in *The Correspondence of Samuel Richardson,* Anna Laetitia Barbauld (ed.), 6 vols., London, 1804, 5:132.
77. Boswell records Johnson's pronouncement: "if you were to read Richardson for the story, your impatience would be so much fretted that you would hang yourself." James Boswell, *The Life of Samuel Johnson,* R. W. Chapman and J. D. Fleeman (eds), New York, Oxford University Press, 1998, p.159.
78. Aaron Hill, 'To Mr. Richardson, 7 January 1744–5', in *The Correspondence of Samuel Richardson,* 1:101.
79. Smollett, *Continuation of the Complete history of England,* 2:160. For Smollett's contributions to the modern part of *An Universal History,* see Louis Martz, 'Tobias Smollett and the *Universal History',* *Modern Language Notes,* lvi.1, January 1941, pp.1–14. As previously observed, a "short, yet not imperfect, system of Ethics" had been the unrealized end of Pope's *Essay on Man.*
80. 'Philocalus to the reader, n.d.', Forster Collection of the Victoria and Albert Museum (hereafter FC) XV, 4, f. 45; 'Frances Grainger to Richardson, 23 May 1754', FC XV, 3, f. 49; 'Anonymous to Richardson, n.d.', FC XV, 3, f. 61, 2v. Quoted by Sylvia Marks, *Sir Charles Grandison: The Compleat Conduct Book,* Lewisberg, PA, Bucknell University Press, 1986, p.34.
81. *Grandison* alone "transcends even as it transforms every familiar genre of writing." Marks, *Sir Charles Grandison,* p.34.
82. Wetenhall Wilkes, *A letter of genteel and moral advice to a young lady,* Dublin, 1740, p.13. The book was printed in London in 1744 and ran through eight editions by 1766, by which time it had more than doubled in length.
83. Samuel Johnson, 'system', in *A Dictionary of the English Language.*
84. Richardson, 'Advertisement', in *Clarissa. Or, the history of a young lady,* 2nd ed., London, 1749, p.iv.
85. Jocelyn Harris, *The History of Sir Charles Grandison,* by Samuel Richardson, Oxford University Press, 1986, p.494. Cheyne was also Richardson's physician.
86. The phrase "solar system" dates from the late seventeenth century; the *OED* cites Locke's *Elements of Natural Philosophy* as its earliest occurrence in English. "solar, adj. and n.1". *OED Online.* December 2012. Oxford University Press. http://www.oed.com/view/Entry/184063?redirectedFrom= solar+system (accessed 15 December 2012).
87. "The strong inclination post-*Principia* was to suppose that phenomena other than the phenomena of motion that Newton had dealt with so successfully could be assumed either to reduce in one way or other to phenomena of motion lending themselves to 'Newtonian' treatment." Ernan McMullin,

'The Impact of Newton's Principia on the Philosophy of Science', *Philosophy of Science*, 68.3, September 2001, p.290. The predicted reappearance of Halley's comet in 1759 did much to confirm the validity of gravitational theory and the universality of natural laws. See also Mark Loveridge, *Laurence Sterne and the Argument About Design*, London, Macmillan Press, 1982, pp.72–3, 81.

88. McMullin, 'The Impact of Newton's Principia', p.290.
89. Ian Donaldson, 'The Clockwork Novel: Three Notes on an Eighteenth-Century Analogy', *The Review of English Studies*, 21.81, February 1970, p.14. The quotation occurs in Boswell's *Life of Johnson*, p.389. Johnson furthermore claimed that, "there is more knowledge of the heart in one letter of Richardson's than in all of *Tom Jones*." Boswell, for his part, found Johnson's "excessive and unaccountable depreciation of one of the best writers that England has produced" surprising. Boswell, *The Life of Samuel Johnson*, p.480.
90. Fielding, *Tom Jones*, p.149.
91. Donaldson, 'The Clockwork Novel', p.15.
92. John Bender, 'Enlightenment Fiction and the Scientific Hypothesis', *Representations*, 61, Winter 1998, p.8.
93. Bossuet, *A discourse on the history of the whole world*, p.a3. In 1728, the edition printed by Richard Reily as *An introduction to, or a short discourse concerning, universal history* replaces "Paris" with "London."
94. History became a regular part of the encyclopedia's purview with the second edition of the *Encyclopædia Britannica*—a development addressed in the following chapter.
95. Chambers, 'Preface', in *Cyclopædia*, 1:ii.
96. Henry Fielding, *Tom Jones*, Sheridan Baker (ed.), 2nd ed., New York, W. W. Norton & Company, 1995, pp.316–17.
97. I borrow the phrase from Bender, 'Enlightenment Fiction and the Scientific Hypothesis', p.10.
98. John Tinkler, 'Humanist History and the English Novel in the Eighteenth Century', *Studies in Philology*, 85.4, Autumn 1988, p.523. Tinkler quotes Gilbert Felix, *Machiavelli and Guicciardini: Politics and History in Sixteenth-Century Florence*, New York, W. W. Norton and Company, 1984, p.225.
99. The use of fictional elements in history, Tinkler observes, has been part of the European tradition for more than a millennium. Tinker, 'Humanist History', p.524.
100. I do not mean to suggest that such gaps or disagreement never occur—merely that if they do, then they are not the result of any external necessity.
101. Fielding, *Tom Jones*, p.259.
102. I follow John J. Burke's argument that Fielding offers "a new form of historiography, history without historical content." Burke, 'History Without History: Henry Fielding's Theory of Fiction', in *A Provision of Human Nature: Essays on Fielding and Others in Honor of Miriam Austin Locke*, Donald Kay (ed.), Tuscaloosa, University of Alabama Press, 1977, p.45.
103. Fielding, *Joseph Andrews*, p.201.
104. Fielding, *Joseph Andrews*, p.203.

105. Fielding, *Joseph Andrews*, p.49.
106. Fielding, *Joseph Andrews*, p.52.
107. Bossuet, *Discourse*, p.a3v. Both might equally have borrowed from a comparison of-the inn and chapter made by Augustine; see John Mason, 'chapter', in *Pantologia*, London, 1813, n.p.
108. The essay on divisions "pays little attention to the notion that a book should be consistently pattered to a moral end, and instead encourages the reader to choose what appeals to him or her from among the rich assemblage of delights separately offered by separate chapters." Bryan Burns, 'The Story-telling in Joseph Andrews', in *Henry Fielding: Justice Observed*, K. G. Simpson (ed.), London, Vision Press, 1985, p.125. James Lynch writes that Fielding treats the divisions as "simply a matter of practicality." His narrators often comment, "tongue in cheek, on presenting too large a joint for the patient reader's carving." Lynch, *Henry Fielding and the Heliodoran Novel: Romance, Epic, and Fielding's New Province of Writing*, London, Associated University Presses, 1986, p.50.
109. Hill, 'To Richardson' (n.d.), in *Correspondence*, 1:98. The letter was certainly written in or after April 1743 and probably several months before the end of the year.
110. When the abridgment "finally brought home to [Richardson] the resolute impercipience of his principal literary consultant, he suspended the correspondence." Thomas Keymer, *Richardson's 'Clarissa' and the Eighteenth-Century Reader*, Cambridge, Cambridge University Press, 1992, p.64.
111. Richardson wrote of his diffuseness and difficulty with forming plans to Aaron Hill, Johannes Stinstra, and Lady Bradshaigh; T. C. Eaves and Ben Kimpel, however, write that "from the first mention of [*Clarissa*] he had its general plan firmly in mind, and he held to his own conception of the story and especially the characters." Eaves and Kimpel, *Samuel Richardson: A Biography*, pp.205–6.
112. Richardson, 'Richardson to Lady Bradshaigh, 9 October 1756', in *Selected Letters of Samuel Richardson*, John Carroll (ed.), Oxford, Oxford University Press, 1964, p.329. In the first letter of *Clarissa*, Anne Howe requests that the heroine write "in so full a manner as may gratify those who do not know so much of your affairs as I do." Richardson, *Clarissa; or, the History of a Young Lady*, Angus Ross (ed.), New York, Penguin Books, 1985, p.40.
113. Hill, *Correspondence*, 1:98.
114. Barbauld, 'Life of Samuel Richardson, with Remarks on his Writing', in *The Correspondence of Samuel Richardson*, 1:xxvi–xxvii.
115. Aphra Behn, *Oroonoko*, Janet Todd (ed.), New York, Penguin Books, 2003, p.9. For the problems of Behn's claim, see McKeon, *Origins of the English Novel*, pp.111–13.
116. Daniel Defoe, *Roxana: The Fortunate Mistress*, John Mullan (ed.), Oxford, Oxford University Press, 1996, p.103.
117. Defoe, *Moll Flanders*, Edward Kelly (ed.), New York, W. W. Norton & Company, 1973, p.49.
118. Richardson, *Clarissa*, p.36. The comment echoes that of Hill referenced in the previous paragraph.

119. Leah Price, *The Anthology and the Rise of the Novel*, Cambridge, Cambridge University Press, 2000, p.13.
120. Price, *The Anthology and the Rise of the Novel*, pp.22, 17.
121. 'To Thomas Edwards, 1 August 1755', quoted in Eaves and Kimpel, *Samuel Richardson*, p.421.
122. Price, *The Anthology and the Rise of the Novel*, p.22.
123. Bender, 'Enlightenment Fiction', p.10. See also McKeon, *The Origins of the English Novel*, pp.25–64. Fielding's narrator opens the final book of *Tom Jones* too much protesting that he "will do no Violence to the Truth and Dignity of History for his Sake; for he had rather relate that he was hanged at Tyburn (which may very probably be the Case) than forfeit our Integrity, or shock the Faith of our Reader." Fielding, *Tom Jones*, p.570.
124. Clifford Siskin, *The Work of Writing*, p.175.
125. Robert Morison's *Plantarum historiæ universalis Oxoniensis* was printed at Oxford in 1679; John Ray's *Historia plantarum* (1686), a similar work, became a "universal history of plants" when James Petiver referred to it as such in his 1716 proposal to expand the original. The author of *A philosophical enquiry concerning the nature, use and antiquity of hemp* (1733) recommends a "universal history of bell-ropes" attributed to Johannes Goropius Becanus. Daniel Defoe, writing under the name Andrew Moreton, published in 1729 *The secrets of the invisible world disclos'd: or, an universal history of apparitions sacred and prophane, under all denominations; whether, angelical, diabolical, or human-souls departed*. Periodicals going by other names than "magazine" had been circulating for decades before Cave's.
126. "universal, adj., n., and adv.". *OED Online*. September 2012. Oxford University Press. http://www.oed.com/view/Entry/214783?redirectedFrom=universal (accessed 17 September 2012).
127. 'To the Public', in *The Monthly Review*, London, 1754, 10:161.
128. Urmi Bhowmik, 'Facts and Norms in the Marketplace of Print: John Dunton's *Athenian Mercury*', *Eighteenth-Century Studies*, 36.3, Spring 2003, p.347.
129. Bhowmik, 'Fact and Norms', p.346. Bhowmik cites Michael McKeon, 'The Origins of Interdisciplinary Studies', *Eighteenth-Century Studies*, 28.1, Fall 1994, p.17.
130. Bhowmik, 'Facts and Norms', p.354.
131. John Dunton, *The compleat library*, London, 1692, p.a2r. Stephen Parks suggests that Dunton viewed *The compleat library* as not only continuing but also perfecting its predecessor. Parks, *John Dunton and the English Book Trade: A Study of His Career With a Checklist of His Publications*, New York, Garland Press, 1976, p.127.
132. Robert Mayo, *The English Novel in the Magazines*, p.15.
133. Dunton, *The compleat library*, London, 1693, pp.143–4.
134. Dunton, *The post-angel, or Universal entertainment*, London, 1701, p.a2r.
135. Hunter, *Before Novels*, p.317.
136. Quoted by Hunter, *Before Novels*, p.317.
137. *The Grand magazine of magazines; or, A public register of literature and amusement* (1750) reappeared as *The Grand magazine of magazines, or Universal register* in 1758.

138. William Fadden, *The Literary magazine: or, Universal review*, 3 vols., London, 1756, 1:iv.
139. Fadden, *The Literary magazine*, 1:iii; italics added.
140. Benjamin Martin, *The general magazine of Arts and Sciences, philosophical, philological, mathematical, and mechanical*, 14 vols., London, 1755–65, 1:iv. "Never" may have overstretched the truth. In 1747, the first issue of *The Universal magazine of knowledge and pleasure* explained that, "In the course of this work, the reader may expect *a whole body of arts and sciences*, a system of husbandry, and other advantageous improvement in art and nature." 'The Author to the Readers', *Universal magazine*, 1, 1747, p.ii; quoted by Yeo, *Encyclopedic Visions*, p.72.
141. The magazine remained a means by which to disseminate general knowledge. In the Victorian era, for example, the *British Penny Magazine* (1826–45) sought "to provide moral, cheap and, crucially, useful literature through 'the imparting useful information to all classes of the community.'" Its footnotes and cross-references "created an encyclopaedic feel," and subscribers were encouraged to bind issues together and keep them as single annual reference works. The magazine was not, however, designed for reconstruction into treatises after the fashion of *Martin's Magazine*. Toni Weller, 'Preserving Knowledge Through Popular Victorian Periodicals: An Examination of *The Penny Magazine* and the *Illustrated London News*, 1842–1843', *Library History*, 24.3, September 2008, p.201.
142. Martin, *Bibliotheca technologica: or, a philological library of literary arts and sciences*, London, 1737, p.a2r. The arts and sciences covered include Theology, Ethics or Morality, Christianity, Judaism, Mahometanism, Gentilism, Mythology, Grammar and Language, Rhetoric and Oratory, Logic, Ontology, Poetry, Criticism, Geography, Chronology, History, Physiology, Botany, Anatomy, Pharmacy, Medicine, Polity and Oeconomics, Jurisprudence, Heraldry, and Miscellanies (mathematical arts and sciences).
143. Martin, *Philosophia Britannica; or a new and comprehensive system of the Newtonian philosophy, astronomy and geography*, London, 1747, p.i.
144. John Millburn, *Benjamin Martin: Author, Instrument-Maker, and 'Country Showman'*, Leyden, Noordhoff International Publishing, 1976, pp.20–1. I am very much indebted to Millburn's study for his detailed overview and assessments of *The general magazine*.
145. 'Advertisement', in *The philosophical grammar*, by Benjamin Martin, London, 1735, p.xxx. Quoted by Millburn, *Benjamin Martin*, pp.5–6.
146. Martin, 'An Account of the Plan and Design', in *The general magazine of Arts and Sciences*, 1:iv.
147. Martin, 'An Account', 1:v–vi.
148. Martin, 'Contents', in *The general magazine of Arts and Sciences*, no. XLV (June 1758), n.p.
149. Millburn, *Benjamin Martin*, p.71.
150. Martin, 'An Account', 1:vi.
151. Pope, *Iliad*, p.56.
152. Martin, 'An Account', 1:iii.
153. Millburn, *Benjamin Martin*, p.69.

154. Martin, 'Introduction', in *The general magazine of Arts and Sciences*, 14:iv.
155. Martin, *The general magazine*, 14:iv.

5 Collapse and Reconstitution: Epic and Encyclopedia Revisited

1. Samuel Johnson, 'No. 91. Saturday, January 12, 1760', in *The Idler*, 2 vols., London, 1771, 2:217–18.
2. Society of Gentlemen (eds), *A new and complete dictionary of arts and sciences*, London, 1763–64, 1:a2r.
3. Curzon, *The universal library: or, compleat summary of science*, p.a2r.
4. 'Proposals for printing, by subscription, a work, intitled, Encyclopædia Britannica; or, A new and complete dictionary of arts and sciences', Edinburgh, 1768, n.p.
5. "For a Renaissance humanist," Passannante observes, "the word '*spargere*' would have had notoriously negative connotations—the scattering of tradition, the scattering of Orphic limbs, the dispersal of Petrarch's Rime sparse." Passannante, 'Homer Anatomized', p.137. That negativity inheres in the sense of scattering conveyed by the proposal despite a lack of necessary connection between it and the philosophies of earlier humanists.
6. Hill, *Correspondence*, 1:99.
7. Sterne, *The Life and Opinions of Tristram Shandy*, p.107.
8. By the nineteenth century, the *Britannica* was "considered to be *the* British encyclopedia," and "of all eighteenth-century dictionaries of arts and sciences, the Britannica is the most recognizable as an encyclopedia by a modern reader." Frank Kafker, 'Smellie's Edition of the *Encyclopædia Britannica*', in *Notable Encyclopedias of the Late 18th Century: Eleven Successors of the Encyclopédie*, Frank Kafker (ed.), Oxford, Voltaire Foundation, 1994, pp.170, 176.
9. William Wordsworth, 'Preface to *Lyrical Ballads*', in *William Wordsworth: The Major Works*, Stephen Charles Gill (ed.), New York, Oxford University Press, 2008, p.197.
10. Laurence Sterne, '23 May 1759', in *Letters of Laurence Sterne*, Lewis Perry Curtis (ed.), Oxford, Clarendon Press, 1935, p.74.
11. 'An account of the Rev. Mr. ST****, and his writings', in *The Grand magazine*, 35 vols., London, 1758–60, 1:309–10.
12. 'A genuine letter from a Methodist preacher in the country, to Laurence Sterne, M. A. Prebendary of York. Printed from the Original Manuscript', London, 1760, p.2.
13. 'Interesting Trial, Harrison against Cooke', in *The Weekly entertainer*, 59 vols., Sherborne, 1794, 24:107.
14. 'The Character of Laurence Sterne', in *The North British Intelligencer; or, Constitutional miscellany*, R. Dick and A. Belshis (eds), 4 vols., Edinburgh, 1777, 4:35.
15. John Aikin and William Johnston, 'Sterne, Laurence', in *General Biography*, 10 vols., London, 1814, 9:242.
16. Ian Watt, *The Rise of the Novel; Studies in Defoe, Richardson, and Fielding*, Berkeley, University of California Press, 1957, pp.290–1.

17. Northrop Frye, *Anatomy of Criticism: Four Essays*, 1970; reprint, Toronto, University of Toronto Press, 2006, p.284.
18. Warner, *Licensing Entertainment*, p.242; McKeon, *The Origins of the English Novel*, p.419.
19. Patricia Meyer Spacks, *Novel Beginnings: Experiments in Eighteenth-Century Prose Fiction*, New Haven, Yale University Press, 2006, p.254. Spacks quotes Viktor Shklovsky, *Theory of Prose*, Benjamin Sher (trans.), Elmwood Park, IL, Dalkey Archive Press, 1990, p.170.
20. Thomas Keymer, 'Sterne and the "New Species of Writing"', in *Laurence Sterne's Tristram Shandy: A Casebook*, Thomas Keymer (ed.), New York, Oxford University Press, 2006, pp.50–1.
21. Sterne, *Tristram Shandy*, pp.11–12.
22. Dirk Vanderbeke, 'Winding Up the Clock: The Conception and Birth of Tristram Shandy', in *Fashioning Childhood in the Eighteenth Century: Age and Identity*, Anja Müller (ed.), Aldershot, Ashgate, 2006, p.182. See also Louis A. Landa, 'The Shandean Homunculus: The Background of Sterne's "Little Gentleman"', in *Restoration and Eighteenth-Century Literature: Essays in Honor of Alan Dugald McKillop*, Carroll Camden (ed.), Chicago, University of Chicago Press, 1963, pp.49–68.
23. Sterne, *Tristram Shandy*, p.7.
24. Aphra Behn, *Oroonoko, or the Royal Slave*, in *Oroonoko, The Rover, and Other Works*, Janet Todd (ed.), New York, Penguin Books, 1992, p.75. Julie Park describes *Oroonoko* as "the most protypically novelistic of narratives—if not 'the first' novel—written in England's long eighteenth century." Park, *The Self and It: Novel Objects in Eighteenth-Century England*, Stanford, Stanford University Press, 2010, p.14.
25. Sterne, *Tristram Shandy*, p.129.
26. Sterne, *Tristram Shandy*, p.130.
27. Sterne, *Tristram Shandy*, p.6. For "scattering" and "semina" with respect to Bacon, Politian, and Homer, see Chapter 2.
28. Chambers, 'Preface', in *Cyclopædia*, 1:x.
29. John Freeman, 'Delight in the (Dis)Order of Things: *Tristram Shandy* and the Dynamics of Genre', *Studies in the Novel*, 34.2, Summer 2002, pp.144, 145–6.
30. See Christopher Fanning, '"This Fragment of Life": Sterne's Encyclopedic Ethics', *The Shandean*, 13, 2002, p.55; Edward Bensley, 'A Debt of Sterne's', *TLS*, 1 November 1928, p.806; Bernard Greenberg, 'Laurence Sterne and Chambers' Cyclopædia', *Modern Language Notes*, LXIX, 1954, pp.560–2. Sterne may also have taken some of his knowledge about knowledge from the *Cyclopædia*, which in turn owes a great deal to John Locke: "the nine-column entry on 'Knowledge', one of the longest in the work, is a summary 'according to Mr. Locke' of the various comparisons and contrasts between ideas that constitute knowledge." Yeo, *Encyclopedic Visions*, p.158.
31. Fanning, 'This Fragment of Life', p.56.
32. Sterne, *Tristram Shandy*, pp.432, 303.
33. Sterne, *Tristram Shandy*, pp.77, 75.
34. Sterne, *Tristram Shandy*, p.74.
35. 'Proposals (by the proprietors of the work) for printing by subscription, in Twenty Volumes Octavo, *an Universal History*', p.9.

36. Both volumes, coincidentally, were published in 1759, the same year as the first book of *Tristram Shandy*.
37. Sterne, *Tristram Shandy*, p.64. Joseph Drury notes that the progressive and digressive motions of the work were suggested to Tristram "by the two movements of the earth in its diurnal rotation and annual orbit." "Despite the fact that Tristram has moved from the microcosm of the body to the macrocosm of the universe for his analogy," Drury explains, "the structural elements are the same." Joseph Drury, 'The Novel and the Machine in the Eighteenth Century', *Novel: A Forum on Fiction*, 42.2, Summer 2009, p.338.
38. Sterne, *Tristram Shandy*, p.323.
39. Judith Hawley, '*Tristram Shandy*, Wit, and Enlightenment Knowledge', in *The Cambridge Companion to Laurence Sterne*, Thomas Keymer (ed.), New York, Cambridge University Press, 2009, pp.37–8.
40. Sterne, *Tristram Shandy*, pp.256–7.
41. "Take away the sex-urge and Richardson and Fielding fall to the ground." Loveridge, *Laurence Sterne and the Argument About Design*, p.12.
42. Sterne, *Tristram Shandy*, p.8.
43. Sterne, *Tristram Shandy*, p.204.
44. The original page was not borderless; the marbling was contained entirely within a white and numbered page. See W. G. Day, '*Tristram Shandy*: The Marbled Leaf', *Library*, 27, 1972, pp.143–5, and Diana Patterson 'Tristram's Marbling and Marblers', *Shandean*, 3, 1991, pp.70–97.
45. As Fanning points out, the marbled page may represent "a response to, or even a struggle against, the fixity of print," which Elizabeth Eisenstein identified as a defining feature of the technology. Fanning, 'Sterne and Print Culture', in *The Cambridge Companion to Laurence Sterne*, p.133. See also Eisenstein, *The Printing Press as an Agent of Change: Cultural Transformation in Early Modern Europe*, 2 vols., Cambridge, Cambridge University Press, 1979, 1:113–26.
46. Sterne, *Tristram Shandy*, p.204.
47. "Paralipomenon, n.". *OED Online*. September 2012. Oxford University Press. http://www.oed.com/view/Entry/137457?redirectedFrom=paralipomena (accessed 3 November 2012).
48. "Readers have frequently observed that death hangs heavy over Tristram's tale, which is, for all its comedy and wit, a pathetic account." William Holtz, *Image and Immortality: A Study of Tristram Shandy*, Providence, Brown University Press, 1970, p.127.
49. Bacon, *The Great Instauration*, in *Novum Organum*, p.9.
50. See Chapter 2; *A Manuall: or, analecta, being a compendious collection out of such as have treated of the office of Justices of the Peace*, p.a3r.
51. Harris, 'Introduction', in *Lexicon Technicum*, 2 vols., 1710, n.p.
52. D'Alembert, *The plan of the French Encyclopædia*, London, 1752, p.137. This text is an English translation of the preface to the *Encyclopédie*.
53. Wordsworth, *The Prelude*, in *The Major Works*, l.542.
54. The proposal for the *Britannica*, published 8 June 1768, gives it a slightly different title: *Encyclopædia Britannica; or, A new and complete dictionary of arts and sciences*. The phrase "new and complete" does occur in the final version beneath the title and above the first entries of the body proper.
55. James Creech, '"Chasing after Advances": Diderot's Article 'Encyclopedia"', *Yale French Studies*, 63, 1982, p.189.

56. "Moment" here includes both the publication of a complete edition at once, and the appearance of it in numbers/volumes over a period of several years.

57. Smellie defined "acanthus" as "an ornament representing the leaves of the acanthus, used in the capitals of the Corinthian and Composite orders." The most recent *Britannica* records the following: "in architecture and decorative arts, a stylized ornamental motif based on a characteristic Mediterranean plant with jagged leaves, *Acanthus spinosus.*" William Smellie, *Encyclopædia Britannica*, 1st ed., 3 vols., 1771, 1:12, 466; *Encyclopædia Britannica Online*, s. v. 'acanthus', http://www.britannica.com/EBchecked/topic/2749/acanthus (accessed 10 January 2014).

58. *Encyclopædia Britannica*, 1st ed., p.10. The error may have been the result of oversight rather than ignorance; the practice of excising material from other and often much earlier works came with risks to accuracy. James Tytler corrected the mistake in the second edition.

59. Yeo, *Encyclopedic Visions*, pp.189–90.

60. Temple Henry Croker, et al., 'Advertisement', in *The complete dictionary of arts and sciences*, 3 vols., London, 1764–66, 1:a1r.

61. See Herman Kogan, *The Great EB: The Story of the Encyclopaedia Britannica*, Chicago, University of Chicago Press, 1958, p.39.

62. Bruno Latour, *Science in Action: How to Follow Scientists and Engineers through Society*, Cambridge, MA, Harvard University Press, 1987, pp.25–8.

63. Smellie, 'Preface', in *Encyclopædia Britannica*, 1:v.

64. See Lawrence Sullivan, 'Circumscribing Knowledge: Encyclopedias in Historical Perspective', *The Journal of Religion*, 70.3, July 1990, pp.315–59.

65. Colin Macfarquhar and George Gleig (eds), 'Preface', in *Encyclopædia Britannica*, 3rd ed., 20 vols., Edinburgh, 1797, 1:viii.

66. Kafker, 'Smellie's Edition of the *Encyclopædia Britannica*', p.151.

67. *Encyclopædia Britannica*, 2nd ed., 1:iv.

68. This figure includes front and back material, pages of errata, etc. Amongst its many other problems of both content and form, the first edition suffered from gross errors in pagination that make an accurate count challenging. The approximation of 2400 derives from Kafker's account of the errors. Kafker, 'Smellie's Edition of the *Encyclopædia Britannica*', p.150. By *Britannica*'s count, the first edition contained 2391 pages, four folded leaves of unnumbered tables, and 160 copperplates.

69. *Encyclopædia Britannica*, 2nd ed., 1:175.

70. Jonathon Green points out that "Sir Thomas Elyot was born in Wiltshire, the son of Sir Richard Elyot, a lawyer. Some claims existed for his having been born in Suffolk, and this spurious theory lasted for at least nine editions of the *Encyclopædia Britannica*." Jonathon Green, *Chasing the Sun: Dictionary Makers and the Dictionaries They Made*, New York, Henry Holt, 1996, p.84. Biographical information, then, was not beyond reproach. If, moreover, the entrant was not the subject of ongoing research, as would likely often be the case with the biographies of "lesser" historical figures, such errors could be amongst the longest lasting. The perpetuation of error equally demonstrates the Latournian model of establishing certitude.

71. *Encyclopædia Britannica*, 2nd ed., 1:a4r.

72. *Encyclopædia Britannica*, 2nd ed., 10:8612.

73. *Encyclopædia Britannica*, 2nd ed., 10:8776.

74. *Encyclopædia Britannica*, 2nd ed., 1:175, 177.
75. Yeo, *Encyclopedic Visions*, p.192.
76. 'Preface', in *Encyclopedia Britannica*, 3rd ed.,1:vii. See Thomas Reid, 'A Brief Account of Aristotle's Logic', in *Sketches of the history of man*, 3:207. A different version of the same quotation also occurs in 'Essay 1', in *Essays on the intellectual powers of man*, Edinburgh, 1785, p.71.
77. Adam Smith, *An Inquiry into the Nature and Causes of the Wealth of Nations: A Selected Edition*, Kathryn Sutherland (ed.), New York, Oxford University Press, 1998, p.18.
78. 'Prefatory Note', in *Encylopædia Britannica*, 11th ed., Cambridge, Cambridge University Press, 1910, 1:viii.
79. 'Preface', in *Encyclopædia Perthensis*, 23 vols., Perth, 1796–1806, 1:i.
80. On Wolf, see Grafton, 'Renaissance Readers of Homer's Ancient Readers', p.158. Wolf was not the first to question ancient allegoresis or Homer's sole authorship of the poems—both positions had ancient antecedents—and his conclusions did not go uncontested, but his work did establish a new basis for the modern study of Homer and the epic tradition.
81. Samuel Taylor Coleridge, *Biographia Literaria*, in *Samuel Taylor Coleridge: The Major Works*, H. J. Jackson (ed.), New York, Oxford University Press, 1985, p.355.
82. Marjorie Levinson, *The Romantic Fragment Poem: A Critique of a Form*, Chapel Hill, University of North Carolina Press, 1986, p.24.
83. Mary Poovey, 'The Model System', p.420.
84. Poovey, 'The Model System', pp.420–1.
85. "I absolutely nauseate Darwin's poem." Coleridge, 'Coleridge to John Thewall, 13 May 1796', in *Collected Letters*, Earl Leslie Griggs (ed.), Oxford, Clarendon Press, 1959–71, 1:216.
86. Alan Bewell, 'Erasmus Darwin's Cosmopolitan Nature', *ELH*, 76, 2009, pp.19–20.
87. Erasmus Darwin, 'Advertisement', in *The Botanic Garden; a Poem, in Two Parts. Part I. Containing the Economy of Vegetation. Part II. The Loves of the Plants. With Philosophical Notes*, London, 1791, n.p.
88. Darwin, *The Botanic Garden*, p.97.
89. Darwin, *The Botanic Garden*, p.202.
90. Darwin, *The Botanic Garden*, p.vii.
91. Michael Page, 'The Darwin before Darwin: Erasmus Darwin, Visionary Science, and Romantic Science', *Papers on Language and Literature*, 41.2, 2005, p.149.
92. The period is full of figures that attempted to write science as well as poetry; nevertheless, some authors and critics of the time did insist that the sensibilities that characterized each made them unsuited to doing the work of the other. The chemist and inventor Humphry Davy wrote and published poetry, but he understood there to be a difference in purpose: "the object of poetry, whatever may be said by the poets, is more to amuse than to instruct; the object of science more to instruct than amuse." Wordsworth too wrote of the differences between the Poet and the Man of Science in the revised *Preface to the Lyrical Ballads*. Humphry Davy, *Memoirs of the Life of Sir Humphry Davy, Bart., L.L.D., F.R.S., Foreign Associate of the Institute of France, Etc.*, London, 1839, p.147.

93. Pope, *Essay on Man*, ll.24–6.
94. Darwin, *The Botanic Garden*, 4.83–8.
95. Bewell, 'Erasmus Darwin's Cosmopolitan Nature', p.33. Bewell quotes from John Prest, *The Garden of Eden: The Botanic Garden and the Re-Creation of Paradise*, New Haven, Yale University Press, 1981, p.42.
96. Darwin, *The Botanic Garden*, p.vii.
97. Maureen McLane, *Romanticism and the Human Sciences: Poetry, Population, and the Discourse of the Species*, Cambridge Studies in Romanticism, New York, Cambridge University Press, 2000, p.6.
98. Wordsworth, 'Preface to *Lyrical Ballads* (1802)', in *William Wordsworth: The Major Works*, p.606.
99. Wordsworth, 'Preface to *Lyrical Ballads* (1802)', p.605.
100. Wordsworth, 'Preface to *Lyrical Ballads* (1802)', p.595.
101. McLane, *Romanticism and the Human Sciences*, p.5.
102. For arguments for and against the completeness of *Tristram Shandy* in this regard, see Wayne Booth, 'Did Sterne Complete *Tristram Shandy*?', *Modern Philology*, 48.3, February 1951, pp.172–83; Marcia Allentuck, 'In Defense of an Unfinished *Tristram Shandy*: Laurence Sterne and the *Non Finito*', in *The Winged Skull: Papers from the Laurence Sterne Bicentenary Conference*, Arthur Hill Cash and John M. Stedmond (eds), London, Methuen, 1971, pp.145–55.
103. Wordsworth, 'The Two-Part Prelude of 1799', in *The Prelude 1799, 1805, 1850*, Jonathan Wordsworth, M. H. Abrams and Stephen Charles Gill (eds), New York, W. W. Norton & Company, 1979, p.3.
104. Stephen Gill, 'Introduction', in *The Prelude, 1799, 1805, 1850*, p.ix.
105. Godwin particularly objected to the works of Hume, Robertson, and by implication Burke. Jon Klancher, 'Godwin and the Genre Reformers: On Necessity and Contingency in Romantic Narrative Theory', in *Romanticism, History, and the Possibilities of Genre*, Tilottama Rajan and Julia Wright (eds), Cambridge, Cambridge University Press, 1998, pp.29–30. Klancher quotes Percy Bysshe Shelley, 'Defense of Poetry', in *Shelley's Poetry and Prose: Authoritative Texts, Criticism*, Donald H. Reiman and Sharon B. Powers (eds), New York, Norton, 1977, p.493.
106. William Godwin, 'Of History and Romance', reel 5 of the Duke University microfilm copy of Godwin's papers in the Abinger Collection, reprinted in *Caleb Williams*, Maurice Hindle (ed.), New York, Penguin Books, 1988, p.361.
107. See Chapter 4.
108. See Mark Phillips, *Society and Sentiment: Genres of Historical Writing in Britain, 1740–1820*, Princeton, Princeton University Press, 2000, pp.118–22; Tilottama Rajan, 'The Disfiguration of Enlightenment: War, Trauma, and the Historical Novel in Godwin's *Mandeville*', in *Godwinian Moments: From the Enlightenment to Romanticism*, Robert M. Maniquis and Victoria Myers (eds), Toronto, University of Toronto Press, 2011, pp.172–93.
109. Godwin, 'Of History and Romance', p.364.
110. Godwin, 'Of History and Romance', p.363.
111. Godwin, 'Of History and Romance', p.372.
112. Phillips, *Society and Sentiment*, p.119.
113. Godwin, 'Of History and Romance', p.372.

114. Wordsworth, 'The Prelude of 1805 in Thirteen Books', in *The Prelude, 1799, 1805, 1850*; ll.125–7.
115. Beth Lau, 'Wordsworth and Current Memory Research', *Studies in Literature, 1500–1900*, 42.4, Autumn 2002, p.682. Lau cites the work of John R. Anderson and Lael J. Schooler, 'Reflections of the Environment in Memory', *Psychological Science*, 2.6, November 1991, pp.396–408; David L. Shacter, *Searching for Memory: The Brain, the Mind, and the Past*, New York, Basic Books, 1996, pp.3–4, 81; Jefferson A. Singer and Peter Salovey, *The Remembered Self: Emotion and Memory in Personality*, New York, Free Press, 1993, p.121; and Schacter, *Seven Sins of Memory*, New York, Houghton Mifflin, 2001, pp.187–90.
116. See Elizabeth Parker, Larry Cahill, and James McGaugh, 'A Case of Unusual Autobiographical Remembering', *Neurocase*, 12.1, February 2006, pp.35–49. The term "hyperthymestic syndrome" was suggested for the first time in this article.
117. Siskin, *The Historicity of Romantic Discourse*, New York, Oxford University Press, 1988, p.104.
118. Wordsworth, *The Two-Part Prelude*, in *The Pedlar, Tintern Abbey, the Two-Part Prelude*, Jonathan Wordsworth (ed.), Cambridge, Cambridge University Press, 1985, 1.288.
119. Wordsworth, *The Two-Part Prelude*, 1.257.
120. Sir John Barrow, *Sketches of the Royal Society and Royal Society Club*, London, 1849, p.10. As J. McKeen Cattell, President of the New York Academy of Sciences (founded in 1817 as the Lyceum of Natural History in the City of New York) put it at the annual meeting of 1902, "these societies were offshoots from the Royal Society, and were a necessary result of the differentiation of science and the increase in the number of men of science." 'President's Address', in *Annals of the New York Academy of Sciences*, New York, New York Academy of Sciences, 1904, 15:102.
121. Samuel Taylor Coleridge, *A Dissertation on the Science of Method*, London, Richard Griffin and Company, 1854, p.15.
122. Sullivan, 'Circumscribing Knowledge', p.320.
123. Coleridge had planned to start "with mathematics, proceeding through the physical sciences and concluding with biography and history." Yeo, *Encyclopedic Visions*, p.249.
124. Coleridge, 'On the Science of Method', in *Encyclopædia Metropolitana*, Edward Smedley, Hugh Rose, and Henry Rose (eds), London, John Joseph Griffin and Company, 1849, 1:21.
125. The editors predictably tried to turn this into a selling point: the title page of the 1845 edition advertises the work "comprising the twofold advantage of a philosophical and an alphabetical arrangement."
126. Augustus De Morgan, 'Review of Cyclopædias', in *A Budget of Paradoxes*, New York, Cosimo, Inc., 2007, p.282.
127. De Morgan, 'Review of Cyclopædias', p.284.
128. De Morgan, 'Review of Cyclopædias', p.285.
129. De Morgan, 'Review of Cyclopædias', p.285.
130. 'History of Cyclopædias', in *The Quarterly Review*, London, John Murray, 1863, 113:371.

131. Robert Post, 'Debating Disciplinarity', *Critical Inquiry*, 35.4, Summer 2009, p.751. Post quotes Roy Harvey Pearce, 'American Studies as a Discipline', *College English*, 18.4, January 1957, p.181.
132. Julie Thompson Klein, 'Blurring, Cracking, and Crossing: Permeation and the Fracturing of Discipline', in *Knowledges: Historical and Critical Studies in Disciplinarity*, Ellen Messer-Davidow, David Shumway, and David J. Sylvan (eds), Charlottesville, VA, University of Virginia Press, 1993, p.190; quoted by Post, 'Debating Disciplinarity', p.751.

Coda: The Angel and the Algorithm

1. Defoe, *A compleat system of magick: or, the history of the black-art*, London, 1729, pp.1–2.
2. Mark Horowitz, 'Visualizing Big Data: Bar Charts for Words', *Wired*, 23 June 2008, http://www.wired.com/science/discoveries/magazine/16-07/pb_ visualizing (accessed 19 October 2012).
3. 'Britannica Today', *Encyclopedia Britannica*, http://corporate.britannica. com/about/today/ (accessed 29 December 2012).
4. David McKitterick, *Print, Manuscript, and the Search for Order, 1450–1830*, New York, Cambridge University Press, 2003, p.205.
5. 'Wikipedia: Statistics', *Wikipedia: The Free Encyclopedia*, http://en.wikipedia. org/w/index.php?title=Wikipedia:Statistics&oldid=587963650 (accessed 6 January 2014).
6. The online edition of *Britannica* has entries on *Star Wars* (1977) and *Titanic* (1997), for example – both in the top twenty in terms of gross – but not *Jurassic Park* (1993) and *Independence Day* (1996), which are also in the top twenty and had the highest grosses for the years in which they were released (these films are briefly mentioned within other entries). Wikipedia has full articles on all of them.
7. 'Wikipedia: What Wikipedia is Not', *Wikipedia: The Free Encyclopedia*, http://en.wikipedia.org/w/index.php?title=Wikipedia:What_Wikipedia_is_ not&oldid=589429742 (accessed 6 January 2014).
8. Meta Contributors, 'Association of Deletionist Wikipedians', *Meta, discussion about Wikimedia projects*, http://meta.wikimedia.org/w/index. php?title=Association_of_Deletionist_Wikipedians&oldid=6764342 (accessed 6 January 2014).
9. Meta Contributors, 'Association of Inclusionist Wikipedians', *Meta, discussion about Wikimedia projects*, http://meta.wikimedia.org/w/index. php?title=Association_of_Inclusionist_Wikipedians&oldid=6939662 (accessed 6 January 2014).
10. Those without internet access cannot benefit from the site at all, but my interest here is in the technodeterministic aspects of article creation and consumption that persist beyond the initial hurdle of connectivity.
11. Jean de La Quintinie, *The compleat gard'ner*, George London and Henry Wise (eds), London, 1699, p.a1r.
12. Wikipedia contributors, 'Larry Norman', *Wikipedia, The Free Encyclopedia*, http:// en.wikipedia.org/w/index.php?title=Larry_Norman&oldid=558068891 (accessed 6 January 2014). See also, 'Larry Norman: Revision History',

Wikipedia, The Free Encyclopedia, http://en.wikipedia.org/w/index. php?title=Larry_Norman&offset=&limit=100&action=history (accessed 6 January 2014).

13. 'Wikipedia: Article Size', *Wikipedia, The Free Encyclopedia*, http://en.wikipedia. org/w/index.php?title=Wikipedia:Article_size&oldid=581677074 (accessed 6 January 2014).

14. Chris Anderson, 'The End of Theory: The Data Deluge Makes the Scientific Method Obsolete', *Wired*, 16 July 2008, http://www.wired.com/science/ discoveries/magazine/16-07/pb_theory (accessed 12 January 2012).

15. "Search is how Google began, and it's at the heart of what we do today. We devote more engineering time to search than to any other product at Google, because we believe that search can always be improved." 'Corporate information', Google, http://www.google.com/intl/et/corporate/ (accessed 2 January 2012).

16. According to comScore, a publicly traded internet marketing research company, Google alone hosted approximately 235 million searches a day in July of 2008. Google currently hosts approximately 65 per cent of all internet searches.

17. Randall E. Stross, *Planet Google: One Company's Audacious Plan to Organize Everything We Know*, New York, Free Press, 2008, p.69.

18. Stross, *Planet Google*, p.26.

19. 'Technology Overview', Google, http://www.google.com/corporate/tech. html (accessed 12 April 2010).

20. Battelle, *The Search*, p.46.

21. According to Google software engineers Jesse Alpert and Nissan Hajaj, Google now "downloads the web continuously, collecting updated page information and re-processing the entire web-link graph several times per day... So multiple times every day, we do the computational equivalent of fully exploring every intersection of every road in the United States. Except it'd be a map about 50,000 times as big as the U.S., with 50,000 times as many roads and intersections." Alpert and Hajaj, 'We Knew the Web Was Big ...', in *The Official Google Blog* (5 July 2008), http://googleblog.blogspot. com/2008/07/we-knew-web-was-big.html (accessed 3 January 2012).

22. This "was customarily regarded as including an ability to decipher the nature of every creature from its name." Charles Webster, *The Great Instauration*, pp.15–16.

23. Estimates of the web's current size vary widely and depend on the definition of a "useful" page. As of 5 January 2013, worldwidewebsize.com estimates that the public indexable web consists of over 14 billion pages. The web arrived at the trillion-URL marker in July 2008.

24. David Weinberger, *Too Big to Know*, New York, Basic Books, 2011, p.9.

25. Eric Schmidt, 'Technology is Making Marketing Accountable', Google (8 October 2005), http://www.google.com/press/podium/ana.html (accessed 2 January 2012).

26. See Jean-Noël Jeanneney, *Google and the Myth of Universal Knowledge: A View from Europe*, Teresa Lavender Fagan (trans.), Chicago, University of Chicago Press, 2007.

27. Tim Berners-Lee, James Hendler, and Ora Lassila, 'The Semantic Web', *Scientific American Magazine*, 17 May 2001, http://www.scientificamerican. com/article.cfm?id=the-semantic-web (accessed 3 January 2012).

28. Grigoris Antoniou and Frank Van Harmelen, *A Semantic Web Primer*, Cambridge, MA, The MIT Press, 2004, p.4.
29. Battelle, *The Search*, p.252.
30. 'About Wolfram|Alpha', Wolfram|Alpha.com, http://www.wolframalpha. com/about.html (accessed 13 January 2014).
31. Horowitz, 'Visualizing Big Data'.

Bibliography

Addison, Joseph (1719) *Notes upon the twelve books of Paradise lost. Collected from the Spectator*, London: Printed for Jacob Tonson.

Aikin, John, and Johnston, William (1799–1815) 'Sterne, Laurence', in *General Biography; or, Lives Critical and Historical, of the Most Eminent Persons of All Ages, Countries, Conditions, and Professions, Arranged According to Alphabetical Order*, vol. 9, London: Printed for G.G. and J. Robinson.

Aitchison, Alexander (ed.) (1806) *Encyclopædia Perthensis*, 23 vols., Perth: Printed for C. Mitchell and Co.

Allentuck, Marcia (1972) 'In Defense of an Unfinished *Tristram Shandy*: Laurence Sterne and the Non Finito', in *The Winged Skull: Papers from the Laurence Sterne Bicentenary Conference*, London: Methuen, pp.145–55.

Alpert, Jesse, and Hajaj, Nissan (2008) 'We Knew the Web Was Big...', in *The Official Google Blog*, 5 July, available at http://googleblog.blogspot. com/2008/07/we-knew-web-was-big.html.

Anderson, Chris (2008) 'The End of Theory: The Data Deluge Makes the Scientific Method Obsolete', *Wired*, 23 June, available at http://www.wired.com/science/discoveries/magazine/16-07/pb_theory.

Anderson, P. W. (1972) 'More is Different', *Science*, 177.4047, 4 August, pp.393–6.

Anon. (1641) *A manuall: or, analecta, being a compendious collection out of such as have treated of the office of Justices of the Peace, but principally out of Mr Lambert, Mr Crompton, & Mr Dalton*, London: Printed by Miles Flesher and Robert Young.

Anon. (1729) 'No. 2', in *The Tribune*, London: T. Warner, pp.9–17.

Anon. (1732) 'Grubstreet Journal No. 24. Essay on the *Dunciad*', in *Faithful memoirs of the Grubstreet Society. Now Published for the first time by Mr. Bavius*, London.

Anon. (1751) *An essay on the new species of writing founded by Mr. Fielding*, London: Printed for W. Owen.

Anon. (1754) 'To the Public', in *The Monthly Review*, London: Printed for R. Griffiths, p.161.

Anon. (1758–60) 'An account of the Rev. Mr. St****, and his writings', in *Grand magazine*, London, pp.309–10.

Anon. (1760) *A genuine letter from a Methodist preacher in the country, to Laurence Sterne, M.A. Prebendary of York. Printed from the Original Manuscript*, London: Printed for S. Vandenbergh.

Anon. (1777) 'The Character of Laurence Sterne', in *The North British Intelligencer; or, Constitutional Miscellany*, R. Dick and A. Belshis (eds), Edinburgh, pp.35–6.

Anon. (1794) 'Interesting Trial, Harrison against Cooke', in *The Weekly Entertainer*, Sherborne.

Anon. (1863) 'History of Cyclopædias', in *The Quarterly Review*, London: John Murray, pp.354–87.

Antoninou, Grigoris, and Van Harmelen, Frank (2004) *A Semantic Web Primer*, Cambridge, MA: The MIT Press.

Aristotle (1990) *Aristotle's Poetics*, Elizabeth Dobbs (trans.), Peripatetic Press.

Ayre, William (1745) *Memoirs of the life and writings of Alexander Pope, Esq; faithfully collected from authentic authors, Original Manuscripts, and the Testimonies of many Persons of Credit and Honour: With critical observations. Adorned with the Heads of divers Illustrious Persons, treated of in these Memoirs, curiously engrav'd by the best Hands*, London: Printed for the Author.

Backscheider, Paula (1988) 'The Verse Essay, John Locke, and Defoe's Jure Divino', *ELH*, 55.1, pp.99–124.

Backscheider, Paula (2005) *Eighteenth-Century Women Poets and Their Poetry: Inventing Agency, Inventing Genre*, Baltimore, MD: Johns Hopkins University Press.

Bacon, Francis (1994) *Novum Organum*, Peter Urbach and John Gibson (trans. and eds), Paul Carus Student Editions, Chicago: Open Court.

Bacon, Francis (2002) *The Advancement of Learning*, in *The Major Works*, Brian Vickers (ed.), New York: Oxford University Press, pp.120–299.

Barbauld, Anna Laetitia (1804) 'Life of Samuel Richardson, with Remarks on His Writing', in *The Correspondence of Samuel Richardson*, London.

Barr, James (1999) 'Pre-Scientific Chronology: The Bible and the Origin of the World', *Proceedings of the American Philosophical Society*, 143.3, pp.379–87.

Barrell, John (1988) *Poetry, Language, and Politics*, New York: Manchester University Press.

Barrow, Sir John (1849) *Sketches of the Royal Society and Royal Society Club*, London: Printed for John Murray.

Bate, Walter Jackson (1970) *The Burden of the Past and the English Poet*, Cambridge, MA: Harvard University Press.

Battelle, John (2005) *The Search: How Google and Its Rivals Rewrote the Rules of Business and Transformed Our Culture*, New York: Portfolio.

Bayle, Pierre, and Desmaizeaux, Pierre (1734–38) *The Dictionary historical and critical of Mr. Peter Bayle*, 2nd ed., London: Printed for J.J. and P. Knapton, D. Midwinter, J. Brotherton et al.

Beauvais, Vincent of (1624) *Speculum Naturale, Prologue*, Bibliotecha Mundi, vol. 1, Douai.

Behn, Aphra (2003) *Oroonoko*, Janet Todd (ed.), New York: Penguin Books.

Bender, John (1998) 'Enlightenment Fiction and the Scientific Hypothesis', *Representations*, 61, pp.6–28.

Bender, John, and Marrinan, Michael (2010) *The Culture of Diagram*, Stanford: Stanford University Press.

Benedict, Barbara (2001) *Curiosity: A Cultural History of Early Modern Inquiry*, Chicago: University of Chicago Press.

Bensley, Edward (1928) 'A Debt of Sterne's', *TLS*, 1 November.

Berners-Lee, Tim, Hendler, James, and Lassila, Ora (2001) 'The Semantic Web', *Scientific American Magazine*, 17 May.

Bewell, Alan (2009) 'Erasmus Darwin's Cosmopolitan Nature', *ELH*, 76, pp.19–48.

Bhowmik, Urmi (2003) 'Facts and Norms in the Marketplace of Print: John Dunton's *Athenian Mercury*', *Eighteenth-Century Studies*, 36.3, pp.345–65.

Blackmore, Sir Richard (1697) *King Arthur*, London.

Blair, Ann (2003) 'Reading Strategies for Coping with Information Overload Ca. 1550–1700', *Journal of the History of Ideas*, 64.1, pp.11–28.

Blair, Ann (2010) *Too Much to Know: Managing Scholarly Information before the Modern Age*, New Haven: Yale University Press.

226   *Bibliography*

Blair, Ann, and Stallybrass, Peter (2010) 'Mediating Information 1450–1800', in *This is Enlightenment*, Clifford Siskin and William Warner (eds), Chicago: University of Chicago Press, pp.139–63.

Blair, Hugh (1783) *Lectures on rhetoric and belles lettres*, vol. 3, Dublin: Printed for Messrs. Whitestone, Colles, Burnet, Moncrieffe, Gilberts, et al.

Bloom, Harold (1973) *The Anxiety of Influence*, New York: Oxford University Press.

Blount, Thomas (1653) *The academic of eloquence*, London: Printed for H. Moseley.

Bodin, Jean (1566) *Methodus Ad Facilem Historiarum Cognitionem*, Paris: Printed for Martinum Juvenum.

Booth, Wayne (1951) 'Did Sterne Complete *Tristram Shandy?*' *Modern Philology*, 48.3, pp.172–83.

Bossuet, Jacques Bénigne (1703) *A discourse on the history of the whole world*, London: Printed for Matthew Turner.

Boswell, James (1988) *The Life of Samuel Johnson*, R. W. Chapman and J. D. Freeman (eds), New York: Oxford University Press.

Brown, John (1763) *A dissertation on the rise, union, and power, the progressions, separations, and corruptions, of poetry and music. To which is prefixed, the cure of Saul. A sacred ode*, London: Printed for L. Davis and C. Reymers.

Buckingham, John Sheffield, Duke of (1682) *An essay on poetry*, London: Printed for Joseph Hindmarsh.

Burke, John J. (1977) 'History without History: Henry Fielding's Theory of Fiction', in *A Provision of Human Nature: Essays on Fielding and Others in Honor of Miriam Austin Locke*, Donald Kay (ed.), Tuscaloosa: University of Alabama Press.

Burns, Bryan (1985) 'The Story-Telling in "Joseph Andrews"', in *Henry Fielding: Justice Observed*, K. G. Simpson (ed.), London: Vision Press, pp.119–36.

Cattell, J. McKeen (1904) 'President's Address', in *Annals of the New York Academy of Sciences*, New York: New York Academy of Sciences.

Chambers, Ephraim (ed.) (1728) *Cyclopædia*, London: Printed for James and John Knapton, et al.

Chartier, Roger (1994) *The Order of Books: Readers, Authors, and Libraries in Europe between the Fourteenth and Eighteenth Centuries*, Stanford: Stanford University Press.

Chevreau, Urbain (1703) *The history of the world, ecclesiastical and civil: from the creation to this present time*, London: Printed for D. Brown.

Cocles, Bartolommeo della Rocca (1556) *A brief and most pleasaunt epitomye of the whole art of phisiognomie*, Thomas Hill (trans.), London: By Iohn Waylande.

Cohen, Ralph (1986) 'History and Genre', *New Literary History*, 17.2, pp.203–18.

Cole, Percival (1910) *A Neglected Educator: J. H. Alsted*, Sydney: William Applegate.

Coleridge, Samuel Taylor (1854) *A Dissertation on the Science of Method*, London: Richard Griffin and Company.

Coleridge, Samuel Taylor (1959–71) '13 May 1796', in *Collected Letters of Samuel Taylor Coleridge*, Earl Leslie Griggs (ed.), Oxford: Clarendon Press, 1:216.

Coleridge, Samuel Taylor (1985) *Biographia Literaria*, in *Samuel Taylor Coleridge: The Major Works*, H. J. Jackson (ed.), New York: Oxford University Press, pp.155–482.

Cooper, Thomas (1740) *The universal pocket-book*, London: Printed for Thomas Cooper.

Creech, James (1982) '"Chasing after Advances": Diderot's Article "Encyclopedia"', *Yale French Studies*, 63, pp.183–97.

Croker, Temple Henry, Williams, Thomas, and Clark, Samuel (eds) (1764–66) *The complete dictionary of arts and sciences*, London: Printed for the Authors.

Crowther, Kathleen (2010) *Adam and Eve in the Protestant Reformation*, New York: Cambridge University Press.

Cumberland, Richard (1798) 'No. xxvii', in *The Observer*, London: Printed for C. Dilly, pp.277–86.

Curzon, Henry (1712) *The universal library; or, compleat summary of science*, London: Printed for George Sawbridge.

D'Alembert, Jean le Rond, and Diderot, Denis (1752) *The plan of the French Encyclopædia*, London: Printed for W. Innys, et al.

Darnton, Robert (1979) *The Business of Enlightenment: A Publishing History of the Encyclopédie, 1775–1800*, Cambridge: Belknap Press.

Darwin, Erasmus (1791) *The Botanic Garden; a Poem, in Two Parts. Part I. Containing the Economy of Vegetation. Part II. The Loves of the Plants. With Philosophical Notes*, London: Printed for J. Johnson.

Davies, John (1715) *The origin, nature, and immortality of the soul. A poem*, 3rd ed., London: Printed for William Mears and Jonas Brown.

Davis, Lennard J. (1997) *Factual Fictions: The Origins of the English Novel*, Philadelphia: University of Pennsylvania Press.

Davy, John (1839) *Memoirs of the Life of Sir Humphry Davy, Bart., L.L.D., F.R.S., Foreign Associate of the Institute of France, Etc.*, London: Smith, Elder and Co.

Day, Robert (1990) 'Psalmanazar's "Formosa" and the British Reader (including Samuel Johnson)', in *Exoticism in the Enlightenment*, George Sebastian Rousseau and Roy Porter (eds), Manchester: Manchester University Press, pp.197–221.

Day, W. G. (1972) 'Tristram Shandy: The Marbled Leaf', *Library*, 27.2, pp.143–5.

de Bolla, Peter (2010) 'Mediation and the Division of Labor', in *This is Enlightenment*, Clifford Siskin and William Warner (eds), Chicago: University of Chicago Press, pp.87–101.

de Grey, Thomas (1639) *The compleat horseman and expert farrier*, London: Printed by Thomas Harper.

de Kunder, Maurice (2013) *Worldwidewebsize.com*, cited 13 April 2013, available at http://www.worldwidewebsize.com/.

de Montaigne, Michel (2003). *Apology for Raymond Sebond*, Roger Ariew and Marjorie Grene (trans.), Indianapolis: Hackett Publishing.

De Morgan, Augustus (2007) *A Budget of Paradoxes*, New York: Cosimo, Inc.

Defoe, Daniel (1729) *A compleat system of magick: or, the history of the black-art*, London: Printed for J. Clarke.

Defoe, Daniel (1973) *Moll Flanders*, Edward Kelly (ed.), New York: W. W. Norton & Company.

Defoe, Daniel (1996) *Roxana: The Fortunate Mistress*, John Mullan (ed.), New York: Oxford University Press.

DeMaria, Robert (1986) *Johnson's "Dictionary" and the Language of Learning*, Chapel Hill: University of North Carolina Press.

Dennis, John (1701) *The advancement and reformation of modern poetry. A critical discourse*, London: Printed for Rich. Parker.

Descartes, René (2006) *A Discourse on the Method of Correctly Conducting One's Reason and Seeking Truth in the Sciences*, Ian Maclean (trans. and ed.), New York: Oxford University Press.

Diderot, Denis (2001) 'The Encyclopædia', in *Rameau's Nephew and Other Works*, Indianapolis: Hackett Publishing, pp.277–308.

Donaldson, Alexander (1774) *The cases of the appellants and respondents in the cause of literary property*, London: Printed for J. Bew.

Donaldson, Ian (1970) 'The Clockwork Novel: Three Notes on an Eighteenth-Century Analogy', *The Review of English Studies*, 21.81, pp.14–22.

Drury, Joseph (2009) 'The Novel and the Machine in the Eighteenth Century', *Novel: A Forum on Fiction*, 42.2, pp.337–42.

Dryden, John (1735) 'Of dramatick poesy, an essay', London.

Dryden, John (2001) 'Fables Ancient and Modern', in *John Dryden: Selected Poems*, Steven Zwicker and David Bywaters (eds), London: Penguin Books, pp.398–514.

Dunton, John (1693) *The compleat library*, London.

Dunton, John (1701) *The post-angel, or Universal entertainment*, London.

Duran, Angelica (2007) *The Age of Milton and the Scientific Revolution*, Pittsburgh: Duquesne University Press.

Eaves, Thomas, and Kimpel, Ben (1971) *Samuel Richardson: A Biography*, Oxford: Clarendon Press.

Edelstein, Dan (2010) *The Enlightenment: A Genealogy*, Chicago: University of Chicago Press.

Edwards, Karen L. (1999) *Milton and the Natural World: Science and Poetry in Paradise Lost*, New York: Cambridge University Press.

Eisenstein, Elizabeth (1979) *The Printing Press as an Agent of Change: Cultural Transformation in Early Modern Europe*, 2 vols., Cambridge: Cambridge University Press.

Eisenstein, Elizabeth (1986) 'Print Culture and Enlightenment Thought', in *The Sixth Hanes Lecture*: Hanes Foundation, University Library, The University of North Carolina at Chapel Hill.

Elton, Richard (1650) *The compleat body of the art military*, London: Printed by Robert Leybourn.

Encyclopædia Britannica, 11th ed. (1910) 'Prefatory Note', Cambridge: Cambridge University Press, p.viii.

Encyclopædia Britannica Online (2005) 'Advertisement', cited 16 December 2005, available at http://corporate.britannica.com/library/print/eb.html.

Encyclopædia Britannica Online (2009) 'About the Editorial Board', cited 27 September 2009, available at: http://corporate.britannica.com/board/index.html.

Encyclopædia Britannica Online (2012) 'Britannica Today', cited 29 December 2012, available at http://corporate.britannica.com/about/today/.

Fadden, William (1756) *The Literary magazine: or, Universal review*, 3 vols., London: Printed for J. Richardson.

Fanning, Christopher (2002) '"This Fragment of Life": Sterne's Encyclopedic Ethics', *The Shandean*, 13, pp.55–67.

Fanning, Christopher (2009) 'Sterne and Print Culture', in *The Cambridge Companion to Laurence Sterne*, Thomas Keymer (ed.), New York: Cambridge University Press, pp.125–41.

Feeney, D. C. (1986) 'Epic Hero and Epic Fable', *Comparative Literature*, 38.2, pp.137–58.

Feeney, Denis (2004) 'Introduction', in *Metamorphoses: A New Verse Translation*, David Raeburn (trans.), London: Penguin Books, pp.xiii–xxxiv.

Felix, Gilbert (1984) *Machiavelli and Guicciardini: Politics and History in Sixteenth-Century Florence*, New York: W. W. Norton and Company.

Felton, Henry (1730) *A dissertation on reading the classics, and forming a just style*, 4th ed., London: Printed for B. Motte.

Fielding, Henry (1995) *Tom Jones*, Sheridan Baker (ed.), New York: W. W. Norton and Company.

Fielding, Henry (1999) *Joseph Andrews*, Judith Hawley (ed.), New York: Penguin Books.

Foley, Frederick (1968) *The Great Formosan Impostor*, St. Louis: St. Louis University Press.

Forsyth, Neil (1991) 'Of Man's First Dis', in *Milton in Italy: Contexts, Images, Contradictions*, Mario A. Di Cesare (ed.), Binghamton, NY: Medieval & Renaissance Texts & Studies, pp.345–69.

Foucault, Michel (1984) 'What Is an Author?' in *The Foucault Reader*, Paul Rabinow (ed.), New York: Pantheon Books, pp.101–20.

Fowler, Alistair (1971) 'The Life and Death of Literary Forms', *New Literary History*, 2, pp.199–216.

Franklin, Benjamin (2003) *The Autobiography of Benjamin Franklin*, Leonard Labaree, Ralph Ketcham, and Helen Boatfield (eds), New Haven: Yale University Press.

Franklin-Brown, Mary (2012) *Reading the World: Encyclopedic Writing in the Scholastic Age*, Chicago: Chicago University Press.

Freeman, John (2002) 'Delight in the (Dis)Order of Things: *Tristram Shandy* and the Dynamics of Genre', *Studies in the Novel*, 34.2, pp.141–61.

Frye, Northrop (2006) *Anatomy of Criticism: Four Essays*, Toronto: University of Toronto Press.

Garside, P., Raven, J., and Schöwerlin, R. (2000) *The English Novel, 1770–1829: A Bibliographical Survey of Prose Fiction Published in the British Isles*, 2 vols., New York: Oxford University Press.

Gay, Peter (1974) *Style in History*, New York: Basic Books.

Gierl, Martin (2008) 'Science, Projects, Computers, and the State: Swift's Lagadian and Leibniz's Prussian Academy', in *The Age of Projects*, Maximillian E. Novak (ed.), UCLA Clark Memorial Library Series, Toronto: University of Toronto Press, pp.297–317.

Gleick, James (2011) *The Information: A History, a Theory, a Flood*, New York: Pantheon Books.

Godwin, William (1988) 'Of History and Romance', in *Caleb Williams*, Maurice Hindle (ed.), New York: Penguin Books, pp.359–74.

Goodman, Kevis (2004) *Georgic Modernity and British Romanticism: Poetry and the Mediation of History*, Cambridge Studies in Romanticism, New York: Cambridge University Press.

Goodman, Kevis (2004) 'Magnifying Small Things: Georgic Modernity and the Noise of History', *European Romantic Review*, 15.2, pp.215–27.

Google (2010) 'Technology Overview', cited 12 April 2010, available at http://www.google.com/corporate/tech.html.

Google (2012) 'Corporate Information', cited 2 January 2012, available at http://www.google.com/intl/et/corporate/.

Gordon, Patrick (1693) *Geography anatomized*, London: Printed by J. R. for R. Morden & T. Cockerill.

Gouldman, Francis (1664) *A copious dictionary in three parts*, London: Printed by John Field.

Grafton, Anthony (1975) 'Joseph Scaliger and Historical Chronology: The Rise and Fall of a Discipline', *History and Theory*, 14.2, pp.156–85.

Grafton, Anthony (1983) *Joseph Scaliger: A Study in the History of Classical Scholarship*, New York: Oxford University Press.

Grafton, Anthony (1992) 'Renaissance Readers of Homer's Ancient Readers', in *Homer's Ancient Readers: The Hermeneutics of Greek Epic's Earliest Exegetes*, Robert Lamberton and John J. Keany (eds), Princeton: Princeton University Press, pp.149–72.

Grafton, Anthony (2003) 'Dating History: The Renaissance & the Reformation of Chronology', *Daedalus*, 132.2, pp.74–85.

Green, Jonathon (1996) *Chasing the Sun: Dictionary Makers and the Dictionaries They Made*, New York: Henry Holt.

Greenberg, Bernard (1954) 'Laurence Sterne and Chambers' Cyclopædia', *Modern Language Notes*, LXIX, pp.560–2.

Greengrass, M., Leslie, M., and Raylor, T. (eds) (1994) *Samuel Hartlib and Universal Reformation: Studies in Intellectual Communication*, Cambridge: Cambridge University Press.

Griffin, Dustin (1982) 'Milton and the Decline of Epic in the Eighteenth Century', *New Literary History*, 14.1, pp.143–54.

Griggs, Tamara (2007) 'Universal History from Counter-Reformation to Enlightenment', *Modern Intellectual History*, 4.2, pp.219–47.

Grose, Christopher (2002) '*Theatrum Libri*: Burton's *Anatomy of Melancholy* and the Failure of Encyclopedic Form', in *Books and Readers in Early Modern England: Material Studies*, Jennifer Anderson and Elizabeth Sauer (eds), Philadelphia: University of Pennsylvania Press, pp.80–96.

H., N. (1694) 'Dedication', in *The ladies dictionary*, London: Printed for John Dunton.

Harris, John (1704) *Lexicon Technicum: or, an universal English dictionary of arts and sciences: explaining not only the terms of art, but the arts themselves*, 2 vols., London: Printed for Dan. Brown, et al.

Hawley, Judith (2009) '*Tristram Shandy*, Learned Wit, and Enlightenment Knowledge', in *The Cambridge Companion to Laurence Sterne*, Thomas Keymer (ed.), New York: Cambridge University Press, pp.34–48.

Hill, Aaron (1804) 'To Mr. Richardson, 7 January 1744–5', in *The Correspondence of Samuel Richardson*, Anna Laetitia Barbauld (ed.), London, 1:99–101.

Hinde, Captain John (1650) 'To the Worthy Author His Honor'd Friend Serjeant Major Richard Elton', in *The compleat body of the art military*, London: Printed by Robert Leybourn.

Hitchcock, Tim (2011) Review of *Society in Early Modern England: The Vernacular Origins of Some Powerful Ideas*, by Phil Withington, *The Economic History Review*, 64.3, p.1027.

Hobbes, Thomas (2008) 'Preface', in *Translations of Homer*, Eric Nelson (ed.), New York: Clarendon Press.

Holtz, William V. (1970) *Image and Immortality: A Study of Tristram Shandy*, Providence: Brown University Press.

Horace (1990) *Horace: Epistles Book II and Epistle to the Pisones ('Ars Poetica')*, Niall Rudd (ed.), Cambridge Greek and Latin Classics, Cambridge: Cambridge University Press.

Horowitz, Mark (2008) 'Visualizing Big Data: Bar Charts for Words', *Wired*, 23 June, available at http://www.wired.com/science/discoveries/magazine/16-07/pb_visualizing.

Howell, William (1704–05) *Ductor historicus: or, a short system of universal history, and an introduction to the study of it*, 2 vols., London: Printed for Tim. Childe.

Hume, Robert (2006) 'The Economics of Culture in London 1660–1740', *The Huntington Library Quarterly*, 69.4, pp.487–533.

Hunter, J. Paul (1990) *Before Novels: The Cultural Contexts of Eighteenth-Century English Fiction*, New York: W. W. Norton and Company, Inc.

Hunter, Richard (2012) *Plato and the Tradition of Ancient Literature: The Silent Stream*, New York: Cambridge University Press.

J., W. (1695) 'The Preface of the Translator', in *Monsieur Bossu's treatise of the epick poem containing many curious reflections, very useful and necessary for the right understanding and judging of the excellencies of Homer and Virgil*, by René Le Bossu, W. J. (trans.), London: Printed for Tho. Bennet.

Jardine, Lisa (2000) 'Introduction', in *The New Organon*, by Francis Bacon; Lisa Jardine and Michael Silverthorne (eds), New York: Cambridge University Press.

Jeanneney, Jean-Noël (2007) *Google and the Myth of Universal Knowledge: A View from Europe*, Teresa Lavender Fagan (trans.), Chicago: University of Chicago Press.

Johnson, Samuel (1755) 'Knowledge', in *A Dictionary of the English Language*, London: Printed by W. Strahan.

Johnson, Samuel (1771) 'No. 91. Saturday, January 12, 1760', in *The Idler*, London, pp.217–18.

Johnson, Samuel (1794) *The lives of the most eminent English poets. With critical observations on their works*, 4 vols., London: Printed for T. Longman, B. Law, J. Dodsley, H. Baldwin, J. Robson, et al.

Johnson, Samuel (2000) 'Preface to *A Dictionary of the English Language*', in *Samuel Johnson: The Major Works*, Donald Johnson Greene (ed.), New York: Oxford University Press.

Jonson, Ben (1756) 'Timber, or Discoveries Made Upon Men and Matter', in *The Works of Ben Jonson*, London: Printed for D. Midwinter, W. Innys, and J. Richardson, et al., pp.70–164.

Jung, Sandro (2007) 'Epic, Ode, or Something New: The Blending of Genres in Thomson's Spring', *Papers on Language and Literature*, 43.2, pp.146–65.

Jung, Sandro (2009) 'Thomson's *Winter*, the Ur-text, and the Revision of *The Seasons*', *Papers on Language and Literature*, 45.1, pp.60–81.

Jung, Sandro (2011) 'Print Culture, High-Cultural Consumption, and Thomson's *The Seasons*, 1780–1797', *Eighteenth-Century Studies*, 44.4, pp.495–514.

Kafker, Frank (1994) 'Smellie's Edition of the *Encyclopædia Britannica*', in *Notable Encyclopedias of the Late 18th Century: Eleven Successors of the Encyclopédie*, Frank Kafker (ed.), Oxford: Voltaire Foundation, pp.145–82.

Kastan, David Scott (2005) 'Introduction', in *Paradise Lost*, by John Milton, Indianapolis: Hackett Publishing Co., Inc, pp.xi–lxv.

Keats, John (2003) 'On First Looking into Chapman's Homer', in *John Keats Complete Poems*, Jack Stillinger (ed.), Cambridge: Belknap Press, p.34.

Keevak, Michael (2004) *The Pretended Asian: George Psalmanazar's Eighteenth-Century Formosan Hoax*, Detroit: Wayne State University Press.

Kerr, Robert (1811) *Memoirs of the Life, Writings, & Correspondence of William Smellie, F. R. S. & F. A. S.*, Edinburgh: Printed for J. Anderson.

Kerrigan, William (1983) *The Sacred Complex: On the Psychogenesis of 'Paradise Lost'*, Cambridge, MA: Harvard University Press.

Keymer, Thomas (1992) *Richardson's 'Clarissa' and the Eighteenth-Century Reader*, Cambridge: Cambridge University Press.

Keymer, Thomas (2006) 'Sterne and the "New Species of Writing"', in *Laurence Sterne's Tristram Shandy: A Casebook*, Thomas Keymer (ed.) New York: Oxford University Press, pp.50–78.

Klancher, Jon (1998) 'Godwin and the Genre Reformers: On Necessity and Contingency in Romantic Narrative Theory', in *Romanticism, History, and the Possibility of Genre*, Tilottama Rajan and Julia Wright (eds), Cambridge: Cambridge University Press, pp.21–38.

Klein, Julie Thompson (1993) 'Blurring, Cracking, and Crossing: Permeation and the Fracturing of Discipline', in *Knowledges: Historical and Critical Studies in Disciplinarity*, Shumway Messer-Davidow and David J. Sylvan (eds), Charlottesville, VA: University of Virginia Press, pp.185–211.

Koepke, Yvette (2008) 'Allegory as Historical and Theoretical Model of Scientific Medicine: Sex and the Making of the Modern Body in Phineas Fletcher's *The Purple Island'*, *Literature and Medicine*, 27.2, pp.175–203.

Kogan, Herman (1958) *The Great EB: The Story of the Encyclopaedia Britannica*, Chicago: University of Chicago Press.

Kolbrener, William (1997) *Milton's Warring Angels: A Study of Critical Engagements*, New York: Cambridge University Press.

La Quintinie, Jean de (1699) *The compleat gard'ner*, George London and Henry Wise (eds), London: Printed for M. Gillyflower.

Lamberton, Robert (1992) 'Introduction', in *Homer's Ancient Readers*, Robert Lamberton and John J. Keany (eds), Princeton: Princeton University Press.

Landa, Louis A. (1963) 'The Shandean Homunculus: The Background of Sterne's "Little Gentleman"', in *Restoration and Eighteenth-Century Literature: Essays in Honor of Alan Dugald Mckillop*, Carroll Camden (ed.), Chicago: University of Chicago Press, pp.49–68.

Langley, Eric (2006) 'Anatomising the Eye in Phineas Fletcher's *The Purple Island'*, *Renaissance Studies*, 20.3, pp.341–52.

Latour, Bruno (1987) *Science in Action: How to Follow Scientists and Engineers through Society*, Cambridge, MA: Harvard University Press.

Lau, Beth (2002) 'Wordsworth and Current Memory Research', *Studies in Literature, 1500–1900*, 42.4, pp.675–92.

Le Bossu, René (1719) *Monsieur Bossu's treatise of the epick poem containing many curious reflections, very useful and necessary for the right understanding and judging of the excellencies of Homer and Virgil*, W. J. (trans.), 2nd ed., 2 vols., London: Printed for J. Knapton and H. Clements.

Le Tellier, Robert Ignatius (1997) *The English Novel, 1660–1700: An Annotated Bibliography*, Bibliographies and Indexes in World Literature, Westport, CT: Greenwood Press.

Levine, Joseph (1999) *Between the Ancients and the Moderns: Baroque Culture in Restoration England*, New Haven: Yale University Press.

Levinson, Marjorie (1986) *The Romantic Fragment Poem: A Critique of a Form*. Chapel Hill: University of North Carolina Press.

Lewalski, Barbara (1999) 'The Genres of *Paradise Lost'*, in *The Cambridge Companion to Milton*, Dennis Richard Danielson (ed.), New York: Cambridge University Press, pp.113–29.

Lloyd, Thomas (ed.) (1791) *The new royal encyclopædia*, 2nd ed., 3 vols., London: Printed for C. Cooke, et al.

Locke, John (1706) *An essay concerning humane understanding. In four books*, London.

Locke, John (1708) *Some familiar letters between Mr. Locke, and several of his friends*, London: Printed for A. and J. Churchill at the Black Swan in Pater-noster Row.

Locke, John (1997) *An Essay Concerning Human Understanding*, Roger Woolhouse (ed.), 2nd ed., London: Penguin Books.

London, George, and Wise, Henry (1699) 'An Advertisement to the Nobility and Gentry', in *The compleat gard'ner*, George London and Henry Wise (eds), London: Printed for M. Gillyflower.

Long, A. A. (1992) 'Stoic Readings of Homer', in *Homer's Ancient Readers: The Hermeneutics of Greek Epic's Earliest Exegetes*, Robert Lamberton and John J. Keany (eds), Princeton: Princeton University Press, pp.41–66.

Lonsdale, Roger (2006) 'N.285', in *Lives of the Most Eminent English Poets*, by Samuel Johnson, Roger Lonsdale (ed.), New York: Oxford University Press.

Louth, Andrew (2004) 'Eusebius and the Birth of Church History', in *The Cambridge History of Early Christian Literature*, Frances Young, Lewis Ayres, and Andrew Louth (eds), New York: Cambridge University Press, pp.266–74.

Loveland, Jeff (2010) *An Alternative Encyclopedia?: Dennis De Coetlogon's 'Universal History of Arts and Sciences' (1745)*, Oxford: Voltaire Foundation.

Loveridge, Mark (1982) *Laurence Sterne and the Argument About Design*, Totowa, NJ: Barnes & Noble Books.

Lynch, Jack (2005) 'Johnson's Encyclopedia', in *Anniversary Essays on Johnson's Dictionary*, Jack Lynch and Anne McDermott (eds), New York: Cambridge University Press, pp.129–46.

Lynch, James (1986) *Henry Fielding and the Heliodoran Novel: Romance, Epic, and Fielding's New Province of Writing*, London: Associated University Presses.

Macfarquhar, Colin and Gleig, George (eds) (1797) *Encyclopædia Britannica; or a Dictionary of Arts, Sciences, &c.*, 3rd ed., 18 vols., Edinburgh: Printed for A. Bell and C. Macfarquhar.

Mack, Maynard (1986) *Alexander Pope: A Life*, New York: W. W. Norton & Company.

Maclean, Ian (2006) 'Introduction', in *A Discourse on the Method of Correctly Conducting One's Reason and Seeking Truth in the Sciences*, by René Descartes, Ian Maclean (ed.), New York: Oxford University Press, pp.vii–lxx.

Markham, Gervase (1610) *Markhams maister-peece*, London: Printed by Nicholas Okes.

Markham, Gervase (1616) *Markhams methode, or epitome*, London: By T. S[nodham].

Marks, Sylvia (1986) *Sir Charles Grandison: The Compleat Conduct Book*, Lewisburg, PA: Bucknell University Press.

Martin, Benjamin (1735) *The philosophical grammar*, London: Printed for J. Noon.

Martin, Benjamin (1737) *Bibliotheca technologica: or, a philological library of literary arts and sciences*, London: Printed by S. Idle.

Martin, Benjamin (1747) *Philosophia Britannica; or a new and comprehensive system of the Newtonian philosophy, astronomy and geography*, London: Printed by C. Micklewright and Co.

Martin, Benjamin (1755–65) *The general magazine of Arts and Sciences, Philosophical, philosophical, philological, mathematical, and mechanical*, 14 vols., London: Printed for W. Owen.

Martin, Catherine Gimelli (2001) '"What If the Sun Be Centre to the World?':
Milton's Epistemology, Cosmology, and Paradise of Fools Reconsidered',
Modern Philology, 99.2, pp.231–65.

Martz, Louis (1941) 'Tobias Smollett and the Universal History', *Modern Language
Notes*, 56.1, pp.1–14.

Mason, John (1813) 'Chapter', in *Pantologia*, London: n.p.

Mayo, Robert (1962) *The English Novel in the Magazines, 1740–1815*, Evanston, IL:
Northwestern University Press.

McDowell, Paula (2010) 'Mediating Media Past and Present: Towards a
Genealogy of "Print Culture" Past and Present', in *This is Enlightenment*,
Clifford Siskin and William Warner (eds), Chicago: University of Chicago
Press, pp.229–462.

McKeon, Michael (1994) 'The Origins of Interdisciplinary Studies', *Eighteenth-
Century Studies*, 28.1, pp.17–28.

McKeon, Michael (2002) *The Origins of the English Novel, 1600–1740*, 15th anniversary ed., Baltimore, MD: Johns Hopkins University Press.

McKitterick, David (2003) *Print, Manuscript, and the Search for Order, 1450–1830*,
New York: Cambridge University Press.

McLane, Maureen N. (2000) *Romanticism and the Human Sciences: Poetry,
Population, and the Discourse of the Species*, Cambridge Studies in Romanticism,
New York: Cambridge University Press.

McLaverty, James (2001) *Pope, Print, and Meaning*, New York: Oxford University
Press.

McLuhan, Marshall (1966) *The Gutenberg Galaxy: The Making of Typographic Man*,
Toronto: University of Toronto Press.

McMullin, Ernan (2001) 'The Impact of Newton's Principia on the Philosophy of
Science', *Philosophy of Science*, 68.3, pp.279–310.

Meta Contributors (2014) 'Association of Deletionist Wikipedians', *Meta,
discussion about Wikimedia projects*, cited 6 January 2014, available at
http://meta.wikimedia.org/w/index.php?title=Association_of_Deletionist_
Wikipedians&oldid=6764342.

Meta Contributors (2014) 'Association of Inclusionist Wikipedians', *Meta, discussion about Wikimedia projects*, cited 6 January 2014, available at http://
meta.wikimedia.org/w/index.php?title=Association_of_Inclusionist_
Wikipedians&oldid=6939662.

Millburn, John (1976) *Benjamin Martin: Author, Instrument-Maker, and "Country
Showman"*, Leyden: Noordhoff International Publishing.

Milton, John (1933) '"At a Solemn Musick"', in *The Student's Milton*, Frank Allen
Patterson (ed.), New York: Appleton-Century-Crofts, Inc., p.19.

Milton, John (2003) *The Christian Doctrine*, in *Milton: The Complete Poems and
Major Prose*, Merritt Hughes (ed.), Indianapolis: Hackett Publishing, Inc., 2003.

Milton, John (2005) *Paradise Lost*, David Scott Kastan (ed.), Indianapolis: Hackett
Pub. Co.

Mitchell, Peter (2007) *The Purple Island and Anatomy in Early Seventeenth Century
Literature, Philosophy, and Theology*, Madison: Farleigh Dickinson University
Press.

Molyneux, William (1708) 'To John Locke. 20 July 1697', in *Some familiar letters between Mr. Locke, and several of his friends*, London: Printed for A. and
J. Churchill, pp.225–31.

Moore, Clarence King (1935) 'L'accademia Della Crusca: Some Historical References', *Italica*, 12.2, pp.128–9.

Moretti, Franco (2011) *Pamphlet 2: Network Theory, Plot Analysis*, Stanford: Stanford Literary Lab, available at http://litlab.stanford.edu/LiteraryLabPamphlet2A.Tex.pdf.

Moretti, Franco (2013) *Distant Reading*, London: Verso.

Morison, Samuel (1936) *Harvard College in the Seventeenth Century*, Cambridge, MA: Harvard University Press.

Mungello, David (1989) *Curious Land: Jesuit Accommodation and the Origins of Sinology*, Honolulu: University of Hawaii Press.

Naddaf, Gerard (2009) 'Allegory and the Origins of Philosophy', in *Logos and Muthos: Philosophical Essays in Greek Literature*, William Wians (ed.), Albany: SUNY Press, pp.99–132.

Newton, Isaac (1995) *The Principia*, Great Minds Series, Amherst, NY: Prometheus Books.

Noyes, Russel (ed.) (1956) *English Romantic Poetry and Prose*, New York: Oxford University Press.

O'Brien, Karen (2001) 'The History Market in Eighteenth-Century England', in *Books and Their Readers in Eighteenth-Century England: New Essays*, Isabel Rivers (ed.), London: Continuum, pp.105–34.

Ovid (2004) *Metamorphoses: A New Verse Translation*, David Raeburn (trans.), London: Penguin Books.

Page, Michael (2005) 'The Darwin before Darwin: Erasmus Darwin, Visionary Science, and Romantic Science', *Papers on Language and Literature*, 41.2, pp.146–69.

Park, Julie (2010) *The Self and It: Novel Objects in Eighteenth-Century England*, Stanford: Stanford University Press.

Parker, E., Cahill, L., and McGaugh, J. (2006) 'A Case of Unusual Autobiographical Remembering', *Neurocase*, 12.1, pp.35–49.

Parks, Stephen (ed.) (1975) *The Literary Property Debate: Six Tracts, 1764–1774*, New York: Garland.

Parks, Stephen (1976) *John Dunton and the English Book Trade: A Study of His Career with a Checklist of His Publications*, New York: Garland Press.

Passannante, Gerard (2011) *The Lucretian Renaissance: Philology and the Afterlife of Tradition*, Chicago: University of Chicago Press.

Patey, Douglas (2005) 'Ancients and Moderns', in *The Cambridge History of Literary Criticism: The Eighteenth Century*, H. B. Nisbet and Claude Rawson (eds), New York: Cambridge University Press, pp.32–74.

Patten, William (1575) *The calender of Scripture*, London: Printed by Richard Jugge.

Patterson, Diana (1991) 'Tristram's Marbling and Marblers', *The Shandean*, 3, pp.70–97.

Peacham, Henry (1622) *The compleat gentleman*, London: Printed by [John Legat] for Francis Constable.

Pearce, Roy Harvey (1957) 'American Studies as a Discipline', *College English*, 18.4, pp.179–86.

Pepys, Samuel (2000) *The Diary of Samuel Pepys*, Robert Latham and William Matthews (eds), 9 vols., Berkeley: University of California Press.

Pétau, Denis (1659) *The history of the world, or an account of time*, London: Printed by J. Streater.

Petty, William (1647) *The advice of W. P. to Samuel Hartlib. For the advancement of some particular parts of learning*, London.

Phillips, Mark (2000) *Society and Sentiment: Genres of Historical Writing in Britain, 1740–1820*, Princeton: Princeton University Press.

Picciotto, Joanna (2005) 'Reforming the Garden: The Experimentalist Eden and *Paradise Lost*', *ELH*, 72.1, pp.23–78.

Poovey, Mary (2001) 'The Model System of Contemporary Literary Criticism', *Critical Inquiry*, 27.3, pp.408–38.

Pope, Alexander (1741) 'Letter xxxiii', in *The Works of Mr. Alexander Pope, in prose*, London, pp.72–4.

Pope, Alexander (1956) *The Correspondence of Alexander Pope*, George Sherburn (ed.), 5 vols., Oxford: Clarendon Press.

Pope, Alexander (1963) *Essay on Man*, in *The Poems of Alexander Pope*, vol. 2, John Butt (ed.), New Haven: Yale University Press, pp.501–47.

Pope, Alexander (1963) *The Dunciad Variorum*, in *The Poems of Alexander Pope*, John Butt (ed.), New Haven: Yale University Press, pp.317–460.

Pope, Alexander (1967) 'An Essay on Criticism', in *The Poems of Alexander Pope*, John Butt (ed.), New Haven: Methuen.

Pope, Alexander (1967) *The Iliad of Homer*, in *The Poems of Alexander Pope*, vol. 8., Maynard Mack (ed.), New Haven: Methuen.

Pope, Alexander (1969) *Peri Bathous; or, the Art of Sinking in Poetry*, in *The Poetry and Prose of Alexander Pope*, Aubrey Williams (ed.), Boston: Houghton Mifflin Company, pp.387–438.

Pope, Alexander (1999) *The Dunciad in Four Books*, Valerie Rumbold (ed.), New York: Pearson Education Inc.

Porter, Martin (2005) *Windows of the Soul: The Art of Physiognomy in European Culture 1470–1780*, Oxford Historical Monographs, New York: Oxford University Press.

Post, Robert (2009) 'Debating Disciplinarity', *Critical Inquiry*, 35.4, pp.749–70.

Prest, John M. (1981) *The Garden of Eden: The Botanic Garden and the Re-Creation of Paradise*, New Haven: Yale University Press.

Price, Leah (2000) *The Anthology and the Rise of the Novel*, Cambridge: Cambridge University Press.

'Proposals (by the proprietors of the work) for printing by subscription, in Twenty Volumes Octavo, *an Universal History*' (1746), London.

'Proposals for publishing the modern part of the *Universal history*' (1758), London.

Psalmanazar, George (1764) *Memoirs of ****. Commonly known by the name of George Psalmanazar; a reputed native of Formosa*, London: Printed for R. Davis.

R., E. (1691) *The experienc'd farrier, or, a compleat treatise of horsemanship, in Two Books*, London: Printed for W. Whitwood.

Rajan, Tilottama (2011) 'The Disfiguration of Enlightenment: War, Trauma, and the Historical Novel in Godwin's *Mandeville*', in *Godwinian Moments: From the Enlightenment to Romanticism*, Robert M. Maniquis and Victoria Myers (eds), Toronto: University of Toronto Press, pp.172–93.

Ralph, James (1728) *Sawney. An heroic poem. Occasion'd by the Dunciad. Together with a critique on that poem address'd to Mr. T–D, Mr. M–R, Mr. Eu–N, &C.*, London: Printed and sold by J. Roberts.

Ramsay, Rachel (2001) 'China and the Ideal of Order in John Webb', *Journal of the History of Ideas*, 62.3, pp.483–503.

Rauch, Alan (2001) *Useful Knowledge: The Victorians, Morality, and the March of Intellect*, Durham: Duke University Press.

Rawson, Claude Julien (1994) *Satire and Sentiment, 1660–1830*, New York: Cambridge University Press.

Rees, Abraham (ed.) (1802–19) *The New Cyclopædia*, 45 vols., vol. 1, London: Printed for Longman, Hurst, Rees, Orme, and Brown.

Reeve, Clara (1785) *The Progress of Romance*, 2 vols., Colchester: Printed for the author.

Reid, Thomas (1774) 'A Brief Account of Aristotle's Logic', in *Sketches of the history of man*, by Henry Home, Lord Kames, vol. 3, Dublin: Printed for James Williams, pp.191–272.

Reid, Thomas (1785) 'Essay 1. Preliminary', in *Essays on the intellectual powers of man*, Edinburgh: Printed for John Bell, pp.9–74.

Richardson, N. J. (1992) 'Aristotle's Reading of Homer and Its Background', in *Homer's Ancient Readers: The Hermeneutics of Greek Epic's Earliest Exegetes*, Robert Lamberton and John J. Keany (eds), Princeton: Princeton University Press, pp.30–40.

Richardson, Samuel (1749) *Clarissa. Or, the History of a Young Lady*, 2nd ed., 7 vols., London: Printed for S. Richardson.

Richardson, Samuel (1753) *The History of Sir Charles Grandison*, 6 vols., London: Printed for S. Richardson.

Richardson, Samuel (1804) 'To the Reverend Mr Hildesley, 21 February 1755', in *The Correspondence of Samuel Richardson*, Anna Laetitia Barbauld (ed.), London: Printed for Richard Phillips, pp.130–4.

Richardson, Samuel (1964) 'Richardson to Lady Bradshaigh, 9 October 1756', in *Selected Letters of Samuel Richardson*, John Carroll (ed.), Oxford: Oxford University Press, p.329.

Richardson, Samuel (1985) *Clarissa, or, the History of a Young Lady*, Angus Ross (ed.), New York: Penguin Books.

Richardson, Samuel (1986) *The History of Sir Charles Grandison*, Jocelyn Harris (ed.), New York: Oxford University Press.

Richardson, Samuel (2001) *Pamela: Or, Virtue Rewarded*, Thomas Keymer and Alice Wakely (eds), New York: Oxford University Press.

Rose, Mark (1993) *Authors and Owners: The Invention of Copyright*, Cambridge, MA: Harvard University Press.

Rosenberg, Daniel and Grafton, Anthony (2010) *Cartographies of Time: A History of the Timeline*, New York: Princeton Architectural Press.

Ross, Trevor (1992) 'Copyright and the Invention of Tradition', *Eighteenth-Century Studies*, 25, pp.1–27.

Ross, Trevor (1998) *The Making of the English Literary Canon: From the Middle Ages to the Late Eighteenth Century*, Montreal: McGill-Queen's University Press.

Rudd, Niall (1990) Commentary in *Horace: Epistle II and Ars Poetica*, by Horace, Cambridge: Cambridge University Press.

Rudy, Seth (2011) 'Pope, Swift, and the Poetics of Posterity', *Eighteenth-Century Life*, 35.1, pp.1–28.

S., A., Gent. (1697) *The husbandman, farmer and grasier's compleat instructor*, London: Printed for Henry Nelme.

Sale, George et al. (1736–44) *An Universal History, from the earliest account of time*, 7 vols., London: J. Batley, E. Symon, T. Osborne, and J. Crokatt.

Sale, William Jr. (1950) *Samuel Richardson: Master Printer*, Ithaca: Cornell University Press.

Scaliger, Julius (1740) *Scaligerana*, P. Desmaizeaux (ed.), Amsterdam.

Schmidt, Eric (2005) 'Technology is Making Marketing Accountable', *Google Press Center*, 8 October, available at http://www.google.com/press/podium/ana.html.

Schroeder, John (1669) *The compleat chymical dispensatory, in five books*, William Rowland (trans.), London: Printed by John Darby.

Schuler, Robert (1992) *Francis Bacon and Scientific Poetry*, Transactions of the American Philological Society, 82, Philadelphia: American Philological Society.

Schulz, Kathryn (2011) 'What is Distant Reading?', *The New York Times*, 24 June.

Scott, George Lewis (ed.) (1753) *A Supplement to Mr. Chambers's Cyclopædia*, 2 vols., London: Printed for W. Innys.

Scott, John, and Hoole, John (1785) *Critical essays on some of the poems, of several English poets*, London: Printed and sold by James Phillips.

Scott, William (1639) *An essay of drapery: or, the compleate citizen*, London: Printed by Eli. All-de.

Scriblerus Club (1988) *Memoirs of the Extraordinary Life, Works, and Discoveries of Martinus Scriblerus*, Charles Kerby-Miller (ed.), Oxford: Oxford University Press.

Selcer, Daniel (2010) *Philosophy and the Book: Early Modern Figures of Material Inscription*, New York: Continuum.

Serres, Michel (1982) *Hermes: Literature, Science, Philosophy*, Lawrence R. Schehr (trans.), Josué V. Harari and David F. Bell (eds), Baltimore, MD: Johns Hopkins University Press.

Shackleton, Robert (1984) 'The Encyclopædic Spirit', in *Greene Centennial Studies: Essays Presented to Donald Greene*, Paul J. Korshin and Robert R. Allen (eds), Charlottesville, VA: University of Virginia Press, pp.377–90.

Shelley, Percy Bysshe (2002) 'Defense of Poetry', in *Shelley's Poetry and Prose*, Donald H. Reiman and Neil Fraistat (eds), 2nd ed., New York: W. W. Norton & Company, pp.509–35.

Shklovsky, Viktor (1990) *Theory of Prose*, Benjamin Sher (trans.), Elmwood Park, IL: Dalkey Archive Press.

Simonsuuri, Kirsti (1973) *Homer's Original Genius: Eighteenth-Century Notions of the Early Greek Epic (1688–1798)*, Cambridge: Cambridge University Press.

Siskin, Clifford (1988) *The Historicity of Romantic Discourse*, New York: Oxford University Press.

Siskin, Clifford (1998) *The Work of Writing: Literature and Social Change in Britain, 1700–1830*, Baltimore, MD: Johns Hopkins University Press.

Sleidanus, Johannes (1563) *A briefe chronicle of the foure principall empyres. To witte, of Babilon, Grecia, and Rome. Wherein, is compendiouslye conteyned the whole discourse of histories*, Stephan Wythers (trans.), London.

Smedley, Edward, Rose, Hugh, and Rose, Henry (eds) (1849) *Encyclopædia Metropolitana*, London: John Joseph Griffin and Company.

Smellie, William (ed.) (1771) *Encyclopædia Britannica; or, a dictionary of arts and sciences, compiled upon a new plan. ... Illustrated with one hundred and sixty copperplates. By a Society of gentlemen in Scotland. In three volumes,* 1st ed., 3 vols., Edinburgh: Printed for A. Bell and C. Macfarquhar.

Smith, Adam (1998) *An Inquiry into the Nature and Causes of the Wealth of Nations: A Selected Edition,* Kathryn Sutherland (ed.), New York: Oxford University Press.

Smollett, Tobias (1761) *Continuation of the Complete history of England,* 4 vols., London: Printed for Richard Baldwin.

Society of Gentlemen (eds) (1744) *A Supplement to Dr. Harris's Dictionary,* London: Printed for the Authors.

Society of Gentlemen (eds) (1763–64) *A new and complete dictionary of arts and sciences,* 2nd ed., 4 vols., London: Printed for W. Owen.

Sowerby, Robin (1997) 'Early Humanist Failure with Homer (II)', *International Journal of the Classical Tradition,* 4.2, pp.164–94.

Spacks, Patricia Meyer (2006) *Novel Beginnings: Experiments in Eighteenth-Century Prose Fiction,* New Haven: Yale University Press.

Spenser, Edmund (2006) *Spenser: The Faerie Queene,* A. C. Hamilton, Hiroshi Yamashita, Toshiyuku Suzuki, and Shohachi Fukuda (eds), New York: Longman.

Spingarn, Joel Elias (1976) *A History of Literary Criticism in the Renaissance,* 2nd ed., Westport, CT: Greenwood Press.

Sprat, Thomas (1667) *The history of the Royal-Society of London,* London: Printed by T. R. for J. Martyn.

St. Clair, William (2004) *The Reading Nation in the Romantic Period,* New York: Cambridge University Press.

Stalnaker, Joanna (2010) *The Unfinished Enlightenment: Description in the Age of the Encyclopedia,* Ithaca: Cornell University Press.

Starr, G. Gabrielle (2004) *Lyric Generations: Poetry and the Novel in the Long Eighteenth Century,* Baltimore, MD: Johns Hopkins University Press.

Sterne, Laurence (1935) *Letters of Laurence Sterne,* Lewis Perry Curtis (ed.), Oxford: Clarendon Press.

Sterne, Laurence (1997) *The Life and Opinions of Tristram Shandy, Gentleman,* Melvyn New and Joan New (eds), New York: Penguin Books.

Stross, Randall E. (2008) *Planet Google: One Company's Audacious Plan to Organize Everything We Know,* New York: Free Press.

Sullivan, Lawrence (1990) 'Circumscribing Knowledge: Encyclopedias in Historical Perspective', *The Journal of Religion,* 70.3, pp.315–59.

Swaim, Kathleen M. (1986) *Before and After the Fall: Contrasting Modes in Paradise Lost,* Amherst, MA: University of Massachusetts Press.

Swann, Marjorie (2007) '*The Compleat Angler* and the Early Modern Culture of Collecting', *English Literary Renaissance,* 37.1, pp.100–17.

Swift, Jonathan (2003) *Gulliver's Travels,* Robert de Maria, Jr. (ed.), New York: Penguin Books.

Tankard, Paul (2005) 'Samuel Johnson's History of Memory', *Studies in Philology,* 102.1, pp.110–42.

Tasso, Torquato (1724) *Opere Di Torquato Tasso,* Firenze: Nella stamperia di S.A.R. per li Tartini, e Franchi.

Thomson, James (1726) *Winter,* London: Printed by N. Blandford, for J. Millan.

Thomson, James (1730) *The Seasons,* London.

Thomson, James F. (1954) 'Tasks and Super-Tasks', *Analysis,* 15.1, pp.1–13.

Tillyard, E. M. W. (1958) *The Epic Strain in the English Novel,* London: Chatto & Windus.

Tinkler, John (1988) 'Humanist History and the English Novel in the Eighteenth Century', *Studies in Philology*, 85.4, pp.510–37.

Turchetti, Mario (2010) 'Jean Bodin', in *The Stanford Encyclopedia of Philosophy*, Edward N. Zalta (ed.), available at http://plato.stanford.edu/archives/sum2010/entries/bodin/.

Tytler, James (ed.) (1783) *Encyclopædia Britannica; or, a dictionary of arts, sciences, &c.*, 2nd ed., 10 vols., Edinburgh: Printed for J. Balfour, et al.

Vanderbeke, Dirk (2006) 'Winding up the Clock: The Conception and Birth of Tristram Shandy', in *Fashioning Childhood in the Eighteenth Century: Age and Identity*, Anja Muller (ed.), Aldershot: Ashgate Publishing Company, pp.179–88.

Voltaire (1759) *An essay on universal history, the manners, and spirit of nations, from the reign of Charlemaign to the age of Lewis XIV*, Mr. Nugent (trans.), London: Printed for J. Nourse.

Wall, Wendy (1996) 'Renaissance National Husbandry: Gervase Markham and the Publication of England', *The Sixteenth Century Journal*, 27.3 (Autumn), pp.767–85.

Ward, Richard (1710) *The life of the learned and pious Dr. Henry More, Late Fellow of Christ's College in Cambridge. To which are annex'd divers of his useful and excellent letters*, London: Printed and sold by J. Downing.

Warner, William (1988) *Licensing Entertainment: The Elevation of Novel Reading in Britain, 1684–1750*, Berkeley: University of California Press.

Warton, Joseph (1806) *An Essay on the Genius and Writing of Pope*, 5th ed., 2 vols., London: Printed for M. Cooper.

Watt, Ian P. (1957) *The Rise of the Novel: Studies in Defoe, Richardson, and Fielding*, Berkeley: University of California Press.

Weber, Harold (1999) 'The "Garbage Heap" of Memory: At Play in Pope's Archives of Dulness', *Eighteenth-Century Studies*, 33.1, pp.1–19.

Weber, Harold (2008) *Memory, Print, and Gender in England, 1653–1759*, New York: Palgrave Macmillan.

Webster, Charles (1975) *The Great Instauration: Science, Medicine, and Reform, 1626–1660*, London: Duckworth.

Weinberger, David (2011) *Too Big to Know: Rethinking Knowledge Now That the Facts Aren't the Facts, Experts Are Everywhere, and the Smartest Person in the Room Is the Room*, New York: Basic Books.

Weinbrot, Howard D. (1993) *Britannia's Issue: The Rise of British Literature from Dryden to Ossian*, New York: Cambridge University Press.

Weller, Toni (2008) 'Preserving Knowledge Through Popular Victorian Periodicals: An Examination of *The Penny Magazine* and the *Illustrated London News*, 1842–1843' *Library History*, 24.3, pp.200–7.

White, Hayden V. (1987) *The Content of the Form: Narrative Discourse and Historical Representation*, Baltimore, MD: Johns Hopkins University Press.

Wikipedia (2014) 'Wikipedia: Article Size', cited 2 January 2014, available at http://en.wikipedia.org/w/index.php?title=Wikipedia:Article_size&oldid=531001444.

Wikipedia (2014) 'Wikipedia: Statistics', cited 6 January 2014, available at http://en.wikipedia.org/w/index.php?title=Wikipedia:Statistics&oldid=587963650.

Wikipedia (2014) 'Wikipedia: What Wikipedia is Not', cited 6 January 2014, available at http://en.wikipedia.org/w/index.php?title=Wikipedia:What_Wikipedia_is_not&oldid=589429742.

Wikipedia Contributors (2014) 'Larry Norman', *Wikipedia, The Free Encyclopedia*, cited 6 January 2014, available at http://en.wikipedia.org/w/index.php? title=Larry_Norman&oldid=558068891.

Wilkes, Wetenhall (1740) *A letter of genteel and moral advice to a young lady*, Dublin: Printed for the Author by E. Jones.

Williams, Aubrey L. (1955) *Pope's 'Dunciad', a Study of Its Meaning*, London: Methuen.

Wilson, Thomas (1654) *A complete Christian dictionary*, John Bagwell (ed.), London: Printed for Ellen Cotes.

Wolfram|Alpha (2014) 'About Wolfram|Alpha', cited 14 January 2014, available at http://www.wolframalpha.com/about.html.

Wordsworth, William (1979) *The Prelude, 1799, 1805, 1850,* Jonathan Wordsworth, M. H. Abrams, and Stephen Charles Gill (eds), New York: W. W. Norton & Company.

Wordsworth, William (1985) *The Two-Part Prelude*, in *The Pedlar, Tintern Abbey, the Two-Part Prelude*, Jonathan Wordsworth (ed.), Cambridge: Cambridge University Press, pp.41–77.

Wordsworth, William (2008) 'Preface to *Lyrical Ballads'*, in *William Wordsworth: The Major Works*, Stephen Charles Gill (ed.), New York: Oxford University Press, pp.595–615.

Yeo, Richard (2001) *Encyclopedic Visions: Scientific Dictionaries and Enlightenment Culture*, New York: Cambridge University Press.

Yeo, Richard (2007) 'Lost Encyclopedias: Before and After the Enlightenment', *Book History*, 10, pp.47–68.

Index

CPSIA information can be obtained at www.ICGtesting.com
Printed in the USA
LVOW04*0253180315

431006LV00012B/63/P

9 781137 411532